The Marrano

The Marrano

A Novel by

Howard Rose

Raymond Saroff
PUBLISHER

for

Victoria de los Angeles

THE MARRANO

Copyright 1992 by Raymond Saroff for the Estate of Howard Rose.
All rights reserved. Manufactured in the United States of America.

Published by Raymond Saroff, Publisher, Acorn Hill Road, Olive Bridge, New York 12461. Typeset in Monticello by Delmas Typesetting, and printed by McNaughton & Gunn, Lithographers. First edition.
1 3 5 7 9 10 8 6 4 2   1992 1993 1994 1995

ISBN 1-878352-08-3 hardcover
ISBN 1-878352-09-1 trade paperback

Library of Congress Card Number: 92-060817

The characters and events in this novel are fictitious.

The paper used in this publication meets the minimum requirements of American National Standard for Information Sciences—Permanence of Paper for Printed Library Materials, ANSI Z39.48-1984.

Distributed by McPherson & Company, Box 1126, Kingston, NY 12401.

Marrano. *Obs.* exc. *Hist.* ... [Sp. *marrano,* of unknown origin.] A name applied in mediaeval Spain to a christianized Jew or Moor, esp. to one who merely professed conversion in order to avoid persecution.

—*Oxford English Dictionary*

"It is an ironic consideration that, notwithstanding the assistance which the Marranos had given in the discovery of the New World, they were not safe from persecution even here. ...They still continued to cherish their ancestral faith in their hearts, and the enforced outward change of religion could not affect their natural proclivities."

—Cecil Roth, *The Jewish Contribution to Civilization*

The Marrano

I FIRST REALLY KNEW GORDON CHARLS ABUL, THOUGH IN POINT OF FACT WE HAD GROWN UP TOGETHER

I first began to know Gordie Abul well

I am was a plain-looking man

Chicago city of

It clotted my blood

It curdled the blood it clotted the hair it braided the veins it harried the mare

To see them to see so much beauty torn loose from the world and returned to its own pure devices

It came as an almost physical violation

Battered by beauty I lay

Beautied by batter

In that still dim hallucinated air the gorgeous screen crashing over and the barbarous intoxicated words shrieked out had an almost physical impact, and I sensed that Emily

It made us me one it made you boil to hear such things in an army hospital ward   there we have it

It made you boil to hear such things in even the normally hallucinated air of an army hospital ward, because however bitterly disillusioned et cetera about ultimate blah and blah, one *had* killed destroyed taken human life, shed human blood, and to have killed destroyed taken and shed the way *he* killed destroyed took and shed—twenty-three the citation said he shed including stray cats and mad dogs—without some trace of

In fact just to *write* without some trace of

In fact, I sink back into the depths of my genius without a trace of

Here lies.

* * *

...and last but not least the room in which I spend twenty, often twenty-four of the twenty-four hours, and again I quote from *Penthouse and Villa:*

> In this exquisite guest-room the embroidered silk used for the Louis XV bed canopy and drapery and also the window curtains (Scalamandré from an 18th century design) inspired the pattern for the custom-made carpet (William T. Pood of Dallas and Mexico City). The color scheme is rose, white and pale green with accents of deeper green and bittersweet. Eight panels in a monkey design, painted in the 18th century manner, were executed by the celebrated artist, Paulding Rotborough. Some of the furniture is Italian and painted in a design of blue-green and yellow. Outstanding pieces here are a Louis XV desk with ormulu and two Venetian serpentine commodes with green marble tops from French and Company.

Another six-color plate, half a dozen detail insets, et cetera. Cost her a little fortune though of course she insists P. and V. bore the expense of the whole spread, including color—"considered it an honor, I assure you. Hounded me for months. Since when have I paid to get into those magazines anyway?"—haughty as a cat. "Since we went to sleep and woke up old, Sister Dolly!" She stared and broke into tears, and I can never forgive myself. She's such a horror when she cries.

But oddly enough I think she's brought it off. Darling little thirty-room chateau in the French style; grounds piled with nymphs and satyrs (Florentine craftsmen); artificial lakes; picturesque islands—one with a ruin; barbecue pits; gay pavilions; night-lighting. To date $700,000, Jerrold confides, with some large bills still to come. It will go well over a million. And the great thing is it's a charming place!—comfortable beyond belief. A damn outrageous fact. I don't know when I found a strange room so easy to be in. Possibly because it's beneath contempt? Possibly nothing. Witless, hopelessly vulgar and sensing it, goo-goo-eyeing for your approval as though you were the shining catch of the whole damn century. I swear the place positively wriggles when you look at it. Well, what of it. If it's a bit over-dressed I'm a bit worn and we make a touching couple. I'm past being a snob about such things. Comfort is all I ask. This very minute a maid sets beside me a silver tray with muffins and plum preserves and a pot of green tea. An hour ago, while I dozed, the flowers were changed and the afternoon papers—Dolly gets me about a dozen—laid out. Big, vulgar, generous, comfortable—the perfect slut for a desponding man. Only of course I am not desponding. I really must remember to feel that. *Was but am not.* The clouds are shot through with dawn, as I keep assuring Dolly. — "What clouds, Matthew? Why will you have clouds? The family was never subject to clouds, except Cousin Estelle, due to the Democrat administration. But unfortunately you *are* a Democrat, a perfectly stinking one. I simply can't see why you of all people should have clouds." Et cetera.

Heart of mold, really. I swear the comfort part must be coincidental. I can't imagine Dolly caring a hoot about anyone being comfortable, though on the other hand (I tend to be unfair to my big sister) I can't honestly imagine her objecting *too* strenuously, if anyone had thought to bring up the point. Do decorators tizzy themselves over that sort of thing? I mean, "Oh no, Mrs. Wexler, obsolutely no George One chairs in a *friendly* chateau, Mrs. Wexler, obsolutely one sprouts great purple piles in half an hour on George One, Mrs. Wexler"? I wonder. I also wonder why decorators never have any backs to their heads. There, I've tired myself.

* * *

Apropos of wondering about decorators, I've most recently been wondering to what extent if at all they consult with their clients on the subject of commissioned decorations. Specifically, Paulding Rotborough's monkey panels. They seem pretty sniggering stuff for the T. Jerrold Wexlers, powers in the Dallas Citizens Council and the rest, to be founding a claim to social leadership on. Dolly's as blind as a bat—though she can spot you a pauper at fifty yards—but Jerrold must see, which raises delicate questions about Jerrold. But then of course he's Dallas bred, and I'm not versed in Dallas breeding. Dirty monkey pictures in the guest rooms may be de rigueur in Dallas. In Los Angeles I know they put geranium petals in the champagne. In Milwaukee—no, in Chicago. Sooner or later Chicago so maybe now? In Chicago—well no.

* * *

I am haunted today, sickened nearly to death with an old passion. The green French draperies have done me in—the sun never touched them in such a way before, or not that I noticed. Dead of green French draperies—another scandal for my poor family to face. Well, they would have understood me in Chicago, that home of the ancient wisdom. Lord, what didn't they understand in Chicago? And where but in Chicago, that blackened graveyard of all rich young eagerness, could sunlight on green French draperies take hold in the soul forever? Certainly not here, where miles of the stuff enfold one, though for a moment a certain triangular shape of light took my breath away. But on a dismal street, in an old small blackened house, that brilliant patch of green was a heart-leaping sight, while inside, those incomparable creatures ...

Hudson would have found my monkey panels amusing, though badly painted, I suppose. He would lay his tapering finger on the heart of the thing at once: "An old joke needs better telling." He would smile and then he would frown, for he was a just man—as he always said—and gave things their due. But he was never kind. Kindness has to do with separate small affairs, such as have always occupied me apparently, and Hudson lived in the higher reaches of the spirit where all is connected and the least compromise spells disaster. Or so he always said. Yes, that's the way it was. Bright and knifelike. A shining year in a small blackened house. Dolly in her worst moments was never so trivial or ridiculous as those sublime pretenders ... or a hundredth so dangerous to the PEOPLE. Irene scowling and saying something fierce and splendid and absolutely upside-down; Hudson smiling, then frowning, and after an hour of patient analysis everything on its feet again. Tell us, Hudson!

"Yes? Matthew, my wrung heart, my good socialist soul!—after all these years?"

"Talk."

"I mean, I thought you had gone on to more useful things—."

"Talk."

"No, I won't talk. Your Paulding Rotborough is a thorough beast. What should I have to do with a celebrated monkey painter? Call the zoo for pity's sake."

"Paints monkeys—."

"Monkeys *would*. Did you expect him to be scratching his fuzzy little ass over Emma Goldman? I mean, that would be madness. A socialist monkey painter! Well, I won't have any in *any* form. This Paulding Rotborough fellow may be the finest monkey painter of his time, but why must *I* care? Suppose a horse counts up to three, it makes him a monstrous wise horse, but everyone one knows can count up to three or very nearly, and how many wise people does one know? Purely and simply that. I'm a plain talker. I don't mean to be unkind, but I have enough to do provisioning my fall-out shelter with sufficient olives for five people for six months—do you realize the calculations involved?—without running off to see every new animal prodigy who sets up as a genius. Yet I won't have you putting me down as a belittler of animal talent either. I've had first-hand experience of it. When I was a lad in Oak Forest, we had a dog soprano, a foul fat basset bitch, who did the most telling mad scene out of *Lucia* I have ever heard. Admittedly I never heard the great ones—my first was old Melba's; the first really good one, Galli-Curci's; Barrientos was a small neat bore—but my dear parents had heard Patti, and Jenny Lind in her great days at Covent

Garden, and they swore the ladies were no better, and even somewhat inferior in pathos, especially Lind. Now, did we make a fuss over it? We did not! We asked no questions about where and when she practiced, for she must have practiced endlessly, you realize. Her technique was absolutely secure, spite of a slight break in the registers, and her musicianship was way out of the ordinary for this type of singer. The expressive variety she was able to wring out of grace notes, for example, was a lesson in itself. My father, Colonel Beckwith, was especially struck by her grace notes. All this, then, took practice ... and instruction. Again, did we go about the neighborhood making casual inquiries about Marchesi-type poodles? Again, no. I mean, to what purpose? It might have led to the flushing out of a whole damn doggy opera troupe, and my poor tired mother would have felt compelled to start giving subscription parties and the rest. The whole Chicago Opera thing over again. Like socialism in a way—better not to notice."

"How's that, sir?"

"Never mind 'how's that.' I say we asked no questions, sir, we made no fuss, so who are you? But neither did we put Maisie down. Justness, Matthew, justness is the mark of the gentleman, right in line after incuriosity. We let her sing her heart out, even listened with a show of attention—we fairly well had to, for she had *power*— but afterwards we chased her into the yard for the night, and *no applause*. And let me tell you, it wasn't always easy to maintain our composure, for we were opera lovers and used to rising to our feet after a great performance. D'you remember the Grace Moore films? Heart's truth, lad, you simply couldn't keep us in our seats at the curtain. When the soprano went down we came up. Lord, and we'd *scream*—old white-haired dignitaries with ribbons and wattled grand dames yelling their heads off and jumping up and down in an orgy of appreciation. You should have seen old Edith McCormick go at it, throwing everything in sight. It warmed the heart—."

"McCormick. Of the fine old Haymarket Riot McCormicks?"

"Mmmmm. Middle name of Rockefeller too—."

"Oh what a *lark*."

"Positively Congrevey of its type, eh? Dizzies one just to imagine what the *change* counted up to. But to get on, it wasn't easy for us to sit there drinking our coffee, calm and inward after one of Maisie's performances. It happened oftenest at dinner, as I recall. Yes. There'd be a burbling in the corridor, some hawking and spitting, and in phlumphs Maisie demented as a nut-cake, eyes bloodshot, jowls running drool, tongue a little out, every organ wagging, and stands there bemused, gusts of memory chasing through her tiny brain. She smiles and swings her ears coquettishly, she starts to scratch and then forgets, staring into space with one mud-caked hindpaw foolishly kicking. It was rending, I tell you. Before she sang a note you knew the worst. But when she did sing, the heavens opened. The piano began its reminiscing—never mind what piano—and the Blessed Damozel lamented, pure and sad beyond words: which was fortunate in a way, because her diction was generally muffled. But I can't describe to you the precision of her staccati or the silkiness of her chromatic scales, the lorn, pathetic, sleepy quality of her legato, and when she was in particularly good voice, the reckless flight of improvisation in the cadenzas, though in perfect taste—like Patti, my father said, her fioriture was shaped to dramatic requirements. Oh, and when she rose to that final despairing top E and threw herself down, her stubby legs in every direction, her lips and ears all over the place and her tongue halfway to the corridor entrance, I tell you it was everything we could do to restrain ourselves. We stared at each other helplessly, quivering with excitement. What *does* one do in such a situation? Nothing.

"My mother was once so carried away she plucked a tea rose from the centerpiece, kissed it, and threw it. Maisie ate it. My dear, we nearly cried. It was so sad, don't you see. Maisie had the genius but not the *right*. A fact of life, Matthew. You don't fling roses at a dog any more than you might have booted Melba out for the night. The dog will almost certainly die of insecticides, while Melba of course would have reacted vilely—very low sort anyway, called my dear father such a name once. In the same manner, if your tiresome monkey painted as well as Titian (which God forbid), there'd be nothing to do but hand him an orange peel and turn sadly back to

Titian. There's no breaking the spell anymore. It's too damn late. We are hopelessly superior to everything we know; and if you grouse, well, we don't know very much maybe—sounds like you too, snotty—I cap you by replying, well, that's the point. You can't be hopelessly superior when there's very much to know, can you? You limit the field and claim there's no more. Call the zoo, Matthew. Stock up your own fallout shelter and forget the mysterious mutants of the world. Their day will come as ours will pass, pass without our ever discovering what the strange dreams mean."

"Strange dreams, Hudson?"

"Don't you have them? Oh lord, you are of a piece. A really good sort for whom the earth is sufficient and this way of life ultimately perfectible if only we care enough. You care, don't you, Matthew? You sweat and weep for us just as your good father has done these many years. Comfort and hamburgers and good-will among the nations—folk dancing in the streets, legalized prostitution, free gin for the old folks—these are your dreams, aren't they? Bless you, Matthew."

"And bless you doubly, Hudson, as the one in more immediate peril—."

"Of what, a clear head? Cheer up, lad. Perhaps in the next historic cycle howling stage-door throngs will greet a farting Madame Maisie grandly munching her roses, to your infinite content, and Paulding Rotborough ... now that *is* a damn uncommon name for a monkey. Some pre-vision on the part of his dear parents of glories to come—?"

"Whatever you say, sir, he must be accorded human rights."

"Sir, how dare you."

"But he *paints*—."

"Socialist rot! Because I screw like mad or try to doesn't make me a *monkey* —."

The maid just now started to come in, leaned there a minute looking at me and slipped out again. 6:35. Two hours rigid with despair. A trashy, race-baiting, decadent, mad megalomaniac—everything abhorrent to me—and I all but worshipped him, sat dazzled at his feet, laughing or mute with wonder. Was I such a clown then, or have I somehow dwindled with virtue till I no longer dare accept what I knew? Can this really be all it came to, that vast expenditure of wit—a few cheap drops of poison?—or was it infinitely more, because not everything splendid or fruitful begins and ends in right thinking? A terrible thought. *What was he? Who was he?* Did Gordie know? He fled with them but did he *know*? Too soon, of course. I begin to tremble like a leaf. What's more, I find I've torn some of the bandages loose and picked off the scabs,. No, I understood I was doing it. My tribute.

> In Xanadu did Kubla Khan
> A stately pleasure dome decree

For I was there and this is my tribute. Whatever infamous thing they were. Here's Dolly, frantic.

* * *

> Where Alph, the sacred river, ran
> Through caverns measureless to man
> Down to a sunless sea

The only poem I've ever completely understood. I think we ran around with the same crowd. Bella phoned three times today but I wouldn't talk. That was foolish. It will make her more "understanding" than ever.

* * *

Mrs. Dolly brought me an armload of scarlet and gold books until mine should arrive from home, if ever. It seems she's convinced that liberal politics have brought me to this pass, so a course in nineteenth-century kings and queens may pull me out. She didn't say as much but I can't think what else to make of the damn selection. I've wasted half a dozen hours of perfectly good life amid some of the mealiest boredom the human spirit ever achieved. I'm *numb*. And uneasy—profoundly uneasy. I can't despise the creatures. One look at the photographs of those mean lunatic faces and my eyes fill up. Yet consider this plum from *Through Four Revolutions* by HRH Princess Ludwig Ferdinand of Bavaria, Infanta of Spain: The band then played a Habanera, and we spoke of Cuba, which with Spain gave scope enough for conversation. After supper the King asked me very politely if I objected to smoking. Later he took us to a stalactite grotto; a tiny cascade [Alph the sacred river!—one shouldn't laugh, I suspect] trickled mysteriously, and through a cleft in the roof one could see the moon. After a while we went to the Indian hut near the lake, so as to hear the music better, and as we passed the Hindu towers the orchestra played *Aida*. . . . Just as we were leaving this fairyland the King threw aside the curtain and exclaimed, "Aurora has arrived." Together we stood and watched the first faint shimmer in the sky.

Now I find I like that very much. A vulgar sort—an arriviste at this sort of thing—Jerrold, say, would have ordered *Lakmé* struck up. *Our* Ludwig was the real insolent thing. Mad, too. They killed him, as was proper. Face down in a pot of water. Wagner never turned a hair. Yet Ludwig was a man as I am a man, even lonelier maybe, with an even wilder longing for the witch. I can't despise him. *Aida* by a Hindu tower. Green French draperies in a tumble-down house. Oh, don't hurt them—

* * *

NY Times, Sun Feb 17: We know that Marlowe was apt to attempt "sudden privy injuries to men."

Good.

* * *

I'm being plagued by correspondences and it makes me more apprehensive than I care to admit. So I don't admit it. *But I won't be led.*

* * *

Yesterday and today have been passed in a sort of trance, full of black thoughts. I've made a damn fool of myself. Consequences are still incalculable, everything rolls about uncertainly but that. I almost can't bear it. Almost, I say—nothing more. Even as an exposed fool I'm worth more than most, and not only worth more, become even more necessary to the aspirations of other fools. They will feel they know me now—a sufferer, and irrational like anyone else whose money has brought him no happiness after all. The *coarseness* of it. Well. And how did I turn into this fool? By performing the most inspired, the most calculated, the most foolproof act of my life. It's been the blackest thought of any.

* * *

Somewhat better though still not good. Bella phoned early in the evening and we cried into each other's ear for half an hour. My good loyal Bella. I'm sure she feels she has me now, bless her. After eleven years and four children she has me at last because no one else can possibly want me. Well, maybe she won't either. Am I afraid of what I've done? I don't think so. Curious, is all. The act itself was the fine adventure, the after-effects of very small account, or so I must continue to persuade myself. I never was a vain man that I know of. Otherwise—. My books and private papers arrived at last.

* * *

"The elder J.P. Morgan is delighted, it is said, jestingly to trace his ancestry back to Henry Morgan, the seventeenth century Caribbean pirate; in token of this he named his yacht the *Corsair* and painted it an anarchistic black." Anarchistic black? As against capitalistic white? Well, the Assassins wore white too. Bastards. I'm sure Emma Goldman got pink, blue, and yellow onto *one breast*. Still, Gordie affected black.

* * *

But how did I manage so long without my Stirner—my secret vice—my holidays? I sincerely believe I could not love mankind half so well loved I not Stirner more! Like being raped by the bankrobber in the banker's own bed. What a dog. What a *lay*.

* * *

Bella again, in a real pet. Due to unfamiliarity with exotic names and operetta conventions we have been supporting the wrong side in Gabon for thirty-six hours. She didn't find this amusing—I really shouldn't either—and went down and raised hell with Ben. Being regent for me I suppose she's especially raw about these things. But they do happen, and people forget very quickly. Ben's a fine editor. The whole point is, we shouldn't be supporting *any* side in Gabon. We don't even know if there *is* a Gabon. Here we are backing one faction and describing heartrending conditions under the other in a country that may owe its existence to an error on the AP teletype. Because generally a partisan paper like the *Dispatch* runs easy as a tricycle—at least if the data is correctly understood. I mean, there's never any fine weighing or balancing necessary. We're on the side of *humanity,* damn it. Matter of fact, we have exclusive representation in the middle west. Then along comes Gabon, and for thirty-six hours we find ourselves supporting the forces of colonialism, segregated piano recitals, French cooking, et cetera. It's a goddamn AP plot!

* * *

No, I *am* afraid. I really am. I think it's the confusion in this poor torn head. I can't locate my *platform*. Being considered a fool is a black thought but not, to me, a fearful one. If it were, I could not have have survived the life I chose to lead. *Chose to.* But murk and confusion . . .

* * *

"It is the absolute condition of revolt, it is an exemplary case of love without respite which makes us, the spectators, gasp with anguish at the idea that nothing will ever be able to stop it."

Hair very black, very fine, very thick, in slow silken waves over the top of the head—but down the sides and back beginning to run in minutest ripples and shudders, like green milkweed silk, eddying around the ears and far down the neck

Without warning the screen crashed over and the picture, by fitful candlelight, of the sweated intoxicated face against outrageous silver pyjamas

* * *

I screamed out. I was sitting with a book, not much minding the words, my thoughts as usual melancholy though by no means rash, when all at once I opened my mouth and screamed. It was pure terror. I grabbed my face as if to hide it. Oh lord. Dolly came pounding at the door but I shouted something lame and sent her away. She lingered a moment—I could hear her labored breathing—and I lost my temper. She sniffled maddeningly. I called her—I don't know what—nothing constructive. Help me.

* * *

Better. I begin to get it a little clearer. Bella phoned twice and no tears at either end. Good sign. The doctor said two weeks, maybe three, before the bandages come off, and I said, "So soon?" and he looked at me. I was properly abashed, then annoyed. Who is *he*? What is this Divine Displeasure doctors wield?

* * *

A journey.

MACHEN: And suddenly, each one that had drunk found himself attended by a companion, a shape of glamour and unearthly allurement, beckoning him apart, to share in joys more exquisite, more piercing than the thrill of any dream, to the consummation of the marriage of the Sabbath. It is hard to write of such things as these, and chiefly because that shape that allured with loveliness was no hallucination, but, awful as it is to express, the man himself. By the power of that Sabbath wine, a few grains of white powder thrown into a glass of water, the house of life was riven asunder and the human trinity dissolved, and the worm which never dies, that which lies sleeping within us all, was made tangible and an external thing, and clothed with a garment of flesh. And then, in the hour of midnight, the primal fall was repeated and represented....

COEURDEROY: Forward! Forward! War is redemption! God desires it, the God of the criminals, of the oppressed, of the rebels, of the poor, of all those who are tormented, the Satanic God whose body is of brimstone, whose wings are of fire and whose sandals are of bronze!

PROUDHON: The French worker asks for work, you offer him alms, and he rebels, he shoots at you.... I glory in belonging to that proud race, inaccessible to dishonor!

KROPOTKIN: In order to understand how much I sympathize with the ideas of Tolstoy, it is sufficient to say that I have written a whole volume to demonstrate that life is created, not by the struggle for existence, but by mutual aid.

BAKUNIN: There will be a qualitative transformation, a new living, life-giving revelation, a new heaven and a new earth, a young and mighty world in which all our present dissonances will be resolved into a harmonious whole.

BAKUNIN AND NECHAEV: We recognize no other activity but the work of extermination, but we admit that the forms in which this activity will show itself will be extremely varied—poison, the knife, the rope, et cetera.

CITIZEN SADE: I am appointed magistrate, yes magistrate! By the prosecution! Who, my dear lawyer, would have told you *that* fifteen years back?

WILDE: All association must be quite voluntary. It is only in voluntary associations that man is fine.

KEMPTON: I have come to the Socialist Party (SP/SDF) because I cannot conceive of living out my life in a world without hope.

STIRNER: In the *unique one* the owner himself returns into his creative nothing, out of which he is born. Every higher essence above me, be it God, be it man, weakens the feeling of my uniqueness, and pales only before the sun of this consciousness. If I concern myself for myself, the unique one, then my concern rests on its transitory, moral creator, who consumes himself, and I may say: All things are nothing to me.

RIMBAUD: If you only knew how fucking silly you look with that herring in your hand.

TRISTAN: *Ich war,/ wo ich von je gewesen,/ wohin auf je ich geh:/ im weiten Reich der Weltennacht.*

Eyes black as pitch and so disconcertingly close-set they stabbed at you with nearly undivided brilliance—some thought him cross-eyed, but no—slightly tilted, his father's eyes—under a thick straight black unbroken line of eyebrow. Nose small, sharp, hooked. Mouth curved, almost re-curved at the center, curling at the corners, *red*. Teeth white enough, I suppose, with a charming childish space between the two top front ones. Complexion olive, again his father's—the face itself tending to narrowness but cheek and jaw bones very prominent, deep hollows pressing against the side teeth, especially now after two weeks of coma and by the light of candles, sweeping forward and out into a voluptuous sort of fleshy cushion into which the corners of the lips were deeply sunk and out of which extravagantly ...

I thought I had never really seen him until that moment ...

* * *

The best day so far. Calm nearly all the way, maybe even a thread of land. Maybe not. First thing this morning Bella phoned and blabbed away through mouthfuls of omelet. Her old self again or a good facsimile and I thank her for it. She was in a mad "pazazz" of course. Her morning to work in Memorial Hospital gift shop; then Neighborhood Improvement League luncheon (co-chairman with Lizzie Bontecour) to plan "Persian Garden" ball; then deliver emotional stir-up lecture at Hadassah; then two hours volunteer work insert campaign literature at Dinky's Tower headquarters; then dinner party at Fairfax's to meet somebody big (forget who).

Then the boys get on and gargle their milk at me—"Hope you're okay and all, sir—can I smoke a pipe?—can I quit dancing class?"— et cetera. Their enchanting laughter when I say yes. Then Richard and Frieda and Mary and even the marvelous new gardener—Stan? (who by the way I hope she isn't underpaying as usual—such skilled labor has to be encouraged). Each wishes me a speedy recovery though no one of course says from what, a speedy return though no one says from where, presumably because they don't know. (Am I really so safe from scrutiny here?)

Great hubbub in background now—boys dashing off—Bella scolding—Richard clearing the table—then Bella on again. Drowning in an orange this time; crunch of waves, crash and gurgle of rafts swallowed down. Oh, ghastly!

Softly now—silence of death, I figure—with the barest minimum of reflective tooth-sucking. And a sort of death it turned out to be. She had had a private interview with old N.T., in town for some student discussion group. So *sad,* she said; a dusty waxwork with a harsh raspy record going inside, and yet what he said was as good and reasonable and full of sweetness as ever. But there was no life in it anymore, no real belief. "Most defeated man of my time," he said and laughed. She had been almost embarrassed. Pause: I was at a loss, the description caught so much of Father. At last I said that, well, he was very old, he had done fine service but his time was past—. She wasn't fooled. To what damn purpose? she snapped back. While I fished about for cheery evidence that doesn't exist she shot me through the heart. "Is it all such a dream, Matt?" I could see her eyes full of angry tears she would never shed, for to shed them meant to answer her own question, and one never answers such a question, or how does one go on? How would she ever climb onto a lecture platform again and in her deepest Foxcroft voice exhort the holy rabble to do away with her and hers, or at least vote for someone who would tax her out of existence if he could? I thought of Ludwig II sweeping through the curtains of Xanadu to watch the sun come up. Such princely courage is not for us. But she must have realized that what I least need is saddening, so with absolutely no transition I found myself in the middle of the "Persian Garden" plans, and how she had wangled champagne out of Elizabeth Arden, and $10,000 worth of exotic flowers out of Pletcher's, and bullied Meyer Davis into wearing brocade and feathers, et cetera—all related with eager innocent laughter and a sense of *mission*. Well, there's absolutely nothing in the world like a fine lady, and my Bella's one of the most thoroughly equipped. I adore her, though she'll never believe it. A delicate abstracted air of personal problems lived with and accepted is one of the fine lady's traditional achievements, and no adoring husband is going to be allowed to mess it up. Half the time Dolly sails about with a really noble purification-through-suffering look because of the quality of furniture polish nowadays. I know, because I asked.

I have just been standing at the windows, and what I want to know is, are the reporters occasionally to be seen behind the statuary out there merely inspecting the grounds—which seems unlikely after all that's been written to date—or have they got wind of Dolly's interesting guest? If the latter, how? Bella packed me off here in the middle of the night precisely because she felt this to be the last place on earth people would look for me. Dolly has been denouncing me publicly for years, first in her capacity as Republican committeewoman, and latterly, since her marriage to Jerrold, as unofficial Queen of Texas Bigotry. Can she really be using me to stimulate flagging press interest in her fool chateau? I swear I'll ram a damn pavilion up her ass if I find it out.

* * *

—Dolly kept her foxy look throughout but that's to be expected of so great a huntress. She had ridden out for two and a half hours in the morning—aged 61, mind you—and I suppose the mystique was still upon her. The britches, boots, and stink were. I suspect she was also somewhat stoned, which is a great abettor of mystiques. Anyway, she lounged about and sipped her Southern Comfort and measured me hostilely. Which way would I pounce! Well, I fooled her—myself too—for suddenly, as we sat idly sparring, my brain gave a little jolt and there it was—the platform I had drawn up and then lost, intact, pristine —and I proceeded to read it off with all the cool wonder of Jerrold at the ticker tape. How eagerly I listened may be imagined.

Tell me, dearest Dolly (said I, and I could see her quiver with distrust)—tell me, was I a handsome man?

Not you (said she) with your baggy ready-mades flapping in the wind.

Did I say best-dressed or did I say—?

Don't take that tone with me!

I haven't—*yet*.

Well, what do you want to know for?

Your opinion is always valuable to me as coming from the uncharted ends of the earth. Lands of perpetual darkness. Cannibaldom.

Matt, do you know what you are?

Tell me.

A mean Communist bastard. Can't *abide* you, my dear.

Quick now, was I ever a handsome one?

Not bad, of your villainous type. Family features saved you.

But not exceptional?

No, thank god, not exceptional! That's one vulgarity you spared us.

Good. Now I want you to attend with all your small brain while I explain a fact of life.

Do you know what else you are? A mealy-mouthed hypocrite.

Average-looking man. Rippled blond hair, good figure, but nothing to draw a second look from the disinterested. Commonplace, one could say, more or less at the dead center of things.

The place for people of breeding to be, except *you* were never within miles —

Oh, but I was. I was your common man. Common in looks, ability, view—

Aristocrat to the bone. Conniving royalty. Ha ha!

Ho *ho*. You're getting pretty gay for a thing your age.

Who did you think you were fooling? You long to have them crown you king—King of the Wild West!—King of Downtrodden Humanity!

But that's the commonest longing of all, Dolly. To serve humbly but egregiously—

To sit on a throne of tears in the hearts of spics and nigras—

Exquisite—

Right?

Oh, right—but what of it? The more you dredge up, the more hopelessly common you prove me. To top everything, I married first a waitress, then a plain woman of no pretensions—

—With a pharmaceutical fortune and the connections of a Maria Theresa. Otherwise—

Damn it, stop riding home on the ends of my sentences. When did you get witty? But what's really amusing is that you should have left out sheenies, I'm thinking—

Another thing about you, you *seem* generally to be talking public issues—

Sheenies? I supposed it a very private misfortune—

Matt, don't do that—

No. Public issues. Here we are. Seem to be talking public issues. Right again, Dolly duck, because what I'm really going on about—

Whatever became of Gordie, Matt—Gordie Abul!

—Is the importance of being beautiful.

You do remember him?

One often remembers the man who steals one's wife.

I'm glad. I haven't thought of him in years.

Listen to me. So fearsomely beautiful that ninnies devised law and philosophy in sheer panic—so wildly, insolently, agonizingly beautiful—

Very handsome man. Not one of us at all.

—That plain folk, exposed for what they were, conspired together in mutually protective cells, wounded and provoked into the beginnings of civilization and its million frenzied activities only to keep from thinking of you, anarchic, civilizing beauty!

Well, for heaven's sake, dear. Is this the newest party line? I mean, does the Institute for Advanced Studies approve? Quite unusual—

Simple experience—

But is it—how does Bella put it—*acceptable sociology*?

The profoundest I ever knew, but hardly acceptable. Who should accept it? Those whose peace of mind depends on its careful obliteration? And that's all of us! Dolly—

Now stop your idiot blubbering. You've got the gauze a fright. A soggy mummy, as I'm a big fat cat! Do you hear me, Matthew Lenart? *Stop.* There. You're simply not yourself these days. Do you realize you haven't abused a single vested interest—except of course me—all afternoon? What would Father have said? No, taking this with that, I think I really prefer our old flamboyant Saint Matthew, soul of the oppressed, toast of the Minneapolis beer-swillers, venomous establishment-baiter to this pink-eyed bunny rabbit. I want my reptile brother back! Coil up and *hiss* a little, dear. *Please.* How about a nice medal for Oppenheimer? No? Gas-pellet gumdrops to commemorate Chessman? Civil rights to pollute our blood? Oil-profits tax to drain it off altogether? Still no? Then how about compulsory fluoridation of the water to make our teeth fall out—migrant workers to murder us in our beds—Red China to use what's left in chop suey? Oh Matt, why have you forsaken us! And by the way, Jerrold tells me that, mysteriously, you've seen the light in Gabon, whatever that may mean.

A wild spot in me, calling and calling to something—someone—ages gone —

Dear, I can't hear you.

—Fragment to the body—thrall to the witch—calling, calling—

Matt?

I had to cut it away!

Anyhow, as someone was saying recently, we don't have scandals like that anymore. I mean the whole juicy scream, not just Gordie. Benham, Shem and Edith. Emily. Did you love her very much? Twenty years ago it must be. Heavens, we've changed. But what were you going to explain to me? Facts of life? Ha ha—I *know* those. Wexlers in Texas had damn well better know their facts of life. Let's see now. Oil lobbies are the foundation of stable government. Right? There's too much staked out in cigarettes for them to be that bad for you. Right? Chiang Kai shek is the Rose of Sharon—

Dolly, if you had lived with beauty a while—

Again? Well—

—A very little while, but long enough to discover yourself plain—nothing extreme, not ugly, merely, as regards the visible part of you, precisely undistinguished.

People of breeding—

—Had been shaken by it until unwittingly you had drawn back from all the verges, not of appearance only, but of thought, feeling—*all*—towards the middle—

To what it amuses you to call your commonness. Ah.

And as a matter of fact went on to live there quite contentedly, until one day, with a shock of horror, you understood that if you didn't at once fight through to some sharp ledge you were in danger of tenderly shading off into the big warm central heart, which wasn't at all your picture of yourself.

Ha ha ha!

More important, unless you could match that memory of outrageous beauty with some outrageous *stroke,* some act and consequence to give you a nearly comparable uniqueness, there might be madness waiting too. Do you follow?

Follow?

The logic.

A child could, my dear, your whole life has been a child's version—

Bless you. Now what I want to know is—

What would I have done? Not what you did, if that's what you mean. I think you really must be demented.

Then *what*? Name the alternative! I wasn't handsome, nor of some secretly original turn of hand or head to bring astoundingly into play—

So one night, in a very public place, after much drink and laughter, you took a table fork with you into the lounge. We part company already: I never dine in restaurants let alone get stoned in 'em—and starting at the hairline and continuing to the jaw, very slowly and deliberately, you raked your face in vertical gashes from ear to ear, only sparing your eyes for some reason—

Well, I wanted to see—

And the tiles were so slippery with blood that people rushing in fell screaming—

And I was a sight at last to make people draw back in fear—*exactly in all respects as they had done*. A remarkable discovery. You do understand?

A little, if only to keep from passing out. Lenarts don't do such things, you damn fool—

Need I add that no such interview ever took place?

* * *

Twenty years? No. I began to know Gordie towards the end of the war—'44, so it's very much less. The last I saw of them would have been around '50. I married Bella at the beginning of the Stevenson boom in '51 and Papa died a few months after. I was home at least a year by then. Barely a dozen years.

* * *

"As socialists, we want a Socialist world not because we have the conceit that men would therefore be more happy ... but because we feel the moral imperative in life itself to raise the human condition, even if this should ultimately mean no more than that man's suffering has been lifted to a higher level."

That's early Norman Mailer and perfectly lovely. I found it in a little anthology of "protest" literature Bella included with my books. She can't help proselytizing even her own husband! Such a passionate woman. I wonder if she read through the long poem called "Why I am a Socialist," which includes the haunting stanza:

> I have seen the queens of fashion in their jewelled
>   pride arrayed,
> Ruby crowned and splendid,—rubies of a baby's
>   life blood made,
> Richer than the gems of nature, of a stranger, deeper shade,
> On their snow white bosoms quivered as the dames
>   of fashion prayed.

Bella has a ruby bib from her grandmother that Catherine the Great is said to have had to pass up for lack of funds. Or noted this refrain from "The New God":

> It's Morgan's, it's Morgan's the great financial gorgon.
> Everything here but the atmosphere all belongs to Morgan.

The gentleman was a cousin of her grandfather's! Well, I'm not being fair. One of Bella's admirable traits is the way she's contrived to live with her background, and not only live with it, actually seem to enjoy it.

But to get back to the Mailer piece—lovely, as I say, but what is this "life" that contains this "man"? What is the "human condition" and what exactly does "man's suffering" include? Admittedly I'm in a strange picky mood today, what Bella calls my "arctic state." Still, what do those fine nineteenth-century abstractions mean anymore? Anything? Anything, that is, more significant than a million little local failures precisely balanced by a million little local graduation exercises, yourself figuring the odds like a horse player over a racing form? I begin to wonder if there would be a noticeable wiggle in the course of events if one dark night liberal and conservative, not to say radical and reactionary, switched roles. In fact, I wonder if there would be a wiggle if we stopped all effort altogether and stayed at home with mouths shut and hands in lap. I don't think so, though the quiet would be welcome. We're not *decorative* anymore. The current (Alph?) has got too strong for us. No matter in what direction we face, or what pose it pleases us to assume, we go where we go.

And who is this pitiable "man" thing anyway? I never met him. Does he exist? Papa swore he did. So I go on fighting his battles under the impression that he's too weak with hunger or brutalized by oppression or bound down by injustice or just plain stupid to fight his own, but recently the idea has been nagging at me that he's never actually asked me to. Does that account for the insulting circulation figures of the *Dispatch* since Papa's death? Is he really out there anymore is what I mean. Or are there a million separate Malcolm X's with a million strange desires wondering who the hell I think I am with my "man" and my "moral imperative" and my "higher level of suffering"? The good fight has become a sort of solo dance. ("Socialist Pleasures." How Bella used to hate Laura Riding for that story!) And where is this "higher level"? How high and whose choice and how do we know when we've got there? Census, poll, vote? Psychological tests given by Experts? Governmental proclamation: "We are pleased to announce that tests show the level has at last been attained where suffering can be meaningful; we trust you will remember this Socialist service at the next election"? Does the "moral imperative" light go off then? Yes? But what if it doesn't! What if we've completely misunderstood!—Laugh away, Gordie!

Well, I realize how easy and cheap such an exercise is. I'm the first one to cry it down in others;—only I get into such a cold depression sometimes. I'm better now. Interesting how necessary scorn becomes to one raised on it. An addiction. Ever deeper and more private parts demand it until only oneself can find the way.

* * *

"It is the absolute condition of revolt, it is an exemplary case of love without respite which makes us, the spectators, gasp with anguish that nothing will ever be able to stop it."

* * *

As generally happened with these seizures of his, he rose back into consciousness as suddenly and unpredictably as he went under. Fifteen days (I believe) of deep coma, and without warning the screen went crashing over and he lay there blazing with excitement. There was no one near him, of course—never was at these moments, to hear the family nurse, old Fay Gahagan, tell it. She had been flown to Paris on special priority when the first signs of the malady began to supervene. It seems that virtually the moment we were installed the hospital staff received word from his mother that such a thing might possibly occur, describing the onset and demanding to be notified at once. Senator Parkless was an old lover so there was no question of irregularity. Anyway, Fay, who had tended him during these strange sleeps since he was a child, claimed she had never been able to hit on the signs of return. She could watch him day in and day out and then nod off for a few minutes or go pee, as she had just now, and when she saw him next he was over on his side sipping at her coffee or coca cola, sallow and thoughtful but altogether himself. Sometimes he would attempt a friendly little grin for her; more often, especially in his younger days, the tears would run in silent unaccented streams; but on no account could any word be coaxed out of him for hours after.

This time there was a difference, however. Far from any sallow thoughtfulness, he appeared positively intoxicated and was talking a blue streak. Burbling would be more accurate—the wildest antisocial nonsense. It made you boil to hear such things in an army hospital ward. Men were *dying*. For nothing, you may think—out of no real conviction, trivially even—but god almighty you had to be made of ice to say it there! And the language—the hissing ecstasy of loathing. Delirium, Emily said later. Well, there may be truth in delirium as they say there is in wine. Callous as I've grown to scorners and haters, the memory of the few words caught then can yet sting my humanity. Nor was I some country boy to hump my back at all heresy. Granted I was the pattern of a second lieutenant, manual-perfect and fierce for the honor of home-town and flag—I was at the same time heir of Matthew Lenart, Sr., notorious radical newspaper publisher of Teapot Dome fame, and younger brother of one of the first martyrs of the Abraham Lincoln Brigade. That they took no pride in *me* is not to the point; is in fact another story altogether, which I am never likely to put in writing. All I mean to say here is that I was not altogether an ideological prude. I had read and heard much in my father's house. I had some experience of the forms of public despair but this was was some secret hope.

September, and Paris still wild with joy. Street roistering at its height keeping the grand salon of the Hotel de R_____ where we were being treated in an improvised officer's hospital reverberating around the clock. Street blocked off and signs posted by Red Cross but useless. Wine cellars still to be looted, collaborators and Vichyites still to be ratted out and killed. Humiliated first if possible. Scattered rifle fire at all hours. Screams or laughter. Children at hysterical games. Tanks nearly shaking you off your cot. Sound trucks blaring orders and information and dance music. Cathedral bells going off in paroxysms just when you are about to doze.

—A little low conversation, discreet clatter of breakfast dishes. Two had died the night before—incredibly, it must have seemed to us, to die *then*—and those who might have been inclined to raise a little hell instead nipped at concealed flasks and dozed respectfully. Grey Parisian morning. Even street noises damped off for the moment. Nurses and sisters floating eerily down the dark aisles. In our corner, weak candlelight still flickered behind Gordie Abul's wonderful Chinese screen, flown from Minneapolis along with special nurse and bundle of cash for the formalists. Other screens in the salon—in fact, many handsome pieces of antique furniture pressed into use—but nothing so magnificent as Gordie's, all faded black and gold and maybe as expensive as the Normandy landing. It had been his father's, I believe. The nurse, old Fay Gahagan, had either fallen asleep back there or had not quite finished her mystery novel; she devoured one a night. She hadn't stirred for hours. I knew because I had been awake and thinking since five o'clock. There was much for me to think about. That first mysterious communication from Special Services among other things.

Some time after ten, Emily—my first wife—appeared and pulled a chair up beside my cot, tossing her magazines and purse at my feet. (She arrived, I suppose I must note, on the same undemocratic flight as Fay Gahagan—good old corrupt old Parkless.) She asked dutifully if I had had a good night and when I said no she smiled dutifully and, nodding at the screen, asked if anything was new *there*. I said no. She started—what?

I said, I said no, nothing new.

She sat back. I thought you said—.

Well, I obviously didn't.

Oh Matt, it's too friggin' early in the morning. (She had been a waitress.)

Just then a grating of chair-legs and a big fart behind the screen and Fay Gahagan hobbled forth swearing and yawning and spitting, all crippled up with rheumatism aggravated by the damp morning. Emily rushed to assist her, but Fay waved her away ill-temperedly and ambled off towards the toilet. Emily came back and sat down. Her face was working. She signaled a passing sister and asked her to check Captain Abul's dextrose feeder. She claimed to have heard him groaning, which was a lie. He hadn't made a sound in two weeks, being in the strange sort of comatose sleep he had been prey to since childhood. The sister went behind the screen and reappeared to say all was in order. Had she checked the dressings? (We had both been laid out by a grenade explosion at close quarters.) She had and they were fine. Emily's face went back to working.

Emily, I said, do you have cigarettes?

I'm feeling just fine, she said. Why do you ask?

I didn't ask that, I said, I asked—.

I *heard* you, she said—her eyes playing over the dim imageries of the screen—and I want to know why you ask. Don't I look well?

You look very well, I said.

Slept like a log, she said, How's my makeup?

Pretty. How about a good-morning kiss, honey?

Have a cigarette? she said, her face going dead white under the rouge, her hand flinging out as if to prevent something.

And the screen crashed over and I heard that hellish burbling—and we looked and were lost.

* * *

Not waiting, in fact glad enough to find Leclerc busy, I slapped General Gerow's directive into the hand of an aide—I had already and much against my principles got Father's packets to Colonel Rol—and ran down to the jeep, to find it gone. *Perfect.* I was a very supple sort of youngster and my alibi had jelled in an instant. Forty extra minutes were at once transfused into this escapade of Corporal Summers', and to soften him up with nerves, I started down the street in a fury. As it was, there would be questions back at headquarters, and I was never a good liar. The side trip to Rol took longer than I figured on; the FFI had been cagey with me. *My* caginess, which had had to do with my driver's suddenly interested face, though he supposedly understood no French, must have been misinterpreted.

I raced along shouting my driver's name. Due to the chaos of street barricades and burnt-out tanks throughout the sector, our trip to Leclerc's headquarters had already taken twice the calculated time. The streets were filled up with strollers and a few shops had dim lights at the rear, but not for long. It was getting towards dusk and the sniping would be picking up. I had been warned that the Milice were still a real hazard; in fact Parisians themselves, I was told—those of a certain political color—were firing on their own people in order to keep emergency measures in effect a while longer. Little bands of the Resistance were herding captives to some improvised prison in the neighborhood, and as the light mellowed they began to hug the walls. Passersby threw stones and wonderful French curses. There was much laughter. I of course was a cynosure. The American army had not yet made an appearance, but in spite of Leclerc and de Gaulle the people were well aware who the liberators of Paris were. Women ran over to kiss me, men pumped my hands and gabbled hysterically, while children calmly emptied my pockets of cigarettes and keys—the French are very sophisticated. I was in a rage but excited too. Overexcited. You couldn't help it. Those grateful gray faces—the sudden self-pity for the terrible things we had been made to live through—. And there we were in a knot weeping and embracing (I think it was then they got my watch, not that I begrudged it) then laughing.

—A motor. I looked up to see a jeep and an American officer waving. I couldn't quite make him out through my tears, but the flash of silver bars brought me to an embarrassed salute and his pleasant laughter floated back. I remember thinking I really had never heard so much laughter. About seventy-five feet away, the jeep stopped and the officer leaned over to talk to a couple of rifle-bearing Resistance men leading a collaborator between them—a practically naked woman with her head shaved and the swastika painted across her face. Now the officer climbed out. He was a small steely graceful man, with an incongruous black kerchief knotted around his neck that identified him for me at once. It was Gordie Abul. In fact, my sister had written that she heard he was now attached to V Corps.

A little crowd began to form; and I started over, wondering that he should interfere in these very delicate French arrangements. The Resistance men were plainly not happy with whatever he was saying. He kept indicating their yellow arm-bands and his black neckpiece. I had covered about half the distance when I saw him step up to the woman and chuck her under the chin. The onlookers fell unnaturally silent. She looked down. Her captors visibly ground their heels. Then he tilted his head to her lowered face and kissed her. I was dumbfounded. The poor disfigured thing started to cry hysterically. The crowd murmured and one of the Resistance men upended his rifle and shoved Gordie back with the butt. At which, with the most insouciant gesture in the world, Gordie drew his pistol and shot the woman dead.

A furious cry went up. The driver gunned the motor and called to him by some name or catchphrase I didn't recognize. Now people were running for doorways as other shots, apparently by some chain reaction, began to rain down from overhead windows. The driver, a negro, yelped and fell half out of the jeep and lay there making terrible whistling noises. The two Resistance men still hesitated—they would gladly have blown Gordie's head off if they dared—then turned to dash for cover.

I write what I saw or think I saw, for it was very dark and I was running full tilt. As the men turned, Gordie took aim at the back of one, fired, and as he fell trained on the other, but I yelled out—I was almost to him—and he swung around to meet me, his pistol arm stiff and the pistol lined to my forehead.

"Gordie, it's Matt." I could only mouth the air like an idiot. "Matt, *Matt Lenart,*" I screamed, for I'll confide a great secret, he was about to shoot me. Yes, he recognized me—hadn't he been hailing me up the street five minutes earlier? No, he bore me no grudge that I knew of. No, he had no idea of destroying a witness, for there were a hundred more in the doorways around. But he was going to shoot me. I won't try to explain it, except by saying that I believe he was on the beginning of that arc that led him downward into sleep. Because while his aim was exact, his eyes were all but closed and his mouth sweet in a sort of interior greeting, or so I imagined. I can imagine no further.

Facts. His body was an alert and pitiless instrument, and I was a dead man but for the grenade that tore us down. I did not then know the number of lives —presumably the enemy's—he would be cited for destroying. Soon after, Corporal Summers found us and pulled us to a cellar, dressing our wounds as best he could. It was the night of the German air raid.

* * *

I have had no thought in three days, or only this, that I distrust a head that can pretend to have no thought but this during three tormented days. It is not a proper or a dutiful head to act so. It is a sly head. It is a very *crappy* sly head. I feel this increasingly. So one day soon I shall trade my head to the gypsies for a tambourine and dance and dance until I am pure light. Sly no more. Ha ha ha, I say. I shall eclipse them all with my light. I shall blot out all mere faces and conquer the world with *radiance*.

* * *

A glass of wine? *Somehow.*

* * *

—eyes glittering as cracked-off tar—thrusting bearded obscure face all shadowy malice hating me I felt—and why I wanted to cry out, why because we had never though one looked but how not at the moon in the lake a pearly violet night or that Titian Hudson so fond with thick ivory-colored neck—sweat in diamond points and silver pyjamas blinding me until all senses maddened—there was it— wasn't *well* to hear those things and see such apparition battering at me violating my most sacred as though he knew precisely what and where of me, though as afterwards came out no, completely ecstasied he *said,* but how could I know with Emily doing that and men dying because I tell you it made you boil over to hear those childish swaggering picked up god knows where being totally unschooled, from demented old anarchist leaflets likely or and I had, I suppose, always disliked him for it, people running to have their faces spit in, and I said a little foolishly and it would seem resonantly about his mother and then he being an ignorant half-caste this or that and other foolishness current back home, all being so fashionably educated and pure of blood, and he had stopped and people listening to *me* spew at *him* and then he too, because you understand he didn't know me, not well, hello at dances he would say, what's the latest from dreamland, or what's the News from Nowhere, all at once unecstasied and attentive the way Fay Gahagan said he usually would return and hands nervous as birds about him pulling back his soaked hair, lingering along the neck to inspect a small cyst I too had noticed, plucking his pyjamas straight, especially the collar in front, to touch the breast bone, jiggling the dextrose apparatus because he had dragged up on an elbow to stare at me to make out who I could be and then he started to *laugh* at me don't you see, started to laugh and would never *stop,* oh stop I said, though everyone thought the sisters and nurses were appalled at the bad form there being nothing the least uncontrollable in it, simply pleasant cultivated laughter at me, which was my first birthday, and Emily's hands, and finally Fay pushing in and swearing but it was much too late to save us.

* * *

Which was perfect nonsense. Maybe he had never seen the inside of a classroom, but he was no more *unschooled* than anyone else, whatever his other deficiencies. Stupid damn gibe, really. A myth to cut down his advantages. I don't know what drove me to seem to fall in with it. He was plainly so beautifully schooled—too beautifully in fact to go around disputing the point with inferiors. Still, I knew it could hurt him, more for the aspersion he felt it cast on his father than for any real hit on himself. He reverenced his father —but this later. The only rebuttal I ever heard him make, aside from laughter, was to the effect that even Minnesota has its educational requirements, which I found very sweet, because his tutor from infancy, an immensely learned oriental fellow, probably had the qualifications of the combined chairs of Oxford. He looked it anyway; and there were doubtless others of supplementary office, though I could never decide positively which they might be.

The Abuls, up to the time of Gordie's father's death, lived a life so private and exotic that it was all but impossible to sort out the dozens of figures going their rounds behind the grille of the high stone wall. We had no precedent for it. We spied and calculated but no usable pattern ever emerged. It all had rather the air of a road company between acts of "Ali Baba," with Shem Abul as entrepreneur. Everyone seemed to do everything at one time or another, and the majestic person you pegged down for an emir was likely to be doing butler's work next time you saw him. It certainly appeared that they kept an unusual number of servants—or rather people who behaved as if they were. Shem Abul had that effect on his surroundings. Those near him insisted on looking paid. Actually, prevailing informed opinion (Nurse's, Dolly's, my brother Herschel's, and Skibee Fenshawe's) had it that some were relatives, some political refugees and exposed spies, a scattering of disguised bodyguards, a few vacationing potentates and potentesses (Skibee Fenshawe was humorous), and the rest beyond human conjecture. Years later it would immensely divert Edith Abul to hear some of the guesses about her old household. It was said, for instance, that a certain wicked-looking old woman who stood near and chased the flies off Shem when he sat on the verandah was his unwed mother, and that a little wizened man who sometimes snoozed in a corner of the yard was a famous eastern mystic who could do the rope trick—Axel Stolt saw him do it. This last made her scream. No, all that was clear was that Shem maintained a throng, exotic, deferential, loyal. Fanatically loyal. I don't recall ever hearing gossip said to have come from his private domain. Not that there was much opportunity for it. Nobody worked part-time for Shem Abul. No such thing as a cleaning woman going mornings to him and afternoons to another where she might soften into confidence over a cup of tea. What was his was generally exclusively his, bound up in some thorough fashion. Witness the nurse, Fay Gahagan, who years after the man's death would offer nothing but that she never knew a better husband or father, which was like being assured that the Abominable Snowman loved his cocoa. Well, nothing shared, nothing betrayed. I mean more than wages. I think eastern people understand better than we the nature of that almost brute reverence frozen at the bottom of the heart, as if it had been the first experience of the first morning. I think Shem Abul must have been a sort of minor master in the abuse and manipulation of it. Poor Gordie—.

This is not frivolity, duck. Shem Abul was a bloody sinister man. Don't tell me about all the affection he inspired, because we know he inspired hatred too, and anyway nurses and maid-servants always love a sinister man. I never learned what his interests were but they were certainly powerful and high-staked, and in the prosecution of them he could be baseness itself. Anything at hand became ammunition. Edith's affair with Parkless, then head of a huge federal project, was a pretty fair sample of this attitude, I believe. And the Benham Lake business. Benham's trusteeship over Gordie's holdings in Pletcher's, which almost predictably led to tragedy, was as far as I could ascertain the stipulated payment for a piece of spiteful and ruinous nastiness Benham accomplished against one of Shem's many enemies, Joseph de la Reina—a fine man with a just grievance. Now, Shem measured Benham's worth pretty exactly. He told my father that of all the men he had ever known, Benham was the only one he would not have turned his back on. Yet he casually gave the man that power over his son's future. Among heels a very giant, this Mr. Abul.

But what I began to say is, it is my private—*very* private— opinion that in Shem's sudden decline and death may be read the whole of Gordie's mystery; that all of Gordie's subsequent behavior was pointed towards finding some guide or key which his father, by particular cultivation, had led him to depend on. Shem gone, Gordie was *literally* lost. Sullen, terrified, half mad with the sense of his weakness—tradition and instinct dim—the surviving cub of some sad, nearly extinct species blinking at us from the specimen table. Shem did it. So much in Gordie that was monstrous or just annoyingly wrong-headed here sinks into place;—and then how monstrous in our tyranny must we have seemed to him, this man raised to see black for white in all things.

I say Shem Abul carefully made his son in an alien tradition, and that this, together with Gordie's aching physical beauty, accounted for everything. My reasons here are no one's concern. The reasoning of an obsessed man is not properly reasoning as you want it, and I've had enough of laughter. The reasoning behind my mutilation was of an exquisite quality, yet how would you take it? So I will say that I have brooded and questioned, read and dreamed, consulted the secret files of three great and ancient Orders, and it is only in the idea of such a youthful discipline that the shadowy man begins to show features. I would stake a great deal on it. Because consider the consequences to a boy, if after a period of lonely and intensive training based on some technique of confusion applied to our most commonly held beliefs in the moral and social spheres—political, religious, everything in fact, the tutor a mere academic adornment to this real substance of the schooling—the consequences to this boy, I say, raised to doubt all basic notions, self-renouncing, utterly dependent on his mentor-father as the only reliable guide through the falseness of this world to the hidden place of truth, if that mentor goes and dies! The frenzied search—in *all* worlds! No more, or only this. Once upon a time Fay Gahagan, idly discussing Gordie's comatose sleeps, recalled that they began soon after Shem's death. For some reason I marked it.

Why did Shem Abul raise his son in this fashion—if he did? Was there purpose? Or merely the humor of a debased and cruel man? I frankly don't know. First causes don't intrigue me. Never have. Talk to me of the many small adjustments needful to the proper style for the trip and we shall have a good visit. Only spare me the basic why's. I do what I can. Out of what itch and towards what end God created the world or Shem created Gordie is of no use to me beyond the fact of noting that they *did*. Creators vanish, the created remain. We are here, we suffer, moment to moment. What difference whose bad idea in the first place? Give the man bread! Alleviation is our pressing, unending job. So much to do, so little time—so little *light*.

The hideous dimness of our lives. I now know that Gordie suffered and I sometimes can't sleep for his pain. I helped so many but never him, whom I loved. The price of being much loved; the price of loving, this—now. If he would come back I would tell him. I would hold out my hand. Almost the most important thing a man may do, you see. The most important being the divine madness to refuse it.

* * *

"Writing a book, dear?" Dolly simpering fingers the cover of my journal which I now leave lying out. A dare, and she takes it.

"Certainly not," I say bored. Women. A man would have the grace to be awed. The effect on Jerrold the other evening—I caught him eyeing it—was to make him talk more interestingly than I imagined he could.

"Am I in it?" A cunt, merely.

"I said no book."

"I heard you. Well, am I?" She's had a couple—likewise, thank you—and there is a drop at the tip of her gigantic beak—the only real nose in the damn dim no-nose family.

"Not you—Jerrold is."

"Well, anyway, the doctor tells me your face will be the horror of the ages." We all resented that nose too. You should have heard Father.

"Want to see?"—and I start to separate the bandages.

"Thanks, I'll wait." She never flinches. God what a frog.

"Another thing. If you don't take your hand off that book I'll break every bone in it. Do you know how long it takes the bones in the hand to knit?"

"Why, you're *mad*," she says. "The idea."

* * *

And all should cry, Beware, Beware!

* * *

What strange ingredients went to make the pudding I called Father. (Ha. I can hear him grump. "You and your fat-ass elegance. The Parklesses and the Falls will flourish all throughout this broad and stricken land, and solely because nobody, not one person, will understand what the goddamn hell you are writin' about. God, the poor country—my poor *paper*. What evil thing have I wrought in you? 'Pudding'—you sap!" Well, we're both right, maybe.) Bluff, cynical, hard and straight of thought as a nail, he also had a dithery passion for cloak-and-dagger intrigue that would have put old-maid novel readers to shame. It got worse as he got older, until it reached the point where the crucial difference between him and his mortal enemies on the right fringe was that he *relished* all the hideous cabals going on in the Vatican or in the secret caves under the White House. I had a taste of it in that ridiculous business with Colonel Rol during the war.

Particularly revealing in this respect was his admiration for Shem Abul, of all people, and not for the reasons he gave, though they were cogent enough. He admired most, I think, the dark international plots Shem was thought to be involved in; but as the best will in the world could not connect these plots to anything remotely like social welfare, except possibly of the power combines, or to the overthrow of tyrannies except by worse tyrannies, the admiration was clearly inadmissible. So, stuck with another of his misplaced enthusiasms—like many obsessed with corruption, Father had no talent at all for enthusiasm —he fastened on Shem's astounding rise from peddler of cheap oriental perfumes to one of the Twin Cities' wealthiest merchants. This was solid American goods. No one could really disagree with Father here, except maybe to niggle that such a wildly successful businessman could not be a wholly honest or humane one. (Whereupon Father was perfectly capable of denouncing the niggler as un-American! A real pudding.) Or some may have imagined it all rather too astounding to have been unsponsored, and the scope of Shem's other interests too large and complex to have developed so suddenly, but the truth is, there are always such around to take the edge off things.

Because even so—even in fractions—it was a remarkable accomplishment. Shem had a genius for affairs. There aren't many Jews one knows of who from such beginnings and in a few years time could take over Minneapolis's most fashionable department store, buy up a great walled house near the center of its most restricted residential area, and set over it the blondest, loveliest, most Episcopalian girl in Minneapolis society. Even backed by all the cartels of Europe and South America (and, if you like, all the revolutionary and counter-revolutionary Orders extant), this was a neat bit of business. In fact the only thing like it in the city's social annals was my grandfather's feat with the prestigious *Dispatch;* but even that, with the added luster of founding a dynasty, was not really comparable. Anti-Semitism in Grandfather's time was mild to what it had become after the first war, when Shem Abul appeared. The old stately house shaking out Kiddush into Friday evening dinner parties, its brood of self-conscious children at their strange holiday games, would have been unthinkable on R_____ Street in 1918. And then, once away from house and family, Grandfather could have passed for Edward Windsor. I never saw him, but photos show a cold aristocratic sort, with the light coloring of my family, and all the thinness and mediocrity of detail. Shem Abul was by contrast a big Levantine Jew, fleshy-featured, greasy, black as the ace of spades, with a low mean look to make you reach for your pearled cross. Nor did Grandfather presume to court and marry a Charls. As my darling grandmother used to say: Vot a sgandl *dat* vos. Hardly comparable, you see; in a way not even of the same genre. Grandfather was determinedly making a place for himself and his family in a society he coveted, while Shem Abul worked out of spite and hated us all.

The last time I saw Shem was on a hot early summer morning over thirty years ago—the gross man and his tiny sleek son hand in hand in their lovely garden. It was the day the Lenart clan was finally packing off to the country for the hot months. As always, we were late and the production was colossal. We seemed never to be able to go anywhere those days, even a few hundred miles up into Canada for three months to a house we had been using for years, without forty or fifty pieces of luggage and a vast expense of emotion. No one would be on speaking terms for days after. Already we—Dolly, Herschel, and I—had been chased from the scene for our bickering, so off we ran to torment friends who lived in the neighborhood of the Abul house; and afterwards, being so near and full of the devil, it would have been unthinkable not to do a little spying through the famous grille-work gate. Nurse would never have forgiven us if we hadn't; she would start to scold when we told her but quickly settle down to some hard listening and questioning. Dolly, being oldest, generally took the brunt. "What *color* shoes, miss?—I never knew such a pokey gossip," et cetera et cetera. The Abuls were news down to the minutest details, you see. Though our parents were friendly with Shem and Edith, the Abul residence remained a place of mystery even to them, and I suspect they counted on Nurse to pass on the choicer things. Hence Nurse's bullying. Any odd glimpse could be sifted of nuggets;—and this morning produced a bonanza.

We saw at once that they were preparing to go away too. The entire household was out in its glory and we didn't know where to look first. Dolly nearly wept with excitement. Near the house itself there was mad activity, with what looked like hundreds of people—*personages:* grandees and great queens and high-ranking military types—shouting and swarming from verandah to driveway floating boxes, hampers, luggage of all shapes like wreckage in a torrent. The hub of this frenzy was an array of five white and beige Packards, really enormous machines, lined bumper to bumper in the driveway, and which were being loaded in the most haphazard fashion. Two were already completely filled, another almost, while still another had dark curtains on the windows and was obviously set aside for the family. (Dolly assured Nurse that all had bullet-proof glass.) At the foot of the verandah stairs, in the very center of the traffic and parting it into two currents, stood Edith Abul, distractedly pointing here and there and looking the height of fashion, a maid maneuvering a parasol above her golden head. She was being closely attended by a clutch of olive-skinned "potentesses," each with *her* maid and parasol, nodding grandly to every order and plainly not understanding a word of the language. Edith ignored them, preferring to match wits with Nurse Gahagan, who ran about like a squirrel, interfering with everything and quarreling with everybody. She was a bright-eyed peppery little baggage in those days and wielded some authority. Dolly said—never mind. Edith tossed her head and Nurse Gahagan stamped her foot and some poor sweating generalissimo took a box he had just put here and put it there. Then Edith called out and he put it back again, with a comment of his own. The resultant din and confusion enchanted us.

Now, between house and front gate, on an island formed by the circular driveway, a space no more than fifty or sixty feet across, did Shem a miniature park decree;—in fact it could have been designed for a site above the clouds or below the earth for all the connection it had to the practical life of the place. The hubbub a little way behind it, for example—Gordie and Shem in the garden looked to be wandering in another world, though often a dozen steps would have carried them from one to the other. A matter of optics, and of Gordie and Shem, I suppose. Anyway, it was an exceptionally pretty area, with its ancient potted fruit trees and yellow and pink marble basins, its clusters of tiny dark-leaved shrubs arranged into groves, the waterfall and grotto, the bright dwarf flowers. There was even a minuscule pleasure house in it, blue as the sky, opening away from the gate, a fact which annoyed us, and Nurse even more. Gordie would amuse himself here by the hour, or conceal himself in the pleasure house to play at inconceivably delightful games and feast away on (no doubt) Turkish Delight and Smyrna figs and halvah. And here he could often be seen walking with his father in the cool of the early evening, hand in hand, as now. But with or without Gordie it was a favorite haunt of Shem's. Puffing a thin black cigar, he would roam the ingeniously winding path, followed silently by one or more of his household, lost in thought. I have sometimes wondered why, with all the ground to the sides and back of the house, so secretive a man would choose to build a retreat in full view of his front gate; and I have sometimes concluded it was pure contempt. Like his son, he hunted so much in the mind that perhaps it amused him to let people, strangers and intimates alike, think to see him walking in a small neat garden when he was really walking—where? In some ruinous black and gold paradise? Well, he was a strange man. So full of power and menace, and towards the end so utterly slack. Tired. Particularly that torrid morning, with Gordie chattering and laughing and trying to hurry his steps, the vital forces in him seemed barely sustaining.

But I thought this later. At the time, what struck me was his utter repulsiveness. He had sweated right through the back and sides of an already shapeless white suit. The bit of purply face visible under the wide-brimmed Panama glistened unpleasantly; and though he carried a bunched handkerchief and constantly mopped his neck and cheeks, the sweat drops flashed about him like rain. He was big-framed, had probably been muscular, but recently he had gone to fat in a shocking way. Even his shoulders that had been so straight were humped and rounded with it. He was said to be ill. It was not so much fat as water, Mother told people, and would tap significantly at her heart. Whatever, as he shuffled along before us now, the tissue shuddered and shook under the clinging suit, and the great wattles seemed to coil like snakes in their moisture.

But I repeat, the contrast with his son had something to do with the impression. That slim elegant sprite would have made anyone look his worst. He was dressed as Shem (Edith told me in later years) loved best to see him. Long shimmering white silk coat, white silk pants, and beautiful crimson leather shoes with the extravagantly pointed toes curled up. His oiled hair fell behind his ears in a fine black tumultuous fleece, with a single perfect coil trained along each cheek; his fingers were covered with rings. We had seen him turned out this way on other occasions. Having no companions his age to laugh and mock, he was free to think himself quite as magnificent as he was, and would run about the grounds for everyone to see and admire. I remember he once wore a fantastic silver and turquoise stomacher that had Dolly ill with envy for months. But most of all, on this particular morning, was the brilliant *life* in him. Such wicked flashing *living* beauty—conscious of itself and wild with rapture. "See me, see me, all you homely Lenarts!" He might just as well have; we couldn't have hated him more. (Herschel was always full of plans for trapping him and boiling him in scented oil.) But he had no thought for us, though he knew we were there. He and Shem were being trailed at a respectful distance by two swarthy men, one of whom, aristocratic and absent-looking, with a long yellow-white beard, was generally accounted the tutor, while the other was instantly marked by Dolly as a bodyguard, and he had in fact done something when we appeared at the gate—snapped his fingers, I thought, though Herschel claimed to have heard him whistle—to make Gordie and Shem turn to see. So they knew we were watching, but it made no difference. We didn't exist for them. They continued on their peaceful way, the turmoil in the background and the peepers at the gate equal light years removed.

Dolly gasped. I remember I had been watching Edith, and at the very instant of Dolly's exclamation, almost as if she had heard, Edith's busy gaze fixed itself in the direction of her husband and son. Shem was in obvious difficulties. Already two or three times he had paused to stand a moment with his head lowered. Now he did not move on, and Gordie, who had let go his hand to run ahead, came back and stood looking solemnly up into the fallen face. He made no effort to help. The two men in the rear started forward but a motion of Shem's fingers stopped them dead. With one impulse they looked over to Edith, but she was already crossing the driveway with her walk like a noble stag, the ankles giving a little at each step. She didn't call ahead of her or run—ladies of her school didn't run—but her measured stride, the only half-raised half-stretched-out hand, the long, taut streaming of her dress had an unexpected grief about them that took my breath away. She loved him. And the sudden quiet and attention of the entire scene: the torrent frozen—a hamper put down carried the length of the yard. Each there loved him, I felt. Anything ever said about bribery, coercion, even some weird sort of spiritual abuse of these people —all may have been true, as I think, but the fact remained that they needed and loved him. I still remember my shock at the idea. I was a child and used to taking my ideas on such matters from others and this was not at all what I had been led to believe. Now Nurse Gahagan padding breathlessly but managing to stay somewhat behind her mistress; behind her, wringing her hands, the old lady gossiped to be Shem's mother. No one else. Not a sound to be heard. Gordie looking solemnly up as if turned to stone while the others gathered in.

Edith busy over that great helpless blob, loosening his clothes, pressing herself to him till her gown was dark with his grease. The ice and flame in me. I didn't understand. I couldn't take my eyes off her. It was soon all right, at least for the time being, and we sped home in near delirium. Shem died that summer. It could have come as no surprise to anyone except perhaps Gordie. As I said. They had to pinch me to make me leave.

Delirium indeed and more than they knew. At home Dolly slapped me and called me morbid and Herschel (insufferable martyr) denounced me to Nurse as "excessively" ill-bred and unnatural for wanting to go on watching so private a scene. Gentlemen didn't. Nurse agreed—in some disappointment, I thought—and in fact they were right. Oh when she swept Gordie into her arms. The dreams.

* * *

Edith. Bright-colored, delightful Edith Abul. Cold, indrawn Edith *Charls* Abul too. Old southern stock no longer rich but of immense self-regard and unnerving silences. Tall, narrow, pale-eyed people whose fine hair stirred in the softest breeze. Except for Edith, I never heard a Charls laugh. I rarely heard one talk either. The family doesn't exist anymore, at least not in Minneapolis, but I clearly recall the round-eyed stare and parted lips that passed for social intercourse. Mother worked into a cold sweat whenever Charls's were to be among her dinner guests. Horseflesh was their single passion, from the oldest to the youngest. Edith told me she had her first riding lesson at two and owned her first horse at three; indeed, till the day of her death she kept the best stable in the area, and Gordie himself was a skilled horseman, though he seldom rode. The fact was the Charls's made a fine sight mounted. The animals were not more graceful or silken or a-shimmer with delicate nerves. Centaurs—true horse people. All their joylessness vanished when they cantered out on their splendid horses, and if even then they never quite laughed, you felt they might at any moment commit a smile. But we never really liked them, nor they us.

Edith was often a visitor at our house in the years before Shem's death. I don't know why, but she was a special care of Mother's. Shem's being Jewish would have had something to do with it, and Father's nutty craze for him. There was also the fact that they had worked so closely with each other in the Junior League. Whatever, it was Mother who sponsored Edith's re-entry into Minneapolis social circles, a piece of business for which the Charls's never forgave us. Edith had been a notable, even a spectacular, debutante in whom the declining family had staked much, more perhaps than anyone knew, and their fury at her marriage to the Jewish ex-peddler was proportionate to their utter social ruin. It needn't have been ruin, of course. Minnesota is not Virginia. But they seemed almost to demand it. A queer people. They fought Mother every inch of the return. Poor creatures, it was hardly an equal contest. In spite of our race, we have been of consequence socially almost from the time there was a Minneapolis; and Lenart women, though generally modest and unremarkable, have always known their worth. The Charls's, of a more elegant line, impeccably Episcopalian, were nowhere near as entrenched. It comes to that always. Mother sat on the invitations committee of every important subscription dance and both annual balls—Christmas and Plantagenets—while Father, that muckraking radical, was a founder of Yachters, and a feared component of the membership committee of Dukes and Barons. And where Mother and Father sat not, some Lenart cousin was sure to have a strategic behind. Facts of life. When my parents asked you to a dinner party, you damn well came. And if you met Edith Abul there, you talked to her or danced with her; and once you did either you usually saw my parents' point.

Edith could charm snakes when the mood was on her. None of your witty or intellectual charmer—she was as far from someone like Irene La Fair, for example, as members of the same sub-species could be—but merely and utterly goldenly feminine. All interest and flattering laughter with women, a delicious, cool, half-mocking seriousness with men. Elegant, a little distant, with beautiful manners—the whole Charls quality apotheosized. Done to a luster too. She married virtually unlimited money and loved to look it. Indeed, her high-fashion French gowns might well have told against her during those Depression years and in that anywise dowdy milieu. That they didn't was, I think, owing to a sort of high simplicity of spirit only the consummately self-indulgent really master. You didn't begrudge her her Chanels and Vionnets any more than you begrudge a child its fourth scoop of ice-cream. Such godlike pleasures purge the beholder.

Shem rarely accompanied her in these campaigns. It may have been policy, leaving the spadework to her and my parents who knew the ground, but I think it more likely he didn't come because we bored him silly. Business entertaining was his excuse generally. Once in a blue moon—as we used to say—he would drop by at the end of an evening to pick her up, but mostly one of his lieutenants, Benham Lake (his terribly social front-man partner) or Paul Parkless (later Senator) would do the squiring. When he did appear there was always a flurry of excitement, for he was such an exotic figure. Herschel and I would hear the maids whispering, then the door of Nurse's room opening and closing, and we would tumble out, followed closely by Dolly, her face all creamed to bleach out pimples, and everyone, children, nurse, and maids, would huddle in a covered space near the landing to peer down into the foyer. (The old house was pitted with these "covered" spaces, where remodeling and additions by a certain fashionable but unschooled architect had left absolute caves.) There Shem stood, sending up waves of orient spice, hair slicked back, bowler in hand and feet planted authoritatively, talking to my mother, who always behaved in the strangest fashion in his presence, almost doing a little dance around him and fluttering like funny Mrs. Feingut, the rabbi's wife. (I used to have the ghost of a suspicion here.) In a few moments Edith would enter from the parlor trailing beige- or lilac-colored silks, allow herself to be folded into a cloud of ermine, her head turned to laugh that beautiful cultivated laugh—Gordie learned it from her—at something my father was saying. (And another suspicion here—it would explain much, after all.) I've seen more beautiful women since, but never one that could approach her for glamor.

I remember how exhausted she would look as they started at last for the door. Those evenings must have been a tremendous strain on her, courting the good opinion of inferiors who should have welcomed her gladly. She was very proud. I know she barely forgave many whose condescending nod had been so important to her then, others not at all. In after years it was one of her bitterest memories. She had had no idea, she said, that gently brought-up human beings could be so vile. "Never let them forgive you anything, Matt," she said, "they rub off the bloom. I would not again. I would live in Tunis rather, among the cannibals." (She was not an informed woman.) She felt the sentence had been tenderness itself to the reprieve. So she forgave her family who never forgave her, but not the friends who did. Very Charls-like somehow.

I stress this for a reason. I have never altogether understood how, having taken the wound so deep, she could want to inflict it on another, one far less equipped to deal with it than she had been. She was not a cruel woman, I think, yet in the circumstances, and with her experience, it was a perfectly heartless thing to have done. There was no question of code or that nonsense. Edith was anything but rigid socially (and in such matters as *mésalliance* should certainly not have been). Times had changed since she was a girl and she was loud in her approval of the new informality. Climbers and their breed were in consequence quick to use her; and where she felt there was merit, she blandly allowed it. She liked to be considered a "touch," as she called it. I think it amused her. She had the most outrageous things to say about the pretensions of Minneapolis society and its seventy-five-year pedigree; but, interestingly, she could also be unpleasantly cutting about those trying to break in, often the very ones she was in the process of sponsoring. But sponsor them she did by the dozens, and some very inept propositions too, certainly inferior in respect of natural talents to the daughter-in-law she so angrily spurned.

As I say, I have never altogether understood it. Her adored son returns from the wars a military hero, bringing great honor to Minneapolis, a fillip to society in general, and a bright new daughter-in-law to her, and she shuts herself up like a bereaved woman and sees no one for months. God knows I hold no brief for Emily. I was married to her for three years and though I suspect there were grand cloudy faults three years' time was too short to reveal, the day-to-day defects did more than nicely. But Edith could not have known them. They were chiefly of a wife-towards-husband nature. I bored Emily, and she beguiled the time with little meannesses. It is not unheard-of. Agreed, her manner was pungent and occasionally shrill, her face too coarsely "American" for some tastes, and all the rest of the petty criticisms—she could *invigorate*. She lit up the whole gloomy war for me with her gusty radiance. She had shrewdness and courage too, and when things were going her way, a fey sort of humor. And she was resourceful, as you shall hear. In fact she needed only the guidance Edith gave so bountifully to others to develop into one of our better young hostesses. But again, none of this had bearing because Edith would never see the woman. She had many worse to tea every day in the week, to my thinking, and I told her so, but she met it with silence. I went further. Emily, I said flatly, was the very type of new blood she herself had been claiming society needed.

More silence. Then: "Did I ever claim that, dear?"

"A hundred times, and you know it."

"And did you absolutely believe me?"

"I did. I believe in it passionately myself."

"Ah. All my men have been passionate types. I'm very partial to it. Come here, with your passion."

I blushed and scowled and held my ground. "My mother didn't object to her, Edith." Immediately I regretted this.

"Blanche didn't? Poor darling, in the sweet Lord's lap—." Her eyes grew thoughtful as she touched the ends of her dyed gold hair. "But why would she, Matt?" She was dead serious. It was Edith Charls Abul at her purest.

* * *

Another time.
"Well, it's partly you I do it for, you know—"
"Me! Now no female guile, Edith—"
"Female guile. What an adorable pompous Jew thing it is. I simply want to eat it up—"
"I swear to God I shall never see you again." (My journal swears I swore it.)
"Ha ha ha!"
"Let go of me."
"—Mind your manners, boy. Sit quietly until I dismiss you or *no lemon ice*. Ha—. All right, I'm a saint. Stay. You do bring out the utter ghastliness in me with that grave Jew face. How dare it look so young in my presence anyway? Am I doomed to insolent pouty boys henceforth, like Benham?"
"I'm not a boy anymore, damn it, Edith. That's your whole tragic trouble—"
"Insolence upon insolence. Not a boy? You mean that in all probability I dye my hair now?"
"I'm mean I've been through a damn war, not to mention married and divorced."
"So we're there again. Well, I won't have her, Matt. *No.*"
"Because of me, of course."
"Yes, partly. I can't see why you should make your eyes into circles like all my idiot cousins. I don't at all care for the cheap way she threw you over the minute she got sight of Gordon, is all. You do mean something to me, but even if you didn't, I could not in my heart accept it. No, my dear. There are ways of doing things. You

know I'm not a snob, about inferiors anyway. Gordon could have married an Eskimo peon for all I would care, so long as it was a clean and *proper-acting* peon. I do demand a natural dignity in those people—"

"Who told you she threw me over?"

"Why, everyone, I suppose. I really can't think. Benham, certainly."

"Did it never occur to you as a possibility that Gordie *stole* her from me?"

"Well, no, it never did. Why on earth should it?"

"Because it would have been so kind of you."

"Nonsense. We all know that the only thing Gordon has ever had to steal in the way of physical gratification is respite, the insufferable pup. You and I steal; to Gordon Charls it is *given*. Besides, I've glimpsed her—"

"He married her. Conceivably, more than physical gratification was involved?"

"Yes, but what? *What?*"

"Love?"

"—Well, of course, you would dare say that to me. I've handed you the right, you suppose, just as Benham warned. Glad you could come, my dear. You're a nice boy whom I fear I've somewhat spoiled. Still, I hope we may see each other again, and do bring Dolly. There shall be lemon ice for all."

* * *

". . . However, even the success of Mrs. Pommery Fetiss pales before the mercurial climb—achieved without any of the latter's claims to beauty—of the remarkable and tragic Emily Lenart Abul, late of Minneapolis. Hers, indeed, is one of the classic *contes noires* of recent social history. Variously called the 'Minneapolis Pretender' and 'Bad Emily' [maybe, but I never heard it], she was born Marion Emily Reis, the daughter of a plumber [skilled machinist actually] in Bloomington, Indiana. [Follows here the usual blah about teenage elopements, minor league umpires, drugs, miscarriages—all pretty factual but totally *unreal*.]

". . . Early in the year nineteen hundred and forty-two she found herself stranded in Little Rock, Arkansas, with 'exactly thirty-four cents to my name,' as she frankly told one interviewer, 'and misery coming out of my ears. I decided I wanted to go *up*.' Always extremely resourceful and self-possessed, with a 'come-hither' air about her, she marched into the offices of the *Little Rock Eagle* and talked her way into a job as a society reporter! 'I had always been interested in society,' she told the above-quoted interviewer. 'They used to laugh at me about it back in Bloomington, and I suppose I laughed a little at myself, but not deep down. No, dear. Deep down I was getting myself ready to laugh at all of you.'

"Inscrutable, unhappy woman! Nevertheless, her climb from that moment was little short of sensational. One of her first assignments was to interview good-looking young Matthew Lenart, Jr., scion of the socially prominent *Minneapolis Dispatch* dynasty, who was undergoing his army basic training at nearby Camp Robinson; and as matters transpired, it proved to be one of the most fabulously successful cub interviews on record. He married her six weeks later, at the conclusion of his training.

"When he was sent to England soon after, Emily followed, taking up residence in London, where she rented a charming town house in Mayfair, one of the few left undamaged by the bombing raids, and whose former owners, the prominent Fitzhugh-Southeys, had been blown to bits while dining out with friends. [As I recall, there was somewhat more romance in the whole thing, but I won't press.] When Matthew was finally ordered out [I swear I went as willingly as any] to North Africa, Emily returned to the States, visiting Minneapolis briefly [Dolly and mother saw to that] to meet her new family, but settling down to wait in New York, at the Plaza. It was during this wearisome sojourn in war-time Gotham that she first met and became friendly with Speranza de la Reina, now the popular Mrs. 'Bo' Kinkle of Virginia, daughter of the very social Joseph de la Reina, late of Minneapolis, later still of Southampton, and important stockholders in her future husband's very swank Minneapolis department store; however, this is to anticipate.

"Meanwhile, some months before the conclusion of the war, Second [First] Lieutenant Lenart was gravely wounded in France, and Emily hastened to Minneapolis to be with the family, but almost immediately [see brackets before last], through the senior Lenart's not inconsiderable influence, was flown off to Paris to be at the side of the injured hero. There, in the grand salon of the elegant and romantic Hôtel de R————, that masterpiece of French seventeenth-century architectural genius which had been pressed into service as a recovery ward exclusively for officers, she met the fabulously handsome Gordon Charls Abul, dashing and popular playboy son of the fashionable and much-lamented late Edith Charls Abul of the horsey Virginia Charls, one of the oldest and most impeccable families in America, or indeed in any country of the world.

"Here was a dilemma! For, as Emily was wont to confide to intimates, it was 'love at first sight'; and as Major [Captain] Abul was in a condition [fast asleep] demanding constant surveillance, Emily found herself called upon for many small personal attentions, which did not help matters [for herself, presumably]. In addition to his story-book beauty and the glamor of his name and fortune, Major [Captain] Abul was one of the great heroes of the North African and French campaigns, having personally accounted for the lives of thirty-three of the enemy [yes, yes]. What must she do? Being Emily, her course seemed clear. Like her soldier-hero, she was never one to falter at the barricades, and perhaps too, recalling her early unhappiness, the terrible briefness of our hours for any worldly fulfillment, she quickly abandoned herself to 'the romance of my life.' She and Major [ ] Abul were married in Paris, and after a honeymoon there of some months, descended on Minneapolis, with their exquisite young son, David Shem, prepared to conquer the city. [Whatever became of me?] But they reckoned without Benham Lake.

"Benham Lake was at this time the city's unofficial social arbiter and a close friend and adviser of Edith Abul, having stood in a similar relationship to Shem Abul during that mysterious and prominent man's lifetime. Not unnaturally, therefore, he was, or had been, on terms of the closest intimacy with Gordon, and had acted as mentor and pattern when the hour arrived for that blithe princeling to assume his social responsibilities. Lake was a bachelor—one of the last of the 'extra men,' that vanished breed of elegant and witty 'singles' once considered so indispensable to the social milieu; and while perhaps not quite so splendidly accomplished as he considered himself to be, apparently did have a cool charm, and a pretty, trivial sort of wit. But most important of all to our little *histoire,* he was in perpetual trusteeship over Gordon's holdings in Pletcher's, Minneapolis's famous, fashionable shopping center and the foundation of the Abul fortune, the principal itself being secured for Gordon's heirs. This, together with Lake's own not inconsiderable holdings, gave him great sway in the board of director's room, to what tragic *dénouement* shall be seen.

"Now, for some occult reason or reasons, Lake seems to have loathed our Emily on sight. Precisely why remains one of the best-kept secrets in recent social history, for according to all reports she went far out of her way to conciliate him, only to have snub after snub greet her efforts. Granted, it was a *mésalliance;* still, Shem Abul—on whom Lake had been alacritous enough to bestow his cachet, and who in return had replenished Lake's dwindled resources by taking him, on the handsomest of terms, into Pletcher's—had been *far* from impeccable. And, then, however charitable one might like to be, Minneapolis *is* but Minneapolis. Flour mills do not a Boston make. Even more distressing, Lake communicated his choler to Edith who, without ever consenting to meet her daughter-in-law, conceived the most violent objection to her and, her fires stoked to white heat by the vengeful Lake, blocked Emily at every turn, going so far as to deny her entry to the Minneapolis chapter of the Junior League, of which Edith was a director, and without which convenient machinery life for the young matron in a strange community can be simply insupportable. Taking their cue from the formidable Edith, the fashionable set stayed away in droves from the Abuls' handsome Pine County estate on the St. Croix River, wittily called 'Luba,' or Abul spelled backwards. Even business friends, cued this time by the powerful Lake were constantly *engagé*.

"In all of this, it may be noted, Gordon Abul played a curiously passive rôle. Before his marriage, he had been one of the more dynamic and promising young socialites of the day, as witness his war record, and earlier, his multifarious social and sports activities. In affairs of business, too, while he could of course take no active part in the direction of Pletcher's until his majority, his very real interest in the firm and his occasional intelligent and constructive suggestions at board meetings, when he could rein in his naturally high spirits, had augured brilliant achievements for the future. As if all of this weren't promise enough, he was in addition unusually cultivated for Minneapolis [Ravel's *Bolero* and all of Van Vechten and E. Phillips Oppenheim rounded off with a few of Emily Brönte's poems—interesting but surely a bit spotty] and had been respectfully attended to, when he could control a youthful propensity to fun [like atheism in the dining room at Yachters or duelling with guns at Eveleen Rectem's funeral or punching Skibee Fenshawe's nose and Munnie Svendsen's jaw no matter where including baptisms and presentation parties and endless other hilarity], by the more artistically inclined heads of the community.

"Apropos of this last, let it be stated at once that for all its shortcomings in other areas of endeavor, and they are serious, Minneapolis indubitably has an *eye*. It seems the least one can say for a community that erects not one but three art museums for a population of under five hundred thousand souls living in extremes of temperature amid a waste of *Mille Lacs*. [*Fou le camp, ma chérie.*] Indeed, before returning home after the war, Gordon had bought up [raving drunk] the most artistic *figures nues* of the famous French painters Fortunée and de St. Clair, and these masterpieces, considered by experts to be the finest examples outside of museum walls, still hang in Pletcher's in the imported shoe salon, and may be seen there [a little off to one side, in the stock-room in fact, and should be asked for].

"But times had changed. The young Phoebus Apollo of the fashionable set was all sicklied o'er. Some will-to-live appears to have been left behind at the superb Hôtel de R_____, in Paris, burned away in terrible fevers, perhaps [no mean guess this]. Who can tell? Certain it is that here stood not the spirited 'Gordie' of the early brilliance and promise. He appears to have been perfectly devoted to his family and estate, and oblivious to all else. As one friend puts it, 'He gave the impression of being neither happy nor sad, pleased nor angry, merely *indifferent* as to the frightful snubs being piled on them. It was extraordinary. A vegetable, you know, a sort of eggplant thing, or artichoke-heart. Did he love her? No, I don't think so, to any extraordinary degree. How could one? Depended on her, you know. Like an invalid on a nurse thing. She *was* capable, you understand. A perfect dynamo sort of thing.' [Some of Axel Stolt's flap, if I'm not mistaken.]

"'Depended on her'—well, Gordon could have done worse, certainly. That she was capable is pure understatement, for she apparently was equipped to take over the country had that been necessary to secure her marriage and fortune. About this time word got to her that Lake, whose malice knew no bounds, was up to some treachery behind the doors of Pletcher's board room. Emily never hesitated. Leaving her precious family—an enchanting daughter, christened Victoria, had been added but three months earlier—in the care of one of their few remaining friends [me], she flew to Southampton, where she went immediately to work on the family of her old New York acquaintance, Speranza de la Reina, Pletcher's largest shareholders after her husband. It may be imagined that Speranza, or 'Sperry' as she is known to all the social capitals of the world, who detested Lake scarcely less than did Emily, was not unhelpful; but the family, conservative to a degree, showed initial resistance, until Emily alarmed them by some not altogether accurate information about the firm's recent unsteadiness, confirming this with cleverly forged 'secret' financial reports [engineered by me], sent on by Pletcher's legal staff [whose youngest member, Asher Friedlander III, was a first cousin of mine and owed me a number of important favors besides]. Old Joseph de la Reina himself harbored no love for Lake, who years ago had driven him out of Minneapolis on a wave of scorn [at Shem's behest, who broke with Joseph for refusing to do for him the very thing Joseph now did for Emily—sell]; but more important were those reports, and the fact that the continued tie to Pletcher's had kept open a wound that could revive old pain and bitterness even now.

In short, Joseph agreed to sell his interest in Pletcher's for ten million dollars [actually about 8½ as I later discovered, Emily pocketing the rest]. When Gordon told her he didn't have that much, Emily herself went out and, pawning her jewelry [some from me], begging, borrowing heavily from Gordon's few remaining friends [me], from banks, et cetera, miraculously managed to scrape the sum together. Finally, in nineteen hundred and forty-seven, she had the satisfaction of sending her husband to a stockholder's meeting which had been convened to oust him, and having him oust the ousters. Five months later, Lake stepped out of his bathroom window. His youthful valet was inconsolable, and gave a heartrending account of Lake's final hours, before disappearing with a valuable collection of Byzantine ivories.

"So our Emily had her triumph, but as often occurs when the battle exacts such a toll of chicanery, bitterness, and cruelty of the combatants, neither side reaped happiness. Needless to say, Lake's suicide closed the last remaining doors to the young Abuls. They were welcome nowhere, and 'Luba' became not so much their home as their prison—at least for Emily. Gordon, of course, continued in his usual bland routine, clipping the magnificent trees and formal hedges in which 'Luba' abounds, planning new wings to the house and improvements in the stable, attending board meetings in town and occasionally relaxing over an evening of bridge at Yachters, spending endless hours in the nursery with his children, whom he loved with an overwhelming passion. But Emily grew increasingly morose and shrewish. *She* had no board meetings to attend or club to relax in [besides which, her bridge was atrocious]; after the fourth or fifth redecoration, the house began to bore her to distraction; and though, indeed, she loved her two small darlings, they were scarcely sufficient company for a dynamic young matron at the height of her powers. As for her relations with her husband, it seems safe to conjecture that all the disparity in their interests and backgrounds must now have reared up with a vengeance. Peace, as has been noted by wiser than we, is not an unmixed blessing. That she loved Gordon there can be small doubt. 'But,' as a former 'Luba' domestic puts it, 'she began to hate him too, bit by bit, you could see it comin' on, but funny, you know, because one minute she'd be cooin' in his arms, as who wouldn't, gorgeous as he was, and the next throwin' half the insides of the house at his head, or hidin' things from him, like the big prunin' shears, screamin' as how he was ruinin' her trees—*hers,* if you please. But he was a saint, and a damn good man with a tree too.'

"Early at 'Luba,' Emily had begun to take riding lessons—being a Charls, Gordon kept a good stable, though nothing so grand as his mother's—but after two nasty spills, she conceived a violent dislike of horses, and never ceased agitating against them.—'Said the stink and all was bad for the tots besides givin' her the headache. But David loved them and rode about proud as Napoleon himself, his father's eyes sparklin' like fine champagne when he came passin' by, and even the tiny Miss Victoria showed a dear foolish delight in them, gurglin' like a little brook, a way she had.'

"Well, matters had progressed in this fashion for over a year, when tragedy struck. Both children contracted the Asian flu and died within a month, two of the earliest martyrs to that then dread disease. Once again we have recourse to our domestic:

"'It was a black, black day when David left us. The girl had gone two days before, poor helpless soul. I must have used up near my quota of tears then, for I have never cried so for my own since, and I always was notable in grief. Mrs. Abul took it hard enough, sobbin' the nights through or poundin' the arms of her chair in a fit, but it was him who made no sound at all that tore you up. When they came and told him, they said, he was in the middle of lookin' for something in his study, and he just nodded and went on lookin', only harder, as it were, pullin' out drawers and books or runnin' his hand under the carpet, his face red as a beet, for it was excessively hot weather, June or July. One said she thought she heard him say that he was lookin' for some keys, though to what I couldn't tell you, as there was no lock in that house but Mrs. had the key to it.

"'Well, they left him there finally and came back up. We were all standin' outside the door then, some cryin' and others talkin' a little about their positions and what might be now, when he comes runnin' up beggin' our pardon to let him through. His face was still red, like they said, but excessively calm and sad now. Well, he goes in and closes the door, and we hear talkin', and all of a sudden the door opens, and there stands Mr. Abul with David's poor corpse in his arms, that calm sad look in his eyes, and begs our pardon again, and goes a little way, then turns around to us, smilin' the shyest small smile you ever saw, and says givin' a little shake to his head, "This is my *son*," as if to tell us that's how he come to be carryin' him, poor man. Then he goes a little more, and again he turns—"My *son*," he says, as if to be sure we understood, and turns down the stairs out of sight.

"'Well. We all stood there dumbstruck, as you may imagine, till suddenly the doctor and the nurse come flyin' out—Mrs. had fainted and was stretched out moanin' with compresses inside—and hurry down the stairs and we after them, except for Nellie Manners, Mrs.'s maid, who goes in to her. Well, we search that house, and then we search the grounds with flashlights and candles, and everyone shoutin', "Mr. Abul, Mr. Abul, it's contagious, sir—he's *dead*, sir—take heed of the contagion"—and so forth and so on. Nothin'.

"'*Then*—then the windows of the big bedroom light up and there's Nellie callin' down to us, though not too loud, tellin' us to come up quick, he's there, and so we all go up, and sure enough, there he is on his bed, the corpse tight in his arms cheek to cheek with him, fast asleep. Nellie had been helpin' Mrs. to her room, and they come in and saw them like that and bang, Mrs. goes down again, and there was some to-do, I can tell you, between helpin' Mrs. to her bed and consultin' about how to get the corpse away without disturbin' him, for we all thought he had left his senses, of course, and wanted no trouble. Besides, there was the contagion, you understand. They—him and Mrs.—had always slept separate. [Not true, not *always,* and anyway a gratuitous piece of gossip.]

"'It was about this moment that this Mr. Lenart appears, sweatin' like a pig and breathin' hard from runnin' up the driveway, afraid to have missed somethin' you know. He was always underfoot at 'Luba,' and the plain fact is it was like workin' for three married people 'stead of two. [Balls.] Anyway, he takes one look at Mr. Abul and goes up and takes the corpse out of his arms and hands it to the doctor, without him so much as flickin' an eye, Mr. Abul, that is. As it turned out, he was in a *coma,* which he would go into now and then ever since he was a child, though nothin' serious. So they undressed him, and the doctor called up and got another nurse to stay in the room with them that night, and Mr. Lenart and the doctor made arrangements about the corpse.

"'But the very next day a van pulls up outside, and they drag out this big, dirty, black screen, ugly as sin and just as old, and bring it and put it up in front of Mr. Abul's bed, to everyone's indignity, and only a few hours later comes the old shanty-Irish b_____ of a nurse, breakin' wind all over the place and cursin' us out and demandin' to see her 'Gordie.' So we take her up, because Mr. Know-it-all Lenart grandly informs us that she's from his mother, the screen too. Well, she and Mrs. can't *stand* each other, you can see that at once, but she stays, and Mr. Abul is in this coma for one week and four days, straight through the funeral and all, arranged by Mr. Do-it-all Lenart.'

"And now our tale hurtles to its lurid *dénouement,* as the story of a high-life *mésalliance* quickly degenerates into a veritable *roman policier!* [Oh, excuse me, must have dropped off—have we finished *Jane Eyre?*] Gordon emerged from his coma abruptly. Indeed, according to our informant, he was probably conscious a long while before anyone became aware of it, a day or even two, perhaps, the doctor thought. His old nurse was well beyond her years of competence. In any case, when it was discovered, he sprang from his bed as light and silent as a feather and resumed his routine as though there had been but an over-night hiatus. He went back to his board meetings [not true], he worked on the lovely grounds or in the stable, but no word was ever heard to pass his lips concerning the children, and no one had the heart to mention them. One morning he picked up near the stable a colored marble dropped there at one time or another by little David, rolled it for a minute in the palm of his hand, then tossed it to the stable boy with a gay admonition. Quite literally, he went his way as if they had never existed, as if he had not adored them, young David in particular, almost to distraction.

"The effect must have been unnerving, to say the least. But not only did he not talk about the children, he said virtually nothing at all on any subject. He lived in a sort of globe of silence which all of Emily's vehemence could not pierce. She, indeed, began to have fits of hysterics, until not a day passed without some painful scene marring 'Luba's' golden summer calm. Her threats, according to our informant, were of the most violent nature, and couched in language doubtless learned in the dens of Bloomington, Indiana; but Gordon only retreated deeper into silence—'pleasant as you please, but watchful, like he was expectin' someone and nothin' could be done meantime. He was *not* depressed the way the newspapers made out later.'

"Then one night Gordon vanished. For seventy-two hours nothing was heard of him, though Emily alerted the police forces of both cities together with the constabulary of the surrounding small communities. She appears to have worked herself into an absolute phrensy of wrath. About twelve-thirty o'clock on the morning of August ninth, nineteen hundred and forty-nine, our informant, who was a light sleeper [where other people's business was concerned], was awakened by the sound of the telephone in the drawing room, directly beneath her room. As the telephone was kept in fairly constant alarum in those days what with the police—Gordon Charls was a considerable figure in the area—and reports from sundry private agencies being employed by the distrait woman, our informant paid it scant attention, merely remarking, before falling off to sleep again, how Emily, upon hanging up, sighed exultantly, even laughed a little to herself, then immediately left the drawing room and came upstairs, her face wreathed in smiles [divine Jeanette Slade!]. At five minutes past two o'clock of the same morning, our informant was again awakened, this time by the sound of tires on the driveway. Her room being at the back of the house [ears], she hurried up the corridor to a small window at the front, arriving in time to see Emily enter a car about fifty feet off the entrance, which then drove away. It was Gordon's black Jaguar [though it was the darkest night of the year and the outdoor sconces were off—who says our faculties are deteriorating?—but which happens to have been the fact].

"And that was the last to be seen or heard of Emily and Gordon Abul. The Jaguar, with its real jaguar skin upholstery and onyx and gold accessories, was located the next day among shrubbery along the shore of Lake Minnetonka, near its junction with legendary Minnehaha Creek. A sodden shoe, identified as Emily's, was eventually discovered by truant boys half a mile upstream, while later, a blue [black] silk neckpiece, sometimes worn by Gordon, was reeled in by a fisherman casting among offshore reeds for bass, in which the icy blue water of the lovely lake abounds, but no amount of dragging or diving ever produced the bodies. They, for all the 'glitter and the gold' of their mortal hour, continue to molder with shells and slugs in Minnetonka's oozy [pebbly] bed.

"But as if this were not tragedy enough for fashionable Minneapolis, as if the jealous Gods had determined to obliterate every vestige of the proud Abul name, the very night that witnessed the terrible final hours of Emily and Gordon, witnessed the last of Edith Charls, who disappeared without a trace from her superb snow-white, fifteen-room Minneapolis apartment, one of the last and finest examples of the art of Syrie Maugham, never to be seen again. No violence or untoward circumstances were in evidence here. The faithful Syrian couple who had been in her employ since the early years of her marriage, a Mr. and Mrs. Toolkakian, heard her leave the apartment about twelve-thirty o'clock; though being venerable, they completely forgot she had been at home all evening, and in their senility imagined she was *coming in,* so neglected to investigate. Her companion, Fay Gahagan, the old nurse who had been sent to watch over her son during his illness, had taken a Nembutal and retired early. The garage attendant, Hollis Doernheimer, who at twelve-twelve o'clock received the call to deliver her white Mercedes Benz, noticed nothing unusual in her voice, though he confessed to thinking the hour strange; while the doorman, a Mr. Weigert [Weigert, one g, Gregory Weigert, damn it] recalled she looked as she always looked, and was even somewhat gay with him as she passed through the lobby, playfully snatching a rose—how like the gallant thoroughbred she was!—from the vase he was carrying to the new manager's office.

"*Le reste est silence.* The white Mercedes Benz was never recovered. She simply slipped behind the wheel and drove away forever into the night—and into, one likes to imagine, some finer, fairer social whirl above, where—can one doubt it?—she sits prominent and ever-lovely among the first families of history.

"Well, it must be a jaded reader indeed who would not agree that the story of Emily Lenart Abul is one of the more provocative in *A Closet of Gilded Skeletons*. But 'picaresque,' even 'macabre,' to a certain degree, though it be, it cannot compare in sheer 'frisson' with the haunted destiny of Gladys Spurgeon Schrumm...."

* * *

The night he vanished was full of surprises. First off, on the verandah, he says distinctly and unequivocally, "You mean my boy, don't you, Matt?" It came as a totally unlooked-for response. I had been babbling along discursively, captivated by the rich, oily sound of my after-dinner voice—not unlike Benham Lake's, as I recalled it—and accepting as a matter of course the vague grunts and nods that made up the larger part of his communication those days. I lit here or there arbitrarily. He seemed to grasp nothing, so nothing was forbidden. God knows where I wandered. I suppose at some point I may even have been tempted into a little delicate malice about the children. Yes, I think so.

If this smacks of unspeakable cruelty, remember I had cause for it. The point is, I hadn't dreamed he would understand—though by this time I had formed the highest regard for his head, if not his heart, and already had my first glimmering of that inner discipline. But I also realized the fragmentation in that head just then, the tiny lights gathering and scattering across choppy waters and never quite cohering in an image, and I had no sympathy with it, at least not any longer. Neither did Emily. He made no effort to pull himself together that we could see. Worse, he asked no help. He simply endured, a monument of patience, and we couldn't bear it. The temptation was to *sting* him into some sort of propriety. I mean, there were obligations. The children were scarcely cold in their graves. Isolated at Luba though we were, we did have a small world of domestics and country people, with a fashionable spy or two a week from the city, for whom appearances simply had to be kept up. Emily did her bit with tantrums, and I with deep breathing and bursts of bitterness at the table and a little becoming inwardness. And what did he do? Smiled, and put in tulip bulbs, and lost his damn memory. It was impossible. He had practically no memory since the seizure. If one could believe Fay Gahagan—which I am of successive minds about on successive days—such a thing had never happened before, or only once, or twice at most, and in so minor a dose that it could not really count as the same thing, a few unimportant facts confused or lost, names mostly. Nothing nearly so extreme as this, where for a while he couldn't remember his children, let alone their deaths. I have the clearest picture of him receiving the condolences of Axel Stolt—*blushing*. I had to walk away.

But it wasn't only the idiotic untimeliness that vexed me, it was his refusal to be helped, or even to admit. We had had to infer the memory-loss, which we didn't do for several days after his awakening, so cunning was he. What he apparently did was to listen for names, and address himself exclusively to those persons until more names were dropped. He developed a nagging little cough to induce us to finish sentences for him. He peered around him constantly to ascertain the duties of various members of the household, what he might expect of them and they of him. I forget who it was that first found him out, but by that time he had got together a sufficient body of fact to defy us, and though we might make him stumble, we could never bring him down. Pride or mistrust—whichever, I didn't care for it, and cared even less for the way he appeared to take my magnanimity for granted. For example, about the children just now. To my knowledge this was the fist time he had referred to either of them. Plainly, he had been gathering up material, though they were scarcely mentioned anymore in his presence and then in the most veiled terms. By his tone he clearly intended that we take up in as normal a manner as possible, that I treat him with a delicacy he had no right to expect of me—that I appear to let him fool me! Disarming in the perfection of its egoism, but really too insulting. Why no, I thought, and had to smile. In fact I thought his eyes went so dark with pain that I had trouble not to laugh. "Yes, poor sweet Robert," I said, working to keep my voice steady. He sent me a pleading glance but I would not see it. "Poor sweet Robert," he echoed finally, helplessly, under his breath, and looked away. "Dead," he ventured presently. "The girl too."

"Mm," I said, admiration and resentment pulling at me like wild horses in the old torture. The sensation was delicious. It demanded brandy and I called in through the window for some.

Profile to me (he was looking well—while comatose, his body had used up most of the disfiguring flab of the past few years and his hair had somehow regained its old fullness and luster), head lowered, and mouth pressed to the backs of curled fingers in an exquisitely fine, sad pose: "Be my friend," he said with surprising warmth in the tone.

"It seems my fate," I replied, apprehensive of some touching confidence to ruin everything.

"Or mine," he mused.

"More could get embarrassing," I returned coldly, meaning, I suppose, to his sense of gratitude.

"Ah, suspicion vile," he thoughtfully agreed!

"I should think you'd blush to make a cheap crack like that—."

"I blush. Original rat. Anything you say, but be my true friend."

"Perhaps it's your turn?"

"*Oh I tried.*"

"Tried what?"

"Tried." And that was the whole luminous confidence! I breathed with relief at so transparent a shift; he had not tried anything at all, in my understanding of the word, and this was one more mark of his taking me for granted. Then softly: "Matt, what was his name?"

"Whose, Robert's?"—and now I really had to laugh out; his position was so *ridiculous*. He realized this too. He snorted and gave a little appreciative shrug of the shoulders and returned to his rags of thought. By now his suffering had reached the sublime point of imperceptibility. Perhaps a stranger would have sworn he was not suffering at all, but I knew better. He was undiluted suffering, through to the bone. He sat there limp with it. But thinking how a stranger could not savor this talent of mine for hurting him simply because I could hurt him so profoundly, I began to grow dissatisfied. I wanted some visible sign for my invisible stranger.

He was sliding off into reverie. I wished to hell Emily would turn off that mood music she was so crazy about. The damn whorish strings had been crooning and sobbing at us ever since I arrived at a little past five; it was now past *eight*. Even here on the verandah at the back of the house, a faint cheap perfume of sound found its way through the brain. (I am very susceptible to cheapness in certain of my sense areas. It excites me. Bella for one knows it and uses only honeysuckle or lily-of-the-valley scent, to everyone's horror. She claims it's out of deference to the colored and Puerto Rican leaders she's always conferring with, but it's for love of me; they, I'm sure, wear Tabac Blond.) I got up and strolled the length of the verandah to the far corner of the house, came slowly back, and sat down. He hadn't moved. His great shadowy eyes swam dreamily. In the distance, marking a boundary of the estate at the St. Croix, stood a line of dusky trees, every outer spray cut clear upon a cold rose sky. He appeared to linger there. Before us, in the miniature garden, his private blue pavilion glowed like a jewel. Or was it here? I picked up a magazine crossly.

A few minutes later, Emily came out to join us. She was wearing a strapless orange gown with a train of Spanishy ruffles halfway to the Pacific coast, which she handled better than one might imagine. Her hair, fluffed into a mane, was a light brown that month—it changed often, like the interior of her house—and her skin was tawny and faintly dusted gold. Not everyone's idea of taste for an intimate little dinner, but marvelously, sexily leonine. "Where's my brandy?" I demanded, studying her wickedly.

She stared as wickedly back. "Do I look like a damn waitress? Jeanette'll be out in a minute."

"Why, you used to do pretty well in that line, I believe."

"You fart-face slug. Pull that chair over here for me before I kick you sillier than you already are." I did, placing it between Gordie's and mine and somewhat to the rear. As she sat, I bent and ran my tongue up the nape of her neck, at which she reached back and deliberately dug her golden claws into my knuckles. "Dear," she said to Gordie, with an edge in it for me, "your wife has just come in."

"Out, I think." Moveless, talking into his hand, "Welcome, my wife," he said, and rolled his eyes to see. "Emily is the damn sun."

"Damn daughter, I think," said I.

"Whose damn daughter?" said he, ever in profile, his eyes strained to their corners.

"The bloody King of Lions," said I, licking my knuckles. "Her talons."

"Talonts," said he. "Oh a bloody true-life fact. Mad splendid talonts, by god. Talonted to point of pain. Struck me forksibly first tine we met. Only tragic is—mark me—b'long the hole world, such talonts—"

"Whirl!" cried Emily staring at him. She seemed as amazed as I, after weeks of near-silent evenings, to find us spang in the middle of this old word game of ours—but nothing daunted. "Life's whirl left we to bury selves in Luba gloom —"

"Whore'll," said he. "Whore'll clap you blue-balled, Matt, say dripping Uncle Sam—."

"War'll," cried I. "War'll make strange deadfellows."

"Ah, suspicion vile," he sweetly commented!

"Vial!" rapped I. "Vial of ingratitudes poisons friendship true—"

"In platitudes," said he. "In platitudes lurk latitudes of attitudes covert —a triple *fouetté,* darlings!"

"Bravo!" cried Emily.

"My dear," murmured he, lowering his eyes in acknowledgment.

"Since prattle rudes," said I.

"Rudes?" said Emily uncertainly.

I insisted. "Since prattle rudes in addled moods one must forgive, yet *warning clear—*"

"Christ's teeth, Mattie. Jesus. Got me right here. Treat me gentle in my condish or I *break,* lad." I thought he laughed.

"You break? I begin to think maybe you don't even chip, except for public viewing."

"That what you begin to think? Well, maybe you're right. Maybe I don't chip. Maybe I am the living diamond they slaved so hard over. Gleam eternal. Good as new, except for everything. Catinka, lioness, am I a diamond?"

"To me you are, dear—all the virtues."

"I love you for your values. But tell us about the sweet cubs, Cat."

Fantastically, she missed it. My guess is that the manner threw her. It threw *me.* He hadn't done this high snotty line in years, really not since that post-war spree in Europe when from week to week he was never less than dazzlingly fizzed; and so eager was she to get them back on some version of it —poor thing, how she despised the husband in him—that it could not immediately occur to her he might take it up only to be more solemn than ever. She was too starved for fun. "Perfect little beasts," she rattled, "and listen — you'll never guess who they ate today!"

"Tell us, dear," he drawled, surveying the view off to the right.

"Little Alvin Ape!—finished every bit, I was so proud."

"Apestein," came the languid voice. It made me crawl.

She whooped. "You know it! Alvin Apestein! Ha—"

It's not that I categorically object to Yiddish humor of this type, but that Gordie's tone with it was always so much that of the gentiles who used it on *us* —pissily unctuous—Benham to the life. However, I was more put out by the fact that even through the swiftly gathering dark I could catch glints from his curled hand, which because of her rear position Emily could not. Crying there— trading puns with her and quietly sobbing out his heart for his babies. And my god how the katydids shrieked (my notes for the night particularly mention this). Suddenly everything seemed wrong, strange and vulgar and confused. I hate confusion; fear it maybe. After having for months felt myself in absolute control of things, I sensed once more that old elusive something clouding up, enfolding them—not me. Not me, you understand, never me. If ever a proper history of villains comes to be written, I suspect this will be seen as the deep common factor—this bitter exclusion from mystery. And then to turn the scene utterly sour, I became aware of Jeanette Slade, dwarfish and goose-eyed, standing behind my chair, my brandy forgotten on a tray, watching with all her vicious *Nibelungen* might. I rapped the side of the seat and told her she might serve the brandy if it hadn't all evaporated. She didn't reply, but immediately came around, opened a folding table with one fat hand, and banged the snifter down. I looked into that pouchy bleary face. "Been sipping a bit, Jeanette?" I said, for of course she had been. She always was.

Says she blinking evilly, with a breath out of her mouth to blight all vegetation for miles: "If I was—*if* I was—it was surely from no damn bottle of yours, sir."

Enough. "Emily," I said in a real rage now, "when will you turn off that sugar-tit crap? When I want cat-house charm I know likelier places to go."

"And so it's been rumored too," soughs an effluvial wind beside me.

"*Em-i-ly*." She turned to stare. "The music, woman. Give us some *peace*."

"There's always the grave, sir," wheezes Effluvia.

"You shut up and beat it, Jeanette," said Emily; then to me, "and put what on? The Red Hatikvah or something, you screw? Listen, Matt, just for a change, why don't you leave us alone tonight?"

Way too much. *"Oh you cook,"* I muttered, starting to rise.

"What did you say?" said she coloring and rising too. "Do you hear me?—what did you just say!—Jeanette, I told you to get out."

"But Mister's weeping," snivels the thing, shooting out a fat arm with a digit waggling at the tip.

Do you know these moments? I simply left them and went down

for my brandy, wordless with fury at myself and the whole greasy peasant broth. When I could bring myself to look again Emily was leaned over him, her face tilted to bring their eyes level—it was very dark now save for light from the drawing room windows—saying gently, "Darling?" touching the back of his head, his arm—"Gordie, dear?"—to no response; whereupon she returned to me. "What's wrong with him?" she said, fixing me with those shrewd Yankee eyes. The katydids raved like toothache. I thought my head would split.

"It seems he's crying," I said, near nervous tears myself.

"Why is he crying?" she said.

"Life—" I started to say, praying for control.

"Why is he crying?" she dared to say again in the same insulting monotone.

"Robert—probably over Robert. Yes, exactly." I suddenly could not be spiteful enough.

"*Robert!*" she yelled slapping the snifter out of my hand and clear over the railing. "Who in blue shit—?"

"Shh," I cautioned, making exaggerated eyes in Gordie's direction. "We were discussing the boy—*Robert,* you know?" and gave her a conspiratorial wink and a quivering gay bit of mouth.

And after a second or two of dawning she gave *me* a face of such horror and grief, with a yowl out of the pit of her stomach— "David!" ("David!" I heard him echo ecstatically)—that for all my experience of these outbursts I went backwards in alarm. Jeanette, who had been whining into a snotty brown rag, actually sprang behind me, as if I could be counted on to protect her! I wish it had come to the proof. But Emily's passion blew the other way, and the next minute she was on her knees beside Gordie, her face in her hands. And Gordie was down with her and his arms around her and they were kissing wildly, now forehead to forehead, each other's head in each other's hands, like children themselves, gasping the mournful names, again, again, as if to take them indelibly through all transmigrations, with more clinging, clutching, and those pummeling kisses, and tears to fill up a lake. Oh, my adorable boys, whatever my crimes, let strangers requite them—never hurt me so!

—Well, I have been honest about my small villainies, but that wasn't all of the relationship. I loved them—consumingly, you might say. I wept with them now. It would have taken a monster not to in the face of such desolation. David and Victoria had been dear to me, Victoria especially, a tiny cool snowflake of a creature, who loved me to hold her. David was his father's child. But I would have fantasies of stealing Victoria away and raising her in some exotic land, for in those days I was determined never to marry again. No, we all did our share of grieving then, I think. At last I noticed a falling away in Emily, though Gordie had her locked against him like a second soul and continued to say the children's names into her cheek, her hair, her neck, whichever part of her came to his mouth, for his swollen eyes were closed. Still, I felt it was over. I roused Jeanette, and between us, very carefully, we pulled them apart. There was no resistance. Gordie relinquished his grasp instantly, almost gratefully, hanging his head and bracing his hands on his thighs like one exhausted; while Emily, even as I took her shoulders, fainted dead away. With Jeanette's aid I hiked her into my arms. I then motioned Jeanette to help Gordie up, but he shrugged her off.

"Get along, Nell [sic]. Help her. I'm fine, I'll come." When she persisted, he hit viciously at her hand.

"Oh, sir!"

"I said get"—a surge of that buried violence. Then ash again, barely audible. "Get."

So I carried Emily to the sofa in the drawing room, accompanied by Jeanette, her nose high with chagrin, holding the train of the dress from under my feet. Practically treading on our heels came Nellie and Edsel, the first with aromatic spirits and a pillow and the second with a tray of strong tea. One of the other girls followed in a few seconds with cologne and towels rolled with ice cubes. Emily's emotional releases often ended in faints and the routine was pretty set. Of course they had all been observing us. Every eye in the room was red, and without turning to see I knew there were more such peering in from the corridor. I could hear the whispering. It began to grate on me to have been part of so touching a scene, like an extra in the movies hanging near in mute sympathy while the stars emote (the music was perfect for this at least), or one of those small reddish-brown figures in old wall-paintings clustered about some great white king and queen. It was simply not the part for a Lenart, not in Minneapolis anyway. And now to be waiting anxious as the servants for their low-born lady to revive. Oh damn them, I thought, and poured myself a cup of tea, taking care to slop some on the ecru carpet. Then I walked up and down in a careless, thoughtful fashion, humming along with the music, until I became aware, though very gradually—the idea was so mad—that the hairs of my neck were standing on end.

I was *freezing*.

Now, it was a warm August night. Clouds had closed in a little before dark to make it breathless besides. A faint moldy coolness had begun to move along the verandah but as yet the house was an oven; a few minutes in the drawing room and every face went shiny. Not only the heat but all the emotion. Emily lying there looked cut out of brown lard. My shirt-front buckled in and out like some old clown suit and my maroon cummerbund was wet black under the jacket. I smelled foul. I longed for some of the rose water they were using on Emily (I was very fastidious in those days) but didn't have the nerve. Besides, the intense discomfort of the thing bemused me. Somehow—and I've never been able to run this down—it had a teasing quality for me. I had been in such heat before—in a dream?—whiteness, a paradisiac whiteness trembling and melting with heat, some hot secret valley in a mountain, many of us, waiting, struck dumb. Even now—. It was as I stood puzzling this that I felt the bitter cold. But for an instant even then, so anomalous was the sensation, I thought my pain —it *hurt*—due to a sudden increase in the heat. Then I knew. Instinctively I went for a mouthful of tea. Ice. An actual film of ice on liquid that not two minutes before had scalded my throat.

I looked over at the sofa expecting to see I don't know what and saw in fact a group of greasy domestics laboring over their greasy mistress, whose head was just beginning to roll and moan on the pillow. I was terrified. "Jeanette," I said. She was standing behind Nellie and Edsel with a wet towel in her hand, watching as usual.

She didn't hear me. "Jeanette," I said again. She looked over her shoulder. I stood between the windows across the room where I had gone to catch what air there was. I pushed the cup and saucer towards her—I can still hear the clinking—and in spite of her black looks at being called from a sick couch for such work, I persisted in my mute demand. Emily had begun to cry and burble the children's names. Well, the thing took one quick look at the couch, threw down the towel and lurched over towards me, her face a vision of wrath.

Almost to me, she stopped, dead white with surprise, like someone shot. In an instant her lips were purple with the cold. She stared at me and I stared at her. I tilted the cup to show the ice, and she peered delicately in with eyes of glass. She looked a hundred years old. So, I'm sure, did I. The goose-bumps on her arms were fantastic. Why neither of us spoke I have no idea; instinct, or shock. Conspiracy of fright. But a suspicion of some tasteless trick began to dawn in her—her face always a graph of her mind—she (rightly) never trusted me—and made a motion as if to turn back;—when through a flash of sympathy we both looked towards the nearest window. And together moved, as if wanting to get there before thinking prevented us. The sheer silk curtains were webs of frost.

Full in light from the window, and as he came up he spun towards the garden in a slow spiralling turn—an utterly graceful dancelike motion, such as one performs in dreams, unhindered by bone and flesh, all joy. Surely some dream part continued on and through the clouds.—Ecstatic. Even though during those brief seconds we could not see his face, there was such sense of wild feathering —*richesse*— all the cherries of the soul spilled out and wild birds eating them. Have you seen it? Fluttering off, falling back, drunk with juice? *Lewd* to unraptured or unhungry eyes. Swaying on the balls of his feet, hands gripping the railing as if to keep him earthward, now leaping a little against them. And I said, Don't—stay. I said, Oh, one can't—, and yet the darling did. Light as a dream he vaulted the railing and fled. The heat broke over us, the katydids screamed, and I stood there listening to Jeanette's hoarse whispers nearly out of my mind with happiness.

Propped on a pillow, her face liverish and puffed, fanning reflectively, Emily said he would be back in a while.

"No—" not wanting to sound as absolutely certain as I was.

"Yes. Probably no farther than his damn pavilion anyway."

"Probably much farther. I heard the car soon after."

She batted her lashes mockingly. "Did you." But was angry. "I don't care where he thinks he's going. I said he'll be back and he will. I know a little about that bunch by this time. I'm not blind and I'm not *dumb* and *they* know *that*."

"Bow-wow-wow!"

"Sorry," she said and blew out her lips as though to blame the heat.

"—What bunch?"

Impatiently, with half-humorous, half-amorous fingers in my hair: "Oh you baby."

"—Who's 'that bunch'?"

"Come *down* here."

Towards morning, her head in the hollow of my ribs while I twisted one of her great brown nipples between thumb and forefinger: "You've really improved, Matt." She munched a candied apricot—she had a passion for them—from a glassine box on the night-table.

"Well, I've been in practice."

"What Jeanette tells me."

"Not with her!"

She chuckled. "No."

"It doesn't take great talent to excite another man's wife, you understand."

A brief pause as she swallowed the last of the apricot and wiped her fingers in my pubic hairs. "And when may I look forward to the excitement of another woman's husband?"

"If you mean me, never."

"Big word, never, Matt."

"I love *you*." My voice cracked like a boy's. It was true—the only one I ever loved. After all these years I long for her.

She rolled her head to look at me and I started to cry. "Oh, dearest

Matt, I'm sorry, sorry.—Ye gods, what damn station are you trying to dial?" she laughed and slapped my hand off her breast. "My aching tit! Aii!"

"I tell you, he's gone for good—"

"And I tell you, he'll be back—"

"Trampy liar! Would I be here if you believed that? You're *alone,* you miserable rich doxie."

She sat on the edge of the bed and licked at her nipple, cradling the breast in both hands lovingly. "Sadist bastard you."

"We would be happy this time, Emily, I swear to you." But she didn't hear. All night long, through the love-making and snatches of talk, she had been quietly sucking her resentments much as she sucked her breast now, and suddenly nothing could cut through the loud thought in her. The mattress thrummed with it.

"Killer. Jesus—um um—this is delightful. Who needs men?"

"Who's 'that bunch'?"

She raised her head to study the gleaming nipple. "He'll never get away from me, never in a million years. Let them try. I still have a few tricks left. You'd think they would know me a little by this time, wouldn't you? I mean what do they take me for?"

"*Who?*"

She looked around in mock outrage. "*Who?*" And before I could pull back, she flung herself on me and pinned my arms—she was as strong as any man—kissing me all over the face and mouth until I lost my breath and started to yell. She rolled off laughing and gasping. "Rich doxie, am I?—oh, I'll kill you with tainted kisses—I'll give you a dose of clap'll make the headlines in China—mean Commie whoremaster like you—what was it?—trampy liar?—I'll eat your subversive heart!"—and she tried to mount me again but I got her by the shoulders and wrestled her down, and we struggled and howled there until exhaustion set in, and we lay prostrate, groaning, trying not to laugh for the ache in our middles.

After a while she flopped a hand into the glassine box and noisily disengaged an apricot; soon another. Then one into my mouth and two more into hers. Then, an arm crooked under her head, eating apricot after apricot, she began to talk about him. Her tone was casual enough, but what she said was appalling to me. In those years I was innocent above most. Love was *love*. When one said to me he loved, I understood a very particular thing. It had to do with satisfaction. Regardless of beginnings, the end was a surface tumult of marriage and children and quarreling and occasional unfaithfulness, and underneath a counterpoint of dark, rich satisfaction, never heard or seen maybe, but making the harmonies of our lives. This had been the case with Father and Mother, Grandfather and Grandmother (so far as I knew), their friends and relatives, and mine. This is the case with Bella. So what I heard from Emily that morning made me prickle with discomfort.

She talked about his looks. "The most beautiful object in the universe, Matt. You have no idea. From any angle, in any light, absolute perfection. A slap in the *face*." It embarrassed me. She said the sight of him had become as necessary to her as drugs to the addict, and yet to come upon him accidentally, in some rare peaceful moment, her head full of everyday thoughts, was a thing she dreaded. Seen fresh that way, he so clearly didn't *fit,* either in the present moment or in any future she could imagine. It was agony. "I have him," she said shrugging, "but I've never known what to *do* with him. I feel like the man who stole the Mona Lisa, you know?" She laughed. "He's always polite and considerate, of course." With a roguish stare: "I mean he's so well brought-up. He accepts everything at the door *smiling.* It's a sure sign. But even that would be bearable if he would ever vary it to show when one thing pleased him more than another. But no, everything with the same charming smile, because everything is *nothing* to him. My man-in-the-moon. But oh god, the sight of him." Very serious and quiet: "The mere ravishing sight. *Damn.*" She slapped the mattress with the flat of her hand. "Matt, I'm suffering. Do you realize that? I'm not well. I can't stand the idea that other people may be looking at him and feeling what I feel. It will be light in a few hours, hundreds of strangers will be ogling him as he walks down some street. Thousands of eyes will caress him. I don't want that. He's mine. Where is he? Find him for me!"

"No, you're not well," I agreed, utterly revolted. I got up and started to dress.

She heaved over on her side to watch me, reflectively chewing what must surely have been the last apricot, unless there were two boxes, I didn't notice. "He knows how I suffer. I've told him, screamed it at him, often enough. He'll come back. He won't let me suffer. He's a Charls. And his mother's a great lady —isn't she? She'll show him his duty, won't she? She's such an authority on proper behavior." And she gave a low and very unpleasant laugh. I was at the dresser brushing my hair, and without knowing I was going to do it, I spun and threw the silver hair-brush at her with all my might. Fortunately, I always was a rotten shot and the brush sailed over the bed.

I wondered if possibly she had gone a little mad with trouble and loneliness. She certainly sounded it that morning. I won't preserve what she spat out at me after I threw the brush, but it was vile. A small core of truth —yes—was blown up into a mountain of filth and unwholesomeness. I got out as fast as I could. I suppose I was angrier than I should have been. If it had been a pack of lies—but like many of her class, like Irene after her—she knew how to mix in just enough truth to choke you into silence. She had no honor about her, no delicacy you could count on in the pinch.

Well, I fumed. I was ready to strangle Dolly for some remark she made over breakfast—Emily had a habit of leaving "roses" high up the neck—and only Father's sarcasm saved her. I actually turned on *him*. We were all flabbergasted, and Dolly later told me it was one of the few times in her life she admired me, for she loathed the old man as much as he loathed her. I of course instantly regretted it. He didn't speak to either of us for days which, added to everything else, was a great oppression to me. But at the moment I was in too much of a turmoil over Emily to think about apologizing. I busied myself with some "pop" articles on Gene Debs I was doing for the Sunday supplement of the *Dispatch* (Father's idea of entertainment for the masses), long overdue. It did me good.

As I say, I realized from the first that what had really incensed me were the bits of truth in her accusations. The rest had been simple hysteria, and the poor woman had plenty of excuse there. As I cooled down, which I always do fairly rapidly, I began to be sorry for the few choice words I myself had got off at the door. It made it difficult to resume as fast as I would have liked. By the following morning I was ready to forgive but still far from the mood to beg forgiveness. Emily would never phone, I knew, so I phoned there and asked for Nellie. She talked in a whisper. Mr. Abul had not returned and Mrs. was in a temper. There were detectives—private-like—she had to go. I was neither surprised nor comforted by this last—she often employed detectives, Benham had been under surveillance for months, and even Edith for a while—but the first item really elated me. He was *gone*.

On hanging up, I phoned Edith, and pretty plainly took her by surprise. I had an idea that she and Gordie were in touch but soon felt otherwise. She wanted to know everything. She questioned me closely—rather severely, I thought; her loftiest vein, yet intensely eager; and *not* friendly. I understood. I was well acquainted with this tone. I had been neglecting her, and gave what satisfaction I could. I was all patience. We went over the evening in ferocious detail. It was not a pleasant task, but I did it—save for one thing. I could not bring myself to touch that moment of ice in the drawing room. The more so perhaps because I had the impression that that was exactly what she was fishing for, and either didn't realize she was, or didn't know the nature of it and so how to ask. Besides, though I am aware of the reality of such phenomena, I don't like it. It has nothing to do with me. Well, she covered the same ground over and over, each time—so it seemed to me—poking in a different corner. But I wouldn't help. She seemed moved at their grief over the children (she had refused to attend the funeral); expressed mild surprise that someone of Emily's background should faint; wondered that it should have been so hot ("the country is always cool or what's the good of it?"); that Gordie should have been so exhausted; that, considering the heat, all the domestics should have been indoors; that Gordie should have jumped over the railing instead of using the stairs; et cetera, et cetera.

"How did you say he looked?"

"I said I only saw his back." My patience was thinning. She had been at it nearly forty minutes.

"So you did. But what I don't understand is why the girl was at the window too, or why either of you went to the window at all at that particular moment." She felt she was close now. "The woman of the house is in a perfect *condition* on the other side of the room, and here are her dear friend and her bawd to whom she pays a large salary idly staring out of the window. I mean, did you hear something, or—?"

"Or?"

"*Anything,* you little beast."

"No-o."

"No-o! What does that mean? Maybe?"

"It means I have no more to tell you, Edith. I don't understand what you want."

"I *want* to *know* what *happened.* Good heavens, what a clod it is."

"Well, you know." I was finding it hard to be civil.

She heard it too, and softened her tone. "He's my son, Matthew—no lectures, please. We are all aware of my deficiencies, what we're after are his. I simply must be interested when he engages in a strange stunt like this."

"Strange? Men have been running away from their wives for years, though not in so literal a fashion, perhaps. Still, it's a custom."

"Do you really think he's done that? That's what I've been trying to find out, you see. Nothing strange? Just that?" She fairly trilled, and I was to understand that she had decided to make do, and we were friends again.

"Well, Emily does. She's sicked detectives on him, I hear."

"Oh—oh that's ill-advised of her—"

"Is it?"

"I mean, well, you simply can't hold a man that way. You can't hound him into loving you, or even into seeing you occasionally, can you?"

"I can't say. I haven't really tried."

"Don't be cavalier with an old woman, boy."

"Not I. With the old ones I'm all respect. It's the fierce mellow beauties who would wither me with a glance that sting me into attitudes. You're too splendid by half, lady."

"I don't know if I care for 'wither' in the context, but the rest seems nicely said. But what must I do then—plead old to get respect?"

"If respect is what you want, as it appears to be."

"Why, damn you, what a nasty child you are. You know I must have it. And yet I must have the other too, somehow. Oh lord, what it is to grow smooth and sphinxlike, so that people have lost your meaning, and everyone comes to stare and admire, and no one to stay, no one to lag behind and strike a pose and call up, 'Woman, you desire me. Come here, you ancient idol.'"

"Why, would the sphinx obey?"

"Oh, she would shake off her dust and descend on him and show him such rare eastern arts."

"Edith—"

"Matt, come to me."

I could scarcely talk. "Half an hour." She could do that.

She laughed her Charls laugh, but darkly. "It would have been so kind of *you* to say, 'Tomorrow, if you can.' Well, we're even."

At least she had the memory of a sphinx, and the wiles. She let me sleep on *my* memories, which were of a suffocatingly feverish quality, and by the next evening I was abject with longing. Maybe Emily's taunts spurred me, but Edith didn't need help. She was the most accomplished and exciting woman I have ever had. Shem taught her—but the devil knows what she taught Shem. These high-bred Nazarenes can be surprising.

She looked marvelous, having lost weight since I last saw her—she had a tendency to stoutness in her latter years; otherwise, time had dealt well with her. A certain early radiance had vanished maybe, and her public generosity for people and causes was backed by an increasing private intolerance, distasteful to a degree and one reason I went less and less to her. But physically she was a wonder. She must have been well past fifty but not a crease betrayed it, and I always looked, snot-nose that I was. Even her new pale hair seemed more a fashion than a development. Since moving into her splendid white apartment (which in my recollection was Elsie de Wolfe's, not Syrie Maugham's) she had switched from gold to platinum, and while one could suspect it had been gray for years anyway, one still found it unusually becoming. She kept it long, pulled straight back and folded into a loose bun at the side of her neck, all ready to fall apart at your touch. She wore some billowing smoky silk with violet flashes in the folds, a few pale flowers at her waist, a pale stone on her finger. Her bared shoulders gleamed like pearl.

She was reading when Aram showed me in, and she rose to greet me with so natural yet expert a grace that I had to blush for my poor Emily, who worked so hard and stayed such a duck to this mother of swans. The fact that everyone else did too made no difference. My concern those days was for Emily, only Emily, and I felt Edith understood this and took special pains to embarrass me. Don't ask me specifically how; women have ways. I don't imagine she was ever really fooled by those claims of disinterested justice for my ex-wife. Discarded husbands aren't generally notable for that sort of thing.

I blushed, as I say, and of course she caught the import at once. "Welcome home," she said, and came close to beat the air with an ivory fan.

"Cut it, Edith," I said.

"But you look so warm, dear." I brushed the fan aside more decisively than I intended, but she wasn't taking offense that evening, for which I was immediately grateful; the gesture had purged me. Demurely, with lowered eyes, she closed the fan and tapped my shoulder with it. "All right"—saying really, well don't show it then.

I kissed her quickly on the lips and by the little pressure of her response knew to what I could attribute my luck. We would not linger over dinner that night. As I drew back, her eyes were looking into mine with such cool, silken familiarity, such a refinement of depravity, that not only did I forget to blush again for Emily, I forgot her altogether.

It usually went this way. There was an Emily-land to be crossed before the evening could properly begin, and sometimes it took a longer and sometimes a shorter time. It rested with Edith. I would come on defensively and, depending on whether she was more or less accommodating, our evening was long or short. There had been times when it never began at all, and others, rarer, like this evening, when she let it begin at once.

She was in high spirits. I wondered if she had been puffing hemp, as she occasionally did to calm her nerves—her eyes were unusually large and clear. She even had a sherry with me. She had been recently to New York, and while we waited for dinner she took me around to show me her purchases. The ivory fan had been one. There were a pair of small jardinieres filled with porcelain flowers and a Meissen parrot. Aside from personal adornments, her taste had never been startling. Also I think the famous white apartment awed her. She never added a stick of furniture that I know of, only these innocent ornaments pushed into out-of-the-way places. Before she had been able to bring herself to buy the little Renoir landscape hanging over the Adam console, she consulted every decorator in town about the color: this immensely brave and opinionated woman—this cosmonaut among grandes dames—reduced to a jelly by the imagined frown of some pock-faced fairy. I think of Dolly too. Strange about us nowadays. Anyway, the jardinieres led her to speak of Ethel and Sam Einhoern, old Minneapolis friends of ours now living in Chicago, whom she had run into during lunch at Countess Széprényi's and taken on to the shop for their opinion ("not that they have a *right* to one"). Before the war Gordie and I had been rivals for the favors of Durie Einhoern, a wildish girl, since married and buried in Seattle. Sam had asked after me. Ethel was growing the most beautiful moustache —"looks like a pork butcher, but grander than ever, the very best clientele, *mein schatz*—." She frowned. "Now what's wrong with me? I *like* her."

She poured us each another sherry. One was rare for her, two an occasion. The skin on the bridge of her nose and under her eyes had flushed as pink as a girl's. She went on to make a joke about the white décor, a liberty no one else ever dared take, at least in her presence. She apologized for not having vichyssoise for me, saying she had had to give up serving it because the last few times it had been hours before anyone found it. I laughed along with her, taking care to taper off a second or two before. But she hadn't finished with the Einhoerns. They had been brought to lunch by one Agnes Dupres, also of Chicago—"a Millbank, good stock [with Edith that signified Jamestown at the latest], and therein, dear Matt, lies a story. You were too young to have known Cydneye Bissche, of course?" I shrugged; the name meant nothing to me. "He hasn't been here in years. But he used occasionally to come and stay with poor Benham. They were college cronies, I believe." And that was all. Aram appeared for the fourth or fifth time that evening to call her to the phone, and when she returned dinner was announced, and the Einhoerns and friend were forgotten, or purposely dropped.

About those phone calls. They were a major irritation of any visit with Edith. Everyone complained about them. They rarely lasted more than a few minutes but they were *constant,* and she never refused one. Serena Stolt used to say that the only way to have an uninterrupted talk with her would be to meet her midway up the tallest tree in the park—too high or too low and someone would be sure to have the number. Well, she was enormously popular, besides being committed to any number of the usual causes and cabals. She was also very busy those days whipping up support for Harry Truman. She and Bella's aunt Sherly were co-chairmen of a committee, with Dolly and her hags as the enemy, and simply everybody in town was having a delicious time with "dear Harry." So if the phone rang and rang it didn't seem odd. What did seem odd, and what caused the irritation, was that however breathless the moment she must be off to answer it. Never once in my experience did she ask Aram to take the message—and I was her damn lover! There was something else too. I won't speculate on it, just state it. I never heard it discussed but I'm sure others noticed. She told small fibs. She would come back and say so-and-so sent regards when you knew so-and-so had left for Florence that morning. Once she detailed an entire conversation she had just had with old Iain Fenshawe, and he laid up with a stroke for days. She needn't have said anything at all, was the point.

Well, whatever her purpose, it was no great sin. I only mention it because as we sat down to dinner that evening, she announced she had just been talking to Father. I nodded without comment, imagining he had unburdened himself of that scene over breakfast the previous morning. I hadn't come in contact with him since, but Dolly told me he was in a white rage, and Edith of course was his confidante. But when she went on to say how pleased he seemed to be with my work on the paper those days, and "really, for the first time, a little bit proud—I told you—*patience,* darling," I suppose I was startled enough to stare disbelievingly. Which she caught, and with a straight glittering look and covering smile cut the fib short. No more of this though.

The dinner was splendid. A galantine of duck as good as I've eaten, and a warm buttery lemon tart with cream to nearly kill a man. Amara Toolkakian was an exceptional cook. I sent my compliments back with Aram, and she came hurrying out to give me a hug and kiss—to Edith's mild disapproval. Edith was generally strict about such things. No airs here; she simply did not know how else to live. Even in these informal times, with her staff cut to a minimum, the gold service was out for the two of us, and behind each chair a hired footman waited for her to tinkle the little gold bell. (She never spoke to domestics except through Aram.)

Fay Gahagan joined us for coffee in the livingroom. She was at her most manic, besides being dressed up in some ancient electric blue rag that set the room vibrating. "Matthew, you goniff!" she shrieked, then flung her bulk down beside me and launched into a bawdy story about Skibee Fenshawe and his latest negress. Edith poured in silence and I, feeling some analogy with Gordie must be inevitable, tried once or twice to head the thing off, but you didn't do that with Fay. However, the story turned out to be pure fiction, with a very funny twist at the end, and in spite of herself Edith chuckled.

I was relieved, but more puzzled than ever about the evening. The conversation skipped along amiably now. We touched on all the current gossip and there was much laughter at Fay's comments. All very easy and apparently spontaneous, except that not once that evening had Gordie figured in the talk, which took some doing for three people who ordinarily talked of little else. I had begun to find it interesting that Edith should so pointedly avoid the subject, especially after yesterday's orgy of questions; but that Fay Gahagan should whoop it up for nearly half an hour without a single reference to her beloved boy seemed queer indeed. Discretion be damned where Fay figured of course. She said what she liked. No, it was queer. Certainly she must have heard by now about his running off. As she gave me her hand on leaving, I tried to read it in her face, but she neatly avoided me. Still she must have known. Even if Edith had decided against telling her, she had a grapevine second to none. And Jeanette Slade was broadcasting it all over town—even Father, who was the last to hear local news of any sort, had heard it as early as yesterday breakfast from one of the maids. So why? Had they been contacted by him after all? They were altogether too spirited, I began to feel. I was not not precisely uneasy about it—*puzzled,* as I say. Intrigued.

In her bedroom wildly—puking with it—as I stood baby-bare a window seat behind white velvet draperies very slightly parted. My god my god. Since a moment earlier when out of silence a cry, small and trembly, deep off in the apartment, another closer, together wailing, mixed sobbing and laughter, always closer. Edith bolt upright listening. Fay and the Toolkakians? Seemed, but could make out no words. Something. About eleven-thirty, to reconstruct from J. Slade's narrative.

I had lightly dozed to dream my ever and glorious dream when I heard the cry, and lay there with my eyes open, and Edith sitting up beside me. I touched her long white hair. She did not respond. I thought I had dreamed it and, feeling some guilt, thinking her hurt, I tried pull her down to me, but she shivered not budging. Then I cocked my head to look up at her face by the light of the small pink-shaded lamp burning near the bed to gauge, if I could, the degree of displeasure there to be overcome by exactly what effort and no more of these oiled and weary thighs, and saw not displeasure but something more profound. *Not* pitiable, or how could I bear to write this. Oh even so. But there is a soft sadness of regret, sweet grave twilight thought sometimes on fierce or hard or noble faces could make us shudder if we heard the cause, maybe. Chin firm and eyes like still water towards the door, indescribably lonely, near the end. Edith. I somehow saw, and started up, confusion.

The cry again, more than one entwined, much nearer, and without warning she thrust me from her with terrific force, dizzying and wheeling onto the bear rug where always love began, gesturing at the window, saying something I couldn't understand, though she repeated, *Not one word,* her face so calm. But laughing and weeping nearly to the door, and I fled in sudden and absolute terror to perch ignominious behind the curtains. That they stayed parted a crack was no thought or provision of mine. I could swear. I had no thought. I wanted no sight. I wanted to vanish. I wanted to scream for the door to open and when it did I vomited duck on my foot.

Then stopped. All sounds. Click the light on overhead. I nearly passed out. So young, my god was ever so young to faint with terror who seeks it now, or any gothic extravagant thing? With happiness now, with happiness! But then I would have been anywhere else. The crack held some of the bed, her on it, and some floor with piled-up white animal skins. Closet doors, opening hangers squealing along rods as some heavy breathing one searched through while she was holding the sheet up over her breasts and following with eyes quite unafraid and thinking, really, other things. I believe I had a plan. Ho ho leave it to Matt. The PEOPLE as shrewd as good. Well no less than cowardice my cheek. Anyway no need.

Her following eyes almost reaching mine when they turned away. He moved (by the path of her eyes) retracing slow to the closets then, slowly, to her. Sudden hands palm down on skins. He, someone executing a profound reverence. Many seconds she let him there, watching with utmost unflustered reserve as having known how for all anger it must come to this. Not a word the while, but now still abject, at least the hands, something said after a moment, very softly, something answered, and he sprang to take her in his arms, and for all her composure and his presumable outrage wept, he supporting the sheet delicately at her back, in each other's arms deep at the root of each other's neck, sweet rain for two parched hearts, O. Words, a broken few, but I caught only "David," and "Benham," after which particularly increased sorrow from both. Again again, "Benham," and each time great woe. Well to be sure. So presently talking to her, grave in her ear, still grasping the sheet behind, she listening close, at first yet gustily sorrowful, then gradual silent radiance. Kissing his neck as he most seriously and clearly with deepest urgency instructed her, nuzzling the deep bristled cave of his cheek, her half-closed eyes softer with richer love than I knew them ever. Had I a gun—I swear to god so unnatural it looked! The PEOPLE raged. Even he must deprecate such and once drew back to chide her but she seemed so drunk with him. Knew who stood in the window needless. I saw when she told, anyway he must know my clothes. His foul, same as last, white jacket et cetera but disarrayed and streaked filthily. She said, and over his shoulder slanted such roguey swagger—electric, those glittering close-set black stone eyes tilt and bold as a fiend's and cruel curved mouth open to eat. Soon in words or voice I could for the first time hear, said he, *Who's there?* Said she, I swear, *No one.* Said he, *I'll wall it up or speak!* Said she, *Do, I desperately need more wall space.* A game of me—they dared! Said he releasing her, turning while she adjusted the sheet, standing towards me his most arrogant, *Was he no good then?* She didn't look, arranged her sheet, said, *Very good, but it was long ago, leave him. Dress,* he commanded, and she went obediently. Back and forth he goes, eyeing my cave increasingly angered. I standing nowise, intimidated now feeling common decency at least for her, must spare me. But. Stopped.—*What do you want?* I think genuinely puzzled. Collar open, black tie knotted high up the neck, ends hanging a way I hadn't seen of him since once in a Paris dusk when first with dim surmise, nor this menace. I his benefactor, great and only friend, but two days since! Decency required years and reasons. Yet *he* puzzled. *What do you want?* he says. *Don't play with us, Citizen. We eat such. Strike from dark bellows at height of noon. Oh Jaysus such filthy dumb blond!* Forward on toes raging. *Must be some congenital brand of dimwit never to see—! Now hush,* says Edith somewhere near. *This blithering fool?* he cries. *But listen, what if it's no fool at all?* (The PEOPLE did shake then.) *An Observer, sure!—Mat-*

Mattie, your a dead 'un!—and leaped, but Edith there to put a hand on him and say some soft decisive thing. Tug from him and into the pocket of her suit—*You are not to. Phone her then,* he bites out chalk white. She: Outside I think. He: Here now, if he's a fool it's no such difference *hein? Phone her,* and she obedience again. Then he again to me breathing purest malice: All my women all my life but never me. What about me, Matto? *Gordon* she called, *phone* he said, *I won't hurt him.* She: Then lower your voice or she'll. To me, lower, eyes driving into mine through crack playing, violating: What I began to say, I like an occasional boy or did dumb blond not see this either? Not often, they be a bore, but once in a while you see some trick you got to take. Pair of murderous hands, mean wet mouth, hard little ass very willing two-fifty, three bucks depending on the lateness of the hour. So? I so revolted I. He: My wife my mother all my girls, every one of them. Hey you me too, mister? Grand slam like? Edith back frowning: I've told you I won't have your swinish comicalities here. He: O sweeter than the cherry! She: No low verses in the bedroom, Gordon, do you hear me? He: Why what pretty window boxes virtue tends. She: Well a healthful thing for a lonely woman. He: Well not for lonely woman's lonely son if he can't pluck too. You want me pale into normal happy cluck like him—? She harsh and cold: As you tried, dear. He: Hilariously tried, you mean to say. God you're ice. But you really want me be what I said after my so exquisitely looped and twisted boyhood? Do seem a waste. She: Oh you whine, child. He: No, m'um, sometimes think, only that. Even we diamonds. Only—. She: Only only! He: Sure only— only all my dames got this same cute-shaped window box and I wanna know where's the sale so's I can spend cozy healthful hours plucking too, only that! She: Will you never outgrow that appalling jargon? He: Sure, when elders and betters more merit emulation. Till which I talk baby and pee with the women and rob banks. Down with big peoples. She: If Shem could hear you—. He: Or see you—or *this*—. She: *Stop it.* He: How could you do this to *me*! She flaming, shrill: Stop it stop it! He abashed: Sure. She sorry I think but not another word, turning with hauteur to go. Wait, he softly says and from an inner pocket draws a duplicate black handkerchief to tie, kneeling, around her waist under her jacket, she in noncommittal silence, tightening the bun of her hair, but once—a moment—to cast down eyes at his bent head so *beautifully*. Then *exchange of car keys,* his up a block I think he said.—Brake her easy, hear?—Then went. —Mourn us good and proper, baby—laughing, she not looking, and went. I heard the door.

After a moment I sprang from the curtains into Aram Toolkakian's restraining arms at which last outrageous straw the PEOPLE blanked out. He may have clipped me though almost needn't have. I could not have made it to the phone.

Awake next morning in my bed about ten o'clock on pillow soaked with tears. I had dreamed of Emily. Last night. Had such and such been said, or had only I heard what I desired to hear, or dreamed it? And what was irrecoverable between then and now—*that, that.* Poor innocent Emily I never told. Gave him my darling and now never—he was right, I played with them. But not they, who kept her. Dragged up at last filled with such black fears yet stay alert, I knew. Suspected everyone or how else had they got me to my bed? Bathed, dressed, pushed gagging food down my throat. Nothing in either paper. Dolly and Father gone of course. Back to my room with a pot of coffee, ostensibly to work. I had no courage to phone. Would I even to answer? I never found out. No phone knell broke that long hot noon, longest of endless life, dreadest. I listened to house sounds for possible gossip. Nothing. The maids did their rounds, vacuum cleaners, quarrels and laughter on the stairs, along the hall, above around below me an ordinary hot summer day, and in me—oh god in me. Emily! I couldn't, and sometime after one ran down for my car but it was away at the garage being something. Dolly's and Father's were out though Father almost never used his, an ancient Packard of Shem's old fleet, but that morning he had. I ran like a madman for half a dozen blocks till I found a cab willing to take me to Luba, about two hours then, though improved roads through Anoka County (thanks to Father's editorial campaign) have now reduced the time by nearly half. Interesting footnote to history. Well, the cabbie told me. Remember, Abul is an important name locally and the two out at Luba a popular diversion, Gordie especially admired by such as cabbies, war record et cetera. Not a great deal yet, surmise mostly. Gordie's car found at Minnetonka and Emily missing. J. Slade, her story. Empty rowboat on the lake with chipped oar nearby.

Not a great deal but enough. I took the cab to Minnetonka. Some police and a couple of Emily's detectives, a group of rubbernecks behind a line of wooden horses. Far down the lake more police in boats dragging near the empty rowboat. *Hot.* Reporters, two of them ours, introduced me to officer in charge who wanted anyway to talk to me as being the closest friend, but of course I had nothing to tell. Said I had not seen them a few days, said yes of course it was Gordie's car, said in response that in my opinion such violence between them was out of the question though by his arch look J. Slade felt otherwise. I shrugged. Later they let me poke. Minneapolis police about on par with Dallas's. I retrieved one of Edith's long white hairs from the upholstery of the driver's seat. I have it still. It delicately smells of her. I wind it around my finger now as she used my body, face—.

It occurred to me, though apparently to no one else, that there was not a necessary connection between car and rowboat. Two tragedies possibly. Neither of my ladies rowed so far as I knew, and the boat lay near the center. Emily would shriek with terror when I took her out on St. Croix, while the picture of Edith plying oars was ridiculous. Of course they thought Gordie, which I didn't. Anyway, very casually, I strolled along the shore in the opposite direction. More people arriving, dignitaries now and such. Comptroller Wally Sorsen, a couple of Fenshawes, some Pletcher brass. Father too the last I looked, at least the Packard. I continued idly out of sight, watching carefully but not apparently the shallow reed-grown water off-shore. After a while no one, and I pulled down a dead branch and began to poke all the thickly reeded places. I don't know how I had the stomach. Even now I quail. Out of my mind, I think—very quietly feverishly out of my mind.

About a quarter mile away, near the junction with Minnehaha, in small bay dense with willow and reed, I found them. Struck something softish and fished up a foot, Emily's. Her shoe nearby, a turtle sunning on it. Then the hem of Edith's skirt. Stood back half dead, how long I don't know. When I started to leave, there on the rise behind me was one of Emily's detectives calmly watching. I went straight in a fury and threw, literally threw, what money I had in his face, about twenty dollars. Instead of angering, he bent and retrieved it to the last nickel. With my toe I looped a quarter off and he went and got that too. I laughed at him but he could not be ruffled. Grimly, quietly said else he'd starve. I suppose working for Emily accustomed one. He said he too had seen the white hair but had not been permitted near the car unaccompanied as I had been. He saw me take it, but would not say what else he saw or knew, at least not then.

I arranged to meet him there that evening and returned to the *Dispatch* offices. By that time, Fay Gahagan had reported Edith missing. A lot of juicy talk. Questions I shrugged off. I must have looked as queer as I felt because no one pressed. As I was leaving, Father came in but barely glanced at me. Bring him Truman's idiot Seattle talk I heard him snarl.

I went home and slept until dinner. Dolly did most of the talking. Terribly upset. In her way she was fond of Edith and of course Gordie, an old secret crush. More than anything, though, she loathed scandals and without quite saying so implied fears that I might be implicated. I could not look at her. Father laughed mirthlessly once or twice but he too was upset. Edith was god knows what to him, and whatever he may have known or to what degree he was involved—not deeply I think, like his son he played—the fact remained. He looked old. This and Truman too whom he despised but a little less than Dewey. He never slept a full night after Hiroshima. They called to him was all he'd say. Well so did I, so did I. I went out as soon after dinner as I dared. I had instructed the garage to return my car repaired or not.

At the lake they were still dragging for the bodies. Swimmers there now, and the police boats were gay with flares. On shore they were drinking beer and talking in shrill voices. It was like Venice. I cruised slowly by and on, then circled back watching for the green station wagon I had been told would mark the location. I found it midway between two widely spaced lights. No lovers to fear that night, not with such famous exemplars at the bottom of a lake. It was altogether a bad week for lovers. I walked straight back from the cars, feeling carefully at each step, for while it was a brightish night this particular area was thick with trees and brush. When I reached the top of the rise I stood a moment looking out over the gray waters. The air warm and soft, honeysuckle in it. I felt I wanted to die. Emily gone. All time to come without Emily, with some strange woman, some conventional Bella to—. I couldn't bear it. Yet all these years I've borne it.

I must have cried out—though I think it was my only outward emotion during the entire business—for a flashlight clicked on in front to my right and a voice said, Here, here. Jack Dreifort it was. He had brought hip-boots, blankets, a set of stretchers. Lord they were heavy. I think the soul must lighten the body, for neither was half so heavy alive. I could scarcely support my share of the stretcher weight. He had wrapped and tied them into blankets at the lakeside, in darkness, to spare me as I suppose. At least he didn't ask me to guide with the flashlight and I didn't offer. When they were stowed in the back of the station wagon he returned for the gear. It was while waiting for him that I noticed the shovels, and up came my dinner, very quickly and quietly. By the time he got back I was recovered.

We drove tandem out to a lonely place I knew below St. Croix Falls where at various times I had lain with both my girls. I still occasionally go there to relax for an hour and talk to them. It is my favorite spot in all the world. I once took Bella fishing there. Well, we dug a large grave in a plot of wild ginger. It took over an hour for the tree roots and buried rocks. At last they were in, side by side, and Jack Dreifort suggested we stop for a smoke before covering them. We were both panting by then and I at least sweated through. So we put the shovels down and lighted cigarettes and after two puffs I asked for the flashlight. He said he thought better not, but I insisted and he gave it to me. I had no idea which bundle was which. The first I opened was Edith's. I saw a patch of bloody scalp where hair had been torn out, then part of the forehead savagely raked by finger nails. An embedded fragment glinted in the light. I covered her again. Warily I opened Emily's and, being reassured by a space of unbroken skin, opened more and more, until I'd exposed her to the waist. I was astonished. Absolutely no mark on her except where a snapper had been at her lips. Jack stood across in darkness. Drowned? I asked him. He grunted dubiously, came around, and squatted peering very particularly. He reached a forefinger down to explore the neck. I nearly screamed. Here, he said, and with the nail of his little finger raised a bit of fishing line so tightly looped it had cut below the skin. Lovely people, he said. I said I wanted a piece of the line and he disengaged and handed it to me. I then asked in some heat what he meant by lovely people, whereupon he led me around to Edith again, uncovered and unclasped one of her elegant hands. The palm and sides were blue with cord burns. I tell you I reeled. Then we filled in the grave, and while he replaced clods of moss and ginger which had been carefully put aside at the beginning, my mind for the first time raced ahead.

Until this moment I had no idea what must be done afterwards. I had only known I had to get them away and bury them. A wildly compromising thing, but had to. They were mine, don't you see, or if you don't it is no matter. I had to simply. But all at once standing there, watching a hired man pack them off to hell, I felt they should be paid for with more than money, Emily at least. Edith had done as instructed. Edith was at peace, with Shem maybe, in some black and gold. Wickedly escaped me taking all. Or not quite all. I had not thought of Gordie but suddenly could think of nothing else. I felt I had to see how fetching he might look, his mouth eaten off by snappers, who had carried such a message. The notion obsessed me. It would give Emily peace too. Literally out of my senses with misery, as I handed Jack Dreifort his check I proposed that he locate Gordie for me. I thought I put it matter-of-factly. I did not say why. I offered, I thought, a good sum. He kept silence.

We drove back to the city. At the first stop-light he pulled alongside and suggested I wash up at his flat before going home. We were clay up to the eyes. His fat grim-mouthed wife, watching me with intensest curiosity, made iced coffee. God knows what they surmised. When at last she left us I repeated my offer. He seemed embarrassed. Said he didn't know what I had in mind but that none of it was Gordie's doing. Angrily, I retorted that I knew more about it than he but in any event was not asking advice, just offering cash for services, simple business deal. He said he understood that and was in addition a great lover of cash, mine *or* Emily's. For the first time it occurred to me that he too may have been affected by events. Not professional chagrin only. He had worked on and off over a fairly long stretch for Emily, and I gathered liked her.

His voice was tired, bitter. He had traced Gordie by the second morning of his disappearance, had gone to where he was and kept tab of him every minute of the next thirty-six hours. They (sic) were making him eat dirt, he remarked. Then Gordie had been some way contacted—Jack wasn't certain how, but it took place on the beach about three in the afternoon among mobs of people—and had driven full speed back to Minneapolis and Edith's place. Jack had waited down the block, and—he smiled—for one of the few times in his career proceeded to follow the wrong car. Sonovabitch you, he addressed himself. He had arrived back an hour or so before I turned up at Minnetonka.

What, I asked, about the other? For I knew Emily generally retained two or even more detectives. In fact I had recognized another at Minnetonka earlier that day. What had he been doing all this time? Again smiled. Helping everyone, he said. A great talent. Anyway pulls in a hell of a lot more cash than me with all my munificent patrons. I suppose I colored at this, because he went on to say he hadn't slept in three days and was nearly gone with exhaustion. He looked it too, eyes blue-ringed, pale. But he wanted me to understand that Gordie had very little to do with anything. He had tried to explain to Emily but she wouldn't believe it. Watch Gordie, she insisted, and he had, and this was what had come of it. After all his delicate work. Sourly shook his head and fell silent. I said perhaps he didn't realize I was a very close friend—. He cut me abruptly. The man didn't have friends, the only man he had ever come across without one real friend. He looked at me. He wondered what they (sic) could have done to Gordie in the past, what they would do—.

Who! I finally had to burst out. He blinked his eyes as if to keep off sleep and said good night. Damn romancer like you, I shouted at him, portentous hints about big dark "they," and the only proof of existence is two tons of ingenuity to get rid of a couple of weak pretty women—. His nearly closed eyes opened at this. A couple of weak pretty women? he repeated, was that all I really knew of it after so many years? He looked sceptical and I didn't like it. I said I considered him a rascally fool who mystified to cover blunders and extort unreasonable fees. He was very angry. He said all night he had been aching to let me know that he by no means considered *me* a fool—.

I hit him but not too hard, saying it was for his driveling, that I hated driving with such passion that the next I heard from or of him I would likely kill him for. Now how much, I said, recovering myself, and once again though figuratively he bent to pick up pennies. He named a reasonable price. I said, too much. Understand that by this time I knew where to find Gordie. I had caught "the beach," which together with approximate number of hours to return full speed to Minneapolis—more than once in recent months I had occasion to verify it—and small speculations and dribblets of information concerning things the past year, gave me Chicago, with point of contact at Oak Street Beach. Which I had thought but not known. My "dribblets" had dried up recently. Chicago I would have tried in any event—the beach was what I proposed to pay for, and only the beach. The rich do not throw money away nor should they; the poor must learn how to *take* it. I offered half and the slavish brute accepted. He would mail information when cash received. I could barely conceal my disdain. You should organize, I admonished as I left, the union would have got you more. Not, said he, with such as you arguing and judging the case, then questioning the verdict. The workers have given themselves into the vilest bondage yet. A thinking slave, by god! We should have been friends in other circumstances.

The next week, so strange we are, turned into one of the happiest of my life. I let it be known that I was going away for a while and everyone shed blessings, including Dolly who would miss me most.

Gordie and Emily had been my dearest friends and the relationship with Edith not entirely unguessed. All agreed it had been the kind of wound travel alone could heal. Father himself, ordinarily a dragon about time off (though he gave me little enough to do at the *Dispatch* those days), approved to the extent of staying the entire week at the club so as not to have automatically to object. Dolly thought it over-delicate but I understood. He had his problems. I finished up the Gene Debs series, smoothed out a few miscellaneous pieces that had been lying around for years. I read through my journals and locked them away. I was thoroughly relaxed. I spent part of every day fishing the St. Croix below the Falls, as may be imagined; evenings with Dolly and a few friends like the Stolts and Condies who came to condole and drop a little gossip. The town was stirred up over more than the sensational aspects of the case. Economically and socially the Abuls were intricately woven in the fabric of the place and could not be pulled out without a drastic change in the pattern.

Towards the end of the week, when it began to appear likely that for whatever reasons Edith would not return, Serena Stolt (this from Dolly who Serena came to butter up) started her play for Edith's mantle, only to find herself face to face with her former ally *against* Edith, old Alice Ishply, all girded for the coming battle. Poor Harry Truman was quite forgotten. In addition there was the titanic power struggle getting under way in Pletcher's board room (this of really serious import to the town's economy) with Serena's husband, Axel, Sr., pitted against *his* former allies et cetera et cetera.

I relished it all enormously but felt no part anymore. My life here was over, I grandly imagined. I gave my deposition the day before I left. I realize the pressure applied by my family was considered fairly unusual at the time, but there was no question of my involvement and much as to my health, for happy as I felt I was looking wretched. Dolly seemed genuinely worried. Furthermore there could be no inquest without the bodies or the reasonable certainty, which could mean months or even years if the insurance people had their way. I promised to keep in touch. As for Jack Dreifort, I had sent the cash off the next afternoon, and three days later received an envelope enclosing a blank sheet of paper. What I expected when he insisted on cash but my honor was preserved. The revolution will never be carried through by such. I didn't bother to contact him, being pretty certain he was "away." Besides, I already knew what he could tell me, in addition to which my "dribblets" were again at full flood. So the morning of departure arrived. The car had been packed the night before. At precisely nine o'clock I got on my way.

Oh it is a gorgeous thing to be on one's way. In the most leisurely fashion I cruised south as far as Rochester, then veered to the Mississippi, following down the west shore to Dubuque, roughly on a latitude with Chicago, where instead of crossing the river (as may or may not have been expected of me) I turned west, stopping outside Cedar Rapids for a late lunch and going on to Des Moines, which I reached about midnight, weary, eye-sore, but utterly exalted. The next morning, at nine sharp, I got back into the car and continued more or less due west through the most broiling heat I can remember, arriving in Lincoln, Nebraska, a little past noon. I remained in Lincoln the rest of that day and all of the next, strolling about the streets, going to air-conditioned movies, eating tons of the first crop of sweet corn—nothing else in those parts being remotely digestible—and *sleeping*. Pretty green city, Lincoln, I suppose.
Nine sharp the morning of the third day I was on my way out of Lincoln traveling in a southeasterly direction. I lunched (so to speak) near Leavenworth, then veered west again towards Topeka, where I spent the night. Or no. Half an hour out of Leavenworth I suddenly pulled off the road, cut around and raced like frenzy back to the luncheonette to recover a book I had left on a shelf under the counter. The conceit amused me. Then very leisurely to Topeka, amid a swarm of luncheonette flies. Prompt as always, at nine the following morning I was back on the road, traveling due east to Jefferson City, Missouri. Thus far, perfect.

Two more days here, spent pretty much as those in Lincoln, with the addition of a Policeman's Benevolent Association Fair, where I picked up a bowl of goldfish and a shaving kit for tossing coins into a plate. Also someone named Mary. My nerves were fine, you see.

The evening of the second day I squired this Mary to a late movie. I got back to the hotel after midnight. I had a drink in the room, standing at the window in my underwear top (which went against my grain but was usual in JC and anyway absolutely necessary) and idly staring up and down the empty street. On my way up I had informed the desk that I would be leaving at nine in the morning. I asked for a porter at quarter of, and particularly requested that my car be brought from the garage in plenty of time, for one runs into trouble about these matters in smaller towns. I finished the drink, stood a few minutes longer surveying the street, then went to pack my bags. This done, I washed up, pulled the shade and drew the curtains as I always did, switched off the lights, sat heavily on the bed and listened for a few minutes longer. It was then twelve-forty-seven. I was dressed within five minutes, in clothes I had not yet worn, and at one on the head (how well it went!) met the service elevator at the back of the building, and left by the delivery entrance two minutes after that. By a connecting series of alley-ways and basements I traversed four blocks without a single window having been locked on me and by one-fifteen was behind the wheel of a fresh car. By three-thirty-five crossed the toll-bridge at St. Louis.

Time was the thing now. I had calculated on five and a half hours from St. Louis to Chicago via the Springfield-Bloomington route, and so it worked out. I passed through Cicero at nine-ten and by ten (about, for by now I was too excited to make entries) I had left the car in Washington Square Park and was turning into Division Street on my way to Oak Street Beach. Sheer insanity, of course. Had I a drop of sense just then I should have expected to be stopped at a dozen points along the way. I should have proceeded with the greatest caution and called attention to myself by every imaginable clumsiness. Instead, in my half-demented state I walked boldly up the center of the sidewalk straight to my destination.

It was one of those fantastic bits of luck desperation metes out to her pale ones. The chance had been so *slim*. By driving on to Chicago instead of the rendezvous in Joliet, I had put myself in jeopardy of at least two very fish-eyed Orders. Had I bided my time, had I continued a while longer in the carefully laid plans ... but I didn't, and never had any intention of doing so where this particular phase was concerned. Perhaps they suspected as much. They had held notably aloof after my discovery of the bodies, waiting for me to get control of myself, as I imagined. As so often in the past I had had to force their hand by scrounging up my own information. Well, they would never have let me touch him. He was too valuable. If it came to a choice, I would have been the one to go. I had no doubt of this. So on I walked, reaching the underpass at the Drive without incident. It was of course *cloudy*. The first cloudy day in weeks, and many degrees cooler than it had been. There was not a reason in the world why Gordie should be on Oak Street Beach at ten of such a morning. Yet he would be, must be—was.

I saw that black scarf the minute I stepped from the underpass. There were less then a dozen other people on the sand, none near him. He lay on his stomach on a white beach towel, his clothes rolled up in a ball near his head. I removed my shoes and socks and went directly over. When I was almost upon him he looked up. I think he had been asleep, certainly he was alarmed. He glanced swiftly around but there was no one within thirty yards. He was deeply tanned and had a bit of curling hair on his chin. Very becoming. I reached over and chucked it. His eyes glittered at the movement but he didn't flick a muscle. On more than one occasion I had remarked this inner control of his that encompassed the minutest physical reactions. Cute, I said. He laughed. Didn't think I could get prettier, eh Matto? He rolled over on his back and languidly stretched himself, one hand reaching nearer his rolled-up clothes than I liked.

I fell on him playfully—so I hoped it looked—pinning his arms. I was a good twenty pounds heavier and proportionately stronger. Leave it, I warned. It would have been a knife, I think; he was an expert knife-fighter. He peered up into my face, the only time in my life I knew him frightened. Don't be sore, Matt, he said with a sort of broken grin, I got lots more girls I'll give you.

I released one of his arms and slapped his mouth with a short hard stroke—not nearly as hard as he had coming but I feared drawing attention by any larger motion. He merely looked at me. Then I drew the fishing line from my pocket and before he knew what was happening I had looped it about his neck beneath the scarf and was drawing the ends tight. For just an instant he grabbed my wrists and struggled. Then suddenly he locked his arms around me, in agony ground his forehead against my jaw and rattled hoarsely, Do it, do it quick before they, oh please, please, please—*Tateh*—.

I had every intention of complying, but my incredible luck had run out, and a blow on the head stayed us both from felicity awhile. I say both; when I regained consciousness, my clothes had been taken from me together with the three green tablets in the pocket watch, and all trace of the madness that would have used them.

* * *

Literally translated excerpts from two Gestapo file briefs in my possession:

Major Hudson Beckwith (Claudius) OSS, Sept 17, 1896, Chicago in the State of Illinois, USA, of wealthy and distinguished parents, both dead. Two younger brothers, Noble and McGeorge, both long and bitterly estranged from Major B, believed to be commissioned naval officers attached to the Far Eastern Command, with homes respectively in the State of California and in the State of Maine; the numerous cousins, many of prestige and influence, likewise and without exception estranged and valueless. Twice married, once a widower, once divorced, the woman re-married to a public official in Buenos Aires and unfriendly. No children recorded. Male, white, Protestant, 5'11¼," 156 lbs., crosswise shrapnel scar 1½" below right elbow and approx ½" in length, appendix scar 3," small hairy mole in right armpit, skin on soles of feet notably hard and cracked as perhaps from early scarlatina, circumcised. Luxuriant, graying light-brown hair, expressive blue eyes with charming gold flecks surrounding the indigo iris, teeth complete and of a sublime whiteness and sharpness, form splendidly muscled and constructed throughout and of notable measurements... [et cetera et cetera *ad nauseam*]... believed to have been one of Moulin's closest advisors, and for a time intimate with Vroons and the traitor Poldowski.... Of fierce cunning despite easy charm and elegant manners.... Three escapes, two from Montluc and once from Caluire, the latter in broad daylight with the aid of degenerate German officers, the which were liquidated.... See Falkenhorst, Baroness Iren. RHSA-IIIA2, Gestapo Field Office, Montluc, France.

Baroness Iren Falkenhorst, pos. Renée Frankel, pos. Irene Fairweather (Madge) OSS et al., June 22, 1918, 1916, or 1912, Miami in the State of Florida, USA (doubtful), of peasant family of outrageous depravity and criminal activities, entirely liquidated by the authorities for heinous crimes against the State (doubtful though thus far impossible to check out). Never married (doubtful). Female, white, Catholic or Jewish, 5'5," 108 lbs. (with considerable var.), bullet scar left front rib-cage bet. two lower ribs, knife or bayonet scar on right back 2½" below bottom rib. Under-arm hair reddish though head-hair notably black and cut short, for she will on occasion masquerade as a boy, towards which end she in addition keeps herself excessively thin. Teeth complete except top two wisdoms, eyes violet, form (as noted) thin, skin color of a notable, almost Irish whiteness, similar to "Bridget" of infamous memory. Altogether of extraordinary beauty for a woman, with a *délicatesse* of feature to belie her low heritage, and indeed her temperament, since she is utterly ruthless, and is considered one of the most dangerous and vicious agents in the European theatre.... Skilled with explosives, and to be examined with the utmost caution, for she has been known to conceal grenades in the cups of the brassière, or in even more disgusting niches, being totally devoid of code of honor.... An interminable and crushing talker, until the head splits with false informations, bestrewn with grains of fact she is aware we already possess, so that one is left mindless with fatigue and indecision, and remands the liquidation order for the nonce, and the next thing one hears is that she has exploded a dozen guards in a particularly vicious manner and made her escape, taking half of the prisoners with her.... No fewer than eighteen known escapes in Poland, Holland, and France.... Three successful raids on prisoners.... Reports of her, or one closely resembling her, in Cairo and Haifa.... See Beckwith, Major Hudson. RSHA - IIIA2, Gestapo Field Office, Montluc, France.

Interesting point number one is the A2 designation on both briefs. This was the special Nazi "communist" file, though both are flatly stated to be OSS agents. Stats of the originals came into my hands in 1955. An old contact of mine in CIA ran across them in a pile of declassified and inactive war records, and, recalling my involvement in the 1949 Chicago case, sent them to me on the chance I might be interested or at least amused. Oh indeed. They had been turned up by OSS in 1945 among masses of captured German files, and doubtless would have been tossed aside with other Gestapo material on American agents but for the the A2 business. This, though by no means serious considering Nazi paranoia on the subject of communism, was yet provocative. At the time and in the context, *all* American agents were in a sense Russian agents too. Russia was an ally and presumably there followed some coordination of intelligence between OSS and NKVD—pertinent material gathered by either side was theoretically at the disposal of the other. Why then would the Gestapo bother to keep entries on these particular American agents in their A2 file? A redundancy (German enough) or last-minute spite (both, it seems, were unusually troublesome) against the probability of the records falling into OSS hands? *Or.* Consider the amusing "et al." following OSS on Irene's brief. What, not only American and Russian, but Japanese, British, Egyptian, Palestinian, et cetera? An octagonal spy. Not even Irene had the wits for it. *Or.* In Poe's "The Rue Morgue" a chattering ape is positively identified to have been speaking in a dozen dissimilar tongues for the reason that no one understood ape. Or, I ask, were they up to something no one understood?—But, you ask, why neglect the simple possibility that they were communist agents after all? The answer is as simple as the possibility. I know they were not.

Now for interesting matter number two. There is no specific material in either brief to explain the cross-referencing. Likely they worked together, or were considered to do so. The peculiar A2 designations and the Montluc Field Office origin fortifies the guess. Yet there is one point not common to both and it, in my view, profoundly divides them. I have copied out the briefs exactly as returned to me by the German teacher I employed to translate them, with the exception of that one point, which I was interested to see meant nothing to him as a German and was omitted. I have taken the liberty of restoring it. I myself remarked it instantly, that point or dot in the ΘSS entry on Hudson's brief, but dismissed it, as apparently numerous others did, and as I believe it was meant to be dismissed by all but a few Nazi hierophants as one of the ink droppings defacing the top of the sheet. Irene's was scrupulously, Germanically clean. I say I remarked it and dismissed it. But when I received the translations from Herr Hessler and began with the aid of an English-German dictionary to collate for omissions or interpretive liberties, I was struck by the lack of that point. Cleaned of its Θ the brief hit a different note entirely. ΘSS was not OSS and logic be damned. Now let me state at once that I was under no illusion I had discovered microdots or the like. The soiled sheet would have been processed immediately for such as these; ink droppings were a common ruse. No, I had no idea what I had discovered, only that I was being haunted by Θ, and the more I tried to lay it, the more insistently it rolled about the inside of my head like an ominous runic wheel.

Well, I finally got off some letters of inquiry. As I anticipated, my chum at CIA put it down to accident. There was of course no microdot, and the spatterings as a group conformed to no known type of Nazi code pattern, for with the exception of Θ, the other marks fell along the margin and top of the sheet. Besides, to what purpose would the Nazis be passing code messages within their own Intelligence stronghold? Even German pens occasionally drip, he observed. But my inquiries to Hamburg and Paris bore fruit. *"Freimaurerei." "Maçonnerie."* Not ΘSS, only Θ. Freemasonry.

I wanted to laugh. Freemasonry! Bella, I said, how would you react to my becoming a Mason? She looked up from *Studies on the Left*. You mean like Laurance and Axel? Why, I would pee laughing, I suppose, so spare the carpet, do.—Exactly. Why not Elkery and Shrinery too!

My French correspondent, a scholarly journalist sort, was laconic about it, but my German one (of course) went on at length to explain how it had been the code reference of a long-defunct German sect of Freemasons that had flourished just prior to the French Revolution, the Bavarian Illuminati, a powerful and sinister body feared by Freemasonry itself. Strange designation, he thought. He had not turned up another in all his months as clerk at the *Reichssicherheitshauptamt*. He conceded however that certain among the Nazi hierarchy had a passion for these occult references, and that ʘ probably signified nothing more than how they at one time found a Masonic key mingled with Hudson's dog-tags. Why they should bother to note such trivia at all, let alone secretively, was a matter buried deep in the Nazi mystique, and never having been a Nazi, as I was certainly aware, he did not feel qualified to deal with it. Well, maybe he wasn't and maybe he was. Anyway I was soon over my ears in the history of Freemasonry. I won't go into my discoveries; for one thing they were less discoveries than deep dim personal shocks—cloudy apprehensions —most inexplicit. The books I consulted are in every library in the world, and the shocks are there for all to experience;—not in the accounts of Freemasonry *per se,* for it is an innocent inspirational body for all the right-thinking men— George Washington took the presidential oath on a Freemason Bible, Ben Franklin would have if he could have, and if Hudson was a Freemason I'm a flamingo;—but from a sense derived from footnotes and passing references, of the busy whispering depths underpinning us, of the rich underneathness of the history of the race, where right and wrong and good and evil dissolve in the Divine exhilaration of *the story*.

My German correspondent was misleading in one respect, though in all innocence, perhaps. He stated that in his eight months in RSHA-III he had never seen another such designation, but I prefer to think he was unobservant. OSS was not at the head of every card and the dot would then have been concealed in the body of the brief. It was not, in my estimation, for every eye to read. Like all essentially secret societies, the Nazi Party consisted of ring within ring, with the true aims and fullest intelligence reserved to a small inner nucleus. I am ready to allow that ϴ in its original signification had little meaning here, but I can't allow that it had no meaning whatever, and I know for a fact it was not unique with Hudson. In the relatively small number of Gestapo briefs I was subsequently to study—under 2,000 of the hundreds of thousands that comprised the five divisions of RSHA—I turned up three further ϴ's, two which I had been particularly searching for, the other by chance during the course of the search. The first of these dealt with a Russian agent, a Jew, NKVD typed plainly at the top, but again, as in the case of Hudson and Irene, there appeared to be some uncertainty about his real allegiance. He was active throughout most of the war in the Balkans and Middle East—assassin and saboteur of great skill—Bryan Younglove by name. The second dealt with another Jew, ϴSS and A2: Captain Gordon Abul of Minneapolis in the State of Minnesota, active in North Africa and the Middle East, taken in Iraq, tortured, escaped in an FFI (JÜDISCH) raid. I must here state my conviction that, ϴ notwithstanding these men had no specific contact with each other, certainly not Gordie with Hudson. Later events made no sense at all otherwise.

Whatever information the Germans thought they had, whatever they intended to signify by ϴ, did not involve a specific concerted action. For consider my last ϴ, the prize I had been searching for, and by fantastic luck found. It dealt with yet a third Jew, ϴSS, First Lieutenant Matthew Lenart, of Minneapolis in the State of Minnesota.

* * *

—The next I knew, I lay on my side in a rancid-smelling bed, staring at a yellow wall figured with pink and silver nosegays, unbearably thirsty. Carefully, so as not to antagonize my head—someone must have used a hammer on me (I did not at once remember the beach)—I eased onto my back. I could not face that wall longer. God knows what ages I had been studying it, for I was sick at my stomach with the graffiti scrawled at bed level and which I noted in some detail. I however held the gagging back until I could place myself. A tiny cubicle in some fourth-class hotel it seemed. A dresser with pitcher and glass on it, mirror above and chair beside made all the furnishings along with the bed. At the single window to my right a man stood peering out through half-drawn curtains. Ghastly pink oilcloth curtains, full daylight blazing in. My eyes ached with it. There were street noises—raucous, clanging—street-cars—a thoroughfare. My fool head roared. Still carefully I rolled a little over on my right side for I seemed to recollect a pitcher and glass on the floor beside the bed. Yes. Over-eagerly I reached for it alerting the bedsprings. Eeee! The man at the window turned.

"Now don't you drink that."

Gordie. Quickly and efficiently he brought water from the pitcher on the dresser. When I finished he brought more. While waiting this time he thoughtfully regarded the pitcher near the bed. "Nasty sleep-water," he observed, tilting it with the toe of his shoe. "You been waking up and putting yourself back for time out of memory, love. Bearded Sleeping Beauty in enchanted Joe's Hotel. Trusty Prince Desire hacking through. Cute, *hein*—?" and there was a hissing intake of breath as he sent the pitcher banging and spilling under the bed. "Oh I am sick to fucking death of these mean cute games. I feel over my eyes in baby-stool. Can't see, can't breathe. How much damn longer, tell me? When do we grow up? Matt, tell me if you know—" but I handed him the glass and rolled back to the wall.

I was overwhelmed by the memory of our last encounter. I found this familiarity of his inhuman, villainous. It struck me as so unfeeling that it nearly succeeded in reviving my anger, which in fact would have eased me considerably. I had tried to *kill him*. For a moment I even had to doubt he understood this. I mean, one does not wield one's utmost thunder to have it go luckily unheard, or what is there?—what does one do to be damned? or even saved? I mean, if all those tremendous sweeps of the soul we fear but love to dream about come to nothing in the proof, then *we* are nothing, for what are we more than the worst or best we dream to do? Surely, I felt, surely I merited something more glamorous than a bleak starving-to-death by my own hand and a rescue full of tender solicitation by my victim? Oh I was upset. I wept.

Had my anger been intact ... but it was gone. Without it, and without the bracer of a sounding and immediate repercussion, my behavior was simply unaccountable to me. The whole direction of my life the past few years, all the heartbreaking work, the risks, ended. Worse than ended, betrayed. Half a dozen dedicated years in one mad squib of an act. I was suddenly nowhere, and those who had depended on me, and on whose dependency I based my own esteem, were in wild confusion. I could not accept it, I could not. *Why?*—Oh human nature divine. Why, indeed. There plainly was no reason. No mere *reason* could have been sufficient, you see. *No reason at all,* was the only justification of sufficient breadth to hold my shame. The idea a little intrigued me, if nothing else, and I grew gradually calm. I had been mad. Well. It did for the moment.

If pressed to name it now, I suppose the word would have to be revulsion—a madness of revulsion for the terror of our lives, all the degradation, darkness, corrupt eternal darkness—an impulse to crack back into day—to save us! Because oh I could have screamed with laughter at the thought that our inhumanity was serving some high cause. Emily and Edith slaughtered in the higher cause of mankind. Hooray and Hooray.—Something of the sort infected and deranged me. Whatever reasons I originally had were overlays to it. At the last minute Gordie caught it too. Our only escape. He understood. He generally understood me very well. He never questioned me about it, then or afterwards.

As I lay with my face to the hotel room wall sobbing with weakness and despair, he sat on the edge of the bed gently massaging between my shoulder blades and discoursing in a quiet, almost comforting vein. A valedictory of sorts, and of a more nearly sentimental color than I would have associated with him. Perhaps to distract me but I think not altogether. Boyhood things mostly—scrapes, dances, secret engagements, early deaths, madness (there is much madness in Minneapolis) rolling them out like paragraphs in an almanac, name after name and scene after scene, scenes necessarily involving Edith too, for until the war they had been inseparable, more like lovers than son and mother. (There I sound like Axel who god knows had no right to talk.) About the recent scene between them he said nothing, not even by implication. Certainly he shed no tears at her name. Well, as J. Dreifort said, they were making him eat dirt. He had a surprising stomach for it too, or at least so pretended. There was not the slightest resentment in his tone, he used her name sweetly and openly, yet he knew I had compromised (fatally, did he know *that*?—it would have been too appalling for him then, yet I think he knew) her and Emily both and as much as anyone forced the crisis. But he didn't blame me, instead was tender, comforting. Edith, you see, had taken me as a lover and raised me closer to their level. Equals in that thin air answer only for their frailties. You may laugh but I swear it was a factor. For all his low bohemian ways he was worse than she about such things.

Presently, when I had quieted somewhat, he announced he was going down for food, and advised me meanwhile to empty my bladder and maybe take a shower. He left, and when I staggered up on my feet I understood the reason for the advice. The bed sheets were as yellow as the wallpaper with urine. I fled to the bathroom retching up water on the way (it appears I retch the way others sweat —I never realized it before) and practically fell into the tub underwear and all in my frenzy to get clean. When I emerged a little later with a towel around my waist, he was back at the window sipping from a paper container and peering down. On the dresser was the watch, and on the chair beside it a blue sport shirt, white duck slacks and tennis shoes, their wrappings strewn over the floor. Without a word, I dressed—stumbling a little, for I was exhausted by this time, but I would brook no help and he didn't offer it. Then he handed me a comb, which I used and returned, still without a word. God knows I longed to talk. An unequivocal exchange just then would have done me all the good in the world. Yet training was too strong;

I must take, never give, whatever the circumstances. At last I sat and, with his hand steadying mine, gulped down two containers of beef broth thickened with stale crackers. When I finished, he offered me brandy from a hip flask. It was glorious; I sucked long and deep. All right, he said, and bruised my nose wresting it back. Then he placed a cigarette between my lips and lit it. *Draw,* love, he said. After three or four puffs, amid further silence, my composure broke. The brandy, I suppose. I went forward on my elbows, dropped my head, and broke into sobs again. With a start I felt his hand moving over my hair.

"Davey's was a lighter color," he observed quietly, "but it would have deepened. So they said. You were almost platinum as a kid, I believe. Disgraceful. A fancy platinum Jew—green-eyed and skinny. Oi. Sure, I remember you rubbernecking outside our gate. I used to think you were some kind of awful freak. Say, love, did they even bother to circumcise you? They didn't me. I did Davey though—cutest little mushroom thing. I about swooned at the ceremony. They said it was my boy's screams that unnerved me, but there was something else too—something *touched* me—a hot bloody finger on my pagan heart! And a cosmic voice—'You, Gordon Charles Abul, are *cheesy!*' Why, it was an impudence without equal in all polite history! Can you wonder that I nearly swooned? Some total utter *stranger.* I mean, one *doesn't.* I mean, a real fuckaroo *ci-devant* thing—you know?" He paused.

The next thing I knew a handkerchief was being applied to my cheeks. I opened my eyes to find him squatted before me mopping with tender concentration. He gave me a divine smile. "You going to cut the water soon, love? I have things to say but I run out of breath with this upstream swimming." For some dim reason, I swung at him, but he caught my wrist and nearly snapped it; then dropped it. He sprang up. "What's got into you of late? Hitting my face and choking my neck like a real nut. Someone dip you in eternal life brother? Listen, I won't be touched—you hear?" I started to my feet but sank back. The brandy had dissolved me. So, to put my intention another way, I spat with all my might in his direction. "Well, fudge," he growled, and went and threw himself on the bed, where he diverted himself with wadding up pieces of the wrapping paper and pelting them at me, meanwhile studying me with spiteful half-amused eyes. Finally I shifted in my chair so as not to face him. This brought on an endless stream of the vilest imaginable epithets, along with a shower of coins, keys, pen-knife, sunglasses, cigarettes, et cetera, until I felt I had to stop him or go mad.

"You have no right!" I screamed in a cracked voice.

"—To do *what*?" he said in surprise.

"To treat me this way—to do this—" but I trailed off weakly as he went into shrieks of laughter.

"Jaysus—oh Jaysus what a godlike thing is Matt!—He he he!—No, you really are sublime in your way, love. No damn body but you has the *right*. You destroy me. Ha ha ha! Dearest innocent in all the land, so watch out! Mingles with us saying right and doing right and each right word knocks off a cause, and each right act brings down the roof. Oh you odious goddamn saint! You holy terror! Listen, I've lived out my time with the scum of this earth, black-souled slobs you never turned your back on twice—villains to the tenth generation, real *family*—but nothing I knew, *nothing*, ever gave me a sense of such absolute danger as the sight of this cute midwestern face coming ablaze with right. Strong men weep, conspirators scream and scrap all plans. Matt's come to help! Save the children! Well, Jaysus. The creeps who tapped you for undercover stuff should have their brains replaced with custard. You and your right. You're driving us to the goddamn *moon* with your right, you asshole dumb blond!"

Stung past endurance, I lurched to my feet and managed to get as far as the window, helped along by a storm of chocolate-covered raisins and unspeakable taunts from the bed; but I could get no further. I caught a raisin and ate it loftily or so I intended. My head swam. I lay it to the window frame and closed my eyes.

"Well," I heard presently, "the trouble with you fags is you ain't got no stamina.—Hey, who guv you the darlin' slave bracelet, love?"

With strength I didn't have I pulled the curtains from the wall, fixture, plaster, everything in a great dusty crash and, freeing the rod, breathing stertorously, I started across the room for him.

"Help!" he screamed, "help, help, help—here comes Matt—head for the moon, men!" jumping up and down on the mattress like a chimpanzee. Just before I reached him, the bed collapsed, and as he sprang lightly off the end I fell like a stone where he had been and lay there half-conscious with rage and exhaustion. Meanwhile bedlam. He was smashing every object in the room—pitcher, glasses, dresser drawers—all the while gibbering insanely.

"Burn the papers!—Where's my moustache?—Here—there—shove the fucking *code book,* someone!—Jaysus I can't, I got a assfull pencil bombs already, what's if I cough?—*You* shove something, Maya, you got the grandest hole in all the Russias.—Here, the transmitter—quick! Bravo! [Applause.] Now the operator—Mitya the midget—easy—fwoop! Wonderful! Great spy, that Maya!—Help, he's here! Who? Mighty Mouse Lenart! Miserere! Bang bang! Zap!"

He pulled me onto my feet and hurried me to the door where there had been a furious pounding for some seconds. "A minute, loves, a minute," he called, scrambling about to retrieve his valuables, "I can't locate me goddamn emeralds —I never opens up undressed." Outside, a pale little man with celluloid cuffs and a green visor, flanked by two gigantic negresses, blocked our way angrily, but Gordie waved them aside with the cocked pen-knife. "We was *jist* leavin'," says he grandly. "Niver in me born life has I set foot in sich a manqué dive. Them yellow *sheets*. Me nerves is shot with horror—"

At the staircase he paused to threaten one of the negresses back. "Honey, you be about your business or I'll cut you into coconuts. You know me."

"Yeah, I know you—*stupid*!" she hissed, and went trailing a wake of abusive language, which he stayed a further moment to match. Furious, she swung and fired off one of her shoes. He caught it and tossed it through the hall window. "Why, you *mean* little cocksucker," she yelled.

"Oh, you cruddy black fart-sniffer," he returned.

"Hah, I know what's good," she said.

"Pervert," he said.

"Beach trash," she said.

"Head-hunter," he said; then we started down.

"Racist bastard," I muttered, feeling somewhat better. "Oh, Mae Moon's my friend," he said, "she's just too sloshed to remember the cash I slipped her a couple hours ago. It makes me sore. You okay?" I nodded. "I'm sore anyway. I mean, they waltzed me something rank the first time around. This was one of the first flops I tried, and Alf—the little pimp-type gook with the visor—said no, never saw no big dumb blond in company of little dark Haganah types, not he. Why, that Catholic pig."

We rounded the second-floor landing and while I stopped for breath, he flashed over to the window to take part in the bellowing match between Mae Moon on the floor above and people in the street concerning her shoe, which had evidently landed out in traffic. He climbed out on the fire escape. "Don't touch it," he yelled down, "it's filled with things—a bomb, you fool, a bomb!" A universal groan, pierced by a screech from Mae Moon, told the worst. It had been run over. Gordie ducked back in just as a rain of yellow liquid descended to shouts of hilarity from below and Mae's wild howls: "I will destroy the world—I will make all mankind pay with *blood!*"

"Son, she's really gone," he said as we started down again. "Well, I'm getting even. I'll teach 'em. I *knew* you were in the area. Someone saw them bring you. It took me a whole goddamn day to figure that Alf was a fervent Catholic and *never* saw Jews, except maybe the size of their cocks. So I came back this morning and said, 'Listen here, Alfie, I'm gonna bring in the *poh*-lice, and even if we don't find my dumb blond pal, we'll find something, don't you know, you unutterable old fiend.' He belched vulgarly and took a pill. Meanwhile I count a hundred twenty-five bucks on the edge of the desk—which you now owe me, payable soon—and finally Mae grabs it and says, 'Oh come on, we got something upstairs what's slept so long it's got a odor.' She's Anabaptist or some shocking thing. So through religion I found my soul at Joe's Hotel—."

Gordie supporting my elbow, we passed through a peeling yellow lobby, among half a dozen ghostly derelicts slowly swatting flies, to the glass entrance doors. There I stopped again. The glare and racket of the street appalled me. "I can't," I said covering my eyes, but he pulled down my hands and jabbed his sunglasses over my ears. "I am patience on a pedestal," he muttered, pushing a comb through my hair, "and you are the god of all pigeons. Stop crapping on my head and *get*."

He shoved me full tilt through the doors. Well, life in its richness came near sending me straight back. It was a broiling August noon on Clark Street near Division, one of the wonders of civilization for stench and noise and just general unsavoriness, at least in those days. Knots of boozy idlers along the curb, patrons of Joe's and of the bars that flanked it watched with interest as passersby nudged me out of the way. There were comments and some laughter. "Gordie," I called, but he had lingered inside the doors to argue with someone I couldn't see. I stood there overwhelmed. "No," I suddenly shouted, "I can't—" drawing cackles from the curb. I meant everything. I wanted my small darkened room again—that potion—sleep.

But: "Yes you can," said Gordie quietly into my ear. "This way, love,"—and he took my arm and walked me away. I went, in an anguish of light and all things in it, my true self unseen, that can touch me even now, more than touch me. I never forgave that pain. From that moment light was no friend of mine.

We had nearly reached Division when I felt a pressure on my arm. "There's Haganah. Across the street, three doors from the corner. Yoo hoo! Itshak—over here! Ha, look at him go—"

"Don't, please."

"Boob like you. What did you want to get mixed up with that Bible-study group for?"

I shrugged. My pride was too bruised for more. Had I been free to talk, as I say. I could have told him much to make him admire me. In spite of his parody of my reputation, I had done good work for my cause since the war. But I was not free, and I could not understand why, plain as I had made this, he yet persisted in his taunts. They could serve no practical end and in his perverse way he was a very practical man.

"—Lehi [he used a gutteral *h*]—now there's a crowd. They'd

have drilled your head instant for choking their best lead and you'd have been sweet and clean by now. Fierce elegant boys—an aesthetic experience to have them at one. But Haganah. *Rabbis, politicians.* Sleazy goddamn *citizens.* Set you up to starve in a flophouse room because taking life is *sinful,* my dear. Then they light candles and consult the Talmud and pray you'll do it for them, slowly, vilely. Citizens! What do you mean consorting with such?"

We had not turned down Division as I dimly expected we would but continued north along Clark.

"I mean, why not a room at the Drake? *Hein?* Citizens, I tell you, wholly without style."

I had no idea where he was leading me and at the moment didn't care; I only wanted to get out of the light, and several times tried to draw aside into doorways, but he kept a firm grip of my arm and moved me along. "We're being fiercely tailed, love," he said at one point. "Half Clark Street's out in fright wigs." It seemed more and more to irritate him, though all his life he had proved a generally complacent host to swarms of what he called "observers." "—Now stop your flutterings, Matt, you're safe." Oh, he read my disgust of light as fear. He was concerned for *my* sense of security. I began to wonder why.

"—Tactically, your position is ravishing. Enjoy it, for the love of god. In one breathtaking action you crossed up exactly everyone—beautiful, I tell you. Only an angel of right and progress could have conceived it, let alone brought it off. You divinity you. No one will come anywhere near you for fear of exposure. Better yet, you won't be touched because no one knows what the bejaysus to *make* of you at the moment. You might explode, or turn into a dragon. I mean, you're the queerest. Besides, there is the small matter of protocol. You realize, of course, that your rabbis pulled a most fatal boo-boo. They should have tapped your head and moved gaily on, but they got carried away with their dark Jewish passion. Now FBI'll show 'em whose territory this is. No sonovabitch foreign types is gonna skim *our* scum—pardon the similitude of course. All I mean is, you're safe, love, absolute dead center of the storm. God looks after his saints. No mortal man present has the imagination to imagine—. Ha ha. Listen, what do you suppose walking arm in arm with me this way is doing to those acid stomachs now?" He leaned against a tree and roared.

We had crossed North Avenue and were strolling eastward along the edge of Lincoln Park. The shade and relative calm of the paths somewhat revived me, and of course what he had been saying set my mind up as nothing else could have done. I was alarmed at the amount of information he'd managed to nose out in so short a time—and as we resumed walking he continued in some detail, much of it bluff but quite enough of an involved and exact nature. I simply could not fathom his purpose in telling it. To gloat?—not like him. To impress me?—well, there was that side to him, but it seemed hardly the time or place. I puzzled it bleakly. I was feeling a little revived, as I say, but in no sense cheered—if anything increasingly morose. Pare away the cuteness and his view of my immediate safety was valid enough. Only safety did not concern me. I should not have got myself involved to begin with if I had been a fearful sort. I was as brave a man as he, maybe braver, given my temperament.

What did concern me to distraction was the very consequence he pretended to find such a lovely bit of luck—the neutralizing of Haganah. It was not. It was, for me, catastrophic. FBI and CIA meant nothing to me, but as long as I continued to follow up their leads and pass them information they obligingly closed their eyes to my Haganah connections, whose presence, needless to say, had been known right along; and used. All three organizations were involved in a search for the same hidden beast, but each having interest in a special and separate aspect of the case—criminal, political, religio-political—and, in the initial stages at least, with specialized knowledge and skills to contribute to the common effort, there had been no real trouble until now. Such cooperation is not unusual in cases of an international reach. The hitch, generally, is protocol; doubly so where, as in the present instance, the understanding is tacit. However, CIA and Haganah had maintained an exquisitely deferential air throughout the course of their work. FBI's paranoia is legendary. No, they were guests and acted it. There was no doubt in anyone's mind that FBI would step in for the kill and apparently no question of their right to it, or to the ensuing publicity.

The quarry, man or woman, was infinitely extended, infinitely troublesome, and infinitely obscure. Some hateful and hating Hebrew renegade—some fierce messianic throwback of such cunning that not only his nature but his very existence was still (though considerably less so by the summer of '53) a matter of surmise, patched together out of faint but measurable traces throughout the world, from an unidentifiable shadow near the Mufti of Jerusalem, to a sub-communist element in the diffusion of atomic information among the nations. He was, shall we say, the arch-enemy of nations—of all established order. Various unlikely cells of his—or her—organization had been under surveillance by security units for over two decades, but the dispersion was such that not until the war, and a general strengthening and pooling of Allied intelligence, did a sort of pattern begin to appear. Since then the problem had been to narrow down the field to an operational center—which now seemed almost certainly to be in or near Chicago—and for this much, painstaking and often irregular undercover work had been necessary, and delicately tolerated.

The whole thing had been a marvel of cooperation. Now that was finished. FBI would never brook so open an affront to its authority, even if, as was likely, it approved of the act in principle. Haganah had behaved like hysterical fools —sleazy goddamn citizens, as Gordie called them. It was true in this instance anyway. But then what could be said of me, who had provoked them to it? That I had run mad? That I was not properly responsible? That I had *personal* problems? Well, it seemed pretty thin stuff when measured against what our brothers-in-arms, each with personal problems far surpassing mine, were bringing to pass in Palestine at that very time. Not a month earlier Ben-Gurion, in an address to the Provisional State Council, spoke of those ten glorious days in July during which untrained men and women, out of a background of unbelievable personal tragedy, "smote the hosts of Egypt and Trans-Jordan, Babylon which is Iraq, Syria, and the Lebanon and the famed

Kaukji, and slew more than five thousand men, adding a thousand square kilometers to the State." Against that, I say, I came off criminally small. My brother's face leered down at me from his martyr's paradise. I was the lowest of the low.

Yet I had to laugh. I sat on the edge of a bench, looked straight into his eyes and laughed. He picked a bottle cap off the grass and tossed it at me.

"What's wrong?" he said, uncertain whether to be offended or not.

I tried to stop but couldn't. It was so *funny*—*he* was so funny.

Half-amused, he began to circle me. "You're no good to anybody else that one can see. Exposed agents get a strictly limited sympathy in this unfairest of all worlds. You stink in the public nostril, kid. Face it, you're no Mata Hari. Jobs won't come easy—"

I controlled myself. "I'm not arguing the point—"

"But you're not facing it either. Your whole trouble is you're *ornery*. I, a benevolent-type employer, stand here offering a job utilizing all your unwholesome experience, at a fantastic salary considering the odium and things —and from which a hundred twenty-five dollars will be deducted, not in one cruel lump, but in five painless thirty-dollar installments—and you laugh! I mean, you got hidden assets or something?"

"Well, you're more than half a Jew, I think."

He shaded his eyes to study me. "Love, I am chairman of the goddamn *board,* remember?"

That started me off again and this time he joined in. I loathed and despised myself for it but there was nothing else to do. The sheer fantasy of him was irresistible. No, not fantasy—he *was* chairman of the board! Every wild thing he said could be traced down to ordinary fact. It was more than enough to make a serious man hysterical. And then the gall—to propose I now begin to spy for him, sensing something in me that *might*—fantastic to the point of genius, absolutely sublime! I could have slit my throat for the horror of us both.

We were walking again, heading out of the park in the neighborhood of Astor Place. He kept peering over his shoulder at a certain dowdy couple, the man with an armload of old newspapers and the woman with a torn shopping bag, who had been wandering in and out of sight behind us since we left Clark Street. In fact, the man had been part of the curbside group outside Joe's Hotel. Another of that group, a young tough in dungarees, was sprawled asleep on a bench a dozen yards to our right, but apparently Gordie didn't spot him. Instead he grunted with satisfaction as the couple entered a path leading back into the park.

"You don't have to say yes now," he took up. "Think us over. I'm bringing you around to the Einhoern's—remember them? They live here now and damn well better be enchanted to see you. They'll put you up, anyway. They're so fearsomely polite. Ethel'll say, 'Matt, how well you look!'—and you draped on the fence looking two weeks dead. Then as they heave you in the front door courtly old Sam'll say, grinning into your unshaved yellow-green face, 'Vell, boy, are you enchoying your stay among us, *hein*?' But they're decent people"—Edith's accent to the life—"and if you can arrange to survive the preliminaries, they'll take proper care of you for a few days. I hear they have two cooks, one company and one private, when they dine *à deux* in a foul underground crypt on stewed gizzards and pickled carp. Cryptos, my dear. Euch. Be sure to tell them you're *company*." He giggled delightedly. "But remember me, love."

I turned my head to look at him.

"I sorely need another pair of eyes. Trained, practical eyes—yours, if I can hire them. My black beauties won't do for anything but show. Too lumped together in the middle of my face."

"No," I said, praying it might stop him. I felt I could not hear more of this with safety. I had no self-defenses left.

"Oh, I am a fucking hopeless Cyclops," he went on undeterred. "I mean, for example, your head always looked flat and commonplace to me, though now I figure it probably isn't. I figure it may be a very round head, packed with strange treasure. Well, I grew up one-eyed and foolish. What comes of staring long at a fixed, invisible point—anyway, no more of that. *Isolement, spectres, adieu.* Gordie Abul sleeps no more. He seeks—he finds—he joins! When? Where you come in, if you will. They choose to play it coy. For how much longer I can't say, though I hope not longer than I can bear, which was about a week ago. I walked into a police station and said, 'I am Gordon Charls Abul, and I strangled my wife and drowned myself, and we are both at the bottom of Lake Minnetonka. It's in all the papers. Here is my identification.' And you won't believe it, but the commie cluck looked embarrassed and threw me out! So I rushed back in screaming, 'Help, I just shot Greta Garbo, the national idol!' And they threw me out again. No one'll touch me! So—I must touch them. When you're ready you can find me at the beach, unless of course I finally spot them on my own, in which case I won't be there, the deal's off, goodbye. But it seems unlikely anymore. I've been looking down their throats for weeks without getting through, aside from that charming message for Mother, which I found in my towel one day. Well, they don't *trust* me. I've been untrue. I've tried to help—to love. *Awful,* you know. Still, I am a prince of the blood, as you guess, and they may discipline but not deny me. I insist on meeting my uncle Khan at last. I come prepared to work in all the ways demanded of me. But, in exchange, there is something I must know. When will be the end of days. I must know, I must know. I am an unreasonably fragile bit of humanity—fragile as Melisande, with as still a soul, in spite of what you may think—very, very still, and sad, and, well, I am not happy here. Davey—. Oh, Matt. He was so dear to me—"

Gloomily, not unsympathetically but filled to the top with my own dark fortunes, I somewhat snappishly remarked that he seemed pleased to be mercurial. It must have sounded colder than I intended. Through his tears he flashed me a look of that violence which was never far from the surface. I could actually hear the grinding of his teeth, this Melisande of the still soul; but he quickly worked it off. As I say, he was a practical man.

We were walking along Astor Place, a neat leafy street lined with small dark elegant houses and polished brass ornaments, clearly expensive. A fifteen-minute stroll from Clark Street had put us in another world. The passersby in their sensible Chicago clothes and their extravagant French poodles clipped in the Paris style eyed us distastefully. Porters trimming hedges or shining hardware turned to stare as we passed. A few late bees haunted the miniature flower beds. Behind us, on the other side of the street, the young tough sauntered aimlessly, a rolled-up towel under his arm.

"—Just sit around the beach and look. Watch those who watch me. I'll pay ninety-five per, or about ten times what Haganah pays, which makes me *less* than half a Jew. Theology! Anyway, I think fresh eyes could pick them out;—they're *human,* I hope. It doesn't signify that you're known. It may even unnerve them into some foolishness, though I doubt it. They are gorgeously trained. Same old Arab that turned me out probably. A *serpent,* my dear. But they prowl there. Somewhere among the agents and hustlers and cruddy clerk types I claim a subject or two. So—?"

I said there was not a chance and that he should make other plans.

He clapped my shoulder and offered "a solid one hundred! Ruin myself but put *you* in clover."

I said I was not interested.

But why? It was too unprofessional of me. I was de-committed to all the world—

"To all the world, and you. I am not your friend," I said at last—at last. "No."

"Aw, sure you are, love, my very own best friend. It's almost a scandal—"

I was drenched with sweat. Casting about for a diversion, I spotted a small dignified woman leading a small dignified Pekinese up the block and asked if it was Ethel.

"Herself," he said, "or Teddy Roosevelt. Jaysus what a moustache. And here is her place." He began to move away but returned to snatch the sunglasses from my eyes, bruising my ear in the process. "I'm off for the sun," he said, slipping them on. "Today may be the day. Who knows? *Entre nous,* love, don't mention I brought you. Remember, I'm dead. I think it may embarrass them. You never know in this preposterous town.—See you at the beach, love!" He leaped the bit of lawn between sidewalk and street and started across.

"—I can't let you *live!*" I cried after him. I tell you I was wild.

I heard him laugh. "—The end of days—!"

I wept frenziedly for a few seconds, feeling suddenly terribly weak again, almost ill. People hurried by, forcibly dragging their interested dogs. I came near blanking out, but wouldn't. I braced myself against the lawn railing. Gradually I grew aware of a yapping at my feet and someone insisting that I move away. It was Ethel. "—Go and stand over there, why don't you," she was saying, "the family's out of town until after Labor Day. Over there. I'll cause a piece of cheese to be brought to you. Do you eat cheese?"

I started (of course) to retch.

"Over there, person, over there! Immediately! In front of that *ugly* house —!"

With a great effort I controlled myself. "Ethel, it's Matt."

"—Wheuuum?"

"Matt—Matthew—Lenart."

"*You* are?" She came closer. "Why, so you appear. Matt, how very nice to see you, dear!"

* * *

After something to eat—not cheese—I was helped upstairs to a quiet room at the back of the house where I slept through to the following noon. Two or three times I woke up weeping, and once I was conscious of Sam and Ethel whispering at the foot of the bed, but for the most part it was a blessed deep sleep. When I finally sat up, I realized I had been under anxious observation, for there was a bustle in the hall outside the door, and when I emerged from the bathroom a few minutes later an enormous breakfast had been set up on a folding table beside the bed. I ate half of it, then lay back and slept again.

When I awoke, the food and table had been removed. After some confused reflection I got on my feet and walked about the room to try my strength. I found it improved if not restored. There was some shakiness. There was also an uncertainty about the exact distance between the sole of my raised foot and the surface of the floor. My eyes were off; I had slept too much. They glittered unnaturally at me in the bathroom mirror. Well, I was a grim thing altogether. My face was haggard and waxy and my collar bones looked as if they could be lifted right out; I must have dropped fifteen pounds that week. I shaved and bathed carefully, and dressed myself in my Clark Street robes, which I found hanging in splendor in a huge closet. My tennis shoes had wooden trees in them and had been beautifully brushed.

Ethel was arranged over a vase of flowers in the drawing room waiting for me. With the insanest grand manner, she handed me a chrysanthemum the size of my head, which I threw behind a chair the minute she turned her back. Presently she ordered tea to be brought in. I asked for whiskey instead. Her tiny eyes grew round.

"Whiskey for Mr. Lenart, Gerhardt—the *old* whiskey."

"And a sandwich," I said, "if I may." I was ravenous again.

"What *manner* of sandwich, dear?" I could see her throat working; I was being odiously un-teatime.

"Oh—cheese," I said.

She gave me a straight look but I was all innocence. I'm sure at that moment Minneapolis loomed even bleaker than she remembered it. Gerhardt, I gathered, was new and impressionable and it would require ten bank presidents to re-orient him after this. But she was polite and really very companionable, for all her nonsense. We were soon deep in talk of mutual friends—rather, she was. I was in no mood for chatter. I answered all her questions adequately, but no more than that, I think. I listened to a long jeremiad on Durie's neglect of her; I kept a composed face as she confided her disappointment that Durie, one of history's all-time bitches, had not married *me*. And so on. Not one word of course about my appearance or condition, or the unusual circumstances of our meeting; no question as to how long I might need or want to stay. This was old-time grand manner of the acquired kind; my paternal grandfather had had something of it, according to Mother; that uneasy high style that a breath of naturalness or plain sense might at any moment violate unless one stopped up all the chinks. Little Ethel Klein from Pittsburgh who had married her boss—it was rather magnificent, you understand. But wearying; and at last I was wearied beyond endurance.

I hoped she would notice, but she didn't, and so I told her. She looked concerned, then uncertain, and finally, with an obvious effort and a sepulchral tone, put out a hand and asked me to sit a little longer. I saw immediately what was coming. She had counted all along on my bringing up the subject. She couldn't bear to let me go without some mention of it. Edith and Gordon. It was too appalling she said. They had seen Edith not two months earlier in New York, on their way to Switzerland, and thought she had never looked so well or happy. They had done perfectly delightful things together, as one can in New York, though of course it is so vulgar anymore. And Gordon, that *interesting* little beauty. How did one even talk of it? What really did happen—did I know? I said, really no more than appeared in the papers—was it given much space here? Was it not!—and she caused Gerhardt to bring in a book of clippings. I glanced over the material casually, enlarging on one or two minor details for politeness' sake, and also to allow myself to dwell over the photographs.

I was struck by how little Gordie's photographs resembled him. I had never remarked it before. I don't mean they looked *unlike,* only that they could have been a dozen other dark young men. I suppose vitality, a sort of brilliancy of presence, which was one of his most striking features, is not capturable on film, but it was more than that. I realized that in each of the likenesses before me he had managed to be taken in a three-quarter view, his least characteristic. All was neutralized—the close set of the eyes, the high-strung winging of the nostrils, the fullness of the mouth. Even profile would have been preferable, for then one had the short hawk nose and incredible re-curving of the lips. Enough. I begin to sound like his Gestapo description. I mean to say I think his posing so was purposeful, against just such a time as this maybe;—which is not to rule out the likelihood that AP was talked into circulating his least descriptive snaps. I have no doubt they were. *Both* suppositions help to explain why he could walk the streets of Chicago practically unrecognized—a fact that eventually would have put me to some thought—except by the police, and they, as he discovered, would not touch him.

Well, I finally escaped to my room, and stayed there. Dinner was sent up, and afterwards Ethel and Sam came and drank their coffee with me. Sam was many years older, a fat courtly little German-Jewish banker, whose pyjamas came above my ankles and nearly to my elbows, to his infinite merriment. He laughed until the tears came to his eyes. After they left—still without a word about why I should be in bed at all, let alone in his pyjamas—I found a roll of cash on the dresser. God knows what they thought my sickness was.

The next day I felt altogether revived but continued to keep my room. Ethel was in and out constantly but I feigned sleep as often as I heard her coming. I was in a quandary. I had fully determined to go home when I recovered enough appearance not to scare Dolly half to death, yet as the time drew near I felt less and less inclined to it. In fact, I knew I couldn't. I prickled with so much frustrated energy, so much forward movement still unused. My life for years had been trained on the present moment and its hopeful issue. It was my *adventure*. I had to face it finally. My private story had not faltered, it had merely taken over.

I had had an inkling of this personal element at the instant of Gordie's flight from the porch a month earlier—that strange frozen scene—when I was staggered with such dizzy plunging release, such sheer happiness, that I feared myself—I did. I had felt, at that moment, such a *twinge* for the enemies of the People. It is a terrible thing to happen to a public-spirited man.—But honestly, my public spirit was doing nicely too, thanks. For all the mental anguish I enjoyed afflicting myself with, my abasement in the eyes of my co-workers, and presumably the People whose representatives they were, had sunk far beyond my inclination to follow anymore. I mean, I would go on spinning pages of self-indictment for weeks, but emotionally I had begun to turn quietly back. I had always had a certain pride. I was a Lenart before I was an agent, after all.

It began to appear to me that, in an ideal sense, it simply was not possible for one man to have made all the mess laid to my account;—

I was scarcely that important to the operation which at various times had involved hundreds of men and women working in mutually exclusive patterns; or if I was, then some others stood at fault in never giving me my due, in treating me always with a cavalier hand. If I was centrally placed I ought to have known it. Holes can be picked in this, but at the time it served. Besides, how could any single action be felt to balance my entire previous contribution together?—The reasoning of an amateur; but as I say, it served, it served. It set going that most saving of our graces, a faint, unacknowledged tingle of contempt for the injured party.

I would stay, I realized, and for reasons of my own. But being me, I had of course to flaunt some grander justification, ideally some re-entry along adjacent lines that might eventually converge on the main action and reinstate me with honor. If I had indeed compromised Haganah out of the operation, I would represent them solo. Let them hurl great Hebrew curses at my head. After what they had tried to do to me, I could afford to play it angry awhile too. Needless to say, I could not think of facing my other contacts, even if, improbably, they could be faced. Gordie's proposition was simply insulting.

Some new lead was imperative—and late that night I had it handed to me. It was a fantastic piece of luck, though quite how fantastic didn't become apparent until days later. Still, I had no doubt I was back in business.

I woke up sometime after midnight with a sharp hunger, and knew I would get no more sleep until I satisfied it. I wanted cheese. Ethel had given me a passion for cheese that verged on obsession. I had eaten pounds of ementhaller that day, and now I was faint with desire for brie. I knew they had brie because it had been offered me at dinner. I had been dreaming of it. I lay ecstatically on a soft, yellow, creamy woman with bad skin, and it had been brie. I only mention the degree of my emotion because it was the direct cause on my meeting Agnes Dupres that night, not to say Cyd Bissche. I put on Sam's blue silk robe and went out into the hall, but stopped near the head of the stairs at the burst of light and voices coming from the drawing room. Ethel and Sam had gone to a dinner dance that evening and apparently brought people back with them. Now, given my appearance and state of mind, I would most certainly have turned back, had I not been visionary with brie. I had to have some; there simply was no choice. The vestibule, save for a glow from outdoor sconces falling through the stained-glass panels bordering the door, was fairly dark, and the drawing room entrance was several feet removed from the bottom of the stairs. I descended carefully—the staircase was fashionably uncarpeted but I was barefoot—rounded the newel-post, and made my way back and around to the kitchen. There I gorged on brie, drank a quart of milk, wrapped more brie in a towel, and started back for my room. I had nearly gained the staircase when without warning this great grand figure of a woman comes sailing out of the drawing room, and we both stand thunderstruck, I clutching my towelful of cheese and she her triple strand of pearls.

For but an instant; the next I was caught under the arm and swept into a small powder room that had been let in under the staircase. She switched on the light. Her head to one side, her eyes welled with tears, she studied me. For my part, I must say that, chagrin and mystification aside, I have rarely in my life so immediately liked a person. She was between fifty and sixty, tall and regal, with a great bosom, no hips, and skin like white rose-flesh. Her features were large and nondescript—well-bred, as Dolly calls it—save for the eyes, which were a quite impudent porcelain blue; her thinnish hair, circled by a faded headache band, was a small shapeless soufflé of an indeterminable color somewhere between pink and buff; her gown was "Chicago," black, long, and nothing else; her pearls were magnificent; an emerald-cut diamond on her finger was incredible. In short, everyone's idea of the old-line matron—with this exception, that benevolence folded her like a summer cloud. Such an unaffected sweetness and softness of expression is rare in any milieu, but nowhere so rare as among old-line matrons. My mother and my father's mother had it but I can think of no one else. I had in fact been musing this when with a deep sigh, clasping her hands before her, she said, "My poor, poor boy—I knew your mother—I understand—" And immediately I felt she did, that sort of woman always does; it all had to do with the untimely death of Mother;—yes;—I was a comfortless orphan. (Remember, please, that I was still in something of a befuddled and beleaguered state and here unexpectedly was *tenderness*. No man is immune.) She stepped forward and embraced me, pressing my head to her splendid bosom, and then I did melt.

"—Poor child," she murmured, "I *told* Ethel you could not be well, but she has this dreadful fear of embarrassing people. 'He has not said so.' Fancy! 'He's just tired, perhaps.' 'Indeed, indeed, Ethel,' I cried, 'tired near to *death,* perhaps.'"

I was; I was. Oh I wept.

"You must have a doctor at once—"

I worked my head in the negative.

"Dear, you *must*—"

"No—"

"Very well, but then you simply must take medicines. I have some very good ones at home I'll have sent over in the morning."

"Thank you," I murmured, adoring her.

"To lose a mother so tragically. It's enough to unhinge a stoical philosopher, and which of us is that anymore? I met her only once, you understand, but I loved her instantly and forever. Such charm, such wit and beauty—oh, she was a scarce commodity for these plain days. I mean, of course, *entre nous*. Among us. I know of one who *pretends* to it, but that's another story."

For some reason a slight chill blew over me. Perhaps it was the unfilial view that while Mother had prime qualities, wit and beauty were not among them.

"I begged her to stay longer and visit with me, but she would not, you know. Her charities cried out to her, she had been away too long already. Oh, a deeply good woman. My friend, Mr. Beckwith, joined with me in urging her, and he can be very persuasive—*I* should not have been able to resist—but she would only shake that lovely silver head and murmur, "My work, my work—"

I drew coldly back. "My mother had brown hair till the hour of her death."

"Oh, well, perhaps—" She waived the problem with a toss of the hand.

"She was neither beautiful nor witty."

"Monster—!"

"I am not Gordon Abul."

"Poor child, you are ill—"

"And *you* are thoughtless, and Gordon Abul is worse off than either of us. *He,* madam, is perfectly *dead.*"

Her confusion was entire. From forehead to fingers she went a spectacular pink. "—But Ethel said—"

"Evidently you didn't listen." Had I not been so vexed with my own ridiculous behavior, I should have let her off. There was more than one reason for doing so. But Mother had been dead a dozen years; given the idiocy of the error, what right did I have to fall in with it? No, I regarded her implacably.

"Ah," she softly said, crushed but dignified, "it's true, I don't listen. Of course you could not be Gordon Abul. Oh, I shall *die.*—Well, I entreat your pardon, young man. I am given to somewhat foolish inspirations. I believe I am what they used to call an 'enthusiast.' I barge about armed with the most frightful misinformation, and put everything at sixes and sevens—"

"Well, that makes a pair of us," I said, weakening carefully. "In part, anyway. But even if Ethel did claim to have Gordon Abul upstairs, would you not have questioned her, knowing the story, as you seem to?"

She shook her head, with the most charming little flash of guilt out of those blue eyes. "I fear I don't think, either. I sometimes wonder what substitute machinery I do run on, for I always have things coming and going in my head, quite like thoughts—" She tried a tentative smile, exposing a row of enormous yellow teeth; and I had to accept and return it. I found her enchanting. She laughed. "There, now, no one was ever the worse for a few tears, especially in the cause of motherhood. Yours was a paragon in *other* respects, I trust?"

"Angelic."

She reached out and patted my cheek approvingly. "I can believe it, by the luminous child she has left us. Now don't be impatient with me, please, but just who was Ethel supposed to have said she was caring for upstairs?"

"Matthew Lenart."

"She did, too. Of course. Well, I am delighted to know you, young man. I —."

There came a gentle rapping at our chamber door, and Ethel's voice saying, "Agnes? Wheum are you talking to in there—?"

"You," I said, "are Mrs. Dupres. Agnes Millbank Carson Pirie Dupres."

Her eyes grew round with astonishment. "To the syllable!— Which is a syllable more than I generally manage. I'm always forgetting poor Pirie, who was so quiet. How—?"

But before she could question me, the door flew open, and in crowded Ethel and Sam, followed by a plump owlish man about Agnes' age and Ethel's height with wisps of golden hair and round, gold-rimmed spectacles. It was a tiny makeshift room, nearly half of it taken up by a dressing table on which stood one of those theatrical mirrors ringed with hot, naked light bulbs and, in spite of the ventilator overhead, five bodies on a warm night made it distinctly uncomfortable.

"Ve tought you had been kitnapt," Sam said.

"And abused," said the owlish little man.

"Ah, *tais toi, drôle*," said Agnes. "He means to be elegantly decayed, and always ends up with Tom Swift behind the barn instead."

"Unfortunately, *not* always," chirped the little man, trying to squeeze past us.

"Phew, he reeks too. He's got everyone tipsy on whaddayoucallems—"

"Egg crêmes."

"Bouffon, I mean, he kept adding brandy to our champagne all evening, to poor Millie's total despair.—*Toi, où vas-tu, ouistiti terrible*—?"

But he was already there, plunked down at the dressing table and screwing his face this way and that an inch from the theatre glass.

"—Wherever did y'get one of these, Ethel? I always thought, with all that *mahn*ner, you must've kicked in a chorus line once—"

Sam went into one of his gentle laughing fits, while Ethel, her nose on a level with Agnes's great bosom, addressed that lady in suppressed fury. "But what were you doing in the powder room with our Matthew, dear?"

"Powdering, dear," said Agnes, "powdering, powdering."

"But what could *he* have been doing?"

"Cydneye," said Agnes in a thin cool voice, "I want you to meet a charming acquisition. Mr. Bissche, Mr. Lenart.

"—Hullo," said Cydneye Bissche, lost in his eyebrows. "Sam, d'you have your tweezers on you? I've got a wild hair here that's like to devour me—."

Sam was by now in teary hysteria, but Ethel was pale with French 75's and all the slights she had ever received. *"I must know,"* she said rather foolishly, poor thing.

"Must you?" said Agnes. "Well, he was holding this—this cheese for me," and with a forefinger she poked my towel to verify her guess.

"That's what effluviates so!" said Ethel.

"Does it? Effluviates?" muttered Cydneye Bissche, spreading the skin under his eyes by pressing back with a finger on each cheekbone. "I think I may have my eyes slit! Look how it would be—."

Ethel stared down at him, then to Agnes, "But how do you come suddenly to be possessed of such quantities of cheese?"

"You do go to the heart of things, dear. Well, as you may guess, it *is* a story, but I won't tell it now. Oh, I must go," saying which, she swept out into the entrance hall, leaving us all flattened against the walls.

"Cydneye, *venez!*" To me: "Good evening, Mr. Lenart. Shall you linger long among us?"

"I fancy now I may—." The style was very catching.

"Excellent. Come for tea one day soon. I can be had at the Drake—."

With a howl of despair Cyd Bissche went scurrying after her. "I can't bear it, I can't bear it! You all begin to sound like a coopful of demented Lady Wishforts! What on earth do you mean, 'you can be had at the Drake'? Are you mad? Oh, it's too *distressing,* my good chaste old friend, really it is. Irene Fairweather has ruined the town with her preposterous language—."

Both women bridled perceptibly at the mention of this name, which was not new to me.

"Well," said Agnes, "one would not know it is my birthday, by the way I am mauled. I am trapped by my own cheese and teased with my own words. Irene herself could not have abused me better. I am sorry she is away, indeed I am."

"Who?" I said, emerging from the powder room.

"Ach!" said Sam, following and rubbing his hands together.

"She is nobody!" said Ethel, lingering stubbornly behind, glowering out upon us like a small dragon from a fiery cave.

"Unfortunately," said Agnes with a neutral expression, "she is somebody. I grant you, it would be easier if she were not."

"She is the empress of cant—high-styled, impenetrable cant—and here are some ladies of her court," said Cyd Bissche. "Her sway is such, that you go places nowadays expecting to understand about one fifth of all the conversation —on a lesser night, that is. On a really great night it's like being in Boston or some other exotic outpost. Not a single syllable sounds to be anything you ever heard before in your life. I mean, it's perfectly inhuman—*birds-of-paradise* communicate that way—on holidays! Our Irene is the finest bird in town—"

"Lies! said Ethel, thrusting forth her head and screwing her eyes to make us out. "You're all in a cabal against me!"

"Now dear," said Sam, going to her, "ve vere destroying La Fairvetter—"

"—Leave me, you pirate."

Agnes smiled tolerantly and tapped the crown of Cyd Bissche's head with a fond finger. "You do exaggerate, *ouistiti.* Now come along."

He held back. "Pray, in what sense have I exaggerated?"

"Why," said Agnes, "for one thing, Irene talks very well indeed and you know it—"

"*She* knows it—."

"And so do you. Modesty is not an issue here. If we come off thick-tongued and ponderous, we do her less than justice. She is a goddess in her way." And with the air of one who has performed dutifully, she turned quickly and walked off, motioning Cyd to retrieve her things from the drawing room.

* * *

Agnes Dupres and Cyd Bissche were of course known to me from a few words dropped by Edith during our last evening together. I had put the names through a check immediately. At that stage in the game, Edith had rarely spoken idly; our relationship had grown too complex, too almost exquisitely dangerous, to waste the little time left us with the old chaff. It would have been wiser to do so but she had never been wise—

She had been tired, desperately tired, I think; and I—well I had been interested. It seemed to refresh and flatter her to be able to command this interest so easily. From the moment she guessed or was apprised of my role—I can almost pinpoint that moment—her talk took on meanings, colors, allusions. It got to be very exciting. To the degree that, as Swann with his lily, we found she could rouse our physical passions simply by feeding me bits of forbidden information. It became a strange and irresistible game, not really necessary to the love-making, yet a piquant accompaniment.—No. I must guard against this charm. I suppose I mean by saying "accompaniment," by saying "Swann," to shade into a common and quite charming experience, a fragrant *jeu de boudoir*. But it won't do. There was no charm; there was fever, morbidity. It was more than accompaniment. The increasing danger of her position did actually intensify our desire, hers more than mine perhaps, for I was always a little behind her in this, having Emily; until near the end she was wild with love for me and I, virtually destroying her! *In fact* destroying her.—Still, she was a cunning woman. I could not have done it without her wanting it done. I mean, I used all my guile to draw her out, but she was an experienced hand at this sort of thing and could have parried me, *and* had me, with small enough effort. She parried all of Minneapolis for years. That she so often seemed to muff the match with me was less to my credit, or blame if you like, than would appear. She could be indiscreet beyond anything I deserved—gratuitously so. She seemed tired, as I say; the game excited us;—and then she always had her enigmatical brooding side, that inheritance from her inbred family. There was the persuasion in some quarters that Shem's death was neither as natural nor inevitable as it was given out to be. If this was true, she must certainly have been aware of it, and I would question if she ever forgave it. Her family would not—"family" to them was the first allegiance. She and her two men had been almost preternaturally close. That scene of ice;—her inspired questioning. And if she never forgave it, what of Gordie, who worshipped his father as he would some god?—for I did sometimes wonder why he so suddenly, and obsessively, came to seek his "Uncle Khan." If *true,* as I say.

—Speaking of which—truth I mean—though her talk was rarely idle, it was rarely wholly truthful either. And I know she was crazy about me. *Women.* The strange creature led us many a wild goose chase. Yet there was much that after careful sifting and grading and triple-cross-checking yielded up its useful little fragment, and to an operation of such breadth and obscurity this was no trivial thing. My instructions were to report in toto—not to weigh or select, but to turn in every word she uttered. (They by no means considered me a master agent.) So as a matter of course I had Agnes and Cyd put through a check, and the results were given me over lunch in the *Dispatch* commissary before I left Minneapolis—as much as it was thought necessary for me to know. I was never told everything, you understand.

Cyd, they felt, was an obvious blind. He was a notorious spy-lover and quite without value anymore. He simply and frankly adored spies, and his converted coachhouse on Dearborn had at one time been a haven for every spy of whatever ideology passing through Chicago. "Lev," my Haganah liaison in Minneapolis, a skilled mechanic who I was able to consult at length while having my car overhauled for the Chicago trip, likened Cyd to the Egyptian Raphael Sadovsky, the hapless spy-lover involved in the FFI assassination of Lord Moyne a few years before. They were a distinct psychological category, he said, not unlike the little girls who flock after "your Sinatra," only even less bearable since their need was less healthful—voyeurs with little courage and no real loyalties except to some fantasy of the moment. "Oh they are very loyal to their fantasies." They preferred half-light where the hands could play unseen—but no more than play; they do not like to "come"—where whispers are exchanged and secrets, any secrets, are passed in clever ways. Spying was to them an end, a sufficient life, "not as for us the unfortunately necessary means of establishing that life by protecting the Fatherland"—he pronounced the word gravely, with a belligerent dark flush along the cheek that touched me—"for they have no Fatherland, they have only a Motherland, the womb, from whose glamorous dreams they decline to emerge." Consequently the ugly heartbreaking realities of the work were abhorrent to them, even surprising, and at the least pressure they would break down in tears and tell what they knew and often what they did not know, what they had dreamed. So beware. Of course they were generally cultivated, intelligent, amusing to be with, even, in their eagerness to be of service, appealing. Sadovsky had been a most charming man. But, said "Lev," beware. The time for charm was in the future, when Israel was rock-solid among the nations, and "then, my boy, we shall go Sephardic and out-charm them all, eh?" He very nearly smiled.—Ah Europe. I try to picture some FBI contact briefing me in this fashion and am appalled.

Anyway, there seemed to be little left to beware of in the case of Cyd Bissche. By now his reputation was worldwide and his activities of very small account. No agent on a mission would dream of being seen in his vicinity. Yet it seems there had been a period during the war when the smart little coachhouse on Dearborn was a fen of subversion, literally the "letter-drop" of the hemisphere, numbering among its callers some of the most resplendent traitors of the day. Alan Nunn May, during his residence at the Argonne laboratories, had been one of its prize celebrities (though, of course, at the time a strictly "in" one) and had come every other Sunday for bloater, which Cyd had specially imported. Bruno Pontecorvo came, and many others. Even the great Colonel Zabotin, Russian military attaché in Ottawa and director of the entire Soviet espionage network in Canada and the U.S., was thought to have felt compelled to pay his respects —and what an ecstatic occasion it must have been for Cyd! But all that was in the golden age. Nowadays, he was reduced to a few tacky international whores and déclassé playboys who might occasionally pass stock-market tips from one client to another, along with the clap. It was believed—though I was given to understand that no real check was kept on his activities anymore—that he had taken to entertaining underworld types to eke things out. He seemed perfectly uncontaminated; at least, so I had to gather from the fact that while he must often have been questioned, *closely* questioned, about his former guests, his name was never cited at any of their trials. God, was I a fool!—Yet even so I couldn't quite swallow it. Surely he was implicated by knowingly associating—? The man shrugged. He was relaying specific information; he knew no more about it. I let it pass.

For the rest, Cyd came of an old Chicago family and was well connected in the city; socially, in spite of his disreputable tastes, he was acceptable nearly everywhere. He had no occupation. He once wrote, and had published at his own expense a tiny volume on Mozart. Though he lived on a fairly high scale, he had little money and was thought to borrow heavily from friends, especially one Hudson Beckwith, and Agnes Dupres who, since the death of her last husband, he had been serving as steady escort. In spite of all, he was not completely to be written off—as I pointed out—if only for the connection, mentioned by Edith, with Benham Lake. The man shrugged.

Agnes Dupres was also pretty much of a false lead, they felt. For reasons concerning Edith's state of mind I could not accept this, but I kept my thoughts private. She had fed us enough spurious material to make incredulity here practically automatic. Agnes Dupres was merely one of the richest women in the country, listing among her assets about two-fifths of the City of Chicago. There was no dossier on her whatever. What information I was given apparently came from the society editor of the *Chicago Tribune,* Glenna Turdey Cutice, the same who later wrote *Skeletons in Gilded Closets,* which I have already dipped into at length. According to this source, Agnes' family, the Millbanks, spanned the entire history of the city, and before that the entire history of Philadelphia. Not only were *they* hugely wealthy—colonial shipping—but of the three elderly bachelors she married, and who in the natural course of things died, two had been real estate tycoons, and the third and last, Cyrus Dupres, a successful competitor of Sir Harry Oakes in Canadian mining. So she was loaded. And she was impeccable. Followed a list of the usual charities, committees, honorary trusteeships, chairmanships, et cetera; endowed hospitals, museums, concert halls; principal properties and estates (breathtaking); politics (what you would imagine); religion (ditto); associates and friends (the oldest and the richest and the dullest); and the one small, enduring scandal of her else blameless existence—a lifelong infatuation for her lifelong friend, Hudson Beckwith. He, it appeared, was perfectly *unspeakable* (my liaison, underprivileged stock if ever I saw it, blushed as he conscientiously recounted Glenna's furious words), a renegade to his class, an outcast from the family bosom, dead to all decorum and responsibility, a libertine, an adventurer, witty after the fashion of such people, handsome the way such people often are, cultivated to the point of vulgarity, wildly desirable to a certain sort of woman—including poor Agnes, who had known and loved him through all vicissitudes, from the time they were children together in Lake Forest. Since the war this utter cur had been living on Franklin Street, a total slum neighborhood filled with vile bohemians, in a filthy blackened pile of slats, simply—it would seem, to further humiliate those friends and relatives who properly snubbed him—with a sort of woman, a sort of low-born insanely pretentious *woman.* It was too excruciating, because of course Beckwith was one of the finest old names in the city, and the family otherwise, particularly in the lateral lines, an ornament of civilization. But Agnes was under some enchantment. She could not keep away from him, she could not keep away from the detestable "pile" on Franklin Street. All of which appeared to be mere apologetics for the fact that she insisted on living much of the time at the Drake Hotel, within striking distance of Franklin Street, to the neglect of the splendid mansion in Lake Forest Dupres had built for her.

Her connection with Cyd Bissche appeared a perfectly innocent, even benevolent affair. He too had been a childhood friend, and the families had been very close. Most of the Bissche money, together with the Bissche father, vanished in the Insull Utilities crash of '32, when Cyd had been a helpless thirty-five or thereabouts; but the Millbanks did what they could to alleviate the distress of the mother, and ever since, Agnes had been alleviating Cyd.

One further item, which was worth all the rest to me, though not, apparently, to my informant, who dropped it very casually, even pejoratively, as if to imply it was but one more proof of the idleness of the whole report. Edith could not possibly have met Agnes in New York that summer for the reason that Agnes had not been in New York. She had in fact been seen with Agnes in Chicago. At the end of May, accompanied by her friends Hudson Beckwith and Irene Fairweather, Agnes had flown directly to her summer place at Seal Island off the coast of Maine, remaining there through the early part of July, when she came directly back, her friends continuing on to a ski resort in Norway. She lingered in Chicago for a week before going up to Desbarats, and it was during that week that she and Edith had been observed together. So—

So, nothing. It had been Edith's habit to give meaningful information in this fashion, and they knew it. She was aware we checked out every "fact" and would catch the more glaring contradictions at once. If she said that she met Agnes in New York in company with the Einhoerns, and research turned up that she met only the Einhoerns there, and Agnes in Chicago, then probably the Einhoerns were valueless, and Agnes *and* Chicago of some significance. I say she knew we would catch this; and that by this time we would or should have realized that her false "facts" were of two orders— wholly and mockingly false, or, when embedded in an otherwise reliable narrative, *italics*. Of course we did realize it, and I felt my informant was being more than usually disingenuous with me. Furthermore, Agnes, during that first surprising encounter, not only verified the Chicago meeting, but added something that positively dismayed me. I knew all along—I believe I have mentioned it more than once—that I was not perfectly trusted by Intelligence, though to their (no doubt) regret I was too invaluably placed to be dispensed with;—that in consequence certain crucial information had been held back from me. I had had no idea until then that they went so far as to feed me a diet of red herrings!—My poor Haganah!—I had been told that afternoon in the commissary that Hudson Beckwith and Irene Fairweather went directly from Seal Island to Norway; yet Agnes had Hudson joining with her in urging Edith to stay longer in Chicago. Well I had little hesitation in deciding which version to believe. A minor point, perhaps of no significance at all, perhaps even an oversight, but it angered me, and hardened my resolve to go on with the case. Where the night is so thick, you don't commit oversights, you don't issue casual falsifications within your own ranks.—I do confess that at the very moment of hearing this report, which I made a great point about having before I left Minneapolis, as much to gull my own nerves into some sort of patience as to lull theirs in respect of my unsettled behavior over the murders—at that very moment I was quietly, with a kind of tender amusement, savoring their rage when I should have taken Gordie and me far beyond the scene of their loveless ferreting. To a clean—a royal privacy closed to the public gaze;—I don't deny it;—only say for me, that my duplicity was fierce, full of love and hate—!

The next morning I breakfasted at seven-thirty and left the house before either of my hosts was stirring—staggering, I should say. I smiled to think of Ethel hungover. Grandeur awash. Imagine calling Sam a pirate. I laughed out loud at the thought, though I knew of course he was—but such a *dear* one. The street was empty save for a watcher in chauffeur livery halfway down the block, elaborately bent over a newspaper. Gordie-like I waved. It was a glorious day. I strolled over to Division, along it to Dearborn. Behind me a block or two lay Oak Street Beach. There were practical reasons for not going directly there, but the bare idea of holding off was exciting enough to justify itself. Besides, I was being watched and felt I may as well make myself interesting.

At the intersection of Dearborn and Division I paused to scrutinize Cyd's coachhouse, which lay half a dozen doors north from the corner and was unmistakable by reason of its extreme narrowness and the old coachlamps flanking the entrance. Elegant, with its coat of black paint, its brass ornaments brilliant in the early sun, the wine-red sashes in the windows. I turned south, however.

I had in mind a small unpretentious apartment-hotel halfway between Division and Washington Square Park. I had remarked it before, and liked it, both for the exposed location and the overall air of quiet; strangers lurking about would be instantly noticeable, and since my disgrace I would not be anticipating strangers with particular confidence. The seedy respectability of it pleased me too; mostly widows and old couples, I guessed; the turnover would be small which, combined with the advantages of a desk and switchboard, made it just lovely. I took a pair of rooms on the third floor front—very modern, with blue walls and kitchen furniture throughout—gave a deposit out of the money Sam had left on the dresser, and told the clerk I'd return in a few hours with luggage. Before going back to Division to buy some, I walked a block to Washington Square Park to look for the car I had left there over a week ago. It was gone, which did not really surprise me. I regretted the loss of my journal but that was not irreparable; the events of the past three weeks were only too vivid in my mind.

Returning, I spotted a Cadillac outside the hotel—my chauffeur friend. I crossed the street so as not to interfere and continued on to Division, where I stopped in a luncheonette for coffee, at the same time phoning the home of my lawyer, a loathsome second cousin of Mother's, in Minneapolis. Among other items, I asked him to get off a cashier's check to Sam's bank, together with certain identification papers and a driver's license, all of which I had lost. I told him I wanted the check at the bank the next day and the identification papers as soon after as possible. He began immediately to argue and raise objections—he always did. I cut him short with an oath. He grunted in a hurt way and asked where I was staying.

I said it was none of his business, to send everything to the bank. He asked if Father knew about any of this. I said that if I found he *did,* I would have a new lawyer, I meant it. Then he asked, "apropos of the Abul business," where could I be reached in the event my testimony was wanted, I had taken an oath to make myself immediately available. I replied, measuredly, that the Einhoerns would always know where to get hold of me—why, had there been a break? A just perceptible pause; then in a low mournful voice:—Found the bodies late yesterday—horrible.—Whose! I nearly screamed.—His, and the woman's.—You, I said, you are a liar, an impotent fat sadist liar! and hung up. I was shaking. If there is a more soulless object in nature than the professional spy, it is the newspaper photographer; but beneath both, beneath nature itself, lurks the lawyer-who-is-the-second-cousin-of-one's-mother—

I bought two canvas bags and enough stuff to fill them—clothes, toilet articles, *and* a fountain pen and some thick composition books. I had much to write up and planned to spend the whole of that day doing it. Back at my rooms I phoned Ethel. She was noticeably distant with me but I put it down to embarrassment over last night's scene. I thanked her for all her kindness, told her where I was staying, and gave her the number, but asked her please not to reveal it except in the case of a reasonably certifiable emergency, I was in retirement for the moment. She said yes and yes. I asked her to tell Sam about the cashier's check and papers and that I would be by the bank to see about them in a few days. She said yes. I said well, goodbye for now—. She said oh, there was a package of what appeared to be *medicines* sent me by Mrs. Dupres. I expressed surprise. She said she would cause them to be left at the hotel desk. I thanked her. She said, rather abruptly, why, are you ill? I understood her humor at once and hastened to mend it. I said, of course I was not ill, and had I been, should *she* not have been the first to know? I was grateful to her delicacy in never having broached the subject, for when one is *not* ill, it is beastly having people fussing.— So it would seem to *me,* she said, thawing audibly.—I was simply *weary,* I said.—I *told* her, I *told* Agnes that!—And, I said, you were, as usual, exquisitely *au fait.*—But, my dear, she said, when shall we ever *see* you again? I said, when she liked. She said well, actually, she was giving a little dinner party the next evening but two—which I translated as Friday, this being Tuesday—and could I possibly come, though the notice was so short? I said I would be delighted. She said oh charming, when she sent over the medicines she would include a written invitation, and if I posted my "response" that evening she should have it in plenty of time, et cetera.

So, somewhat pleased with myself, I settled in with pen and paper for the rest of the day. Late that evening, chastened with three weeks' itemized follies and humiliations, I went over to Division for something to eat. There I caught a glimpse of Gordie, the black handkerchief fluttering at his throat, capering in the window of a bar with a group of outrageous flamboyants. I hurried by.

* * *

"'Dolmancé: Eugénie, how many inches rest outside?

"'Eugénie: Scarcely two.

"'Dolmancé: Then I have eleven up my ass!'—*You will remember from last night's installment that Augustin, the cute young gardener, got a lalapalooza what measures thirteen inches in length by eight and a half around. To continue:* 'What ecstasy! He splits me open, I can't bear it!—Chevalier, are you hard?

"'Le Chevalier: Feel, and give me your opinion.

"'Dolmancé: Then come here, my children, and let me unite thee, let me assist in this heavenly incest. *(He introduces the Chevalier's cock into his sister's cunt.)*'

Shouts of approval.

"'Madame de Saint-Ange: Why, my dears, there I am screwed from either side! By Jesus, what divine pleasure! I tell you there's nothing to match it in all the world. Ah, fuck! How I pity the woman who has not tasted it! Shake me, Dolmancé, pound away—by the violence of your thrusts impale me on my brother's blade, and you, adorable Eugénie, come and study us, regard me in vice; come, dear creature, learn from my example how to relish it, to be transported, to savor it like great food.—Behold, my love, behold all I do in a single operation: scandal, seduction, bad example'—*Isn't that sublime?*—'incest, adultery, sodomy! Oh, Satan! one and only god of my soul, inspire me with more, etch further perversions on my smoking heart, and then shalt thou see me plunge yet deeper, higher!

"'Dolmancé: Ah, voluptuous creature, how you do stir up my jism, how your sentiments and the uncommon temperature of your asshole do urge it to fly'" et cetera et cetera et cetera.

* * *

Night after night I leaned against a tree in Washington Square Park—or Bughouse Square, as it is sometimes known, by reason of the eccentrics who gather there after dark and rant away to small groups of idlers on everything from British-Israelitism to the virulence of oysters—listening to Gordie give a public recitation from the works of de Sade. He had already gone through *La Nouvelle Justine,* and was presently midway of *La Philosophie dans le Boudoir.* Each evening at about nine-thirty he would arrive with his milkcrate and green paperback book, greet the dozen or so derelicts who were eagerly awaiting him, mount up under a street-lamp, and at once, in a loud theatrical voice, launch into the most incredible filth and radical sentiments I have heard outside an anarchist cellar.

Say what you will, de Sade is a dangerous man. It does not do to underrate him. Luckily he was a bad artist, but certain of his words hover much too near the inadmissible truths. Though an aristocrat, he had no honor about him—as even the lowest born of rebels affects *some* idealization of the vision; he had none of it. He drives the general run of rebels right where they belong, inside the establishment, and is perhaps more disturbing to them than to the powerful, for *they* cannot afford to dismiss him as a boring bad writer—what social critic is not?—and yet he is unusable, he is in the purest sense, and after all these years, appalling. I think that is no mean accomplishment.

No, I tell you it was appalling to hear some of those things read out in a clear voice. And the area thick with police!—Well, they moved out of ear-shot fast enough. It was ridiculous, of course, but what could they do? They had orders not to touch him, and he plainly meant to put them to the test. Short of actual physical violation of the law—murder, say, which was certainly not beyond him but which would have been impractical—he was going to force somebody's hand. It had its amusing side. The same police who gave him a wide berth while he reeled out those spumey abominations were forever hauling off some boneless drunk or inoffensive pervert, or silencing a speaker because of the heat of his sentiments—the woman who was sore at oysters could get quite unseemly and was often chased. Bands of toughs from Clark Street, come to prey on the perverts, were quickly dispersed. And there at the center of the small square, in full light, surrounded by a panting, wild-eyed rabble, lounges Mr. Gordie, reading: "'—Cruelty is simply the energy in a man civilization has not yet altogether corrupted; consequently it is health, not sickness. Abolish your laws, do away with your punishments, all your repressive customs, and cruelty will have no further harmful effects, since it will be active only when subject to immediate conflict with, and repression by, competing cruelties; it is in the artificial civilized state that cruelty is dangerous, because the assaulted person nearly always lacks the force or means to repel injury; but in a state of nature, if cruelty's target is strong, he will repulse it, if weak, he will fall—thus there is the small and normal drama of the weak yielding to the strong—Nature's law—'"

"Kill, kill," goes the chant around.

Amusing, but I was not amused. It was a vile little park, littered with garbage and newspapers and stinking of urine. Save for isolated pools of street-lamp light at irregular intervals, the space was oppressively gloomy, lined with spectral benchfuls of decaying bodies and hallucinated minds. And from all sides that shrieking, that madness. Hopeless scum of the earth. I hated it. But night after night I stood nearby in shadow and scanned the crowd, as by day I watched at the beach and after midnight in the neighborhood bars. Everywhere it was the same, filth and violence. He grew wilder by the hour. Of my ten days' vigil, the last three or four had been truly horrific, a sort of witches' sabbath, and if it had not been for an occasional hour of polite talk and rational manners at the home of Ethel or one of her friends, I don't see that I would have held out. I am not especially delicate, I am *human*. But apparently he had done with all merely human behavior. He was once for all going to be jailed for being a public nuisance, or calmed in the only way acceptable to him—unequivocal contact with . . . whoever.

I say apparently, for we did not communicate. He ignored me when he was sober, and when he was drunk, which was every morning, he condescended to abuse and embarrass me in the most vicious fashion. We had had a blow-up. When he finally grasped the fact that I was working strictly solo, that I would under no circumstances give information or discuss my observations, he handed his drink to someone and shoved me through a plate-glass window. Fortunately I took only a few cuts on my arms, but I went back in and got him and knocked him over the bar. I yelled some things and he yelled some things back. Since then, our relationship had been distant.

I was reduced to this simple-minded—and what I considered all but useless —tailing owing to the absence of Agnes Dupres who, on the very afternoon of the day I left the Einhoerns, had gone down to Virginia for an unannounced length of time. Ethel told me it was because she could not bear the town "sans" the company of her two "fr-r-riends" and wanted distraction. "She rides to hounds, you know; one of those"—Ethel did not ride. I was very put out. I had an instinct about Agnes, and her two friends intrigued me beyond all reason. It was the feeling I had years later about Θ. But though Ethel and I got to be on easy terms with each other, she would not discuss them, nor would the people she had to her house. Everyone loved Agnes, but since her life was so bound up with Hudson and Irene, and as everyone hated *them,* it was hard to gossip about her with the proper objectivity, especially before a stranger who could not flesh things out with overtones. But it was not only love that made them cautious, it was *respect,* my dear. Agnes was a power in the city. She was a sort of larger and richer version of Mother, with many of the most important committees in her hands, and connections in all the vital places. And, surprisingly, it seemed she could be vengeful—not as regarded slights to herself, which no one would dream of offering in the first place, but as regarded slights to her pet pariahs. Ethel confided to me her "unease" at having shot off her mouth so that evening; Agnes would never entirely forgive it, she feared. Cyd Bissche was the only one permitted to go on about them in her presence, since he railed at everyone anyway.

As for Cyd, he was very much in evidence—at the beach, at this or that party in Lake Forest, at the "men" bars I sometimes followed Gordie into; but he was not friendly. He would nod and turn away. Well, I couldn't force myself on him, though I had to feel a little slighted, remembering what a spy-lover he was reputed to be. No *eye,* I told myself—though he had one for pretty young men. At the beach, where he sat in a director's chair under a fringed blue umbrella doing his nails, there were generally half a dozen disposed around his feet. Sometimes there would be a couple of fortyish women, very languid and chic and predatory, playing at flirtation with the young men and dropping apparently outrageously funny remarks. It was quite a sight, though nothing to the sight of Gordie's Follies a dozen yards away.

Oak Street Beach is small, roughly triangular bit of sand bordering Lake Michigan spang in the heart of the city, overhung by the Drake Hotel, convenient to the Astor Place and Walton Place and Chestnut Street rich, a few minutes' walk from the moldering shells of the old Gold Coast; and quite as handy to the Rush Street demimonde, the Clark Street and North Avenue packs, and a few minutes' walk from Bug House Square. When all elements converged on a fine day, the view could be spectacular. The patch of sand was small and hectic, but the beach extended itself for miles in either direction by means of a cement parapet separating the water from the Drive, and looking one way you saw, far off, quiet groups of old people fishing up perch for their dinner; looking the other way you saw solitary sad Chicago souls of all ages seated or standing, gazing motionless out over the water; behind you a few yards, the noise and fumes of the traffic on Lake Shore Drive. Surely a unique spot—and the contrast between Cyd's and Gordie's parties took a sort of measure of it.

—What a rabble Gordie did collect. Nine or ten, swelled now by the addition of a North Avenue tough and a couple of Rush Street girls, diminished when some staggered home to sleep so as to make the bars by midnight. None worked, apparently; but whatever the size of the group, the noise and offensiveness were standard. They were all over each other, all over Gordie, men and women, it made no difference, laughing, cursing, shrieking. He would be in Mae Moon's arm one minute and the next be kissing a sailor full on the mouth or practically mounting some squealing whore. There were frequent boozy quarrels carried out in remarkable strings of four-letter words and flying bottles. There were card games and acrobatics. There were farts and belches and storms of insane cackling. There was sometimes a banjo and Mae Moon sobbing out spirituals.

About Mae Moon. Chicago, you must realize, is the Montgomery of the north, at least always was. To say that negroes were not tolerated on white beaches there is rather like remarking that murder was frowned upon. Even a light-skinned Indian or Turkish dignitary strolling the parapet fully clothed received hostile stares from the sand. And Mae Moon was the biggest blackest loudest lowest negro in all Chicago. And Gordie brought her. Under ordinary circumstances there would certainly have been a scene, for the North Avenue vigilantes, like poor whites everywhere, were particularly violent on the score, and there were generally lots of them around. In fact, Mae's first appearance, in a ratty orange bathing suit with a great moth hole on the behind, was greeted by an almost audible gasp and a wholesale clearing off of the timorous preparatory to trouble. But nothing happened. Gordie had also brought, out of precaution or taste I don't know, a pack of the meanest roughest veiniest stevedore types I hope ever to see up close again—*killers*. The police quailed and were plainly relieved at not having to interfere. Mae planted herself grandly, belched, and bent forward to scratch the hole in her bathing suit with an elegantly cocked finger. Then, while Gordie and the stevedores fell to shameless necking, she brought out her banjo and serenaded them with hymn tunes. Since then she had made frequent appearances with his group, and with only the merest hint of unpleasantness.

I don't mean to give the impression that Gordie was a crusading liberal or in any sense antedated the civil rights drive. Good god no. He was a nasty little aristocrat, above even his own class, to whom negroes were every bit as contemptible as his fellow whites, to whom in fact everyone was inferior and to be used for particular ends. He was out to catch attention, to make trouble—vainly, as I thought, since in all my hours of watching I had observed nothing remotely like a "subject," troubled or otherwise, save perhaps some FBI people pretending it, and one CIA woman agent who sat with the bar-girls and occasionally came and joined his group, fooling him as little as she fooled me, though as it turned out I was wrong and he *was* causing definite uneasiness among his people—and Mae Moon or me or Helen Keller, it made no difference to him. We were all material. This was instanced shockingly in Kelly's Clark Street bar one midnight when Mae fondly tried to kiss him, and he slapped her back in a rage, grinding out that he was not in the habit of kissing niggers! I thought she would go through the ceiling. But big and powerful as she was, she feared him. Anyone else using her that brutally would have got a bar stool over his head. Now she only muttered and went and sat at one of the tables. There, after a time, she did begin to abuse him, but in so general and usual a fashion that the incident seemed forgotten. She got red-eyed drunk and turned up at the beach the next day in a foul mood. That night, when I followed Gordie into Kelly's after the reading in the Square, she was back at the table and already far gone. "Gatzangoo," she growled to my greeting. I brought her a rye and ginger-ale and sat down.

"Why do you let him get away with it, Mae? He treats you like some damn cur."

"Mind your shitty business, stupid," she muttered. "Maybe I *deserve* it, for what you know. Spook."

I opened my book and started to read. I had formed the custom of bringing a book with me nights. I had nothing in common with the habitués of these places, and drinking makes me morose and quarrelsome, not to say virtually useless for any fine observation. So I would bring a book and eventually move to a table near a light, where I could amuse myself and keep a broad view of the bar.

"—Mother-fucking Macree! What weak piss is this you bring me! Pha-a-aw! Ch-h-h! Ga-a-a-ach!"

It was a good-sized crowd for midweek, including the young tough who had tailed us from Joe's Hotel that so memorable day. I hadn't seen him since but now I spotted him instantly. The whores were out in force, as were truck drivers. A party of raucous sailors with boils on their necks. A sprinkling of elderly queans in toupées looking and listening like orphans at a family picnic. Mid-bar Gordie hilariously occupied with his current mistress, Rita, and some of her girl friends. Towards the door a couple of detectives in mufti quietly read the racing form. The new bartender was—well, as you may guess.

Suddenly: "I seen him in action," Mae broke out. I looked up but she was watching Gordie at the bar and evidently talking to herself. "I'll maybe get him sometime only not when he's on his two feet. He got more horrible weapons on him than a Jap—"

"Just a knife," I commented.

"*Just* a knife! You ever seen him use that thing, spook? I mean, he ain't like you or me, I mean, he *uses* it. I saw him once cut up a seven-foot marine till I bust out crying. He ain't human, the gorgeous little cocksucker—"

"Well, why are you crying about it now?"

"'Cause I'm a nigger, a nigger, a nigger."

"Listen to me Mae, you're as good—better, yes better—"

"—Hey, Mae," squalled Gordie from the bar, "come over here, you Anabaptist bitch."

"I ain't no Anabaptist bitch!"

"Oh, you atheist!" Snickers from the queans.

"Jesus," she confided, wiping the tears from her eyes, "what he's doing to my reputation is a *shame,* I tell you. Now I'm a atheist. You heard him. They's cops all over the place too. Jesus. They'll be riding me out of town as undesirable, what with one thing and another—"

"*Mae!*"—Gordie again.

"You shut that poison mouth, you runt, or I'll be over there and shove your damn head up your ass till it squeeze right out your brazen gullet—!"

This sent the entire bar into screams of laughter, which really enraged her.

"You filthy-mouth scum with your infaymous Marcus D. Sade!"

Gordie pounded the bar voiceless with glee. I thought his eyes would leave his head. "Excrements!"

Now Rita came wiggling up, apparently to smooth things over. "Honey," she oozed, her voice a little uncertain with laughter, "now don't mind him, he's really *terribly* fond of you—"

"Oh, gatzangoo, dear."

"Well, fuck you right back, dear. Mind if I sit?"

"Extremely."

Rita sat. "My *feet*—"

"Well, they's big enough for *lots* of pain, if I may say so."

"How droll. And how are you, Matthew?" I shrugged. I was reading. She reached over and squeezed my hand but I pulled it back with a warning look.

Mae chortled unpleasantly. "Big secret. Everyone's so busy with secrets around here—"

"Shut up," I said.

Mae laughed, happy to have been of some annoyance. It improved her mood at once. "Hey, Rita, you better get yourself back to number one before Evvie swallows him. She got bigger tits 'n you and you know how he likes tits. Hah, look at them."

"Oh, he likes everything," said Rita, looking. "I never knew a man with such catholic tastes."

Mae was all attention. "Catholic, eh?"

"It's a manner of speaking."

"Yeah, what ain't?"

"I mean, what he needs is a life-sized doll with *attachments*."

Mae slapped the table appreciatively. The next instant they had put their heads together and were quietly giggling. For several minutes I caught only bits of domestic talk—"he likes *that*?—I ain't heard no one doin' that since I left the Carolines—*hah! ha ha ha*—stand on the new console with my—*whoo! he he*—"

Gordie was hanging over us, steadying himself on the back of Rita's chair and slopping his boilermaker in all directions. He was still potted from a day's drinking at the beach. "What awful truffle you two pigs squealing about over here?"

Mae Moon drew back with a face of the most extravagant disgust. "Merely nasty truffly you."

"Oh," says Gordie, his eyes going dark, "Was it discussing me, you were, you pigs?" He flops himself in a chair a little way off, his legs spread, arm over the back, very rakish and spiteful.

"Come off it," says Rita, "I'm getting fed up with your damn moods. Why can't you be nice and normal-acting like your—" breaking off in nervous laughter and playfully slapping his thigh. I could have killed the silly bitch. He caught it at once. His eyes were slits.

"Like my what?" says he, moveless.

"Like your dear old daddy when he was sweatin' gettin' you!" barks Mae helping out. "It's so comfortable-like, they say." I must have boiled up scarlet.

"You fingered it, girl. I didn't have no proper old daddy, dear *or* cheap," he drew out, glancing from Rita to me and back to Rita. Well a whore's a whore and what did he expect, what did *I* expect? "Born," he said, dismissing us for the moment and relaxing back into the luxury of himself, "from conjunction of two great Sade dykes of gigantic—clitori—hoses, goddamn hoses. Very unusual case. The Pope was speechless at their petition. '*Spumoni!—un' altra,*' he was heard presently to sigh, '*ohimé*—something something'—the whole being under dust in the Vatican Archives. Normal, you say? Brother Jaysus, I'm *insane* with myself. Only look at me, you pigs! Three hundred sixty-five New Year's Eves a year! *Think* of it. The Warsaw Concerto on eight radios, colored lights, fabulous favors. Every eve inside my head! A useless god of love—!"

We looked, and so he seemed. There was no exaggeration meant or taken. He was but too visibly phenomenal. I think I may say, of Mae and Rita as of myself, that vanity never crossed our minds. His head swam from shoulder to shoulder in an only half-humorous agony of frustration that was hard to look at. Running grease, streaked with grime from the Square, in a foul tee-shirt (torn carefully up the side to expose the slim beautifully muscled flank) and shapeless sailor pants (raped from some crumpled victim moaning don't, don't, in the dead of night, I standing near, barely breathing, overcome), hair matted into bangs on his forehead and beard flecked with spume of beer and god knows what scum else, and he stung the eye like a fresh-born star. It was true, it was true. That brilliancy, those blue-white fires that numbed but threw no heat *to us*. Simply, we were not equal to it. Tragic, I supposed—yet how much more tragic if any were ever found to match him. How intolerable.

"—What am I supposed to do with this—gift?" he wailed, still only half-humorous. "A miracle of carnal beauty, born to celebrate, and no partners! Where are my superb, accomplished lovers—the great fantasticators—they know what I want—they—" Edith came to mind. From what I had experienced and heard, it had been quite a family. Evenings at home must have been choice.

It was over. He swung in his chair and called for drinks for the house. The racket was deafening, but somehow such an order is always heard, as it was now, and greeted by the usual hollow cheers. Though people had begun to trail out, there were still a dozen to fifteen roiling about the bar. Rita said it was crazy the way he threw his money around. Mae agreed. Laughing, he said they were both sluts who rolled him in a week for more than he spent at Kelly's in a month. Rita was annoyed at the truth of this and said there wasn't enough money in the world to make her go with him again, at which he ducked forward and bit her nipple—she never wore a brassiere. She screamed and slapped him. He grabbed her and bit the other while she pounded his back frantically.

"You're ruining my good dress, you jerk!"

"Bite him back!" cried Mae.

"Sure," he said, sitting again, "go ahead, bite me." He pulled up his shirt and offered her a small brown nipple between thumb and forefinger. "I love it." Rita turned away indignantly and began re-pinning her hair. "She's so awful nice," he explained to Mae, "she's driving me back to boys."

"Well, you always seem to find *some* excuse," said Mae unsurprised.

"Girl, she don't do nothing, I tell you."

"She come from a very toney house," said Mae, patting Rita's hand comfortingly. "But like I'm always telling you, leave the dolls to *me*. They want someone with meat on 'em—"

"I got A-number-one meat on me!"

"I mean all over, son, not that miserable little wrinkly scrap—"

"A thing of beauty to some. Anyway, I don't see why if I bite her titties she won't bite mine—

"It's a small matter, I grant you, but if I don't start her small we'll never get down to the real stuff, you know? Principle, principle! We give you the vote, you got to assume equal responsibilities. We got to pull together to make this country great—."

"There *is* something in what you say," admitted Mae thoughtfully. "We won't *ever* develop no woman President the way she's acting. Right? You got to start with such as tittie-bitin' and stamp-lickin' and other insignificant chores, right? Learn the ropes—"

"Right. All she wants to do is *fuck*."

"Euch. We ain't going *no* place that way."

"Tell her, girl. She is ruining a beautiful thing."

"Rita, you is setting us women back a thousand years or more. I got a art book I'll lend you, honey. It show in word and picture just what men like doin' best through the ages, god help us girls—"

He nudged Mae with his elbow. "I ever had that one, Mae?"— indicating me with a mocking dead-level stare of that glittering Cyclops eye. I yawned and opened my book. Some ragging of the sort occurred almost nightly. It barely flustered me anymore.

I felt Mae looking me over. "Well, you told *me* you never."

He set his elbows on the table and tilted his head to gaze into my face. I raised my eyes above the edge of the book to meet his head-on. He didn't scare me. "Strange," he said.

"He's just your type," urged Mae. "Big, blond, built beautiful. Very fair basket too from what I see at the beach. I bet he'd be good."

"*Je regarde, je regarde*—"

"Now you know I can't—."

"Sure, love, I bet he'd be."

"His type go like wild-fire once you rev 'em—"

Rita stirred herself from a gloomy contemplation of her finger nails. "Get off his back, you two wolves. He's like a breath of fresh air in this damn zoo."

"Honey," said Mae, "you don't say much but what you do say couldn't be dumber."

"Leave her, Mae. It's the way of the world. She's in business like the rest of us. Only I was thinking I ain't had a proper dose of fresh air in god knows when—"

We sat back while the bartender set up our drinks. Gordie swallowed his in great gulps—double whiskey in a goblet of beer—watching me with that in his face which made me feel the subject was far from exhausted. But I had had enough, and though we rarely these days addressed each other directly, I ventured, "We hear you like carving big marines into little ones."

His eyes sprang to Mae. He was furious. For the moment anyway their alliance was at an end. "You tell that traitor that, you bitch?"

Mae bristled at the tone. "None a your fuck-ass business, squirt. Since when did you get so familiar with niggers?"

"You tell him the whole thing, nigger?"

"Such as?"

"The *ear*."

"The one you cut off?"

"No, fool, the one I left on, fool. Tell him then."

"I just told him, for chrissake, you cut off the poor bastard's ear."

"And?"

"Well, I don't know, you *eat* it, that what you mean—?"

"Tell him why, tell him why."

"'Cause I dared you—?"

"Vicious dyke."

Rita was chalk white. "You ate his ear? I mean, swallowed it?"

"Oh, it wasn't at all bad, baby," he said, "something like the gristle in veal breast. Takes chewing, is all—" His attention flew to a quarrel up the bar between the sailors and one of the truck drivers, and he hurried over to join in.

"Listen," Rita gasped, her eyes round with horror, "I've got to get away from him. He's a maniac. Why didn't you tell me, Mae—?"

"About the ear?" Mae leaned forward on her elbows. "That wasn't all he eat either," she whispered darkly. "He's stranger than fiction, my dear."

"Jesus," said Rita.

Mae sat back and cocked an eye towards the detectives up front who were apparently trying to decide whether or not to quiet the disturbance. "What I mean," she intoned righteously, "it's a terrible thing to go around devourin' up the US forces with the world in such a uncertain condition—"

Gordie was back fuming. "Goddamn baseball," he snarled; then noticing Rita's silent pallor and, I suppose, my incipient greenness: "What loose shit you been oozing now, Snow White?" His mood was savage.

"Nothing much," says Mae, batting her lashes, "just about the time you eat the ass off a hundred-day flagpole sitter and *roo*-ined his career—"

Head to foot, he literally quivered with impotent rage. He stabbed the air with a violent forefinger: "You—all of you—" and without warning brought his fist smash down on the table, startling Rita into tears and relieving my stomach of gases. Mae merely grabbed her drink out of the way. It was at this moment that Evvie, a prettyish whore with a fabulous breast development, came reeling over to embrace him indecently from behind, gargling some Spanish syllables into his ear. Her friends at the bar called out encouragement. The sailors dropped the argument and craned their necks to see, beginning to laugh like nervous girls.

He said quietly, "Take your hand off it, you foul Puerto Rican sink. I'm telling you." Instead of which she fumbled at his buttons. I quickly went back to my book, to read again:

Il est un pays superbe, un pays de Cocagne, dit on, que je rêve de visiter avec une vielle amie....

I heard Mae trying to warn her; and the next thing I heard was a grunt, as of someone thumped in the stomach, followed by two reports of the flat of the hand against a face, and right after that a body hitting the bar. An electric silence; out of which, gradually, a sailor murmuring about the ethics of striking a woman. Soon a low wail from Evvie, rising rapidly to a shrill high cackle of Spanish invective, inciting the sailor to increase his volume, and some of the truckers to add menacing rumbles. I read:

Tu connais cette maladie fiévreuse qui s'empare de nous dans les froides misères, cette nostalgie du pays qu'on ignore, cette angoisse de la curiosité? Il est une contrée qui te ressemble, où tout est beau, riche, tranquille et honnête, où la fantaisie a bâti et décoré une Chine occidentale, où la vie est douce à respirer, où le bonheur est marié au silence. C'est là qu'il faut aller vivre, c'est là qu'il faut aller mourir....

Gordie: "—You scandalous pimple-faced wart-hog—sailors with such faces should be wrapped in the flag and sunk, not set loose to assault delicate bellies. It even talks, the nightmare. Baseball, the witch-brat. Tell us, where'd you peel that skin, off the after-birth of a toad some clammy midnight? *Hein,* monster? Your ma rape a whole shrieking leper colony, ghoul? Jaysus, wow. Look at the vomity *lot* of you. The slut here was right, it's like being in a goddamn zoo! Toads, garbage, prunes—!"

Mae: "Now that's a interesting zoo—" I heard him kick out at her, and her little burst of laughter as she scraped her chair back out of reach. Otherwise silence, Evvie too.

Fleur incomparable, tulipe retrouvée, allégorique dahlia, c'est là, n'est-ce-pas, dans ce beau pays si calme et si rêveur, qu'il faudrait aller vivre et fleurir? Ne serais-tu pas encadrée dans ton anologie, et ne pourrais-tu pas te mirer, pour parler comme les mystiques, dans ta propre correspondance?

"—Flaming pansy cops you, who the hell you staring at?"

Silence.

The point of course being he was untouchable, and every other night or so he'd explode with fury at the condition. It needed little incentive, producing little damage. I knew without looking how he was bent double in that fighting stance of his, the knife held just above the floor and well forward; but I knew too it was a shadow-match, that the bartender was unobtrusively busy up and down the bar warning people off, while the detectives kept an eye out to insure the warning was heeded. Presently there was a shuffling of feet as Evvie's group and the sailors started leaving, Evvie gibbering insanely, the sailors, the one with the bad skin in particular, grumbling some very unkind things about Chicago.

"Ya, fuck Greta Garbo!" Gordie yelled after them.

"Try Rita Hayworth," advised Mae, "this ain't the Ritz we're in, honey—"

Vivrons-nous jamais, passerons-nous jamais dans ce tableau qu'a peint mon esprit, ce tableau qui te ressemble?

"—Oh," he said dejectedly, returning to the table, "shit on Schweitzer, you know?"

"Yeah," said Mae, "goose old Ghandi, right?"

"Thank you for that, love—"

"Pollute the Queen!"

"Oh you utter treasure. But it's an age of decay, love. No standards, no awe of the sanctities. Polluting pollution gets to be a drag. Jaysus, even Greta Garbo. I could cry. Hey you, come here a minute!"

"Yeah, he's cute," said Mae under her breath.

I looked up to see him signaling down the bar to the young tough earlier mentioned—who, *entre nous*, was nowhere as young as he was tricked out to be. I had wondered if Gordie recognized him. The bar was practically empty, save for the detectives, a couple of stupefied truckers, and an old whore with bright red hair who had gone to sleep on her elbows. The "youth" stood down at the very end and appeared reluctant. He hunched up his shoulders and lowered and raised his head like a bird in a mating dance. But Gordie was insistent, and finally, after much peering and turning away, and more lowering and raising of the head, he slowly, belligerently swaggered over, FBI printed in big letters on his forehead. He was precisely the type they used on these assignments, crew-cut and all; you couldn't mistake him. I had to wonder what Gordie could see in such a specimen. I thought him notably unpleasant-looking, and that exaggerated masculine walk plain embarrassing. Well.

"I thought I'd invite you over before your damn eyes fell out of your head," said Gordie sprawled regally in his chair, one arm over the back, very Regency-rake.

"I wasn't lookin' this way, mister," drawls the "boy" in a southern accent so very phony, but so very par for the course it made my teeth ache.

"Well, you should have been. You been drinking my liquor all night. Don't you ever say thanks?"

"Thay-unks." I couldn't stand the fool.

"Come here and turn around then."

The "boy"—he was certainly thirty-five—advanced a couple of steps glaring.

"You hear me. *Turn.*"

"Obey the man," says Mae, "he can't do nothin' here. That or cough up the drinks, if you got a shred of *decency* in you."

Slowly the "boy"—more like forty, really—turned, arms akimbo, feet planted wide and manly. I could see the color starting up his neck. Rita was drawing profiles on a paper napkin.

Gordie poked and cupped the buttocks appraisingly. "Not bad," he muttered, as one absorbed in selecting a goose for an important dinner. He patted the hips and pinched the thighs. "Really not bad at all," he said to Mae. "Want to feel?"

Mae reached across the table and jabbed a forefinger at one of the buttocks. *"Hard,"* she said making a face.

"Of course it's hard," said Gordie defensively, "but there's *give*—"

"Me, I like 'em soft and sqwushy." Her disdain exasperated him.

"This is a *man* for chrissake!"

"Shoo, I got a girl friend makes him look like Shirley Temple. Anyway I just ain't got no taste in men no more."

"I loathe specialization," he said. "You used to like 'em well enough I heard—"

"Oh sure, honey, but I got so sick having to fuck *them* with my beautiful rubber dick, that one night I sat me down in tears, I tell you in *tears,* my poor old belly that sore with poundin' them damn hard asses, and I says to myself, now Mae, you just as well turn normal and fuck girls, beside which it's much more socially *acceptable*—"

"Love, the sweep of your thought is astounding. If ever woman was qualified to lead this nation to glory, you're she."

"Well, I'll think about it. I think a lot before I do things."

"It tells in every weighted syllable and deed.—Still, this is a very nice sort of ass, considering the hour and all. How much to a friend, love?"

Arms, neck, face, the "boy" was such a scarlet as I've never seen. He was staring straight ahead of him blinking his eyes in near hysteria.

"How much?"

"Fifty bucks, to a fray-und—"

"—Fifty bucks! Whatta you got up there, the Secret of the Pyramids or some outlandish thing? Listen, I don't want to come out *famous*—"

"Maybe," said Mae, "he got a talented tapeworm does a song and shimmy number whilst you come. You got to pay for those little extras *anywheres*—"

With a shriek Gordie threw himself into her arms. "President Moon!"—and they sat there rocking back and forth wildly ha-ha-ha-ing and tsch-tsch-tsch-ing, the tears streaming down their cheeks.

It was too much for the "boy." He had been hit below his FBI oath. Darting a quick glance at the bartender, who narrowed his eyes warningly, then a maniacal grimace at me who had witnessed his humiliation, he suddenly spun and caught Gordie by the neck— Mae yawped in surprise—and flung him on his back in the middle of the floor, diving after him spread-eagle and flailing with his fists.

Rita jumped up. "I'm going." To me: "You coming tonight?" I gave her the look she deserved, at which she shrugged and whispered something to Mae who, elbows on knees, was eagerly following the battle, and went.

Though like all small men far more assured on open ground where he could dodge and weave, Gordie was yet a fairly effective in-fighter; but by this time he was pretty well stoned, not to say outmatched—the "boy" was a hefty six-footer with fists like hams—and for a few seconds he took a murderous pounding. The detectives watched impassively; the newly awakened truckers with much elation and advice; the bartender nervously, going over to say some kithing to the detectives who only shrugged and went on watching. The old whore slept on. Mae grew more and more excited. Then at one point she called out—as in fact I had been about to—"Cotch his hands—don't let him get at his pockets!" Which the "boy" did, and they lay there a moment panting and immobilized, Gordie rolling his head from side to side to get his wind.

Mae hurried over. "You miserable little 'ristocrat," she said smiling grimly, hands on hips. Gordie stopped rolling his head to gaze up at her. She spat; he managed to return her a grin over bloody teeth: "Marcus D. Sade—*whoo, he he he!*" Again she spat.

"Nig-ger!" he screamed.

Quickly then she stood on one leg to remove a shoe and proceeded to grind the sole of her bare foot into his face. *"Now* say nigger—say nigger—say it —say nigger." She kept hopping off the other foot to throw all of her weight on his face. "Say it, say nigger now, I say—I want to *feel* you sayin' it—"

Well, he had it coming. But the "boy" was not at all happy to be pinning Gordie down for purposes of racial justice and started battering her leg with his head to get her off. Now that he had hold of Gordie's arms he seemed uncertain about letting them go. The white Protestant truckers were likewise incensed at the indignity, and called out some nasty comments, though not daring physical interference, Mae being a notable brawler in the neighborhood.

Finally I got up and went over. "That's enough, Mae. Let him breathe—"

She gave me a mean red-pig-eyed look. "Sure," she said, "I'll let him breathe," and she went down on her hands and knees and fell to beating him all over the face with her shoe. "—Remember my shoe, you robber, the one you cotched out the fuckin' window—best fuckin' shoe I ever had—remember that —?"

This was more than the "boy" could stomach, who suddenly reared back and slammed her in the temple, crashing her over on her side; but up she came, staggering weightily onto her feet, and the two, she and the "boy," of about equal heft, stood into each other trading point-blank blows that had the blood spraying and the walls sounding. The truckers were ecstatic.

Gordie too was on his feet, utterly dazed, rocking precariously, but as always, instinctively, rummaging for his knife. I slid behind him, and just as he flicked open the blade, I reached and took it away. I have mentioned the super-fine meshing of his physical responses, and here, battered nearly insensible as he was, was a first-rate demonstration. Gauging himself—as indeed I gauged him—incapable of wresting back the knife by force of strength, this fainting animal turned *on the instant,* swift as a hurt black cat, to sink his teeth into the thieving hand, at the same time tugging accurately at the blade-case. He could hardly see, mind you. Well, he was not to be counted out ever; I would not make the mistake again. My response was one of sheer muscle. Dropping the knife, I tore my hand from his teeth, and with all the might of a wide back-hand swing, I whacked him across the face, sending him reeling over the floor, past the grunting gladiators, to crash face-down at the feet of the detectives near the door. They gazed down at him smiling serenely. But at once he drew himself onto his hands and knees and swung his lowered head, I suppose to assure himself he still had one. I had hit him hard. He looked up, his mouth and forehead bleeding, one eye a brilliant red—*giggling*. He seemed not to know where he was, until he discovered the leg of the detective nearest him, and letting his head fall back on his shoulders he returned their smiling gaze.

"Hello, you two flaming pansies."

Their smiles vanished instantly, and one of them was unwise enough to reach over with the toe of his shoe and prod him in the shoulder, saying to run along now, they'd taken enough from him for one night; at which, and with the silliest sort of Charlie Chaplin shrug, he lunged—fell rather—against that near leg and bit, nearly collapsing with the effort. Well, that caused a furor, and in a twinkling he was caught up by the hair and the seat of the pants and pitched headlong through the door.

A few minutes later we were all having a nightcap at the bar, including Mae and the "boy" panting mortally but happily, and the old whore who had awakened and was advising me to go with her that night as she had destroyed kidneys and couldn't last another month, when the door opened part way and Gordie's head appeared. The wounded detective roared at him to beat it.

Gordie regarded him amiably. "You know, duck, I never bit a shaved leg before—"

The detective started over to him, and Gordie looked quickly at Mae: "See you, girl"; then at me: "Coming, Normal?"; and vanished.

I found him a few doors up the block propped against a storefront weak with giggling, a soft, incessant, lunatic giggling. Bored children afflict their parents so. I paused briefly, then walked on. He came padding after me breathlessly and stayed abreast by holding onto my shoulder. "—Lord, what a ogre it is—what a unsociable socialist. Listen, you're supposed to be *tailing* me, didn't no one tell you—?"

"I'm calling it a night," I snapped.

"—Chez Rita, is it?"

"She lives the other way, I think."

"Shoo, she lives any which way you tell her. Perfectly untalented in all of 'em too, but sweet. Don't hurt her, *hein*?"

For a moment I felt pique, confusion. "I said I was calling it a night." It was not what I meant at all.

"Which it is undoubtedly," he agreed, "or if it's a day, god help us sinners. No, it's a night sure, a lewd thick night, a time of *love*, Matto." He had stopped and was unscrewing the cap of his brandy flask. He took on a sort of dyingness in the eyes. "To the sonnet!"—and tilted his head to swallow. He handed the flask to me.

I said, "Why should anyone want to hurt her?" Why had I not said "I"! I was nettled beyond all reason. He watched, amused, as I vigorously wiped the mouth of the flask with a handkerchief. "Idiotic damn thing to say.—Why should *I*—?"

"Sanitary sort," he said, "but who would blame you? Never know where these lips have searched—"

I drank and returned the flask. "Like the bottom of Mae Moon's foot."

"Whoo yeah, but did you ever smell her mouth? Jaysus, she tried to kiss me once and nearly guv me a mortal thrombosis. Listen, I think she chews the cheese out of old condoms—"

My reaction was violent. As I plunged over to retch, he laughed and grabbed me around the middle to keep me from pitching on my face. Such a culmination to nights with him was by no means unique, though this camaraderie was. *It,* I began to fear, would be a mixed blessing. I leaned there gagging up curds until my stomach muscles knotted, while he resumed his insane giggling, occasionally breaking off for another swallow of brandy.

Finally I straightened up, and, as I stood with my weight on him gasping for air, he popped some kind of chalky stomach pill into my mouth. In disgust I motioned for the flask.

"*Regardons nous, mon cher,*" he laughed as I drank. "A couple of high society things from Minneapolis. A unique caste—Parisians of the hemisphere. We always try to vomit in the provinces, if we can. A few caned rustics are a nice touch too, *hein?*—maybe a string of ears to counteract suspicions of decadence. Warrior-race. Grandmother had Indians to tea. All we lack for the full picture is Axel, *pour une pointe de rouge, comme qui dirait—*"

I smiled tightly. "Benham, *autant dire,*" I murmured moving off.

I thought he stole me a shadowy look. "You didn't know him," was all he said.

We walked in silence through the silent streets.

"—Won't nothing ever happen, Matt?" It was almost a sigh.

I shrugged. I had begun to have doubts myself.

"Ain't seen *nothing*—?"

I didn't reply; he knew better than to ask. But in fact I had seen exactly that, nothing. A cityful of watchers and nothing to watch. Watchers watching watchers.

"Poor little man," he softly soliloquized, "won't never get home. Big bastard world. Weary little fuck." I suspect he started to cry—I wouldn't look—but he controlled himself. This time of night his moods were as vagrant as foxfires and about as substantial. "—Piss!" he took up cheerily. "Listen, love, let's chuck this vile civilization and open a cute Utopian settlement on the Riviera—"

"I understand they have a pretty fair one going."

"A *serious* one. A rainbow palace of kings and queens and perpetual princes. *No swinish people.* A polar sort of swan and peacock place. Divinely unreal, cruel, pure—oh my dream! A crowd of glories in a palace of flame—blue—a garden—a walled preserve, for all the beautiful and extravagant freaks of the earth—"

"And if some king or queen should chance to be plain?"

"Plain? *Plain?* My boy, you got some dangerous republican nits in them bouncing blond curls. Kings and queens are *au fond—naturalis,* Robespierre—smashingly gorgeous, with lesser divine attributes such as all kinds of cruel wit and cold wisdom and stolen oil paintings. And their greatest joy in life, aside from appearing over-dressed on balconies or impressing the royal seal into scented wax of various pretty colors—blue for the gas chamber, pink for beheading, yellow for burning, how enchantingly they laugh through the long afternoons!—is the cherishment and pamperment of the perpetual prince—"

"You."

"Adorable Matto—"

"But what in god's name should *I* be doing there?"

"*Fourieriste!*—That what you said—?"

"Being a commoner, I used the vulgar mother tongue."

"And so you ought. *Fourieriste!* The dark prince *always* has a golden hireling to stand near and listen in sunny raptures. How otherwise to draw out the sweet, deep nature of the cad? Consider the present moment. Besides, where all are royal, there must be one to mend the robes, bathe the whores, and execute socialists, you know?"

"I know. And that's your Utopia?"

"In large, though by that clouded face I suspect it's not really yours. What's your dream place, love?"

"Mine? Why, a world without you, I suppose. Any world."

He chuckled. "My idea exactly.—Matt, do I bother you?"

"Bother me? No—."

"I mean upset—*disturb* you? Please be frank."

"Not seriously. You appall and disgust me, but it doesn't go deep."

"You gladden my heart. It's why I feel so comfortable with you. Impervious to my charms—what a saint! And what a relief, my dear. Oh, I am hopelessly attached to you. I never had anyone I could talk to on so high a level—"

"I'll try to keep it in mind next time I'm going through a plate-glass window."

"I give you my word I hardly slept a wink that night! I looked *ghastly* the next morning—"

"—Or the next time I'm pulling my hand from your teeth—"

"You? Hey, give back my knife, you unbred crook!"

"I'll mail it to you, my hopelessly attached friend. The thought of you mourning me is too piercing—"

"Can the wit and *give it,* you hear?"

"Yes? Take it away from me, why don't you? A true prince would."

His eyes glittered drunken malice. "Aw, Matt, I've unwittingly offended you —"

"Why, you clown. That you offend me, or attempt to, is surely the least of my life's afflictions. I have no *personal* commitment here. I'm on a *job,* clown. You know that. One meets with all sorts of curiosities when one's on a job, though admittedly you're something of an outlying point in my experience. I'll grant I've never come this far or low before. I'll even grant I'm sometimes shocked. But never forget I'm a merchant where you're concerned. I deal in you. I coolly buy and sell you, and the likes of you. You're goods to me, and wouldn't I be the damn fool to respond in a personal way to *goods*? Wouldn't I now? Wouldn't I be just the ass you try to make me out to boil up at your fantasies and randy overtures? Wouldn't you laugh, as I laugh at you? Aren't you all ready to laugh at my first reaction? Admit it! Wouldn't I be the number one goddamn fool?"

He regarded me duskily, faintly perplexed, from the tail of an eye.

"—Clown like you. I tell you, I don't give a little damn. Offend me? You could not offend me short of presuming to treat me as an equal, *mon très petit seigneur*. But oh yes, you are an *offense,* god in heaven you're that. An offense to all one cherishes of this world, an offense to all one hopes and prays for, works for, fights for—decency and dignity, compassion—an inner beauty unknown to you—love, which asks no features, which pities, sanctifies, a little sweet and holy love of man for man—and for this—in the name of a shivering, bad-skinned world. In the largest sense I deplore you, despise you— I am offended. Oh yes—"

We had reached the corner of Division and Dearborn. I heard him say, after what I began foolishly to figure might be a soul-searching pause, "Thus spake the first homely goy, one supposes. Degenerates. Euch. I got a far more healthful love than holy—"

—I didn't stay to hear him out. I swung around the corner and started up Dearborn for my hotel.

"Matt!" he called laughingly. I walked faster. "Matt!—don't go sore. I'm a silly. Have a nightcap—old time's sake—Mat-tie—Ma-a-at-tie—" He was following at a distance yelling his fool head off. "Matt Matt Matt Matt." Windows crashed open, threats were hurled. He of course replied, but as the threateners were mostly eighty-year-old women the danger seemed negligible. Still, I had to feel I was being as nonsensical as he about it. It did seem the wrong hour of the night to be losing one's temper over ideologies, or whatever we *had* been talking about, for I all at once discovered I didn't clearly know. So I stopped. Any excuse, you see. It was becoming increasingly difficult for me to leave him.

Dearborn was an unnecessarily dark street then, with infrequent street lamps, a third of those unlit. And the night was unnecessarily lovely. A silken breeze wound off the lake, with all its unrest of water-smelling air, and I had seen the setting moon. Coming onto Division, I had paused an instant to watch it—I am a watcher even of moons—mantling and throbbing forth under the swift light clouds, like one turning and turning again—he silent at my back—and though I could not see it now it was a presence. It depressed me; I don't know how but it did. I was suddenly overwhelmingly depressed. Of course I had taken much brandy on an emptied-out stomach. It was past three. Working folk slept. I told myself it was that, I should be asleep, I was a working man too. Malaise of the idle. Only I wouldn't sleep. I now found I wanted desperately to get away. I don't know where to. Certainly not bed. I longed for people, a great plain sunny crowd maybe singing hymns, or assailing the mayor or the price of milk; a piece of silliness that made me smile, though I knew I was afraid. At least I knew I trembled. Yet I stood in place and calmly observed his approach. That is the worst part always, the approach. It seemed to take forever. He sang softly along the way, like a child on a country road, occasionally breaking off to exchange bits of conversation with himself, or peer at something in the gutter. I threw back my head and drank until the flask was nearly empty, hoping I suppose to drink in courage. My stomach took fire and my head a minute after. As I returned the flask, he was watching me very particularly, sadly, I thought, though his manner continued gay enough.

He drained off the remaining drops. With the utmost nonchalance he asked if I had seen who stood just around the bend. Of course I had. It was the FBI fool. I had spotted him behind us when we paused that moment before turning up Division. Most natural, I said coldly, it being his job.

Gordie chuckled as he screwed the cap back on the flask. "Zero for Matt. The Fed's *crazy* about me—"

"I noticed earlier," I hastily replied; thanked him; yawning, murmured I was bushed; said good night; and started to go. I even managed a sort of grin to tie up the evening with some neatness, or so I hoped.

But to my now frantic impatience he said he would walk with me! I assured him there was no need and he said he quite realized it and took my arm. Then in the most intimate and disgusting fashion he proceeded to enlarge on the creature's physical characteristics, which I found not only dull but insulting, fiercely insulting.

To say such to *me*. I rounded on him. I said I would not have him walking with me. I said his conversation was the last thing in the world I wanted to hear just then, or ever, ever. I said there was clearly nothing in common between us but contempt and animosity. I said many other things quickly and poorly. The brandy was in part to blame, so was fear. My voice kept cracking, which further bewildered me, until I stood there wagging my finger under his nose barking out disconnected syllables. I said I was not one of those queer cronies of his that enjoyed foul talk, what did he take me for, how did he dare, I hated it, loathed him, that even as a boy, that all my life, that god knew, that I had no, didn't, none—and I turned suddenly and fled. But though he was unsteady in walking it seemed he could run, for in less than half a block he caught me by the arm and swung me about near a street-light. Weaving and panting he held my arms and looked into my burning face, his discolored, swollen, blood-caked, half the filth of Kelly's floor stuck to it, the white of one eye fiery, yet all of beauty, all. Fantastic.

"Love, you're jealous. You lied to me."

Only that, a conventional stupid thing, a ploy, yet his saying it—guessing it—released, I don't know how, such a music in me, such a slow dark pulling music in me, that I was unable even to make the conventional denial for listening to it. It was so still, so grave. And though strange to me, until that moment so much more of me than my oldest intimate thought. If it had meant my life I could not have disturbed those sacred phrases. I can't recall it nor have I ever wanted to. But it saved me then. I no longer had to fear, don't you see. I had heard myself, I had *listened,* and when one has done that one is a person of sorts. A bad or good or bright or simple person, but a person. There is no place to run to because wherever one runs to one arrives, and again departs as that only person. And in fact I wanted to be no place save where I was.

When he found I did not try to get away, he released my arms and braced the top of his head against my chest face down. I heard little of what he said. "—Dear decent reputable friend, our own sweet virtuous Matt, oh don't—"

I thought perhaps he wept, which surprised me, for my tears, all moisture in me, had dried away. All heat too; my hysteria had lifted like a steam. I felt as cold and dry and hard as marble. I tell you, it was a remarkable tune, yet maybe as common as dust, as the philosopher's stone is said to be. I was formidable, dense.—But jealous? Then say a leopard clawing the heads off half a hundred sleeping baboons is healthily angry; say a freezing man, his consciousness shrunk to a point of light, and within that point a vision of the Judgement Day with God enthroned among Alps of sun-tipped angels and beautiful bored Satan just visible out of a hole, and between them, where they gigantically watch in that perfect weather, all the billions of the tiny risen dead, with one racing furiously among them, holding back the millennium to ask of each and every one if he has seen or heard of such and such a little ardent creature, dark, with close-set eyes and such a mouth, for that he has a heart to give him, and each and every faceless one replies, then give the heart to me, noble Matthew, the good fight is fought and all are equal here, and one is the same as another, it is the great law; and God nods approvingly; until at last the searcher turns and with a desperate trembling reverence towards the throne says, surely, Lord, whose law I ever loved, surely, *entre nous,* all but he? and God smiles guiltily. —Say that man wildly dreams. And say I was *jealous.*

"—Never never mesh yourself in web of Black Gordie, love—destroy you, suck you dry, then fling you in the filth—I know—"

But don't you see, the leopard is *mad,* babooned with reality—so many baboons, so much reality, one cannot in a night, or in a life—the freezing man escaped into a vision but *sane* at last, reality grasped—and I was, don't you see, both, both? Maddened with sanity and that's no paradox. It was something more than jealousy. Yet I must say that for the moment at least I felt marvelous, exalted even, equal to anything, even to the discovery that he had all along been laughing and not weeping as I supposed. It never fazed me.

"—Tragic, I tell you—listen, he's too utterly *swell* for you, kid—I mean, Back Street and all that—" and off he went into cascades of self-delighted giggles, screwing his head against my chest, helpless with it.

My response was simple and mechanical. I put my hand against his shoulder and tipped him backwards over a low iron railing onto a plot of grass. Mechanical I say. Understand I was not angry; was in fact nearly as gay as he, who squirmed about on his back like an ecstatic dog, whining and whuffing. He invited me down. I declined. Presently, when he appeared to have exhausted himself, and lay with his hands behind his head singing some tuneless lullaby— something of the sort he used to put his boy to sleep with, an endless nasal whine filled with shakes and runs. I quietly suggested he get up and go home while he was still able to walk. He rolled his eyes to stare at me as if surprised to find me there; then, in a wild surge of energy, began tearing and pulling at his shirt. When he had got it off he made it into a ball and wedged it under his head, stretching up his arms to me, wiggling his fingers. He said we would sleep there. I grabbed one of his hands and pulled him up on his feet, lifting him bodily over the railing.

"No. Now go home," and I gave him a little shove.

"Kiss me first," he lisped, and when I stepped back in alarm, soberly: "Okay. Good night." He took three wobbly steps and doubled over in laughter.

"Get your damn shirt," I said, still a little flustered but laughing too, "they'll never let you back in the Drake this way."

"Love of god," he said knuckling the tears from his eyes—"such gaieties, and us so blue"—laying a finger along the side of his nose in a fiercely thoughtful way—"the Drake—the *Drake*! Ha ha ha!— Oh don't mind me, love, I don't mind you—I swear, I'm *tragic*— ha—no. The Drake, *hein*? He sat heavily on the iron railing. "Sure and a perfectly adorable place it is, the Drake. Glad you brought it up. Fact is, I've decided to take it for a season. I mean, it's biggish, but the *location,* my dear. Its own *lake*—" Here he closed his eyes and made sucking motions with his mouth indicating he wanted a cigarette. I gingerly put one there. *"Light* it, you odious rustic."

"La, sir is so impatient—"

"Hm. Comes fully staffed, you understand, and such a staff, a *treasure*. Heart-warming, the way we get on. I mean, whenever, *if* ever, I come on indisposed, the way it looks I may have to do this very night—"

"Morning surely?"

"Oh cheerful enough, considering I ain't had no ass in days. But as I say, if I ever should, as I almost always do, the whole darling gang dives behind furniture so's not to notice! Ha ha ha. Adorable little gnomes. The *upshot* being, when dragon Aggie Dupres lodges one of her eight daily complaints against me, no one has the dimmest dream as to what she can possibly be farting about. That thing. Tips *dimes,* I'm told—"

"Dragon who?"

"Dragon Dupres, vile virgin hag of all Chicago, virtuouser than a grape in a bower, than a pea in a pod, than you, even, love. Shits cream-of-wheat, they tell me—big tourist draw every morning at nine—though they never tell me what she *eats.* Hah. May well have one of those rare inverted colons, you know, in case of which, for *heaven's sake.* I *mean.* Anyway she's powerful rich and sure don't love me. Started trying to get me out the minute she clapped eyes."

"Why, is she back?"

"—Whose close enemy is she? Back? Hard to say, of so universal a essence, where she is. She got her a nose for sin can snuff a soiled breach in Almash, while she's eyeing one's very own private keyhole here in town, and vice versa, though they do say the keyholes in Almash is very clogged these days, not to say the—"

"Does she know who you are?"

"Doesn't she though."

"And you are—?"

"Cyrus Dupres, says so in the register."

"No!" I roared.

"Yes, dear, yes. She goes into perfect frenzies over it too. I mean, she may be the *biggest* Dupres in town, but who is she to be the *only* Dupres. I mean, it's a *republic.* I tell you I never been so violated in my Rights of Man, never. Though I have my little ways, you know. I called the desk yesterday, and complained she was odorizing the corridors dismally with those bags of bloody old kotex outside her door, but was informed in a snippish tone that since she wouldn't return until tomorrow it seemed highly improbable, with which *I* said, improbably *high,* for the matter of that, Mr. Snot, and that they had been improbably festering there for utter improbable weeks, and if they were not put to death immediately I would poison her abortionist, I would. Indeed I said it. I mean, how sophisticated can one get, dear—?"

"Tomorrow meaning today, or tomorrow meaning tomorrow?"

"What obtains here? She got a lien on you too? Tomorrow, tomorrow, for chrissake!"

"And so good night, for tomorrow I work. Good night, good night."

"—How *can* you be so insensate, to leave me this way?"

"Oh, it isn't easy."

"Ain't even asking me up for coffee, to which I say yes?"

"No. Union wages, union hours, sweetheart. Thanks for the melody," I called over my shoulder.

"Drinks my brandy, picks my brains, and—. Light o' love! Union onion! Damn the unions!"

"Fascist filbert!"

"Populist pip! Progressive pea! Hah! You know what your flaming progress shakes down to in the end? Fewer people saying fewer people got bad skin, while more and more of 'em have it! It's a fucking *finochio*—!"

"I'm gettin' a poh-*leece*-man!" shrieked a cracked old voice overhead.

"Well, joy to you," I heard him say wearily, "but in the name of decency, control yourself—and while you're up and waiting, madonna, would you mind stepping down here and handing me that bit of a shirt? The unions has destroyed all life in me—"

I laughed all the way to the hotel, thinking how probably the old woman took one look and came running, and how they would sit on the iron railing until sun-up, discussing her grandchildren and his little lost boy. And all the way up to my lonely rooms I laughed, wondering at the power of music.

* * *

I am much relieved tonight. Bella's visit was less of a trial than I had feared. We made love very nicely considering my bandages and her initial hostility. Among other things, she came suspecting me of plans to desert her. Four months to heal a few scratches, she said. Everyone is beginning to wonder. I scoffed—who? Well, she said, your cousins for one, who are constantly at me with stories of your early strangeness and unpredictability. And you listen to them? I said. I am polite, she said. And so you think—. So I *wonder,* she said, that you can bear to remain so long among people you loathe, unless—. Oh unless, I said, unless what? Where would I desert *to* anymore? She regarded me with those proud long-suffering eyes, for which, though I utterly disclaim all guilt, can cover me with guilt nonetheless. I have been everything to her she had a right to expect—which I suppose is the crux of it. Which I suppose is less than nothing. I am a worm. I said, besides I love you. Do you? she said. I just said so, I said. So you did, she said, and so perhaps you feel, yet try to see my side of it. There are times when you do grow strange and out of things —. I laughed—you wouldn't have me otherwise I think. Gives you the chance to re-indoctrinate me—. She raised up her head. Dearest, she said, dearest beloved thrice-precious Matt, I would have you in any way, in any form you deigned to offer yourself—only do offer—never leave me—I won't survive it—.

Innocent though I am, I wept bitterly. I do love her in my way; at least I love no one living more. And I have been faithful. Yet for all one's innocence one is never quite *innocent*. She deserves more of me than I can give, than in fact she could conveniently use anymore whether or not she knows it, for I have shrunk her, in all innocence of heart.—No, she knows it. Being the victim, she is even less innocent than I. Then have I shrunk her or merely civilized her into shrewdness? Perhaps we arm as we oppress?—saintly oppressors, battening victims?—the civilizing process? It seems to me she is fairly content while I am never without some ache about her. Does she dare to take from me what I never offered? Should I fear her? Pleasures of tyranny. "Until one day the Tyrant glanced down and noticed chains et cetera." Meanwhile I gave all that (seemingly) her appetite can manage, and we ended the afternoon in one another's arms. Later we discussed the children. They are getting somewhat unruly in my absence though they seldom mention me now. But their fun is too feverish, Bella feels. They laugh and shout too much and are too impatient of unoccupied time. Well, they have their shifts even as we. She brought an envelope of snapshots and a funny sad note from my youngest, Noah—handed her secretly just as she was leaving to come here. He hopes I am happy and don't miss him! Oh the darling, the darling.—Some talk about the paper though not overmuch. It is an uneasy point between us these days. I have not forgiven her her handling of the Cuban missile business. She continues to blame Ben but he would not have dared without her express sympathy. She realizes this too and is in some perplexity over it. On the one hand she is violently pacifist, and on the other allows a huge spread to be made of Alsop's vile attack on Stevenson for putatively opposing Kennedy's all-out gamble. What purpose could it serve but to further whip a whipped man? She knew how I felt about Stevenson and always will, always. She, who worked like a demon through both campaigns, has nothing but scorn for him in defeat. Very female of her, though I hesitate to point it out. Enough. It gave me a bad week. The paper otherwise hums along with embarrassing smoothness in my absence, which perhaps irritates me. At least so fancies Bella, which *does* irritate me. Head bent to drive the pin through her great floppy leghorn, she remarked offhandedly that Jerrold said I had been writing—was it true? It was. That eternal diary? No. She drew on her gloves, a sight I dearly love to watch in a woman of quality—the absolute authority is hypnotic. What then, something for the paper? Your "features" have been missed—. A memoir, I said. She regarded me long and luminously, deftly pressing the leather between the fingers. Well come home to us soon, she said at last. You don't know how you are loved, my dear—loved and needed. Our people need a future, not of justice only but of a beauty in things, if that is the word—a sort of shadow to *hurt* us in our comfort, and keep us moving on. I think you see that shadow everywhere you look. Oh, Matt, we need you. You can't go back. We mustn't give in yet—. But I am going *forward,* I said—it is a curious memoir. Must be, she laughed huskily. We parted with subdued but deep affection. She left the house at once to avoid words with Dolly. Thinks the new place appalling.

—The *heat* tonight. I have moved the desk to the window where I can look out over the illuminated lawn with its classical groups and little ruined temple and snuff up the faint odor of imported English roses—thousands of them, ungainly bearlike masses, lilac-tinct, brown, dirty white, shaggy and queer as the fantastic teeming gardens they were bred in, and for all their bulk and number not able to match the odor of a single wild rose at dawn. Sad brown roses —sich a accomplishment! Some minutes ago Dolly and Jerrold came out on the terrace and now sit under my window off to the right. They drink lemonade. She is reading aloud, a custom carried over from our childhood, when she would read Herschel, Nurse, and me sound asleep. Jerrold wisely pretends to enjoy it—no, I believe he really does. He adores her. Should, too, with all the prestige the Lenart name has brought him here. But feature adoring Dolly. What a strange, still, mournful passion. Bourgeois passion, compact of many dispassionate small adjustments. Dolly and Jerrold, Bella and Matt. Ike and Mame, Dickie and Pat. Life encysted, unbursting. A weary world.—It must be Miss Mitford. I can't catch the words but she is generally reading Miss Mitford, another throwback to our youth. Does she realize it? Jerrold occasionally comments and now and then they laugh, presumably at some homely jest. Her voice is gentle, almost sweet. Yet not many weeks ago her photo was in papers across the country jeering maniacally at Stevenson during his Texas tour (though to her credit she now regrets it); and only two nights past she had to dinner the executive committee of the Association of American Doctors, in Fort Worth this week to protest Medicare, and this same gentle almost sweet voice was savage beyond belief, filling the corridors of her house with a clangorous wind of hate. It was frightening. I cowered upstairs with my head in my hands. Well, we made her this thinking woman, Father and I. We sharpened our thoughts on her, and thoughts beget thoughts. I tell you, education is a chancy thing. She could have been another woman entirely, *this* woman, quietly reading Miss Mitford, growing brown roses, dispensing an elegant Jewish wit and charm. For she does have charm and she can be quick. She is no fool: she is made simply. We drove her mad with our righteousness. Now she keeps me sane with her madness, good with her badness, and perhaps I have lately wished that she might, just a little, relent, so *I* might just a little, just for the space of a smoke, say. It can be a wearing thing to be always virtuous, always wise. Always on the long-face side of things. It is *tiresome* of Dolly to be so bad—utterly selfish. But let her look sharp. One of these days she must fall into some humanitarian trap or other, and before she can recover, quick as a flash I shall get off so fearful a curse on the race of men that her standing shall be forever impaired. Bella is wrong; I don't loathe Dolly. I don't. She is so much part of me. Her roses are another matter, however. Thornless and scentless. At least Dolly stinks. No, I can't abide them. I look and look and get more and more depressed. Steers. Oh for the sight of a lean mean wild pink rose to terrify the soul. When oh when shall AP flash the word that legions of the swamp rose are storming Sussex gardens? Won't I play *that* up! Page 5 for ye missile crises. Pages 1, 2, 3, and 4—HELEN TRIUMPHANT! TROY THE VICTOR! DWIGHT EISENHOWER ROSE WIPED OUT! HAMLET DENUDATA! STIRNER ADORATA! MESSIAH AT THE GATES OF ROME! HELEN TRIUMPHANT! TROY THE VICTOR! DWIGHT EISENHOWER ROSE WIPED OUT! HAMLET DENUDATA! STIRNER ADORATA! MESSIAH AT THE GATES OF ROME!—and readers, he's a *beauty*—jeweled head to toe, and never a pimple!— But oh—the trumpet vines swarm with swallow-tail moths the pale color of willow leaves. Luna—I've never seen so many together. Underwings too, yellow and crimson in shafts from the concealed flood lamps. Whirling mass of them where the gardener's boy has smeared the boles of shrubs with fermented fruit. I watched him at it this morning while waiting for Bella. Very pretty trick. In honeysuckle a party of sphinx attended by some small white creatures I don't recognize. Perfectly lovely. Hosts of angels sent to comfort me. In the midst of death, life. Now heat-lightning. Rose-gold throbs delicate and still as bloom down a long bluff of cloud. My wild rose, my wild rose!—So like that night. Uncanny. Even to the reading. I grow strange at moments, Bella says. Thinking of it, love.

* * *

Thinking how Satan read Sade to the damned one such weary night and angels came—. (Miss Mitford, M. Sade: M. Sade, Miss Mitford.) Lewd thick night. Night of love, Matto. Heat-lightning over the lake and occasional dank puffs as of coming rain that never did. Bughouse Square in firmamental glory more than usual. Sewer of sewers, hell of hells, thickly iridescent-eyed around its little mad moons. Crush of flesh in the oveny heat. Everyone out for air precisely where none was—all limp brown roses, little ruined temples and cheap new casts of old things heaping together, rolling out odors, gibbering dustily. Festive in a fashion.

NEW CAST: "Some bunch of psychos, eh? I'm from Toledo. John Smith's the name. Yours is—?"

"Tom Brown."

"Ha ha. Wife flew back yesterday. Sox fan, father of three—me I mean. Ha ha. So—?"

"No."

Polite and friendly.

LITTLE RUINED TEMPLE: "Pardon me, sir, which way to the lake?"

"Not down there, anyway."

"Oh excuse me"—crush of flesh—"I didn't mean—."

Even solicitous.

OLD THING: "Don't you never smile, Mattie?"

"Rarely, these days."

"Seen Rita?"

"No."

"—Need any tonight?"

"The galloping syph? Not desperate for it."

"You never got nothin' from me!"

"Including a half-respectable screw, eh?"

"Suvonabitch."

I early lost all count of such indignities and moved back to the fringes of the crowd. Papers, bottles, wiener ends. A mashed sparrow, a bloody tissue. A more contemplative mood.

SAD BROWN ROSE: "Falstaff is my favorite opera. I suppose I'm what the peasants call a snob. Does that offend you? Well, I couldn't care less, you understand. I mean if it does. Do you like opera?—Are you actually comfortable sitting up there?"

I, depression by now so heavy in me I cared as little as he about where or how I sat, was in fact perched on the back of a bench, midway of one of the four broad aisles that cut spokewise from the Square's corners to the center.

"—I usually go standing. No, not for *that*. Economics, frankly. I've run through two fortunes in my time. Do you dislike me?"

Midway, yet no more than a yard or two from the rearmost members of the crowd. There must have been three hundred people in the area—an extraordinary attendance. Most nights this bench commanded a view of the entire Square. At the head of the aisle Gordie would be surrounded by a couple of dozen "regulars," while three other speakers, working the other concrete clearings formed where the aisles met a central bed of scarlet canna, divided maybe twice that number among them.

"I certainly have as much right to sit here as *you*—!"

Now, I was able to manage a fitful glimpse of the fountain that rose out of the canna to the height of six or seven feet, but of Gordie himself not a hair, though his voice came through:

"—English travelers have found this idiosyncrasy in Batavia too."

His audience was not only the most numerous but far the most respectful. Whereas in other parts of the Square gusts of jeering or rebuttal jangled gleefully with the various orations, here rapt silence reigned, with only occasional embarrassed giggles or rumbles of token outrage, subsiding quickly of themselves or fiercely *shhh'd!* away. Nothing was allowed to obscure the pure song of Sade. Or the clear calm sight of *him,* where he stood cradling the little green book in one hand and gesturing interestingly with the other, pausing after some finely poisonous thought—"'I grant you pardon,' said Louis XV to Charolais, who to amuse himself had murdered a man, 'but equally do I here pardon whoever will murder you'"—to stare soulfully into the souls of his hearers. These were charged moments, for he was, as he damn well knew, looking marvelous.

"—I'll cry if I like, do you hear? *Hn hn hn hn.* Do you hear? I'll do anything I want to do, anything. You can't stop me, you flea. I may even gouge out my eyes. See this knife? Who would care? Would you? Look!—Or castrate myself!"

Some there are who turn all things to advantage, or in whom all things design to insult us, changing our blackest efforts to gold, even casual hurts to ornaments of a sort.—Casual? Well no. An empty word. If you hit a man, you kill him. That is certain. The degree of apparent "purpose" in an act is a matter of convenience or deception, the result without importance. The act within the act is all. Our truest genius lies in the variation form. We do maybe five things in a lifetime, over and over and over, but through convenience or deception, with our genius for variation, we appear to each other, even to ourselves, to be doing an infinite casual variety. How have I killed Gordie?—I cannot count the ways.

Or consider Hamlet. Hamlet is everyone's victim-theme. There is no play, no story, no characters, there is Hamlet only, already fulfilled within himself, pared down to the theme at curtain-rise, and he must seem to do, to improvise, to complicate till curtain-fall. The first sight of the audience must be as painful to his poised soul as the vulgar cues of the clattering puppets beside him on stage. He needs no cues, he knows it all. Yet he must do the stations, ring the changes, must seem to love who *is* love, to disapprove who is beyond caring. How like a life it is! The rest is silence? Lord, it has all been silence!—the purest sweetest silence ever falsified with senseless noise. Good night sweet prince?—Good day sweet *night.* Night returned to night. *Ich war, wo ich von je gewesen, wohin auf je ich geh: im weiten Reich der Weltennacht.*

—I say unmotivated acts—"theme" acts—are the purest, inconvenient, incomprehensible, undeceived. ("The boy sits in court unmoved, amused. He doesn't seem to realize what he has done. A moral idiot—") Acts of "passion" are pap for the audience; of "self interest," pap for the actor himself, since no interested self exists where acts begin. But casual acts—why, there never was a casual act. For the general truth of this, you need only observe in yourself, after some casual effort, the incommensurate bitterness with which you accept a casual defeat.

To get back, the case of Mr. Gordie namely. A finochio! No one ever looked so fine in cuts and bandages before. His appearance that night nearly wrung a cry of rage from me, and I hadn't spent a second thought—that I knew of—on the beating we gave him. How, I wondered, evilly nibbling my lip no doubt, had we managed to hit him in exactly the right places? So that a bandage might be cut and dyed and placed with the effect of a beauty patch? Or that a couple of purple eyes (of course the clot on the eyeball had dissolved entirely) should be exactly the tint and contour to set off the brilliance of the pupils and turn the lashes and unbroken line of brow jet velvet? Is it just, do you think? Is it a fair return for a casual slapping around? Could such a flagrant disproportion obtain within a properly regulated socialist community? Never! A finochio of the first flaming water!

"Did you hear me?—What's *wrong* with me? Tell me. Why did you hate me the minute you set eyes on me? Don't deny it!"

He had trimmed his beard away to a beautifully shaped stubble just covering the chin. His fine thick hair was long, brushed and burnished down into those languorous waves on top and dashing little ripplings and featherings down the sides and back. Moreover, he was scrubbed and oiled (a custom in the Abul household) and his clothes were immaculate, if informal—a sort of loose hip-length Russian tunic of some sheer white linen caught in at the waist by a three-inch belt with a spectacular silver and turquoise buckle, pants of a soft clinging brown stuff, and yellow boots to just below the knees, but such boots, a fortune in boots, slim, elegant, folding the leg in a web of delicate reticulation, almost as human skin.—Well none of that. At his neck the black scarf, in his ear a silver ring.

For about a quarter of an hour previous to my moving back, Gordie had been haggling price with the FBI "boy" (name of

Blaffie, I was later to learn, Blafford Fillyhausen IV, Harvard '34) who amid much protest had suddenly appeared in the thick of the crowd off to my right, Gordie glancing smugly at *me*. I shrugged. They were bargaining with the fingers of one hand, each finger from the thumb signifying a cumulative ten, the angle of depression giving approximate intermediate values. Asking had opened full-hand at fifty and by the time I edged away was down to half that. The reading meanwhile proceeded smoothly;—I even heard some comment on the unusual eloquence of Gordie's fingers. "—Almost Indian, my dear." Ah, the history of the dance.

"—I tried to be kind, thinking you looked unhappy. I did everything humanly possible to carry on a decently interesting conversation. I told intimate things about myself, things I've never breathed to another living soul with the exception of course of dear Father Few, yet you haven't seen fit to offer me the courtesy of a single word in reply—not your *name*. *Wart*. Very well, I curse you. *I curse you!* The curse of the Duchess will follow you to the grave—!

"No one spurns the Duchess—the Duchess *spurns*—like *this,* and *this*—!" Kicking and trampling imaginary plebeians.

Outraged shushings and remarks from the rear of the literary society. "Shut yo pansy moufs back theyah!"—"Respect the fucking speaker, you vampires!"—"Grow up!" (At which the Duchess swung and shrieked, "Why, I'm older than *you*!")

I jumped to the ground. God knows I had no thought to touch the lunatic. I wanted—I don't know what I wanted—to shift the brown crush of the place from my heart, to escape the ugliness, depravity—myself. But the Duchess was pleased to imagine otherwise:

"Don't dare—I'm a foundling—help!"

And then, amid really furious threats all around, a voice behind me, a cool, clear, mocking voice: "Ah, touch her not." A delicate restraining pressure on my arm of something hard. I looked down— an ivory fan, leading to long white-gloved fingers. "The Duchess may not be handled during the waning of the moon." Exhalation of Tabac Blond, a laughter of ice blue waters in my ear, and a vision— she seemed nothing less; at such a moment in such a place to have suddenly before you the most striking woman you have ever seen, a classic snow-and-roses Irish beauty, hair like the night, in streaming yellow silk that Edith Abul might have envied, as electric in every coiled insolent inch of her shining surface as Edith's son, was surely not "right"—a vision burned mood, moment, place down to a smoky rubble fathoms below. I was transported, literally. My heart nearly broke with the outrageousness of her—oh my fate, to find this *attractive*. I stared, I trembled. So did some others in the vicinity but not as I, not as I. I hoped, I prayed, I might not vomit. Who would understand?

She for her part was all composure in spite of her friend's distress. After vainly trying to calm him—her method consisted mostly in tapping the top of his head with her folded fan—while he sobbed away in inviolable content, drawing more and more eyes our way.

She turned impatiently on me. "Well, what was it, person?" The style was familiar; with more composed wits, putting together the few grudging hints of the past two weeks, I might have guessed who she was on the spot. She had been perfectly described by default. "What, had you the temerity to asperse Falstaff?"

"I love you," I said. It seemed to me a thing to say as quickly as possible in the circumstances.

Instantly the fan bespread the lower face to mask out her expression while her startled eyes—startling rather, violet, enormous, black-lashed and *violet* —transfixed me for the space of a most lacquered appraisal.

"—And Falstaff, fool?" Amusement flickered dimly beyond my human reach.

"If I must—"

"Rather that you *should,* and offer us at least a polished fool.—He loves Falstaff!" she cried, spinning back to the Duchess. "Preen, darling, preen!"

"*Hn hn,*" wept the Duchess, far too happy in his hopeless distraction to grab at such a lollipop. "—Thank god you've come *hn hn hn* oh thank god *hn hn* thank god *hn hn*—"

"Now hush, you plaguey old gentlewoman," murmured the lady; and tapping and prodding the heaving creature with the end of her fan, she drove him a little way back along the aisle and over to a bench out of earshot of the crowd, and less than gently thwacked him down. She sat herself with infinite grace beside him. Spellbound, I followed at a short distance, but was ignored. "Now—"

"I was, I was ready," blubbered the Duchess, quite as charmed to be sitting as standing.

The lady broke into laughter of a fine metallic ring. Silver in timbre but not in heart. So Nero laughed as his mother lay writhing.

"—A foundling! Ha ha ha—"

"—Save me, save me—"

"—I mean, who would be careless enough to *find* you, dear? Everyone one knows is at endless pains to *lose* you. The idea is too alarming—ha ha ha—" Chin tipped up, she fanned herself ecstatically.

"—The things he said—"

"—'Such a dear fragrant wicker basket, Pandora, I wonder what—ah, *je meurs!*—ha ha ha—!"

"—To the point where I—*lacrymosa dies illa*—I threatened to *castrate* myself if—"

Fan clapped shut and pressed meaningfully to his knee. "Dear, you must. Some dull Sunday.—I'll have a few people in. We'll do you in orange blossoms and toe-bells. I'll follow with a lute, in white linen. The bleeding will be negligible, if at all, and I stand you guarantee of a future fat credit far in excess of your present—ah—mignon capital. Oh, you must! The legends we'll spin—!"

The Duchess was beginning to get the drift. "It seems you find me droll—"

"Droll, my dear?" Fan plying in solemn sweeps to the breast. "'I tell you in all frankness, Miss Fairweather, you should not thus have smiled in the days of its glory. Terror and madness—flight! Oh cry her mercy, mem! This cold dead crater was a savage Vesuvius of pr-r-rick, bearing down vast North Avenue legions in its flood—'"

"Well, of course, you are such an abysmal bitch, one really can't take umbrage—"

"But think of the posthumous fame, darling! Why, what have you living? Tragedy upon tragedy. Dense meat-loaves and loose slipcovers. Tell me, then, have you once in this so precious life of yours, this luminous state of things, things you feel you may no way hope to amend, *once* been favored with a slipcover that does not de-scend on everything in sight like a collapsed parachute?"

"Oh you're low, low—"

"Or if not the fame then the fun. Think of that. God knows you're no fun now. I simply do not understand you anymore.

To me: *"Will* you go away, please?"

I: "I—"

"Stop loving me this instant! Who are you at all?—Now—now where is it, this man-thing I'm so weary of everyone's shrieking about? *Where is he,* Ottoline?"

Ottoline was back on his feet spurning plebeians. "No one insults the Duchess.—The *Duchess* insults—!"

"Oh," she sighed, lowering the great lids of her eyes and fanning indifferently, "scuhrew the peerage."

"Monster! Ruiner of lives!"

"Say to me what you will, I cannot despise you—"

"Sucker of souls!"

"—Nor near so nourishing as your Rome would make it seem, at least the filleted souls that come my way. I find them, in the present state of my acquaintance, the most efficient diet after brain-picking. One dwindles visibly. Indeed, one would quickly starve to death on you. *Vanish.* Ha ha ha. Why, I daresay your soul, like those twenty-nine bottles of champagne poured into Bernhardt's bath that drained out into thirty, may even mysteriously *enlarge* under subtraction. Like clever Rome itself, who somehow gathers up more than she ever leaves behind in her fecundating flood—"

"Blasphemy, blasphemy!" raged Ottoline, sensing rather than grasping it, advancing on her in hoarse foaming madness. "Mother Rome demands satisfaction!"

Daintily, she crossed her legs and deftly wreathed and spun herself in silk, exposing a bewitching little foot shod the yellow of her gown; lay a supple white-gloved arm along the back of the bench; tilted her head thoughtfully, in further emphasis of which she brought the end of her fan to the tip of her fierce dimpled chin, toed the air a little; said: "Satisfaction of me? No. The law no longer allows her these amusements. But *I* won't be cruel. Merely tell Mother for me that I shall stay and play with Father. Say he has got much larger balls—"

Ottoline roared like a demented bull. He flailed his fists, he chattered his teeth, he raved, he danced. A few strollers glanced aside with mild interest but passed on; it was a common entertainment of the place. Those that stopped expressly to study her I sent quickly along. All the while I was myself held off by her utter composure; she had not shifted the fraction of an inch in her lovely tableau, though Ottoline threatened every minute to wind up in her lap. But at last I started towards them. Her blandness destroyed his last reserves and he struck her. Not hard—on the shoulder—but a hit.

I heard it, and lunged, or started to, for to my astonishment, I saw that bewitching little foot swing up and kick very precisely at his knee cap, dropping him like a stone; then, while she bent forward and over him as though to discover what in the world could have happened, neatly obscuring his head with her skirts, I saw that little foot deliver him a very dainty deft kick to the temple, putting him out. "Fool, fool, fool," I thought I heard her croon as she paused a split second to ponder her work. I say I saw it all and she saw at once I had. She stood up and beckoned me to her with a straight sharp glance. A few strollers drew up a distance off to stare. An old couple took one look and spread newspapers on a bench across the aisle, then leisurely disposed themselves like people early for a concert. She was uneasy but full of scorn.

"Don't you see that my old friend has swooned?" she said. "Why do you stand columnular? Get a *policeman,* please. Immediately."

Well, I laughed. Maybe I didn't love her in the usual sense of that word, but I never wanted anyone so much in my life. She suffered my mirth as one suffers the misbehavior of a brute animal, in pained forbearance.

"As I had occasion to observe earlier, you stand in marked need of polish. Plainly you have been barbarized by 'the system,' yet it may not be irreparable. You do have a sort of workable surface. But such inner corruption! What can you find to amuse you in the distress of an aged and lonely man?"

I looked into those astonishing brimming eyes. *Brimming.* "I adore you," I whispered, while she prodded me back a decorous space with her fan. "You are the living flaming nightmare!"

"And you are a nightmare's ass. Who gave you leave to dream me?—But oh, for the love of god, fetch a *policeman,* sir. Here—here lies my last duchess —!" *"Il est un pays superbe!"* I breathed, and broke off trembling. *—Et ne pourrais-tu pas te mirer ... dans ta propre correspondance?* It had not occurred to me. I would not think it now. I laughed and turned to go, and turned again.—So *like.* I suddenly feared to lose sight of her. I wondered, should I carry her off that moment? "—You don't want to come? You'll be all right here?"

She beamed prettily through her tears. "As you may have noticed."

I fled on wings. The few onlookers had increased in number and were slowly pressing in. The last I saw of her, as I turned to cut across the grass to an adjacent aisle, she stood somberly plying her fan, lost in herself, apparently oblivious to the dazzled eyes about her though not, I think, to their potential for insolence, which she would requite as any god—a self-encircled Siva on a dwarf.—Or Gordie on a crate. Was she in fact already listening? Had his voice, unknown to her, I felt, come through on some treacherous dank gust?—Where is this man-thing, Ottoline?—I ran like the wind. I would outspeed all mere gusts. But the platitude is a damn fact: the police—and the Square was full of them—turn invisible with need. A chemical sensitivity, not altogether their fault.

I sped down aisle after aisle, I elbowed, pushed, threw and took a few punches, mounted benches, even the fork of a tree—not a one. But there were a dozen of them somewhere! I was frantic. From my vantage in the tree I was able to spot a patch of the still intact group attendant on my goddess, which calmed me a moment. The next I was coursing the outer pavement bordering the Square. Why there!—of course there. Where but there? I was a fool. Chattering gaily beside a Good Humor wagon, each with its cherry-vanilla bar, slivers of cold dark chocolate ravishing cleft pink Irish chins, lurked no fewer than five of the awesome brutes. Oh what *Din.* I ran up bravely. "There has been a murder, gentlemen.—Boy, fudgies for the house.—Gentlemen, gentlemen, finish your cherry-vanillas! The captain would not—"

Ottoline was gone, the spectators dispersed. My goddess had embarked. A little up the aisle, trailing a wake of foamy comment and turned eyes, I glimpsed her sailing slowly Gordie-wards on the arm of a tall silver-haired man —very erect, broad-shouldered, slim, in dinner clothes—Hudson Beckwith at a guess—and I could hear her laughter. Her face was raised to him and she of course talked. I mumbled something palliative to the law—I really forget what, some hurried nonsense which in the circumstances they were ready enough to accept, though they glowered and crossed their arms becomingly, and followed me with narrowed eyes as I crept humbly away, cherry-vanilla weevil that I was.

At the rear limit of the crowd the lady and her escort floundered. They steered back and forth across the aisle, in and out of "pockets," to no avail. Gordie was short, the crowd tall and feathery with craning heads, and physically impenetrable. Their plight was hopeless but she did not see it. The man would no sooner turn to mop his brow than she had scouted them a new position which proved no better than the last. He began to dart her looks. He seemed progressively out of temper and wanting to be gone, but she would stay. They conferred, or rather he did, while she stood silently by and waited him out. Then what?—how?, he at last demanded of her, his head punctuating his impatience, and after a second's further deliberation she led him to a darkened bench, handed him purse and fan, and, aided by his most scornful shoulder, elegantly climbed up.

She looked. My heart seemed to stop. After a long still moment she shook her head doubtfully. My heart seemed to start. She said something to her companion, who grubbed about in her purse and produced a pair of tiny mother-of-pearl opera glasses mounted *à lorgnette,* which he shot up. Then, while she raised the glasses to her eyes and carefully focused in, and he irritably and unselfconsciously spread her fan and began to work it in tiny beats against the side of his face, I vaulted a bench and moved swiftly across the grass to a tree—one of the close-planted maples behind the benches on either side of the aisles—a few yards to their rear. It was a thick, knotted bole, forking about eight feet from the ground; mounting from the side opposite them, in a miraculous silence, I was up in an instant, out of sight of the law but in partial sight and perfect hearing of them. A miracle indeed, you may sneer, but for the moment admit I had one coming after such a month. Keep in mind also that Irene Fairweather was none of your *tête-à-tête* mumblers; she was a *talker,* and her friend was a *talker,* and when they communed together, it was a sort of grand baroque divertimento. There was no trouble at all in hearing them; the trouble lay in remembering not to applaud between movements.

"—Well, I know him," she drew out at last, continuing to gaze through her glasses. "Think of that." "Blmph," said her friend (a very *distinct* b-l-m-ph), chin to chest, elbow up as he fanned the back of his neck.

"Positively. Haifa, '41. There cannot be *two* men in a century more ravishing than Abe Stern. Would you say?" "Blmph?" said her friend.

"No, it's certain. The eyes. The eyes are primordial. Unique. Beginning-of-the-world eyes. Formed to pierce thick gray mists—the way they say the world was then.—Was it?—Cycloptic. I thought, the first time I saw him, why, dear, damn your wild eyes. They won't *do.* And don't talk so much—"

"—You said that—?"

"I thought it." Glasses down. "Oh, critic." Glasses up. "Never—I thought —never be brighter than teacher or prettier than the chief. I tell you, he's the one! He was dying to work with Abe—"

Head up, fan poised. *"Who* was?"

"The small Fabergé hooligan on display up front. The object Cyd, Otto, *et toutes les autorités* have pronounced the great sight of the season. Ha ha—they'll *perish*—"

"Oh. *That's* why we're here." Head down, fan up.

Glasses down. "You know it is."

Head up. "I know only that I'm agonized beyond what a man of my means should have to endure. Where is the *air* in this place, I'll pay—"

"We'll have air later. We'll go by Agnes's and demand some. I have no doubt she runs the air here too—"

"She'll be along in a minute anyway. Oh good. She's much the richest thing around and I trust will have the nobility to suffer up. Indeed I'll make a point of it. I hope she wears the emerald choker. That's *very* warm—"

The lady glared down at him. "So that's what kept you. *Why* is she coming?"

"Why should she *not*?" snapped he, glaring up.

"—You are going into a temper," said she in some surprise.

"I am damn far along," said he simply.

This, or the tone of it, settled that. Glasses to eyes, she resumed her studies while he took again to the fan.

"—Flung himself at Abe in the most desperate and pitiful fashion, but Abe could not bear the sight of him.—My, he *is* pretty. I wonder at Abe.—Well, Abe was not wide—deep, but not wide. He loved only me, poor thing. And I as you know was wildly in love with him, and had a great opinion of his shrewdness besides, but even so, in such a famine of recruits as we had then, I was forced to see the child's points and challenge the judgment. But he would not discuss it.—Then he vanished.—He could have been barely twenty. Oh, my dear, you should have seen him at that time—."

"Seen who, what? You are a damn Coxy's rabble of pronouns. Simply breathless tale about a family named He who went one day to call on the Hims, unwisely as it turned out, though six or seven were twenty, and one was Abe. Who the wide hell is deep Abe anyway, to spurn a He? Or is Abe a He who spurned a Him? Or is he a Kabbible? Were you making wild love to Abe Kabbible?"

"Abraham Stern, *as you know*."

"Will you stop telling me what I know? You're the great knower of knowledge in the family, I'm the mere endurer of it. I endure heat, I endure knowledge, and whatever pleases providence and you to impress on my soft happy nature, I take, I endure. Now, who is this Abraham Stern? Tell me, that I may endure him with dignity."

"How strange you are tonight. You know he is dead."

"Is he? How distinguished of him. Splendid fellow. I suppose I may infer from this that he once lived."

"He once lived. Yes. And I once lived."

"Never mind about you. I have a full vivid character of you from my creditors. *Him,* then—."

"Let him go."

"When I so nearly have him? No you don't. Tell me—."

"He organized—he led. But I am positive you know—"

"My dear Irene—!"

"The Stern Gang."

"Ah. Ah."

"You do know him, of course. It is cruel of you."

"Know of him, you mean. Stern of the Gang. Yes.—Poor Bernadotte. I knew *him*—"

This last statement gave me a momentary start. Some years earlier the U.N. mediator, Count Folke Bernadotte, in Jerusalem to negotiate a settlement before the uneasy truce of the summer should end, had been shot down in the streets. It was most unfortunate, whatever one may have thought of the ambiguous Bernadotte's scheme that, among other subtly prejudiced adjustments, would have ceded to the Arabs a Negev already in our hands. Ben-Gurion was using the furor as an excuse, long sought-for, to clean out the terrorists for good and all, and most specially the Stern Gang, who bore the guilt in the public mind though there was no proof.—So he knew Bernadotte.

"—*That* Stern. Yes, it occurs to me I have endured him fully. Dead as you say."

"Butchered."

"So you have said. I remember now—"

"—Your brave British butchers, your fierce red Aryan stoats!"

"Not mine, though I perfectly agree. Red stoats—excellent—"

"—Screwed all their courage to shoot him three times in the back as he stood handcuffed, then kicked—*kicked!*—those unbathed phlegm-mouthed rat-toothed freaks of Avon—!"

"Splendid!—freaks of Avon—."

"—*Kicked* that radiant noble form, that splendor of the race, down four flights of stairs into the street, the packed, silent street, only Mrs. Svorai raging—. He fought for the honor of his people, and they never shed a tear to see him so, never raised a voice—not one sanctimonious voice, that could be so quick to curse a hungry dog on a fast-day.—Kicked him."

"Well, his troubled eyes are sand. 'Abraham Stern?—why he was mad.' It is the fate of zealots. I wonder that one should care enough to be one. Strange, to care so much. I wonder how it hap-pens. Anyway, you could not pick him out of a thousand now."

"Yet I seem to see those troubled eyes again. They hurt me—"

Her scrutiny of Gordie had been incessant. Head back, glasses up, she stood perfectly still, looking; and as she looked she talked. Her voice, which could rise with such exhilaration to trivia, was very low and calm, her points made with the barest, though most telling, emphasis. I gathered we had reached an adagio section and crouched a little forward, but in doing so lost sight of them and accidentally brought Gordie into view through the leaves. I held him there.

Back to him across the bed of canna, a lunatic waved his arms and howled at a milling jeering throng. From what I could hear, other audiences too had grown bored and unruly and were beginning to rag the speakers in voices only a little less oratorical than the speakers' own. Well, everyone present was a potential speaker. About midnight, speakers would be erupting like geysers all over the place. Only Gordie's literary society continued to maintain a certain decorum, yet even they were infected, talking to each other or commenting on the story with more than usual freedom. But he was reading poorly at the moment. Sentence after sentence came across garbled or broken-backed. Phrase after phrase was re-done, then done again until he got it right, or almost right, or right enough. It made you itch. The thrust, if it may be said of Sade, had weakened to a kind of issueless tickle. Gordie's vexation over it did not help.

Something was occupying him and it wasn't Sade. Nor was it Blafford Fillyhausen IV, with whom he continued the slow clandestine bidding, but mechanically now, without zest. He kept peering into the far reaches of the crowd. His eyes, as nearly as I could tell at such a distance, *were* troubled. He cleared his throat, he smoothed his hair, he shifted feet. And always, always he nervously studied the crowd. Once or twice I thought he looked straight towards my lady. I felt she probably stood too far back, in too darkened a space, for him to perfectly see her; whatever, he did not linger, as in my romantic way I half expected he would. But I had another reason for wanting to watch him just then. I found it interesting, during the ensuing bit of dialogue below me, to see him *here,* as he was *now*—to see what she saw as she spoke—to recall, or rather, for me, construct, for I had not known of the Palestine episode, or of any facet of him remotely corresponding to it, what he had once been. Why, I thought, did you care after all? I was both angry and very moved.

"—This raw-mouth hooligan fellow. He wanted at one time to join Stern's group, you say?"

"Yes."

"When was it?"

"—1941."

"Impossible.—1941?"

"Yes. Stern died in February '42. Mrs. Svorai raving and foaming like a prophetess: Brethren, brethren, they are killing Yair—!"

"As you have said—."

"—I was on my way to him and had nearly reached his street when I heard the shots. They later said he tried to escape. No. He was neither so foolish, nor, in the event, so wise. I saw the crowds and the British trucks. It was over. I knew by the silence, by Mrs. Svorai's terrible sobs. They were still upstairs—"

"Irene—"

"I was terrified. I would not see him dead. He was not mine dead, he was theirs, those silent staring Jews who never lifted a finger for him, who under the worst disgraces of the White Paper did what they could to hinder him, who, had he been taken alive, would have sighed piously at his hanging. He was theirs. It was as though they might turn and demand him of me, loving no one less, you understand, but he was theirs. That was my terror, that loveless doubledeath. Such as you and I die once, Jews like Stern twice. At the hands of the impious, on the tongues of the pious. I saw him and closed my eyes. All Palestine, all Jewry, was not worth such a lovely brave Jew. I think I have never cared to open my eyes again till now. I said some last things. Though he knew I loved him, he never knew, or I had never said, to what a degree I admired him. He made me finally understand, what he himself did not guess, that heroes don't serve countries, or causes, or even people, though they may seem to. They serve a little bright point in the universal brain. Few of us see it, but all know when it goes out. And if you find it a telling mark against them—this indifferent fire as against our warmth—well, you're right. They don't come to comfort us. They are not a lovable or cozy breed to live with—merely tremendous. I said an ancient Hebrew prayer he had taught me at my urging, for of course I knew, hated as he was, that it could not be long. I said the prayer, and gave him back—."

"You were ever generous—."

"My fragrant holy Yair—."

"I have endured him, my dear, I have *endured* him! I am wrung and branded with him to your heart's content! Who am I, after all, to fight the fine effect of an ancient Hebrew prayer—?"

"Jig around if you like. I speak the truth."

"Godsake, it's turning into a sibyl—an ancient Hebrew sibyl! 'I speak the truth!' Stand just that way till I fetch you the mouth of a cave—"

"You, *you,* are my cave, cold as rock, full of bitter mocking echoes—!"

"Well! I was dragged here through mortal heat to see a pretty hooligan, and I find myself overwhelmed with gnomics, Bible stories, murderous saints.—Yes he *was* murderous, fifty or sixty souls at least on his head—those silent staring Jews downstairs of his place were likely *all dead*—pulverized post offices, for some ancient Hebrew reason.—Berserk children shooting everybody's glass of tea off the table—and to top it all, a certain raving Mrs. Svorai who foams! How did they know when the damn *circus* came to town? And what about the hooligan? I *supposed* by what I had been told that we were out to titter at hooligans. Yet I ask you a simple damn question relevant to hooligans —this one anyway—and I get cantillation—Revelation—everything but hooligation! Enough of zealots and heroes for tonight, quite enough. Now I'll try one further time. Was he not attached to an American unit then?"

"He would have deserted at a sign from Abe. He said as much."

"Oh, a *vile* hooligan!"

"Not really. We were not at war. He was a clerk in Special Services, I believe—much too young for work of any consequence. In fact, if I recall the line Abe got on him, they had to manufacture chores to keep him busy, since he was there at all by dint of some government connection of the family. He enlisted with the express purpose of getting to Palestine. So he said. There was no civilian travel then of course—"

"Yet to leave us for a lot of smelly foreign Jews—"

"Oh, there's probably Jew in him, though not as much as he claimed."

"What did he claim?"

"A hundred eight percent, owing to his father's having been an unusually *large* Jew. He's amusing, or was then, though Abe didn't think so. Rather a dirty American mouth, as you hear—"

Gordie: "—Shodomy—oh triple-pimpled son of a pimpled triple-bitch!—*sodomy*—*sodomy*—sweet dog-fucking *sodomy*—!"

"—Impossible to the saintly."

"If not un-dreamed-of. But you think he's not all Jew?"

"I know it. He's not circumcised."

"How do you know that!"

"One of the Sternist girls. Abe slapped his thigh smugly. The rest of us sat thunderstruck. Uncircumcised in Haifa! She nearly passed out with disgust, she said."

"Ah, but didn't quite?"

"Heavens no. You should have seen the blessed rest of him. Indeed, you should see it now, though he appears somewhat *fallen* at the moment, like a floor-sample angel. He was always fighting then too. A sort of snot. Still, come up and look—"

"Not really interested, my dear, except—to pass time—in the story."

"I assure you he is *exquis*. You know my standards—"

"Oh, Irene, I'm past the age."

"*Hudson.*"

"Well, it's true. I tire easily. I'm here purely at your insistence, that you may be diverted. You have been so low lately. Are you diverted?"

"Wild with schemes, yet—"

"No, it's all I ask. For myself, I look forward to a cool drink, a Schubert modulation, bed, and you—"

"You make me feel so *glittery,* dear—"

"Well, well, so you are, too. But you are young still, in a manner of speaking. There are tastes and consolations for every age. Boys for you, you for me, me for Agnes—come to think of it, ecology *is* depressing in the higher reaches, if you don't find nature unassailable. I don't. Now what do I mean?—I mean, I find her *assailable*. Yes. And fatiguing. I'm fatigued."

"You mean, you are not unfatigued."

"Precisely, more or less. When Agnes comes—I do wonder what can be keeping the woman—we shall go home and be lambent."

"And you really don't care to see?"

"No, no, no. I leave him entirely to you. So Stern wouldn't have him, eh?"

"He would not. I think even you might have been moved by the child's passion —"

"Oh, very likely. I was less ascetic then."

"—To *help,* noble Socrates. He wanted so desperately to be of use. He begged for any work, the most dangerous or the most trivial, message-bearing to suicide missions—"

"Really? Strange."

"He wept, he threatened, he knelt and kissed the Palestinian soil—"

"All to be able to join the circus—"

"It was not a circus!"

"I am teasing, Xanthippe."

"You said it earlier. Don't again, please.—When Stern was immovable, he turned bright-boy and paraded out an absolutely numbing esoteric knowledge—"

"A prince of hooligans! What—?"

"Don't ask what. Some old Jewish mysticism, partly in Aramaic, if you please. Full of huge shadow and longing—not my dish at all. We were fighting a small, bloody war just then. I went back to twisting fuses. The others reacted much the same. A few smiled but most frowned. Stern laughed out loud—"

"Who were these 'others' you keep referring to—?

Glasses suspended in mid-air she glanced down at him. "Do I? I don't think I do. What were their names, do you mean? I don't know—."

"So Stern laughed. Well, who could blame him."

She returned to her viewing. "The boy was crestfallen, as though he had imagined this, of all qualifications, would clinch his case—"

"Silly hooligan. What should a perfect new world, such a paradise, in which Jews may one day rise to the level of their inferiors, need with longing—?"

"—What Stern said, in about fifty thousand words, boiling down to the fact that the boy was obviously unstable. Well, it may have been the fact, but it was not the point. The point was the family—"

"Stern knew the family?"

"He knew about them, at any rate."

"What did he know about them?'"

"That, I can't tell you. It was one of the many things he would not discuss. Like you, he never really trusted me."

"I protest—!"

"You lie. Never mind. I mistrust you right back. For close to thirty minutes you have been precisely questioning me on a subject you take no interest in, merely to pass the time, as you say."

"I did *not* say I take no interest."

"No, you did not. Yet you are here by chance, at my insistence."

"You can confirm it."

"Indeed I can. The very thing puzzling my head. It's why I mistrust you. Anyway, the family—."

"Yes, and as long as you feel you are being precisely questioned, precisely what was said about them?"

"I have reported in full. Nothing."

"Then how do you know?"

"I know. I also know Stern more than hated them, he feared them as he feared few things, and considered the boy's being there at all—the very exceptional qualities of him—a sort of outrageous effrontery, possibly a trick. But I swear I don't know details, though you won't believe it."

"It seems I may as well. What is their name then?"

"I don't know that—"

"The boy's name, damn it. You know *that*—?"

"No more than he or the others knew mine. Only Stern and his aide —Friedman-Yellin—knew identities. Among ourselves we went by underground tags. His was Dawveed, and he was insanely proud of it."

(My little man, my little man.)

"That, I don't believe—I mean, looking the way he does, that you did not trouble to learn the name for future reference."

"Heigh ho!—Why, how does he look?"

"I would guess well. Very well. Like you, in fact. At least, I never saw you stare at anything so long but your mirror—or my wallet."

"Lovely, lovely wallet. I could wish he resembled your wallet as nearly as he does my mirrored desire—though he is not in want. He stands there in a hundred dollars' worth of boots. The trouble is, they may be his only pair.—All right, all right, what is he reading? You might have spared me the humiliation of having to ask. If I have not commented tellingly by now, I obviously fear exposure."

"Something or other of de Sade in a perfectly rotten translation."

"Oh, *her*."

"Her, my dear? Are we about to go through one of those tiresome female things again? Is it to be Miss Lamp-post now, and Miss Policeman, and Miss Newberry Library, and—?"

"—Hudson, Hudson!"

"Ah, Queen Midas!"

"*Irene,*" said Hudson warningly, and turned to greet a very agitated Agnes Dupres. "Agnes, I am very put out with you. You said when I called—"

I had not fully appreciated the height of the woman. She was every inch the equal of Hudson Beckwith, which was rather over than under six feet, and she came on grandly, though plainly in distress. She had on a short lavender gown, ruched and draped into a frenzy, indeed the whole cut of which had been a favorite with my mother's maids when I was a boy, though no doubt the price of it would have covered them and their descendants to the twelfth generation. Her hair looked very curious, and she fingered her pearls somewhat wildly. As she drew near Hudson, she reached suddenly for his arm, like a noble tree that has weathered a storm, choosing to topple—now.

"—Oh, my dear—my dear—I got carried up by a revolution—a—*une Commune de Paris—parmi Socialistiki, Kommunistiki, Anarchistiki, toute la canaille parfumée—euch—*I shall be sentenced to the *cleaners!*—While a woman, my dear, a wild-eyed oyster-hater, shrieked and threatened my pearls, saying they were *unclean*—imagine, at eighty-five thousand plus change, what a lot of *dirt*—until I thought, I don't know what I thought—*tumbrils, tumbrils*—"

"Don't mix your nuts. What did you do?"

"What *should* I do? I swore to throw them out the instant I got home—"

"Clever Agnes! And she?"

"Why, she didn't believe me, of course. Would you? She said, with such a face, 'Lady, you're a liar'—!"

"Tush. Irene said the identical thing to me not five minutes ago."

"Indeed? Why would she call you a lady?"

"Liar, dear, liar."

"Ah. Well, they are not dissimilar, now that I think of it, except that the oyster-woman has finer hands, perhaps. Hudson, she actually grabbed for the pearls—!"

"My dear Agnes! What did you do then?"

"Well, in purest terror, or was it greed, I—I struck her—"

"And then?"

"I don't know, I don't know. She disappeared under my feet and I fled—"

"Right over her, heels first!" Hudson broke into laughter. "But what are you doing here unattended? Where is Paul?"

"Oh, I taxied—"

"Damn it, you know I was counting on a free ride home. Where shall we find a cab here? I suppose you grandly dismissed Paul for the night? Well, you are a thoughtless woman, a great breeder of the revolutionary instinct—"

Agnes was not amused. "Really, Hudson, really"—digging in her purse and extracting a mirror—"the loneliness of suffering—*ciel,* my hair looks like a fallen shrimp soufflé—"

"It pretty generally does."

"—No, it sometimes looks *au Grand Marnier*—or lemon, particularly lemon soufflé, is becoming to me—it falls with such a—say, these pearls do appear unclean, after all. The woman was right. Look here, my dear—now why don't you take my purse when I hand it to you—look here, I say—no, not the mirror, the purse, so I may *use* the mirror—should I dress my hair in my purse?—inspect the *pearls,* as I ask you—but where is Irene?"

Calmly, his jacket bulging with purses, Hudson swept the fan in an upward arc as he dutifully bent to the pearls.

"Irene! Descend at once! What are you doing up there—looking sublime? Where can you have been that sustained such a gown? What was said?—of note, I mean, and *not* by you. Anything? Nothing?"—But before Irene could respond, which there can be no doubt of her aching to do, Agnes had leaned her head over Hudson conspiratorially and was casting suspicious eyes upon the scene.

"My dear," said she somberly, "I do believe I own this place."

"Nonsense."

"No. I am convinced of it. All my properties look this way. I swear Mullan must have cornered the dump-market. Oh, it has the true cachet—"

"Even you cannot own a city park, Agnes."

"Now don't spew socialism at me.—What are you doing down there, dear?"

"Inspecting your damn pearls, as you commanded."

"Come up, come up. With Irene elevated on a bench, and you depressed on my bosom, I don't seem to have a face to talk to."

"Blanchéd, wind-stung face," sighed Irene on her height.

"Well, I am not used to being plucked in purlieus!—Why are we here, in fact? Is it the new place to be seen?"

"For hooligans," said Hudson. "We are here to see a hooligan."

"Well, I'm sure we'll have no trouble. Which sort am I to look at first, or must I look at them all together? Are they interesting?"

"You must ascend to Irene and borrow her glasses, and you shall see a sight, or so she says."

"I? Mount a bench? Are you mad?"

"Merely unobservant, dear," said Irene, "yet unless you make the effort, you shall miss the talk of the town."

"We live in different towns, I fear. Glissanda Hotchkiss has never said a word about it, nor has Carrie Phopps, that I recall—"

"Ah, the nymphs of Water-Tower-dom. What *do* they talk about, that was not totally destroyed in the Great Fire?"

"Money. Money and digestive troubles, both of which survived. And moral rot, which positively *blooms,* they say. I shall not mention where. But who talks of it then?"

"Your adored Cydneye, for one—"

"Cydneye? Strange that he never spoke of it to me—"

"Very strange. And Otto von Ofterdingen—"

"The Duke!" exclaimed Agnes. "I *saw* him on my way here, though he is scarcely recognizable anymore. You would not believe what poverty can work in a person. He's all over *blood*—"

"It seems an extreme case," said Hudson dubiously.

"My dears, we positively must do a little something for him. He was such an ornament—"

"Oh, Irene sends him money for drugs regularly—has for years."

"Has she! So that absolves us. Irene, it speaks better for your heart than your mouth ever does."

"And I, for one, would far rather your mouth was at me, than your heart. So where does it leave us—?"

"Badly tangled up in organs, it seems—."

"Gently, girls, gently," murmured Hudson, resorting to the fan.

"We are conversing," said Agnes. "Now, where is this royal sight?"

"Over there, at the head of the aisle," said Irene, "but you cannot see him unless you climb up—"

"That little bearded thing in the boots? One can see him perfectly well from where Hudson is standing," said Agnes, crowding Hudson aside. "Reach me down the glasses please."

Irene did so, folding her hands at her waist and staring fixedly at Hudson who stared as fixedly at Agnes, who blithely focused in.

"Agnes," said Hudson, "you are getting a very large behind."

"Mm," said Agnes, looking hard. Down came the glasses. "Well, I know him."

"You too!" cried Hudson. "It must be the most egregious hooligan of all time! Does it never stay home? What, were you out behind the kibbutz, bent double to the burning kisses of Chaim Weizmann?"

Agnes turned to look at him. "In the words of Ethel Einhoern, *wheum?*"

"Never mind. I don't want to hear about it. Not one damn word."

"He's wildly disinterested these days," whispered Irene resonantly.

"Is he?" said Agnes. "In what?"

"Ask him, ask him," urged Irene. "Don't let him off. He has been very gay with us both. Meanwhile, if you will favor me with *la glace*—thaynk yaow. I fear his villainy has aged me.—Why, no, it has not! I am lovelier than ever —ah, *tu, tu*—"

"—You've been nothing but trouble from the moment you arrived," gloomed Hudson.

"*I* have?" said Agnes mystified.

"Yes, you. Revolution, treachery—I never knew such a disposition to mischief."

"But what has happened—?"

"You're in league together, that's it! You met beforehand to plot a little trap for me—"

"I? Plot little traps with Irene? Oh, Hudson, I'm past the age—"

"Ha ha ha!" Irene's linked silver laughter froze the blood as she maneuvered the mirror from side to side of her face. "Search your own heart for the subtleties of *that*." She was watching me.

"Subtleties—!" cried Agnes.

"You are a perfect mist of them," said Irene. Our eyes met in the glass.

"Agnes," said Hudson, "there is something so anarchic about you, that I tremble in your presence. If you are not a sly clever woman, then you are simply a very dangerous one, and must be controlled."

"Well, I've heard enough," said Agnes with enormous displeasure. "Subtleties, indeed. When I have occasion to be subtle you will know about it —"

Irene lowered the mirror and shrieked, and Hudson shook his head darkly.

"That's the most menacing thing I ever heard in my life—"

I considered what I should do, and decided to do nothing, until Irene spoke. If she spoke. It occurred to me that with her vain temperament she might not say a word to the others, taking her satisfaction in my awareness of the detection. It had happened to me before. The personal vanity of the quarry can be a most useful tool if the agent has the nerves to give it head. I was by no means frantic; the risk of discovery was pretty exactly balanced by rewards already garnered, and even after the fact should not have proved irremediable, had it not of course been for Agnes Dupres turning up with my name and identity. This posed its problems. Still, should Irene say nothing, I was perfectly undetected, for not only was she ignorant of my credentials, I was convinced that, deep in leaves as I lay, she had not seen enough to connect me with the masher of the Duchess incident;—a shoe perhaps, and my eyes. If she decided to expose me, I had a sort of a plan.

"—All I can remember saying is, I know that person reading

there, and I do. He stays at my hotel. Now what is mischievous in that, aside, perhaps, from the subject himself—?"

"He stays at the Drake?" said Hudson shaking off his pique.

"I have said so."

"Ah, sibyl senior. Mischievous—?

"A disgrace. I have threatened to leave, but they *adore* him—"

"They? The other residents?"

"The other residents are with me. The management and staff, my dear. He literally throws his money around."

"He has much money then?"

"Much, they say, though not so much money as magnetism, perhaps. He attracts people. I can't see why, but the fact of the matter is, he makes no effort to attract *me*. But others, the lower domestics especially, are his total slaves. Night to morning, morning to night, there is a constant flow of chambermaids and porters into his suite, generously doing, I am compelled to think, what no longer needs doing."

"I have the scene. Who is he? What is his *name*?"

"Well, I don't know."

"Aggie Millbank, I'll tell your mother—!"

"He goes by a *tag*, a most insulting *tag*, which you must spare me repeating. What shall I say then? I tell you quite simply I do not know his name, though I suspect you won't believe it—"

"Woman, truthfully, were you perched in that tree fifteen minutes ago?"

"Probably not," interposed Irene, who had been listening with interest, "but you may be amused to learn that something else was. And *is*." Bitch.

"—I wondered about that!" said Hudson lightly and coolly, swinging his head around. "But you have such queer friends, with such queer habits, I hesitated to ask for fear of an indiscretion. It is a delicate thing, to ask about a friend in a tree. So it is not with you after all?"

Pure muck. This was the first he knew of it. As he spoke, his eyes flew without direction over the foliage before finding me out. When he at last did, it was as though he looked leisurely, directly to the spot. Gordie had a similar mechanism of response. ("—They are gorgeously trained—same old Arab that turned me out probably.")

To my plan, which was hardly a plan at all. Merely I would not come down, and they, not wanting to cause undue commotion, would eventually go away. I figured—hopefully—that at least one among them would shy at making too much of the thing. I edged back around the trunk and hoisted myself onto the branch above. As I climbed out of sight, I glimpsed them hurrying back with craning heads.

"The idea! Come down here at once, whoever you are!"—Agnes.

"No," I said in a low toneless voice.

"It is Glissanda Hotchkiss!"—Irene.

"Ha ha ha.—Oh, Irene, you are dreadful.—Glissanda—ha ha ha—what should poor Glissanda be doing—?"

"She's lost the Water Tower again!"

"Ha ha ha—well, well, I have heard it said that she was a climber in her day—"

"Ha ha ha—angel!"

"—Goddess—ha ha!"

"Will the Cherry girls shut their mouths? "Young man,"—by my voice—"do please come down—"

"I won't."

"—Are you unhappy?"

For reply I climbed to a higher branch.

"—Perhaps he is not aware that we have had evolution—"

"—Perhaps he is poverty-stricken, like Duke von Ofterdingen. It can lead to unhappiness. Irene, offer him money—"

"—Something up there, mister—?"

"—A poverty-stricken youth—"

"—Jennie!"

"—Young man, do—"

—Kid up there gonna jump—"

"—No! Wait, I'll get Ralphie—"

"—And I'll get a cop. Meet you here—"

"—Cat up the tree, lady—?"

"—A blood-covered youth about to leap, they say—"

"—No! Roberta—!"

So much for that plan. One could not count on these people. I climbed down quickly. At the base of the tree, I lingered a moment brushing bark-splinters from my clothes, a dozen pairs of eyes upon me. To make a run for it was out of the question. If Agnes should recognize me, I was without chance of redress; it was a clear case of eavesdropping. To go to them boldly as I was now doing seemed scarcely better, until a glimpse of Irene's startled and, I thought, worried face gave me my next move, though with chastened confidence in my genius. I decided that she would not want the scene with the Duchess-Duke aired, and that I might consequently stretch my tenancy in the tree to a time before their arrival. Simple and unassailable, depending of course on her. *They* had intruded on *me,* there for a view of my friend;—the claim of friendship, and the ensuing business about the name, was I felt a necessary sacrifice. It would immediately burn away any quibbling. I would settle with Irene later and in fact did not at all regret the prospect of a little collusion between us.

As it turned out, Agnes Dupres did not recognize me until I had climbed the bench and stood before her with my hand outstretched. I could have *walked* away. Well.

"—Mr. Lenart!" she cried, taking my hand warmly. "Ha ha ha. Why, you are refreshing, dear. The last time we met was in Ethel's powder room—."

"Agnes—" cautioned Hudson.

"It's true! He came in walking an enormous cheese, which Ethel accused of *effluviating,* causing Cydneye, who was also there, to say something rude—"

Perhaps it was not a powder room—?"

"It was a powder room, and a very *small* powder room. Ha ha ha. Now he comes out of a tree. No wonder one can never get him on the phone—"

"I didn't know you had tried," I said. I had left my name and number at the Drake desk.

Without further exchange, she turned and introduced me to her friends. Hudson, who on hearing of my Minneapolis origin at once connected the name with the *Dispatch,* regarded me with great interest, Irene with a sort of measuring, sullen amusement, especially during the course of my little fabrication which, I must say, I brought off with just the careless tone proper to an unlikely situation. She heard me out silently. I could have kissed her—in any event.

"—So you know the man?" Hudson asked when I had finished.

"—Will all of you please go away?" he cried to the remnants of the group that had gathered to see me split my head on the asphalt. "We shall have nothing to say here at all up to the Marquis de Sade. If something promising does get going, I'll call you."—They grumbled but trailed off; he was a big rangy man, and for all his elegance, threatened power.

"The Marquis de Sade?" said Agnes. "Is that what he's reading? In *Chicago?*"

"He is," said Hudson, staring the last and most stubborn of the merrymakers out of earshot. "Now," he said, returning to me, "in god's name, *who is he?*"

"Why," said I, unable to find any really workable dodge, "he is—chairman of the board."

"What board?" scoffed Agnes.

"Never mind what board," murmured Irene, breaking her unaccustomed silence, "where are *they* staying?"

As, playing for time, I laughed rather immoderately at this, I felt Hudson's eyes on me. He was, I should say here, a practically perfect specimen of a WASP, his one defect being the sense of physical power already noted. In fact, except for this defect I must confess he bore a marked body likeness to that WASP of WASPs, Benham Lake—from the back it was positively alarming—even to an outrageous elegance of gesture, in the manipulation of the fan for instance, that asked either the greatest virility or the greatest decadence to bring off in public. In Hudson Beckwith, at least, it spoke virility. A fine golden man. Though his mane of hair was white, one had no trouble seeing in it the light brown of youth; his skin had the prescribed boating look, weathered and very tanned; even the pupils of his eyes were a strange clear amber (I was later surprised to find them *blue* in the otherwise accurate Gestapo report). His big horsey features, while of a rough neighborliness with Agnes Dupres'—the large teeth, prominent nose, and chin fixed on a long narrow face, the "high English" flap of skin draped at the outer eye-corners—were yet, as was the case with Benham, of so different a quality, that what made her a plain (if distinguished) woman make him a strikingly handsome man, one of the few I ever saw fit to accompany his lovely lady. And fit not in looks only, in sheer cleverness.

"Very well then," Hudson said, "I'll tell *you* who he is. That is certainly poor Edith Abul's boy."

This produced a short but distinct pause, which Agnes was the first to breach.

"What, the one who is dead?"

"My dear girl—"

"Oh, you know what I mean. He seems to be a very unsteady fact in my head—if it *is* he. How do you know it is?"

"His photo was in the papers for days last month. It strikes me strange that I should be the only one it has occurred to—pretty damn strange." He glanced sharply at me. "Am I right? Is it?"

I nodded. "You make things even warmer than they are. May I borrow the fan?" I did not add that I considered the photos so unlike as to make the discovery unusually astute; or that he had managed it at such a distance and without once resorting to the opera glasses.—I nodded again.

He slid the fan from his cummerbund and passed it to me. "—So, Irene, you may now understand why you were being precisely questioned. I wanted confirmation of my guess—."

"And why you pretended not to see him at all. It is perfectly neat and clear," she said still sullen. "But did I confirm what wanted confirming?"—barbed in a way I didn't catch.

"You know you did not. I was after the name and you retched me up tags and rhetoric—"

"Well, it is a great mystery," sighed Agnes out of profound thought.

"Now, no hysterics, my dear—"

"But it is. I mean, if this is Mr. Abul, who is the man they found?"

"They have not yet recovered the bodies," I ventured.

"Why," said Hudson in some surprise, "I thought they had, and buried them, side by side. Someone told me—"

"No," I said, "no."

"You are positive?"

"—No," I said, "not positive. But how could they—?"

"—Then it would seem he means to be *thought* dead," proceeded Agnes in a sort of self-communion, "yet no one makes a bigger spectacle of himself. He is offensive to the entire neighborhood. Indeed, by what I have seen and heard of him, I am surprised he has not been clapped behind bars for a dangerous lunatic. No, it is very odd. Even Cydneye has confided some suspicions on the head, and you know how unobservant *he* is—"

"To you?" said Hudson. "But you specifically told Irene he did *not* mention —."

"Did I? Well, I am forgetful. Besides, I never connected it with the terror of the Drake. But what of the police? Why have they not identified him?"

"As you say, it is a mystery," said Hudson. "Yet it is not without its boons. It gives us something to talk about that does not need patching up with new and ingenious phrases. Even you, Agnes, spoke a whole paragraph of straight stark thinking, under the impact. As for Irene, I tremble for her sanity. Already she is speechless with subject-matter. And it also raises the possibility that if the son is alive, perhaps the mother—?" He looked inquiringly at me.

I shrugged. "How would I *know*?"

"Well, you plainly know more than you are free to say, so we won't press you —now." He and Irene had not been unnoticing of my fascination with the ivory fan, nor did I mean they should be. It was indisputably the fan Edith had shown me, among other of her New York purchases, the night of her death. Oh they were a catch indeed. "—But Agnes will bring you one night soon, and we shall all three pounce and suck your blood—"

"Hudson!" said Agnes, shocked.

"It is a *metaphor*," said Hudson.

"Well, I should hope so. The young man does not know us well, and may take fright. You forget what large teeth we have—"

"Well, *mine* are just the size," said Irene, extending her hand for the fan.

"A very pretty fan," said I returning it. I tried to engage her in a smile.

"Yes," she said, staring me sober, "Mrs. Dupres has both the money and the idleness for antiques."

Agnes eyed it complacently. "Perfect condition, too. And very valuable, I might add. It is supposedly the work of Boucher, for La Pompadour—at least the garlands are said to be by his hand. I hesitated giving it to you, but then the bishop said I should. It would be good for my soul."

"And what did the bishop say would be good for the bishop? A gold ingot from the True Cross?"

"Irene, you know I do not like your irreligion—."

"Nor I your a-religion. I will not owe your sweetness to a bishop, Agnes. I have too much respect for you. I much prefer owing it to the Income Tax Bureau, who will allow you a fat deduction under the apprehension that I am curator of the Hudson Beckwith Museum—"

"What!" gasped Hudson.

"So Cydneye told me," said Irene glowering. "Agnes has declared you a museum for the next tax period."

"Ha ha. It is a joke," said Agnes somewhat lamely. "Anyway, you *are* a sort of museum, with all those paintings—"

"Really, Agnes, they'll *get* you one of these years! Ha ha ha!"

But Irene was relentless. "I am not easily fooled, or silenced."

"—Ah. I can vouch for the last," said Hudson, still chuckling.

"—And I," said Agnes. "But do you really think Edith may—? Oh, I should be so happy! The charm of her. Such a sweet and gentle lady—"

Irene gave her a frightful smirk. *"Dead, bloated."*

"Oh, you are a horror—"

"—Speaking of which," said Irene to Hudson, "I saw Otto for a moment earlier this evening, while you were making your call."

"The Duke!" exclaimed Agnes.

"Damn it, must you always shriek that?" cried Hudson. "I jump ten feet in the air—"

"He too has guessed the identity of young Abul."

"Well, that leaves the police," said Agnes.

"—Yet you would not tell me?" said Hudson.

"It was merely an idle guess. You know what a prattler he is. Besides, by your tone I suspected you already had your answer. I will not be used in a game, any game. I was not bred to it, as Agnes and you, or Mr. Lenart here. There is no real fun in me. I could never laugh at Mrs. Svorai, for example, unless I meant to run her through—I could never laugh and move on. She deserves better, or worse, than that. Nor could I laugh at Otto's troubles as some do. I suppose I don't know how to play unless I let a little blood. There is a kind of respect in blood. One has played to the hilt, at least. Well, my world is a darker place than yours, if hardly more interesting these days—"

Agnes was indignant. "I laugh at Duke von Ofterdingen!"

"But of course you do, as you would laugh at me if I once relaxed. Why, what should you do if not laugh? *Feel?*—But you are right about his condition. He's in a dreadful way. Collapsed at my feet." She looked me straight in the eyes, and for the first time favored me with something like a smile. I was utterly fascinated.

"It is because he bleeds so much—loss of blood from poverty! The disease of kings! Oh, poor Otto—"

"Agnes," said Hudson, regarding Irene pensively, "with that single sequence you have reached a crisis in human rationality. Congratulations—"

—Why, thought I, it is not that you are less vain than I had counted on, but even vainer. That was why you discovered me to the others. You are *bored*. You must double all odds—

But then she dizzily tripled them and came to grief. "—Hit his head on a rock and went out, like that"—giving a quick tap of the fan on the back of her hand—"there was some blood and I grew frightened. But suddenly, after I had sent for help, he sprang to his feet and ran off without a word. I think he must be *krank*—"

"Poor Otto! Oh my dear, my dear," keened Agnes, peering tragically up and down the aisle. "A rock, you say—" Her quickness was always unexpected.

"The most interesting things happen to you when I'm not around," said Hudson. "If I recall, you accidentally ran into Djuna Berry not so long ago, who also collapsed—"

"Well, they are friends," said Irene blithely.

"Who is Djuna Berry, that also collapsed?" said Agnes.

"—In the aisle, was it?" said Hudson.

"Of course the aisle. Should I be tramping through the grass in this costume?"

"It makes no difference. This is all filled-in land, as any Chicagoan can tell you. You are rusty, Baronne. I won't ask to be shown the rock, as you realize and count on. It would be too vulgar of me—not of you, who would ask at once, but of me, who may not. You love to taunt us with breeding yet you have made a damn career taking advantage of it. Very well I don't ask to see the rock, I ask only to see *a* rock, any rock, in the whole filled-in park—"

"—The very thing that occurred to me!" said Agnes, "though of course I always hesitate to—"

"When have you ever hesitated? *When*?" said Irene, and glanced ferociously at *me*. Hudson caught it. His head swung instantly, and he searched my face with so benign an aspect that for an instant I fancied he must have other matters on his mind entirely. Not quite.

"—Why, were you there?" It was more statement than question.

I laughed, and opened my eyes wide, and gave him back benignity to spare. "I could not possibly have been if I was in the tree." Well, she would not have pulled *me* out.

He nodded understandingly. "No, you could not have been, of course."

"It was not her fault," I began rather impertinently, as I saw too late.

"We have not *asked* you," he snapped, but quickly controlled himself. "It never is." He stole her a sad, penetrating look. "—So, ladies, home. Here come the People. After the cares of the day, we must have music. What shall it be tonight, Agnes?"

"The three Elizabeths, of Coates—"

"You are mad. Mr. Lenart, it has been a pleasure to meet you. I have admired your father for many years. A good and useful man. Mrs. Dupres must bring you to us soon. We seldom entertain anymore, but we may shake ourselves for you. Do you like music? Never mind, you shall dine well, at any rate. Good night, sir.—Irene?"

The disdainful woman had snatched her glasses from Agnes' hand and was mounting a bench.

"Irene, we'll never get out, damn it—!"

The aisle was in ferment. Gordie was winding up for the night and the crowd, sensing it, had begun to break into little noisy cells swelling slowly back down the aisle. Several sportive individuals had jumped on benches or climbed lampposts to harangue the departures along the way, and the police, newly arrived from the ice-cream wagons to ease the crush, were pulling them down one after the other. This led to a few scuffles, the scuffles to a reforming of groups, some of them hostile, and it was altogether not the place for a beautiful woman in long yellow silk to be flaunting herself. I sprang up behind her.

"You had better go," I said, bending my face to her hair.

She neither replied nor moved away. The glasses were to her eyes and the hand that held them trembled with excitement, exciting me. Her shoulders—purest pearl, all but imporous, glistening.

"Irene—!" Hudson and Agnes had been carried several yards down the aisle in a rush of hilarious hoodlums pursued by police, and were battling their way back to us—quite effectively, I might add, though the going was cumbersome.

"—Or come with me," I whispered, "come with me—"

"Do you know him well?" she asked, beginning to train the glasses from Gordie to the area fronting him, and back again.

"—Yes. Well."

"Is his trouble very great?"

"I think very."

Training the glasses along the aisle: "He begs with such a pride. Can he be —helped?"

"By you? I wonder—"

"Do you help him?"

"I am hot to help *you*—!"

She chuckled derisively. "As you so hotly helped me a moment ago? Your *betrayals* must be fabulous—"

"He had already guessed. I don't deal in lost causes." (—Oh, the dear dead days!)

"Then fly from me, sir. I have a fatal attraction for them. Indeed, I think they keep me young, like one who never finds true love—"

"—May I try to *age* you somewhat?"

"Ha ha ha. Well, one night perhaps. Yes. I like the terrible sickness in your eyes. I have thought more than once tonight that I would not want you for an enemy. Will you have much to tell me of your friend?"

"More maybe than you bargain for. I can be hugely communicative in the right company—."

"Hugely?"

Ah. "They say so. Fantastic, gushing tales—one drowning another—."

"Mercy."

"—But like Scheherezade, never the thing you want to know.—I warn you now—for you may lose interest, and then my head would fall—"

"At dawn, as most heads do. Yet not yours, if I felt there was another tale in you. I can be a hugely capacious bowl to the right gusher—was that your word? Mm.—Look at him.—No, I must have cold facts too, like a raspberry ice between meat and meat. Otherwise, satiety, and the best to come—"

"And come! All right, every fact I can manage to recall, though it may be difficult—"

"Prodding may help? Well, perhaps you shall amuse me—."

"—Irene!—I'll cut your allowance, I swear it—!"

"Now listen," she said in an altered tone, "something is wrong with him. What? Is he ill?" She reached me the glasses over her shoulder.

Something was wrong, though it did not appear to be illness in the usual sense of the word. Acute exhaustion. He looked as if he had run a hundred miles in the past half-hour—or dreamed he had. His face was drawn and full of caves, the way I had seen it that morning in the Hôtel de R_____ in Paris, fresh from a coma. He balanced uneasily on his feet, the breath tore in and out of his lungs, audible as his words. The words themselves were hardly more than rasped breathing, of little sense except when he remembered to glance down at the book, and then a spate of more or less connected syllables suggested that for the rest he was making do.— He was crying. Certainly he was crying. With rage, or some shattering pain, it was impossible to say, he looked so disconsolate, so wild. —The filth of the closing lines—Sade's or his own—was ecstatic— as foul as I've heard, filth on filth, senseless as love-talk at orgasm which his low breathy delivery, even his tears, gave uncomfortable point. Now his eyes fixed feverishly on the page—"Listen— listen!"—he pitched a little forward, neck-cords writhing, bellowing with such command that alarm seized the aisle. Voices fell. Startled, people half turned.

"—Listen!"

—Twice already she had demanded her glasses and now she practically hissed her impatience. "—The *glasses,* you pig!"—but I would not hear—

"—For O," he just then cried, apparently reading from the page, "O my soul waiteth for the Lord—more than watchmen for the morning—yea!—more than—watchmen—for the morning!"

Psalm CXXX. Did one laugh or weep? I was frankly shocked. Though he could be vile, he was rarely vulgar. Clapping the book shut, he stood hand to hip, the other extended at shoulder level with the book in it, bowing repeatedly from the waist to mingled boos and applause, for others had been offended too. However, the sacrilege seemed to have improved him. His glittering eyes no longer stalked us. The grinning wet face he showed recovering from his final bow was far more typical than the preceding emotion, and even went a little way towards redeeming his offense. Hate of such a purity *was* devotional, one felt. Then, with a really lewd gesture of contempt, he stepped from the crate and vanished.—The glasses were torn from me and my cheek whacked. She swung away and frantically refocused the lenses, and when she found he had gone, she turned and whacked me again. She was blazing. And, remembering the collapsed Duke, I began to worry over my knees and to draw away, when providentially Hudson's hands closed on her tiny waist and lifted her, furious and pale, to the asphalt. Agnes came up puffing.

"—Really, Irene—you grow more irresponsible every day—"

"She is a damn homicidal nuisance," agreed Hudson, who in one graceful motion shrugged an apology and waved goodbye as they moved off, Irene wedged like a child between them, into the now streaming mob.

"—But, my dear," I heard Agnes say as they passed out of sight, "did you hear the lovely final words?—Quite inspiring.—Perhaps I should read him. Has the Marquis written much such—?"

"—Much such?—" echoed Hudson.

"—Critic—."

"—You *were* in the damn tree—"

"—But do you really suppose Edith—?"

"—*Hush*—"

"—*Quel mystère*—!"

Well, yes, a catch, but what had I caught, I wondered, turning my attention to the head of the aisle to try if I could locate Gordie. Otherwise I would go directly to Kelly's and wait.

—I spotted him, head lowered in thought, on his way out of the park down one of the adjacent aisles. Close behind, carrying the crate and book, pranced Blafford Fillyhausen IV, eager as a racehorse for the gun. I watched them out of sight, too. Then I stepped to the ground, made a move in the direction of Kelly's, turned on my heel, and wandered off alone.

* * *

Towards morning the storm broke. A convulsion of thunderclaps and shrieking winds—a downpour of vicious waters mixed with hail that piled the streets with leaves—all black hate breaking up till it woke me raging with it, not knowing where or who I was. Weeping, weeping; and battering, I smashed—apparently with bare fists—a small cabinet to matchwood, to a little dust, before coming to myself.—Mercifully, the violence was brief. By dawn the winds had died away, and by noon, when I left the hotel, the sky was a radiant azure, the rinsed air pure and sweet, with a tang in it of green from the bruised vegetation.

Not surprisingly the beach was jam-packed. It was possibly the last fine Saturday of the season, for we were in September now, and everyone was out. *Everyone.* The sun throbbed like a new coin, a fresh breeze stood in off the lake, and the lake—oh the lake! The dinning of it carried clear across the traffic noises—I had heard it as far off as the newsstand as I stood selecting magazines—and the spray itself was reaching large areas of the Drive. You could hear the squeals and laughter from passing cars as some gust brought a shower through the windows. But the sight of it was awesome. Farther out, the water lay a level deep blue, a little pitted, fretted with a few choppy white-caps; but midway it began to roll in fat glassy swells, flaked a hundred spumey greens like bole upon bole of sycamore; and at the shore it went wild. Whipped by the morning gales, the breakers rode in thunderously, heaving high as any ocean waves, certainly higher than was decent for a lake, crashing over the cement parapets in rising coils of spray that the sun set iridescing and children ran shouting to catch. Look! While against this commotion, on the near stretches of the parapets but particularly the length and breadth of the sand, another smaller raged—shrilled rather—nesting birds on an ocean rock at their infinite flickering labor—of milling whites and reds, of shrieking, squabbling, cooing, of alarums at the shore where people danced and flung in the breakers, of mothers berating children and bawling adolescents at their games, pricked out as far as the eye could see with the usual feathered flaunting of the place, with much visiting and parading about, and some gay singing here, and cursing there. And both together there, where a banjo twanged on the sand near the exit from the underpass. Mae Moon in her orange suit on a purple towel singing dirty songs. So ravishingly pure was the air, one of the first vignettes to leap to sight as I came out on the cement walk was the moth-hole on her massive ass, vivid as total eclipse in a flaming sky; while the first sea-bird voice to pierce my ear sang:

> "—I'd marry me an elevator-boy
> And we'd live fair and sunny.
> Oh, he'd go down,
> And I'd go down,
> And we'd go dow-w-wn togethah—"

Quite a nice tune it was too. Cross-legged languorously strumming chords, head thrown back and eyelids lowered with the beauty of it all. Next her, Gordie supine, head sunk in her hip, one arm across his face, his thigh grasped in Blaffie's great paw, his chest a rest for Evvie's head, his fingers under Evvie's bra, Evvie's toes in Willie's crotch, Willie's nose in Angie's navel, Angie's hand in Blaffie's trunks, and so it went, to the number of ten, all similarly at peace for the moment, listening to music. To one side a pail of beer half-covered with a Drake towel, and another pail of those cola bottles plugged with paper that surely contained little cola. Peanut shells in three-inch drifts.—After casually touring the length of the walk I came and sat myself about a dozen yards from Gordie's group, on the top step of the three that led from the walk to the sand.

Though I wore trunks under my slacks, I had decided during the course of my tour against stripping down that day. The clandestine man in trunks is pretty closely circumscribed in the breadth of his movements. Any unusual ranging beyond the limits of the sand is both clumsy and noteworthy. Not that I fooled myself. For all practical purposes I was the man-without-a-country and as surely as Gordie a target for informed eyes; no one of importance to me but had my every move in view, perhaps grimly amused by my pains. I was constantly watched and, I felt, *led*. Yet I took a pride in my skills. If I was being led, I would follow in style. I would behave in all situations as if the Director himself were testing my competence, and the fate of nations hung on my nerve. All my life, don't you see—acting as best I know how in a vacuum, hoping not to end up a fool, never finally knowing.—Of course the very limitation of trunks is desirable for study of the beach proper, especially on such a day as this was, when dense shifting crowds made study from the walk a matter of luck. However, it is not desirable, for example, if there seems a chance that you may want to leave the beach on short notice. I was not upset, merely bemused, uneasy. I arranged my nose-shield and sunglasses, then an inside-out sailor hat to protect my ears and neck. I was burnt way beyond the tolerance of my fair skin, which I had handy as a reply, should any inquire why I was not in trunks. I began to leaf through *The Nation*.

—I tried to figure why Lev was here. He had been my Haganah liaison in Minneapolis, and was a very important figure in Nazi-detection throughout the entire northwestern U.S., which terrain he knew better than any geographer. The particular operation I had been involved in was not strictly speaking his;—we were after something far more important than escaped Nazis;—yet so extensive and subtle were its ramifications that, in addition to the receiving and sending of messages through Lev, I would often ask his advice, or plunk down some bare puzzling bone on the chance that he could flesh it out from his special field, which more than once proved the case. My quarry was not Nazi, but like Irene's great Stern himself, he or she or whatever had not scrupled to bargain with Nazis, even to work with them to a point; and what there was to be known to that point, Lev knew. Now he was here. I had glimpsed him near the water, on a blanket with a couple of girls obviously picked up for the day. He was thick black curly hair all over his body, neck to ankles, and they, pale blondes of course, seemed enchanted with the idea. He saw me too. But *why* was he here? It was not his operation, as I say. A separate mission? I somehow doubted it. I liked him but feared him. He was a tough and ruthless little man, of enormous cunning. I naturally wondered if his arrival had anything to do with my continued interference in the case. I had already received enough warnings, which I ignored; and phone calls in the night, which I heard out in silence, since my rooms had been wired and cross-wired (though by unremitting diligence I managed to keep the phone itself clean) any words from me would have been some sort of exposure. A few of the calls were FBI—one voice was certainly Blaffie's and another the assistant Chicago SAC's, a Tim Malone—but most were Haganah, as their fine English diction betrayed. Now Lev in person, who of all the organization knew me best. To more forcefully persuade me? I repeat, it did not upset me—I did not fear him or anyone to that degree—but I was bemused. Even further, by the appearance of Benham Lake's former valet, of all people—he who had officiated at the suicide and then absconded with the Byzantine ivories—in the bevy of exquisites at Cyd Bissche's feet, under the tasseled blue umbrella. A short stocky enormously muscled young man with long straight yellow hair that had been oh so richly brown and waved—name of Bryan. Bryan Younglove. Cross my heart. With his perpetual smile and the sun's own shimmer. And Cyd looking low—very flushed and nervous, downing endless martinis, and plainly not at all susceptible to the blandishments of young love Bryan, who hopped and tumbled about like a circus clown to the great admiration of all save Cyd, who more owllike than ever eyed him stonily. I suppose I was first put onto Cyd's state when, passing near the blue umbrella during my tour of the area, I saw him waving to me! As clusters of curled heads turned to look, and a smiling yellow malevolent one stayed to stare, I nodded and moved on. Altogether, had it not been so palpably radiant and gay a day, I could have thought it deepest jungle night. *O das licht!* As it was, I kept myself dressed and ready to jump.

—Blaffie was smitten, that was clear. Job or no job, he was, as Mae would say, *turned on*. I mean, it's one thing to move close with your quarry, it's another to swoon away in his arms. America's security did not demand it. It must have been quite a night, to turn this FBI tough into an amorous 180-pound nymphet. I don't care that he was blithering drunk, maybe even partly acting. I could have killed him. He was all over Gordie. His hands were here and his hands were there, he rubbed, he nuzzled, and now he threw a leg across, and now he heaved his buttocks up, and Gordie suffering it wearily, if not without interest. If he *was* acting, it was the performance of a lifetime. I nearly ate *The Nation* for shame. But finally Gordie himself had to protest. It was too tiresome, I suppose. Besides, he was being suffocated. Indolently, he withdrew his hand from Evvie's breast and pinched the government's balls, and the government rolled off *giggling*! Oh I *ripped* into Jewish Studies!

When I could bring myself to look again, the tableau had fallen apart. Mae was up flexing her legs (a sight for the ages) and Blaffie had hung himself over the beer pail and was dipping his face in and out of the ice-water. (No one dreamt of staggering as far as the lake.) Evvie and Willie Ray jitterbugged among an adjacent party of quiet respectable types who were trying not to notice them, Evvie heaving that bust around into everyone's face like a wet feather bed. Not notice her indeed. A miraculous girl. The others—blinking their eyes evilly or stupidly as the case may be, their hair splendid with peanut shells—sat around in various effortful stages of consciousness.

Gordie was over on his side propped on an elbow. His mood had altered drastically and it took me no time at all to figure why. Evidently, he had not seen Bryan Younglove earlier—the boy may have arrived while he lay overcome with music, not many minutes before me perhaps—but he saw him now, and his eyes flashed with violence.—I can't explain it. Though I have pieced together much of the astonishing case, including a series of identity displacements which to my knowledge the FBI itself never solved, "Benham Lake's" exact position and influence, crucial as I know it to have been, has always eluded me; while his personal ascendancy over Gordie has not so much eluded as *mystified* me. A shallow vindictive man, almost pathologically sensitive for all his vulgar socializing, frigid as the ski slopes he frequented in all seasons, effete as his own pale wit—not at all Gordie's taste in people, which ran to the hot and the vivid, certainly to the bold. Bold?—Benham was the most craven man I ever knew, to the point, literally, of having been scared out of his own skin. Yet for all this, and the utterly detestable persecutions that marked his later relations with Gordie, his death came as a blow to Gordie and Edith both. A terrible numbing blow in fact. At the funeral they sat white and unspeaking, stricken to the heart. Gordie never spoke of it, but I always suspected he blamed Emily for publicly ruining the man, though the alternative had certainly been Benham's publicly ruining him. Well. And then what Gordie felt for Bryan Younglove—rather why he felt it, for his feelings were plain enough—is even more obscure to me. Was Benham's suicide, like Shem's heart failure, in some doubt after all?—was it jealousy?—was it the theft of the ivories, that left such a cheap sniggering after the inquest? I say I don't know. But to the resultant loathing I can testify. He lay there, his body as usual at such times relaxed and unimplicated, his eyes riding each dart and flutter of the boy's gay performance like a cat at a moth.

—Mae spotted me and came running up, and then Angie Masuto, her stumpy little legs twinkling, her coarse bass voice a-boom: "Mat-tat-tat-o!" They were in high spirits, loaded in fact, and palavered away at me, after commandeering my cigarettes, exactly as though I had asked for their attentions, strutting in the sand at the base of the steps and constantly cutting my sight-lines. I would have told them to move on except that you didn't tell that to Mae. She was taunting me with Rita, about whom I couldn't have cared less just then. And Angie went on and on about Blaffie's charms, even lower on my list of non-interests. I momentarily considered moving myself but felt there wasn't time. "—I'm trying to *read*," I ventured.

"The fuck you are," said Mae. "You and them busy-busy eyes behind them specs. Hah!"

I had lost Lev and was about to rise to my feet when I saw him again. He was picking his way about, off to my right, wearing outsize sunglasses, the kind found in novelty shops, and good-humoredly fighting off a pack of children who were trying to get at them, making himself conspicuous for someone—and Gordie shifting restlessly now, as he had done in the Square the night before, his eyes still fast on Younglove but with a divided, wary attention.

"—Let's go get a hotdog," said Mae.

"Bring me one," I said digging for change.

"No, you c'mon too—," and she grabbed for my magazines.

I slapped my hand down on them. "I'll tear your head off," I said quietly. " —Get going. I'm busy."

I shouldn't have said it. She slid her hands to her hips and cocked her head. "You threatening me, son?" Gordie was maneuvering a mirror the size of a half-dollar piece in the palm of his hand—I had observed him using it on other occasions to study the walk—his eyes flicking down and up again to Cyd's group. "—Me, a helpless minority segment, you fashis' slops?" Blaffie had cuddled up behind him spoon-fashion and was whispering into his ear, at the same time taking quick note of the mirror, and now Evvie and Willie Ray came racing back and flung upon him hilariously. "—Me, who has killed the supremacis' ass off of so many numerous yous, I can't hardly remember how many, you Huey Long, you Eastland—?" Cyd was waving again. Not at me, at someone passing behind me on the walk in the direction of Gordie, and then, though I heard no rolling cadence, I felt a stirring in the flesh about me, I saw faces turning up, even Mae's and Angie's—I noted Gordie's absolute stillness which in him signaled the highest excitement—and I guessed who it might be. Guessed and knew. Cyd's hand fell despondently. Bryan Younglove, his head against Cyd's unwilling knees, his teeth bared in a truly horrendous smile, watched with undisguised interest, and so did most of the others there.—Where was Lev! " —You *revolting* cunt-fucker—?" Gordie was on his feet—Blaffie spitting out sand and rubbing his eyes in surprise—swung around to the walk, legs spread and arms akimbo, that familiar grinning malice on his thrust-out face. But he was shaking.

"—Hey, lady, them beads real?"

"Watch," whispered Mae, centuries of oppression falling from her soul, "he's gonna vamp her!" Angie Masuto scooted back, but not Mae, who plopped her big bottom down at my feet and leaned forward on her elbows in evil absorption. I was fleetingly tempted to crack her skull then and there.

—Irene Fairweather paused uncertainly, peered, then came slowly over to the top step. Hudson addressed a few dissuading words to her back but did not follow. Towering there above passersby in the middle of the walk, he waited with all his pained passivity, looking unapproachably elegant, tapping his boot with a riding crop. Neither, I think, saw through my facial armor. At least Hudson stared directly at me without notable joy. Both were in riding costume, possibly on their way, via the North Avenue entrance, from a morning's canter in Lincoln Park to visit Agnes at the Drake. Possibly not. (Over the phone that morning Agnes had stated that for the next few days she was catching up on charity work and would be unavailable.) Under the neck of her short-sleeved blouse, Irene fingered a strand of tiny seed-pearls—the "beads." I raised and lowered my sunglasses quickly. She was very subdued, and very beautiful, oh so beautiful—even more fragile than I had remembered, and more breath-catching. The white and rose of her skin was unearthly and her short-cut hair, delicately dishevelled by the morning's exercise, was as black as the thick brows and lashes of her eyes, those violet eyes that washed all colors near her pale, and all other eyes expressionless, by the fiercely brooding mind in them. She *was* a goddess in her way, and far too plainly moved by this near sight of him, I felt. It didn't do with him. Twin outrageous beauties—yet one would be perverse, if only to forestall the other.

He laughed at her meanly, taking her at her most vulnerable, her age. She must then have been a little past thirty-five. There was a line or two, emphasized by the fine light. (I less and less cared for the day.) "—Now ain't I seen you somewhere? Din't you go to school with my ma or some such thing —?"

She gazed serenely down, measuring him almost tenderly. "Mm. Until third grade, I believe it was, when they turned her out for pregnancy. Did she ever marry?"

He loured. Any slur on family, no matter how merrily wide of the mark, drew his nastiest. "—I was conceived of the wind on a wild spring day. She died a virgin, as you live a—"

"She declined men, but could not pass wind, you say?"

"Better than fetid reports—!"

"I merely asked if she married, boy." She appeared not so much outraged as surprised; though more than either *determined,* as he must have seen.

"Did you merely? The difference in chicks. She would never have asked it of you."

"And why not?"

"For two reasons, the second and decidedly politer being how it's a private concern—"

"But for the decidedly public fact of you—"

"—Or the many public facts of you? Perhaps. Lord, they did say the variety of colors and shapes was choice—" This set him up. His assurance returned, and his grin;—there had plainly been a more intricate relationship than she had hinted at.

She chuckled indulgently. "Not bad for a cheap thrust, if not good either. I hate these parasitic tack-ons—"

"Then you're an underbred host."

"But full of nourishment—admit it. By the moist O's of their mouths, your friends here lacked all idea of your true brilliance till now. You owe it to me."

"Well, I thank you—"

"Oh, no need. You suck hard for your dinner—too hard, as I recall. Ha ha ha. Touching. Well, well. Perseverance is not talent, unluckily, for if it were —"

"If it were, Miss, you'd have had me long since, *hein*—?"

"Again! Ha ha ha. Depressing, to be forever re-living one's tadpole days—"

"To ancient froggies, O!"

"Sad enough, yet consider old tadpoles. What must *their* anguish be, to be cutely larval at twenty-nine—?"

"Twenty-eight!"

"Ha ha ha. Well, I shall spare us both. So you remember me?"

"Something of the perseverance of tongue, little else. It was, oh, very long ago, Miss."

"Not so long but I remember *you*."

"Well, I was lovely."

"And I was not?"

"The vestiges intrigue. I would guess you were—"

Though she faintly colored at this, her control was unshaken, or only the slightest bit. "But can't remember."

"No. Like one said—"

"I don't recall your saying anything. What do you imagine you said? Tell us."

"He he he! Miss is upset—"

"Like to *vomit,* dear. Now what is it you said that bears quoting?"

"Just never you mind. Shakespeare in person would come off shit-covered here. A real set-up. One must not spend oneself needlessly—"

"When the account is this low, no. I quite agree. You should hoard, and creep with care. Indeed, you do—very close to the ground, among the ruins." She glanced sweetly around the smirking little group. "I swear, I can't conceive what they are the ruins *of*.—In any case I have been aware of the retrenchment, and I want you to understand that I applaud your lack of pretense, if not its necessity. That pains me. You had such promise once—"

His eyes gleamed guardedly. "And you had such a friend—"

"You don't mean to say you remember—?"

"Him? Remember him? I have the most vivid memories—"

"But none of the substance, eh?"

"All the outworn games! What would you give to be certain, lady?"

"Nothing, for a certainty I own, boy."

"Oh, you lie!" He screamed with laughter, while she regarded him somberly, perfectly composed. At least she seemed the least embarrassed person there;—I must have been scarlet. "—It's killing you all over again—!"

With unexpected mildness, and a little sideward motion, as though to leave: "Oh, I don't kill so easily, David."

The name drew him up, and after a moment of staring he brought out a reply as unexpected in tone as hers. "Well, I'm an aging tadpole, sure. All you said. All you *ever* said, noble frog-ess, for you said much, prodigious much. Which is not to say you're without effect in the right company. Rumor has it that you can even talk to the point on occasion—grandly, no doubt, but with point. Great formal parks of words simply to bury a man in style. They say you buried him good—"

Back with a delicate glitter of teeth and eyes: "Yes?"

"So the rumor reached me, much corrupted in the passage, no doubt. You keep him beautifully planted—?"

"Beautifully."

"Bless ya."

"No, you haven't changed. You are still a vain, teasing boy.— Here—you asked about my beads—" and bending her head she quickly undid the clasp and tossed them on the sand.

With a shriek Evvie dived for them and with a roar Angie was on her back pulling her off, but Gordie was down among them kicking one in the face and flipping the other around by the hair, and after some further scuffling with Blaffie, on whose prostrate body all this had taken place, he rose up radiantly, the pearls gleaming on his chest beneath the black silk scarf. Willie and some others whistled admiringly. Mae chuckled. "—Ain't he the prettiest thing?"

"—Just like Cheri," he lisped, waggling his little ass as he approached the bottom step for Irene's inspection.

She had used the interval to gain control of herself. She inspected approvingly with a certain lingering seriousness. "Better, I think."

"Well, I should suppose *so*. Better than you, perhaps—?" He laughed as his eyes sought hers.

At this she smiled. "Why, no, I am pleased to say, not better. But fine, extraordinarily fine—as fine as one could hope for." Lord how she glowed. "What times they were, David! And are you still as brave—?"

"Sure."

He was not laughing now, he was staring past her into the crowd on the walk, and she too had just turned to look, and I to get up, when a harrowing quivery scream tore from Cyd Bissche's throat. He was standing rending his robe death-white—"Lev!"—*Lev?*— Scream after scream: "Lev—Lev—!"

The beach froze at gaze. The boys at his feet including Younglove had flung back in curled attitudes of horror from the maddened creature. It was blood-curdling, terrifying—the pounding of waters and this lonely cry. No one touching him, no one at all. He fought the radiant air. An agonized wave of bodies arched over the edge of the walk and suddenly, tension breaking, crashed in fragments down the steps and filled the scene with silent hurtling forms.

All broke then. An invisible attacker!—Safety in numbers. The sand became a swirling spraying current of fear towards Cyd. There came Lev catapulting from the walk and spurting straight through, and now Irene, running swiftly and lightly. Blaffie sped by far less drunk than one had supposed. Everyone. Mae had cut out immediately and so had the others of Gordie's party. I was on my feet at the first cry—not to run to Cyd's aid, but to see who might be running from him, and to keep an eye on Gordie, who fronted the stampede from the walk unmoving, and now stood unchanged staring across the deserted space—unchanged yet something changed—something—and my heart jumped to my throat as in a rush of mortification. I started over to him, when I was knocked heels-up into the sand, a powerful shove that sent me free of the bottom step or I should have broken my head, and when after a second or two of dizziness I regained my feet, Gordie was gone. Into the underpass, and much too swift for me. Bryan Younglove over the hedge and up and over the wire-mesh fence hell-bent through traffic, and hot after him Lev, looking like a baby ape in diapers. (A chancy business, trunks, as pointed out.)

I looked over at the silent throng gathered around Cyd into which the police were now muscling their way. By the strangulated sounds coming through he was having convulsions. Hudson—Irene somewhere, I knew—Blaffie, Mae, and the others, all there. Police sirens turning into Oak Street. Swiftly I went to where Gordie had been standing, and under the overturned beer pail, half buried in wet sand, I found that which—or more properly the lack of which—had made my heart jump so: the black silk scarf. I plucked it out, as Blaffie detached himself from the throng and came hurrying over. It had been sliced right through the thick knot.

By whatever instrument, for whatever insolent or ritual requirements, four points were immediately clear. The episode of Cyd's screams had been to some extent—not on Cyd's part certainly—diversionary. Gordie had made his contact. Blaffie's reputation as an agent was totally undeserved. And I no longer knew if I mistrusted light or darkness more.

* * *

Gordie immediately decamped. I should have figured it but didn't. Early evening he fled bag and baggage—on to the next stage, while I dreamed away the night at Kelly's. I was crushed; fiercer than crushed. It ate at me that I hadn't been stationed outside the hotel along with Blaffie & Co., prepared to follow up what was after all a fairly predictable link in the day's events. And then though he went on to elude me as beautifully as Blaffie claimed he did him, I should not have had such pangs; one can't by rights rage at being beautifully eluded.—But he would not have eluded me, you see. It had become my search too, and I should have had the eyes of my passion. You do see? No, I hated not having been there, hated it. How they must have laughed. On the heels of missing a contact made a few yards from me, to dream through this;—it was too much; I lost my head.

—I say dream. Leaving the beach, I evidently wandered the streets for hours in a thick fog of speculation, to emerge near one in the morning at a table at Kelly's. A few truckers howled at the bar. Over the top of his newspaper the bartender eyed me curiously. There was no one else. I jumped to my feet in a panic. While it was often the case that Gordie toured other bars before turning up here, I understood at once that he would not turn up tonight, or ever again. There was no need now. I all but reeled. I started to the door, to the bar, to the table again, to the phone booth at the back on the run. The Drake desk said Mr. Carson Pirie had checked out at seven that evening—no forwarding address, no messages.

I ran the whole way. The night staff came on at midnight and had not observed the departure. The desk clerk had heard there were twenty-nine pieces of luggage. One of the porters had heard of this amusing incident and another of that, legends purely, based on the general picture of him. The doorman heard it took four taxis to accommodate him, each piled to the roof with bags (an old but effective trick). None of the drowsy cabbies lined near the entrance had been of the number or so they said. When I finally got a moment with the night manager I found him all careful smiles and little information, though that little was intriguing. As far as he knew, there had been nothing noteworthy in the departure, thank heavens—in spite of myself I had to laugh—no, as a matter of fact, it had not been sudden, Mr. Carson Pirie had given notice *that morning before leaving for the beach* (my italics);—why no, as a matter of fact, I could *not* see the suite, it had already been re-occupied, and by his harried tone I understood the problem. Blaffy-ites.

The next day I talked to the staff that had seen Mr. Carson Pirie on his way, with foreseeably nil results. Everyone had been warned off by then. The doorman had absolutely no recollection of the cabbies involved, nor did the cabbies themselves, several of whom admitted being in the area at the time. They barely kept down smiles at my discomfiture. Jack Dreifort came to mind, and I could feel the anger moving in me. I phoned up to Agnes from the lobby but was told by a secretary that she was out. I left my name.

I spent that afternoon at the beach and the evening in Washington Square Park. I couldn't think what else to do at the moment. I had my ideas of Gordie's present whereabouts, but there was simply no doing anything about it except through proper channels. Agnes, or a direct invitation. "I may not see till I am shown," Gordie had said. I felt it held for me too. There was much danger involved at this point, and much at stake. I could not be clumsy. Whether by coincidence or plan, none of the usual crowd put in an appearance that day or the next. Not Mae, or Rita, or Evvie, or Willie Ray, not even Angie Masuto, an indefatigable hustler. I hardly imagined they could help, but their absence did make the hiatus doubly bleak. My dreams those nights were deliriums. I both craved and dreaded sleep, for once asleep—

Most of Monday I spent near the chapel where the remains of Cyd Bissche were on view. (A thrombosis, the papers said, under a photo of him at about age eighteen. "The last of one of Chicago's original Gold Coast families.") No one of interest, with the possible exception of Duke von Ofterdingen, insanely bandaged, in the company of a dusty dandruffy Pola Negri type, who I decided was Djuna Berry. Agnes herself arrived shrouded in black veils, supported between a chauffeur and secretary, and stayed but a few minutes. Irene and Hudson did not show, at least during my tour of duty. And though I picked out three, possibly four other observers, Blaffie was not among them.

Out of all control, reasonless, the anger in me gathered head. That night I left the Square early and strolled over to Cyd's coach house with some dim bored notion of breaking in for a look around. Perhaps fortunately, it was still under police guard, and I went on my way;—I could have got myself into serious trouble, as I later realized. Besides, the premises would have been thoroughly picked over by now, even as poor Cyd. Cyd—and Lev. For the hundredth time I fell to wondering what Lev was doing in Chicago—if he had not already departed in fact, for I had begun to have some doubts that he had come on my account. (That, after the FBI interdict on Haganah he was able to operate the area at all, I in some measure ascribed to the Bentley-Chambers circus, which was the true rage of Mr. Hoover and his scout troop, and which reduced a "world-wide conspiracy against the human race," fatuously un-Communistic, to a very minor road show.) And what had been the nature of Cyd's involvement? Nazis? Possible. Cyd had concerned himself with every infamy. Except—except for the presence of Bryan Younglove, except for that. Which always brought me back to my original feeling that Lev was here on specifically Abul business, though why in that case he had not contacted me, for good *or* for ill, was a mystery. In my present state I would have welcomed even his threats. And I would have been interested to discover, on my part, just why he had so played Cyd down during our last talk.

To distract myself, I resorted to an old device: I phoned Ethel. She was at her worst. Evidently, she had been quarreling with Sam, and evidently he had not been backing down. The first words had to do with Cyd. Dreadful wasn't it, she said coldly. So surprising. She hadn't realized he had enough of a heart to make all that difference to the rest of him. (Sam remonstrated in the background.) Anti-Semite that he was. (Sam grew louder: "He vas never"—and she turning from the phone, to him:—"Halt's Maul!—he was to *me*—")—Well, but there did seem a sort of justice in his dying at the threshold of the Jewish New Year, didn't I think? I replied, Cyd's anguished throes still fresh in my memory, that death is a terrible experience for us all, which after a second's pause she repeated to Sam, and complimented me on, as though she had been testing my humanity purely.—Well, if it is true that pity lies under the guard of women, we may rest easy that the bullion in Fort Knox is not safer from squandering.—I said, by way of getting her out—though I hadn't meant to begin on it, at best it would lead to my assuring myself of what I already, helplessly, construed—that I had at last met the notorious Irene Fairweather. —SILENCE.—Vulgar to tears, I added, you hardly prepared me.—Well, she said, well, I do not like to be the cause of undue anticipation in others. I feel the thrill of unexpected horror is one of the great experiences, like meeting Sam's mother for the first time, which made me a strong, if bitter, woman. So you despised her at once? Well, I have always had the highest opinion of your blood. One need never fear the juxtaposition of a true Dorothy Perkins rose and a briary wild thing, I mean that they might accidentally breed together.—You have a way of putting things, I said cheerlessly. Tell me, do they live in the neighborhood?—They do not! Matt, you are not thinking of calling on them?—No, no, I laughed, but I believe I may have passed their house.—Now why should you believe so if you don't even know their neighborhood? she scoffed.—Simply because I do, I said, feeling I deserved leniency for the happiness I had just given her.—Ah, she said, but then what could you have been doing on Franklin Street, dear? It is not a street to do things on.—Getting to know your city, I said airily. A blackish house with green curtains?—*Mold green*—peuh—*yes,* dear. And have you also toured our sewer system—?

As I had already guessed, but which I was sorry to be assured of, as I say. It would have been the height of folly for me to go barging over; the certitude only intensified a longing I was as yet in no position to slake; indeed had been at pains to overlook. And the wilder longing quickened my anger.

That evening I came down about nine. I had eaten nothing all day, which had not improved my mood. My head throbbed sickly. I had washed and dressed in the dark. Now, as I stepped into the overhead lights of the lobby, I drew up and pressed fingers to my eyes to ease the sting. I was aware of some slight commotion at the desk. For a split second I ignored it in that aching bliss of red and blue worlds, but then I looked, painfully looked, to see Blaffie hurrying through the street doors. I glanced at the desk clerk, who shrugged defensively as though to say there had not been time (he was in my pay to signal up to me in the event of these visits) and I was off.

In a flash my head was cleared and my mood purged. He turned right along Dearborn then right again at the first intersection. Fool—I thought, icily amused—in a labyrinth keep *left*. Twice he looked behind him, then halfway to Clark broke into a full run, I in pursuit as he suddenly understood. Past Clark, people drawing aside, staring—Angie I saw, Willie Ray her pimp cheering me on —to Lasalle, left (too late! I cried) along Lasalle to Chestnut, again left by way of a corner bar, alleyway, and three backyards, he twisting and doubling like any hare, to my heart's delight, my heady joy, nearly shaking me once by diving into a parked car just past the turning of a street and doubling back as I sped by; yet I was too keen by then, too *pitched* to him—to the Square, at this hour but sparsely populated, to his hurt, or soon-to-be hurt—on up Dearborn past Division and a policeman shouting, neither heeding, the space between us closing inches, feet—to Lincoln Park all the way, and another kind of hunting.

He could not shake me here, for I felt I knew it strangely well. Forest of my life that I an exile held sacred to some homecoming day or night. No, night. Miles of trees and night and he fled hours it seemed to the very most heartless heart of it—and well it was strange, as I say. I heard him begin to stumble and crash in scrub I moved as shadow through. I heard him raucous for breath and I unbreathing as leaves. At last I heard him fall and not rise up again. I held still. Matt? he murmured. It was a frightened voice. I advanced soundlessly tree to tree. What's it all about, Matt?—I've sprained my foot, help me, Matt for godsake!—No southern accent now, no grand FBI airs now. He was in among some bushes and I stood over him before he knew it.—Matt *what*?

While I silently stared, he began to babble on the only subject he could piece with my running him down, the circumstances of Gordie's flight from the hotel, though cleverly telling me nothing.

It could not occur to him, nor could he ever understand, that I had chased him because I hated him, that I hated him because he was hateful, that every lying word he uttered turned him more irresistibly hateful. So I made no attempt to explain. Instead I fell to hitting him. Hit him and hit him and hit him. Wreaked all impurities on him, all the too-long deferred judgment of my brain. I think I might have stopped if he had asked me but he didn't and I'll never know. It may be he lost consciousness. I beat his face to a blue pulp, and when I got to my feet I was soaked with blood and my hands were raw, but lord I was refreshed. So many *stars* I saw then, and pure lovers laughing on the lighted path a few yards off. I felt marvelous. And hungry, violently hungry. I remembered I had not eaten. Well, there was no striding into a restaurant in this condition. I took side streets to Rita's place, and let myself in with a key I retained from friendlier times.

She was in bed with Mae. They yelled out at the sight of me, but I laughed and told them I had been cut in a fight, nothing serious, and to go on with their fun as if I weren't there. I headed straight for the refrigerator. Later, after changing into fresh clothes—luckily I had never bothered to call for my things—I made myself a drink and sat down for a cigarette. My hand was shaking with excitement. For the first time in many days I was feeling *alive*. Mae forced some desultory talk about Cyd and the beach incident, all the while looking very hard at me. I asked if she had seen Gordie lately. She said no—where had I been cut, anyway. I motioned vaguely at my ribs and turned my attention to Rita. Had she seen Gordie? Nervously she shook her head and whispered something to Mae who got up stark naked and went into the next room. I walked over and sat on the edge of the bed. She looked very fetching in the deep pink light. I reached under the sheet and fondled her elegant little breasts. She grinned in absolute terror. I asked what the matter was, had Mae killed her taste for men already? For reply she stretched for a hand mirror on the night-table and shoved it up to my face. I knocked it aside. What was that for, I said.—You look like some kind of bloody saint, she said. I slapped her lightly twice. She gasped but made no sound. I explained that I had done it on two counts, a slap apiece— one for the disgusting degenerate she had become, and the other because someone had asked me not to *hurt* her. Why had that been said to me? Why would anyone think—? But Mae was behind me ordering me up and out of the apartment. As I turned to look, Rita slid from the bed and ran sobbing into the bathroom. Mae had a small revolver in her hand, and on her face a most determined look. For all her occasional feints my way, I was one of the few people she would never tackle physically and she knew I knew it; consequently the gun was more than show. Yet I could not seem intimidated. I slapped my thighs and got up.—You're lucky you're black, I said crossing the room to finish my drink.—She hooted. Yeah, I figured. It's very comforting. If people knew what was goin' on in you they'd *all* turn black.—Too many blacks, I said, rather liking her for it, and I'd start on *them*.—Well you are interesting, she said, that you damn sure are. Please throw the key on the floor as you leave—*now*.

—From a public phone I called the police and told them where Blaffie could be found. I did not mean to more than hurt him. Later I stopped by Kelly's for a drink, where I ran into Evvie, and after some discussion—she had hiked her prices—went home with her. She was magnificently endowed and always disappointing, a not unusual confluence perhaps. She lay there like a monstrous corpse, and her bed, her very skin under the lilac perfume, was permeated with garlic, but she served to take the nervous edge off my excitement, if leaving the excitement itself intact.

—It was past two when I re-entered the lobby of my hotel. I saw immediately that something was on. The clerk, a dithery type under any circumstances, was beside himself with composure. I went nonchalantly to the desk and engaged him in conversation while he wrote on a slip of paper—lightly, and not on the pad, as I had shown him—that two men had been waiting upstairs since eleven. Foreign.

"—Can it be put inside my apartment," I said of a lobby chair I was pretending to covet, "or must it be left in the corridor till I get home?" Inside, he wrote, *Eddie* [the porter] *saw them, probably pass-key.* "You are sure it is of foreign make?" "Yes," he said, and wrote. I thanked him and asked to be rung at nine, which in our simple code arrangement meant three, in an hour. He nodded, and I went up. I never saw a man so tickled with himself as that silly little clerk.

I closed the door behind me and waited, my hand on the knob. It seemed several minutes though it was possibly less. I there and then took an oath not to be caught without a weapon again. I had no taste for knives or the wounds they inflict, but it was getting deep in the game to go without my gun. At last I said, "Aunt?" (Haganese for Haganah) and a second later the floor lamp was switched on to reveal Lev in my armchair and a young man sprawled on the sofa, his hat pulled down over his eyes and his arms folded on his chest. As the light came on, the young man sat up abruptly and pushed back his hat though not too far. It was a dead give-away. As a man masquerading as a woman will expose himself by clapping knees together to catch an object falling from his hand, so a woman masquerading as a man will expose herself by tipping a hat over her eyes during a snooze *in total darkness.* In the case of the latter, it is a habit observed merely, the utility of which has not been thought out. No, it was a woman in a green corduroy suit and wide-brimmed black fedora—short-cut black hair (though long for a man those days), radiant white skin, and I guessed violet eyes. Irene. I closed the door behind me and came forward into the room, signaling Lev not to speak and pointing to the walls. He broke into gay laughter.

"Adi here is an expert exterminator, my boy. Your rooms have been thoroughly de-bugged." One after another he tossed three small "bugs" at me.

I had known the location of but two. I looked at "Adi." "Very much obliged," I said, "only as they will be around tomorrow with others, I fear you have done much work for nothing." It pleased me to address "him" in the slightly translated tone I generally fell into with my Israeli friends.

"*Not* for nothing," said Lev. "We have a great deal to discuss tonight—no, today. You are the night-owl, lad. And what is that *parfum* you're wearing?"

I smiled. "Lilac and garlic."

"Puerto Rican!" he cried with self-delighted worldliness.

I glanced over at "Adi." "And very good she was too, though I have lately dreamed of better."

"Ach, haven't we all," said Lev. "But do not let us talk of it before Adi. He is a virgin in that way."

"That way?" I said. "Why, are there other ways?"

"Very many other ways, and some of them of far more danger than indulgence," said Lev. "But some schnapps, lad, and let us settle to business, eh?"

"—You *are* virtuous," I said as "Adi" shook "his" head to the proffered glass. "He" shrugged. "And of few words." The brim of the fedora was turned down all the way around, in the fashion of old intrigue movies, and shaded the face to below the eyes. The lips were ravishing, fuller than I remembered, the fierce chin more deeply cleft.

"His English is detestable," explained Lev, drinking down, "though he understands tolerably well."

"Such lips need few words to make themselves understood," I said.

"He is uncomfortably beautiful," agreed Lev. "I refuse to sleep in the same room with him.—No, no more, thank you. I don't hold it well. Later, perhaps. Now—"

"Now," I said, seating myself facing them, "you are here on the Abul case."

"Yes and no," said Lev. "I am here on the Abul case, only there is no Abul case." He studied me with those hooded European eyes. "Did you know that?"

"Know what?" I said blankly.

"The last, obviously. You have already expressed knowledge of the first."

"That there is no Abul case? The words are without meaning—"

"The meaning is, that the Abul case, in an effective sense, ended over a year ago, precisely with the death of Mr. Benham Lake. Now I repeat, did you know that?"

I started to laugh.

"Explain," he said, lowering his gaze to light a fat Turkish cigarette.

"—Explain!" I cried. "Explain that I have been risking my life in a cause you suspect me of knowing to be non-existent? What nonsense. No, lad, *you* explain—"

I meekly submitted to a cocked-head appraisal. These mentalities are so serious, you know, so soul-plumbing. They must know all about one. I was aware that "Adi" too, arms folded, was watching me from under the shadow of "his" brim. Well I let them. I was in a turmoil to say the least of it. Lev couldn't possibly consider me such a gull, yet it was equally impossible that he believed what he said—

"All right now," he drew out at last, softly but, I felt, not kindly, "perhaps you do not know, but let me make myself clear, I do not for one moment consider such a game to be beyond you."

I kept a perfectly impassive face.

"I said, I mean, there is no case. There was, but is not. What we have been observing for the past year are some last futile twitchings of limbs whose brain is dead. For so long a period did we track the hand by its shadow, that the hand turned mythical, like God's if you like, and long after it had been withdrawn we continued happily to ascribe to it any and all unpleasantness. Abdullah's politicking, the Atalena business, flying saucers, even the Bernadotte affair—plainly coincidence, though admittedly the devils would have *approved,* it was surely in their *line*. But that is profitless. As an international power the organization no longer exists. The man known as Benham Lake was the last of the hereditary chieftains, and when he died, the movement was for all purposes nullified—"

"You say hereditary chieftains. Do you imply that Benham Lake was in some way related to Shem Abul—?"

"The brother."

"The brother!" I did laugh. "The Lake pedigree is as pure as Christ's blood, and the name as native to the city as mine—"

"I hope *purer* than Christ's blood, as we say in Israel. But they no longer exist, these Lakes. They petered out in various parts of the continent as completely as did the family of Edith Charls, did they not? A point you neglected to bring to our attention, and which I do not hesitate to say makes you extremely suspect, was that the Lakes had not been resident in Minneapolis for upwards of fifteen years, when young Benham reappeared on the scene a few years before Shem Abul himself. Is it true, this I have discovered?"

"It is true," I said.

"Minneapolitans had therefore not seen Mr. Lake since he had been a tiny boy?"

"They had not."

"So that someone, anyone, with a slight resemblance to the Lake family could have entered into Minneapolis and proclaimed himself Benham Lake?"

"Certainly, if he had troubled to acquaint himself with the intimate facts of the family, for they were still remembered—"

"It goes without saying—"

"In such a case there would have been little trouble. The Lakes had been fashionable, but they had lost their money and consequently all their business connections in the city. An impostor would have appeared to lack motive—"

"Ah, America! But you go through it so smoothly. Had it by chance occurred to you?"

"That 'Benham Lake' was not Benham Lake? Yes, in a dim way—"

"Yet you did not trouble yourself to communicate such information to us, and even now laugh when I broach it."

"It was scarcely information. It was merely a sense, sometimes, that Lake was too shamelessly congenial to Shem's needs. The Lakes had been very proud and notably anti-Semitic. I laugh now not at the fact of the imposture, but at the ascription—"

"As I recall it, you laughed *precisely* at the fact of the imposture, but we shall let it pass. And as for your anti-Semitism, no one in history, not Count Chmielnicki himself, was more anti-Semitic than Shem and Khan—"

"Khan?"

"Lake's familiar sobriquet—"

"One question before you proceed. Did Gordon Abul know Lake's true identity?"

"It would be strange indeed if he did not—"

"So I would think. Yes. Now I gather you picked up much of this from Cydneye Bissche—"

"You have a subtle mind, lad. I wish I understood how it worked. From Mr. Cydneye Bissche it was."

"He was not part of the organization?"

"No indeed. But he was a mine of Nazi material, one of my most fruitful sources, in fact, with whom I had been working for many months. Strangely enough I liked him. We were sympatico on many topics—music, literature. I feel very badly for what has happened to him. But he was most helpful. As I say, he had a fatal weakness," and he indicated "Adi" with a twinkle of the eyes.

Before I realized what I was doing, I had crossed the room and pulled the hat from her—*his* head! It was a beautiful Israeli boy of fifteen or sixteen years. I was petrified.—He galvanically reached inside his jacket, but a word from Lev stayed him. His murderous eyes blazed up at me, his mouth was wet. He would have gladly killed me and I, at that moment, could have bitten through that mouth till my teeth met. Beautiful. In my smugness over the incongruously tilted hat, I had neglected to consider that boys aching to be men might fall into the gaffe as well. I felt darkly betrayed, in a snare of some infinitely clever devising, labyrinthine as the brain. I murmured an apology and went back to my chair. Lev laughed at me.

"Why, who did you think it was? Pretty, isn't he?" I forced myself to nod. "Cydneye Bissche thought so too. He became extraordinarily informative in consequence." Lord, how I was coming to despise the race of men. I thought fleetingly of Cyd, of his helplessness in a shrewd world, of his lack of will.

"And he put you onto Benham," I said, to leave the subject at once.

"He did. He had gone to prep school in the east with the real

Benham, and quite by accident ran into him ten years later. His first inkling of something amiss was that Benham, for all his urbanity, plainly did not remember him, and they had been the closest of chums. The second was that, given Benham's memory lapse, he quickly found that he, Cydneye Bissche, did not remember the man before him either, though there was a distinct likeness. So, being of infinite curiosity, and, well, a lover of spies and spylike ambiance, Cydneye Bissche made it a point to visit Minneapolis frequently—"

"And unearthed the whole business—"

"Not a bit. He thought he was onto Nazis! Cydneye was not clever. Indeed, he was unclever enough to come one day recently to the garage in Minneapolis, word of which got to the wrong—or right, depending whose side you are on—ears, and Mr. Bryan Younglove was dispatched to dispatch, which he accomplished by frightening the poor chap. They piece together as quickly as you."

"But *why*, if the organization is all but extinct, as you say?"

"Why, because it is not at all unusual in a dying organism to strike viciously. Touch an almost dead wildcat once. There have been many gratuitous murders since Lake's death, and I fear more shall be before the last conspirators are flushed. The thing was vast, as you know. Too vast for their own good actually, though the vastness itself was an important element in the effect they wished to achieve, yet too many little nabobs and factions. Even before the death of Benham Lake, indeed since the World War, there have been signs of the structure weakening under its own bulk. In your country alone there were fourteen nerve centers—"

"With Chicago as head—?"

"An Intelligence blunder, I believe. Minneapolis beyond a doubt. The Chicago leads were cleverly laid."

"And why then did Lake die—or was he killed?"

"Neither question can I answer. I am an honest man, lad."

Are you, I wondered. "And Shem?"

"As I say."

"You also say hereditary, yet—"

"—Yet Mr. Gordon Charls Abul lives, or did until a few days ago, anyway. Don't take on—one does not *know* now, I mean to say.

As to your question, I think simply that young Abul did not desire the Messiah mantle. He tried hard enough in his youth to discourage their hopes. A touching business—a real marrano—neither one thing nor another. An extreme version of you, in a way. Imagine a bourgeois Abul, a country squire! Well, they fixed his clock for him. In any event he was of no importance in the organization, and his running off here on some mad escapade or other was in the general pattern of his behavior, was it not? And that whole ridiculous business of his being declared dead? A jape—"

"Before I give you my poor thoughts on the matter, I must tell you I overheard, during the course of a most interesting exchange, certain things to make me believe that the Abul family was widely known in Palestine itself. I had not understood this. I was under the impression it was all fearsomely secret—"

"Ah, lad, Jews cannot keep secrets from Jews, not even you from me. Ha ha ha. It was from the lips of Irene Fairweather you heard it, was it not? She was confiding it in her loud voice to Hudson Beckwith, was she not? And you were in a tree, were you not? Ha ha ha—your *face,* lad! It will crack into fragments if you don't relax it. There now. Irene is an old friend of mine. I knew her at the time of the Stern troubles in Palestine, when she was keeping me plentifully informed of that devil's activities.—There goes that face again! You are shocked?—But she is a born counter-spy, simply cannot help herself. One does not criticize the wind for changing its course, and she is no less a natural phenomenon. She has the most inviolate ideals of noble endeavor of any person alive, and absolutely the lowest practices. I adore her, as I daresay you do also, eh? Ha ha. Well, I have seen her twice since I'm in the city. She spotted me on the beach that most luckless day, and we have talked. She has told me all about you, and that conversation, and Mr. Hudson Beckwith's harmless peculiarities. Even Hudson Beckwith, you see, the one man who in spite of all her numerous effusions she truly and deeply loves, and would defend with her life. I beg you to mark that. She suspects you of suspecting him—but that in a moment.

"About the Abuls then. A long line of the Messiah tradition is in the Abul family, back to the fifteenth century it is claimed, from lonely mad creatures with a following of half a dozen wretched Hasidim to some really important trouble makers who caused no end of pogroms by their insolence. The Abuls have been proclaiming the end of wonders for five wondrous centuries—the end of wonders and the rule of light by the Righteous in the Holy Land. And who are or were these Righteous? The Abuls! You may find Abuls in a variety of spellings scattered throughout hundreds of old codices devoted to the subject. Their existence is hardly a secret. Of course after the Shabbatai Zevi disaster, and the reaction of the Enlightenment, little was heard of them. They would not have been tolerated by even the maddest of our very mad people. But again during Herzl's time, and the first stirrings of Zionism, a discordant but intermittent note, not quite identifiable in pitch, began to be heard. A 'feebler' note as it were, to test the temper of the audience. It would die out for a few years, and then broadsides would appear in London say, but simultaneously in Lisbon, Cairo, and a dozen other centers of the Diaspora, together with curious anonymous paragraphs buried in the back pages of influential journals, all with an apocalyptic purport, at first rather coy but later with increasing vehemence, warning of the folly of a temporal Jerusalem. A temporal Jerusalem *now* was a betrayal of the covenant—we had had our temporal Jerusalem, there was no going back in the forward progress of the Soul to God, and we must prepare ourselves for the homecoming into the *heavenly* Jerusalem. So they had decided. Not quite the old Abul line, you see. They changed even as the rest of us had. When we turned visionary with our griefs, ready to fly up into heaven at the first sign, they had been all for a return to the Holy Land and a rule of light, by them of course. Now that the Holy Land was once more a hope and an ache in our hearts, even as they had once fought to make it, they turned Turk and decided heaven was our only home. Have you ever heard of such a people?—*they* would lead us into heaven. They *knew* someone! *Aiii.*

"Well, but they were little amusing, as you know. Along with a change of destination came a change of methodology. No more primitive Messianism for them, and no more choice for us. It had always been an extraordinarily insane family, you understand—insane and cunning. Apparently during the century and more of their quietude they managed to amass a fortune, which was to be completely at the disposal of one great final push—this we have just been through. Their powers of organization were tremendous. They had genius in their way, and they were convinced, totally utterly convinced, of their mission. Anarchy—anarchy for us. This was as much traditional as criminal, for the legend has it that only at the moment of deepest degradation does the Redemption occur—*ours,* please. They took the color black. Their method was confusion. For fifty years, from the first stirrings of the Zionist movement, which they read for a sign to delay no longer, they pursued a course of steady infiltration, not into the ranks of the Jews, mind you, but into the most sacrosanct holies of gentile society and power.

Strange tactic? Not a bit, considering their aims, which were at the same time to prevent the treacherous establishment of a Jewish State—I say treacherous, for what to us was white to them was black and so on in all things —and to reduce gentile social structures—to a Jew the most important unit of stability, greater than the state or the military of which they have had small experience—to a hollow shell of betrayal and suspicion, self-loathing, destruction. The terrible new bomb itself, though surely not of their inspiration, was just as surely not innocent of their encouragement at various stages in development and diffusion among the nations. Betrayal, confusion, and the fear that destroys.

"Ambitious certainly, but what is really extraordinary to me is how well they *succeeded* in this fantastic ambition. Literally thousands of gentiles the world over, in the highest positions of social and political advantage, became their willing, no their *devoted* tools, secretly eating away at the ground under their own feet! But you have seen for yourself. Morale was the target, degradation. They bore no allegiance to anything human. They worked with the Germans *and* the anti-Germans—for of course a German victory would have established a rival power of uncomfortable similarity. The Russians are particularly beholden to them. Moslems, it goes without saying.

"Yet whatever its skills, Messianism remains Messianism. It is a doomed enterprise, for one cannot expose what a powerful bourgeoisie is in league to hide. It is like making a hole with your spoon to the bottom of a dish of liquid pudding. Who will look in time except a few children? The rest have learned to be slow with their eyes. Yet there were terrible moments. Is it not staggering—the thought of it? I mean, the implications? It was as though the choicest people of the world, in spite of much loud palaver about the future, had been secretly awaiting them, these master anarchists, and wanted nothing so much as to watch a little band of despised Jews ascending above their dying bodies into the heavenly Palace. Do you suppose this is what history has been about—?"

"One thing I would very much like to know," I said dreamily. "Where is the true Benham Lake?"

"—Ah?" He chuckled. "You have not listened to a word. No, no, do not protest. Why should you listen, when you know it all—?"

I was annoyed. "How would I know? Never have I been told more than the barest minimum, and even that of doubtful value—"

"Well, now you know," he said. "Yet can you really pretend I have told you something?"

There was a snideness in his tone that made me bristle. "Explain," I said.

"With the greatest pleasure. I have lately heard the rumor—"

"I want no rumors," I broke in hastily, feeling my color rise.

"Yet you asked me to explain," he said with unctuous patience. "No? Yes. Adi nods yes. The rumor, current it seems when you were a child, that Shem Abul himself was your father."

It took all my strength to sit in place—that and the sight of Adi's fingers playing near his shoulder-holster. "A vicious and long-dead canard, bred and carried by diseased swine. My father had many enemies. The families were close—"

"Dead entirely to *your* satisfaction? I mean, you responded to nothing in my little survey? No small flush of excitement, no quickening of the pulse? I could have sworn I saw the roses bloom—"

I felt if I let him go on I would have to kill him. "—Shall we proceed with my objections to your case?"—blood drumming in my ears.

He had been sitting aggressively forward and now flopped back with a sigh. "Not unless you insist. You have always been a magician with facts—a dismal newspaper man—"

"To begin with," I said, compelling myself to a show of moderation, "I cannot see how you, who little over a month ago were so severe on the likes of Cydneye Bissche, how you can now pretend—"

"I do not pretend," corrected Lev, emphasizing with a forefinger.

"Worse then, seriously accept the evidence of this—"

"I was wrong about him," said Lev simply. "Or do you prefer to hear that of the two we trusted you less?"

I would not let him deflect me. "He could not have fooled you?"

The lids of his eyes swam down. "He was an American," he said discreetly, repressing a sneer. Adi asked in Hebrew for a recapitulation of the last exchange, and laughed heartily, showing blue teeth.

"So he was," I said. "And it can only have been because you are *not* an American, and likely not an authority on prep schools either"—it slipped out in spite of me—"that he would chance that school-chum bilge. All better prep schools have a religious bias. Lake's family were fervent Catholics, and I believe he more than once mentioned his days at Portsmouth Priory, a noted and exclusive Catholic breeding-ground. Bissche on the other hand is Episcopalian, was proudly Groton—"

"And you?" said Lev amused. "Where does the rich dilettante American Jew go, who accepts him?"

"That does not answer me."

"Such as, that Cydneye Bissche is possibly a tool of the Abuls? That answer? I have considered it, you may be sure. But, dear lad, it is less an answer, in the event, than another question, and we are *done* with questions. Whatever the merit of the ingredients, the cake is perfect—a triumph. All quibbles as to procedure and such I leave to you cookbook cooks. *You* may vex your souls with explaining why it cannot be as good as it is. I shall eat."

"You are impertinent," I remarked.

"And *you* are jealous!"

"I have been waiting all night to hear you say it. So you really do feel that is what my probing comes to. It seems foolish to go on. Yet about Hudson Beckwith—"

"Precisely," said Lev sitting forward again. "I meant to talk about him. Irene Fairweather is disturbed that you may suspect him of some deep-dyed implication, and requested me please to disabuse you before you made fools of them *and* yourself—"

"Deep-dyed implication?" I said, and then said what I should never have been able to support, and yet profoundly believed. I wanted to startle him. "Only that he's Khan."

But such was his opinion of me that he was prepared even for this; yet perhaps, by this very preparation, suggesting something of his own deeper thought. "Lad, lad, you do run away with yourself. There has been no hiatus in Mr. Beckwith's life. Even if one hundred incontrovertible evidences pointed to him—and they do not, that I know of—he is *Hudson Beckwith*. Irene, who is *not* implicated, of which I think even you must be convinced"—I was—"and who is anything but a fool, *knows* him to be Hudson Beckwith. She has been constantly with him since she was a little girl, and but for a short sojourn in Palestine throughout most of the World War as well, and surely her jealous eyes would have detected an impostor? And if you still demur, consider Mrs. Agnes Dupres who has known and loved him all of her life, which *precisely spans his*. What, was he replaced in Madame Beckwith's womb by an Abul fetus? Well?"

I kept my silence. As he had anticipated my challenge, I had anticipated the rebuttal, indeed had brooded long hours over these very points. It was plainly an impossibility. Nonetheless.

"So here is what is to be done," said Lev. "I have already informed Uncle [Haganese for FBI] of the Benham Lake exposure, together with pertinent materials for them to check, and now, tomorrow, shall hand over to them a list of conspirators' names—as many as we have been unable to uncover—a hundred seventy-three, though of course some will duplicate names they already have. All day I have been on the phone gathering them from our men around the country. The remainder, I daresay, will kill each other off in due time—"

"Then you feel Hudson Beckwith is no way involved—"

"I said no such thing. He was involved—as were so many of his world-weary fellow fashionables, mildly, very mildly. Irene and I discussed it thoroughly, and we decided his name should be turned in with the others. It is my understanding that there will be no public prosecutions, no publicity. It will all be as if it never was. He may be investigated—perhaps jailed for a few years for the sake of his safety—on two or three minor infractions of the law, income tax juggling and the like, which Irene has put into my hands—"

"Lev, you must not do it," I said.

"And why must I not do it?"

"Because it is not right—you know it is not right. They are our people. They deserve more from us—"

"Aha. I suspected as much. Adi, didn't I tell you? Yet I do not believe in ennobling my enemies, sir."

"They meant to ennoble *us!*" I knew I had best keep my mouth shut, yet I was crushed with grief.

He merely smiled at me. He was searching the inside pockets of his jacket. " —Of course, you are now relieved of any future obligations to society on this score. You were long ago relieved, but you never seem to know your place. Or perhaps you have no place. Do you even have beliefs—American?—marrano? Here.—Here are some papers and valuables taken from you at the time of your first dismissal. Joe's Hotel, was it not? I have been asked to return them to you as a token of our—contempt." He reached an envelope across to me and I tore it from his hand.

"You must not do it, I say!"

"Yet it shall certainly be done."

"Only hold off a while yet," I pleaded. "There are too many flaws, too many facts point—"

"Many more point my way. It is a closed case, accept it."

Wild with dismay, I sat rummaging through the envelope, mindlessly taking out the various contents—keys, driver's license, et cetera—and dropping them back in. And then the tiny fob-pocket watch given me by Edith. I slid it back with the rest. I took it out again. I put it to my ear and shook it.

"What, still running?" said Lev, incredulous. "Here, let me see—"

But at that moment the phone rang and I jumped up to answer. It was the desk clerk. I thanked him and said everything was all right. I placed the envelope on the telephone table and turned back to find Adi and Lev watching me tensely. I explained the prearranged check. Lev relaxed and smiled and said that but for my "romanticism" I would have made a very good agent. He had rarely come across a mind with such quick responses, he said. Then he yawned and said they had to go. Talking to night-owls was not for two such ordinary birds.

"—But one more schnapps to celebrate, eh?—you too, Adi. No, I insist. Maybe we'll even get you Mr. Lenart's Puerto Rican woman one of these nights." His using my real rather than code name was a finely insulting touch. Adi blushed charmingly and Lev roared.

I went into the other room and began to pour drinks at the kitchenette counter. "By the way," Lev called out, "your beautiful Polish luger is here under the sofa pillows, lad. No offence meant. We had no idea of what our reception might be, you understand. You are somewhat unpredictable—"

I closed my eyes and prayed. If I forget thee, O Jerusalem, may my right hand forget its cunning.—I took the watch from my pocket, snapped open the back, and emptied into my right hand the three minute green tablets that so many weeks ago I had brought here to use on myself. One tablet I dropped down the sink drain, one I dropped into Adi's drink, one I dropped into Lev's. I watched them dissolve. So many weeks, veils, lives ago. I believe I felt nothing.

"—A toast," said Lev. "To Israel!"

"—To the Yishuv of Israel!" said Adi.

"—To the glory of Israel!" said I.

The liquor went instantly to Adi's head. He got fiery red and put his arm around my waist affectionately. He rubbed his cheek against my shoulder. "After all, you are fine and brave too," he said. "A pity."

"A pity?" I said.

"That *you* wehr not Cydneye Bissche," and he went into hysterical giggles. A lovely boy, unfortunately for him. I ran my hand through his mop of hair, and when I tempted to withdraw he clapped his hand over mine to keep it there. I did not fight him. Presently he lowered my hand and, clinging to it, looked drunkenly at Lev.

"Layt me stay."

Lev had grown more and more annoyed. "That part of your career is over, my boy. Come on now. I really do have to get you a woman."

Adi giggled and staggered over for his hat.

"—Good night," said Lev from the door after pushing Adi out. "Remember, *accept it*." I thought he was looking poorly, though according to what I knew, the tablet would not kill for yet an hour. Tired probably, as tired as I.

I sat at the edge of the arm chair and finally, near dawn, after blank ages of staring at the door, dozed off on my elbows.

I was awakened towards noon by the phone. A registered letter was on its way up to me. It read: "Come to dinner tomorrow at 7:00." No signature, no return address, no request for a confirmation, just those six vividly scrawled words at the center of a sheet of heavy yellow paper.

He knew I would not fail to be there.